Alan Scholefield was born in Cape Town in 1931.
His first novel, written in the early 1960s, was an
immediate success, enabling him to give up
journalism and become a full time writer.

He now lives in Hampshire with his wife and three
daughters.

Alan Scholefield's many books include: *Great
Elephant, Lion in the Evening, Point of Honour,
The Stone Flower, Venom* (which was filmed in
1982 starring Nicol Williamson, Sarah Miles,
Oliver Reed and Susan George), *The Sea Cave,
Fire in the Ice* and *The Hammer of God.*

A View of Vultures

ALAN SCHOLEFIELD

SPHERE BOOKS LIMITED

First published in Great Britain by
William Heinemann Ltd 1966
Copyright © 1966 by Alan Scholefield
First published in paperback by Pan Books Ltd 1968
This edition published by Sphere Books Ltd 1986
27 Wright's Lane, London W8 5SW

Set in Plantin

Printed and bound in Great Britain by
Collins, Glasgow

For my mother
Margaret Elizabeth Scholefield – in gratitude

Book One

THE PRISONER

'We carry with us the wonders we seek without us: there is all Africa and her prodigies in us.'

SIR THOMAS BROWNE

On a day in April in the year 1806 a small depression began to form among the icebergs of the Antarctic south of the Magellan Straits. At first it seemed it might die there, swallowed up in other weather systems: but it began to grow, and growing began to move. It swung up in a north-easterly direction, passing to the east of the Falkland Islands. By this time it was a cold front a hundred miles wide and getting bigger all the time. It moved crab-wise over the South Atlantic at a rate of thirty knots. Ahead of it raced north-westerly winds of forty knots gusting to fifty and sometimes sixty. Five days later it struck the uninhabited island of Tristan da Cunha and thirty-six hours after that it reached the Cape of Good Hope where it was received with joy.

Someone standing on the top of Table Mountain at that time and gazing down on the neat geometry of the settlement, would have felt the first hint of the coming gale as a slight coolness on his left cheek; a few hours later he would have been blown off his feet.

In Cape Town itself the gale was not unexpected. For the past few days Dutch burghers, who had been born in the Colony, had been aware of the usual signs: the stillness, the sudden clarity of the autumn air which made the granite buttresses of Table Mountain seem close enough to touch: the flocks of seagulls which settled on the lawns of what had been the Dutch East India Company's garden.

Those who understood the signs stared out to sea in expectation, waiting for the first feel of dampness in the atmosphere. It had been a long, hot summer.

No rain had fallen at the Cape for five months. The Salt and Liesbeek Rivers were nearly dry and all that was left for the stock were pools of greenish, stagnant water. For the first time in living memory the stream that ran down the Heerengracht, in the middle of town, had dried up completely. The level in the reservoir had never been lower.

If the watcher on the summit of Table Mountain had faced to the north, he would have seen a desert laid out before him all the way to the Hottentots Holland range; first the stretch of grey-brown sand that covered the Flats and then the tawny, lion-coloured grass that spread to the far foothills.

Beyond the Hottentots Holland, which separated the Cape of Good Hope peninsula from the rest of the Colony as effectively as a wall, the wine farmers of the Drakenstein Valley and farther north the graziers of the Great and Little Karoos, had also had a trying summer. It had not been quite so bad for the farmers who had managed to harvest their crop before the sun shrivelled the berries, but for the graziers it had been a disaster.

As usual, in summer, they had moved their flocks from the parched lands of the Karoo into the cooler gorges of the Rye and Snowy Mountains, but even there the springs had dried and the stock had begun to die. A grazier's journey in search of water could easily be followed from one dead beast to the next.

And there *were* followers. Close behind the graziers came the vultures, the white-necked crows, the jackals and the hyenas. Behind the birds and animals came the Bushmen. It had been a wonderful summer for the Bushmen. Few could remember when their bellies had been fuller: not since the Christians had come to the Cape 150 years before.

But for physical discomfort Cape Town had suffered most. There had been five dry months in which the south-easter had raged, covering the oak trees with the grey dust of the Flats, whipping up flurries of sand in the streets, stripping the leaves of the silver trees above Paradise, snapping away the smoke of the shell-burners' fires on the beach. It had been a summer of dust: dust in the eyes, dust that came through the tight-closed shutters of the houses, dust between the teeth, and the pages of Bibles.

Now another wind was blowing. It blew from the northwest for a full day, getting stronger and stronger, until at noon on April 14th the black clouds opened and rain began to fall. By sunset four inches had fallen in Cape Town making the streets a bog. The gauge at the Governor's summer home at Newlands measured five and a half inches and waterfalls were pouring down the slopes of Table Mountain above Paradise. The rain fell on the shanties of the freed-slaves and Hottentots who lived on the Flats, it fell on the new Union Jack flying above the Castle, it fell on the beaches below Mouse Mountain, it fell high up on the slopes of the Franschhoek Mountains bringing the Berg River down in spate, it fell on the Rye Mountains and the edges of the Karoo, it brought down the Salt and Liesbeek Rivers and their brown mud stains stretched out into Table Bay almost to the lee of Robben Island where Sir Home Popham had anchored his fleet three months before to launch the Highland Brigade at the throats of the Dutch.

It also fell on a vessel of 467 tons, at that moment weathering the gale 145 miles north-west of Cape Town. She was ninety-two days from the Motherbank, and was called the *Babylon*, but to the manacled prisoners who lay in their own filth and excrement in the 'tween deck holds, she had long before been known as The Great Whore.

The *Babylon* had slipped down the Solent in early January carrying a crew of thirty-two, a cargo of 166 male convicts and a Royal Marine guard of one lieutenant and thirty men. Her sailing orders called for revictualling at Santa Cruz, Rio and the Cape before setting out on the long final leg to the convict settlement in New South Wales, but after Teneriffe she had failed to make her westing and had crawled down the coast of Africa either becalmed or tacking to hold what wind she could. Twelve days from the Santa Cruz Roads, when the temperature in the holds was over 100 and the tar had begun to drip down onto the prisoners from the deck seams, the two-pint daily ration of water was cut by half. There had been talk of mutiny. Where the rumours came from no one knew, but the result was that a prisoner called Sykes was hanged from the yard-arm and fourteen others received fifty lashes each. Seven of them died from the beatings. What little deck freedom the prisoners had enjoyed was now stopped entirely and their leg irons were re-fastened to the ringbolts in the holds. The hatches were battened down, three cannons were brought up from the gun-deck loaded with grape-shot and trained at the hatch-covers. The sentries on duty carried primed muskets at all times.

Death was no stranger to the *Babylon*. Even before she sailed there had been corpses. Now, ninety-two days out, with scurvy and dysentery, fluxes and fevers taking their daily toll, the figure was nearer forty than thirty, though no one knew exactly how many because by the time a tally was taken there was always another.

The steerage-hold of the *Babylon* had been divided into cells eight feet square. Each cell had held six men. In one of them there were now five. Four, if only the living were counted. Three and a half, if the boy was classed as a boy and not as a man and he wasn't a man yet.

James Fraser Black was dreaming. It seemed that he was in an eastern country, in a place filled with a golden light. It struck down from a high shadowy ceiling in lambent bars illuminating the woman on the throne. At first he thought she was his mother but the face was difficult to see because the light was so bright. He could sense she was smiling and that her eyes were brimming with kindness. He was kneeling at her feet and slowly she held out her arms to him. He half rose and put out his hand to take hers. He felt warm and very happy. Abruptly she reached forward, grabbed his wrist and twisted it savagely. He cried out: 'God damn you!' Ogle was shouting: 'Lie still!' He wrenched again at the chain, and the handcuff bit viciously into James's wrist.

'You have an admirable turn of phrase, Ogle,' Fitzhenry said. 'But then I've complimented you before, haven't I? Positively felicitous.'

The voice was little more than a croak. It had no resemblance at all to the bantering, over-exaggerated tone that had been one of the irritants earlier in the voyage.

'So the little Celt is with us again,' Fitzhenry continued. 'Good day to you, Sir Jamie. God bless the House of Stuart.'

Ogle turned his big, clumsy body to face the speaker. He was brought up short by the chain that bound him to James. He jerked to bring the boy with him. The guttering light from the lantern which swung above their heads fell on Ogle's face. It was a young face, about twenty-three or twenty-four – Ogle himself could not have put a more definite date on it – wide and peasant-like with close-set hostile eyes.

'Shut your mouth,' he said to Fitzhenry.

'Oh, capital! Remarkable. You have a gift, Ogle.'

'I'll reckon with you yet.'

'I've no doubt you'll try,' Fitzhenry said dryly. 'In a dark street, like a cutpurse.'

Ogle grunted and turned away. He settled himself in the wet straw with his head against the rotting bulkhead. 'Give over!' he said to James, and jerked the chain again.

James could no longer remember the dream, but the warmth and happiness had gone and it was as if he had been cheated of something. He was cold, wet and ill. Reality was being in the cell, in the dreadful smell of death and decay, anchored by his arm to another living person; he could hardly remember anything else. The dream flickered briefly in his conscious mind as some half-formed impression of golden light, and then it was gone forever.

Fitzhenry was talking again but the words meant nothing to him. He had found the ability to close his mind. He looked down at the galling on his left wrist and began to chafe the skin with his other hand. One day he would kill Ogle for this; one day he would kill the second mate whose idea it had been; one day he would kill Loxton; one day he would kill Fitzhenry; one day he would . . . He glanced up sharply and his body grew colder. From the other side of the shadowy cell

Royal was watching him. He could make out the long cadaverous face and the black hypnotic eyes. He shivered.

Around them the ship creaked and groaned. The wind had lessened slightly and shifted a few points to the westward. It blew now on her starboard quarter and she began to take the Cape rollers over her lee rail. Since her keel had been laid in a Thames yard sixteen years before, she had been a wet ship and barely a week had passed after leaving Portsmouth before the convicts had been formed into squads to man the pumps. But after the rumour of mutiny, that had been stopped and the marines took over.

The pumps were unequal to the task. At first the straw and bedding in the cells had been merely damp which, in a way, had been a blessing in the tropics. Now they were awash and each time the *Babylon* buried her fore-peak in a swell, small waves coursed through the cells carrying with them straw, bedding and human filth. The wavelets washed over the legs of the manacled prisoners. Some pulled themselves farther up the bulkheads to avoid the worst of it but most were too ill to move.

'Get him up!'

James started. Royal was watching him again.

'Get him up, boy!' The voice was evil and grating.

The dead man lay half submerged in his sodden straw. His name was Pike and he had been dead for two days. James leant over and took hold of the front of his kersey jacket. The stuff was rotten and tore in his fingers. He tried again but the man's body was too heavy for him.

'Ogle!'

'What?'

'Give the boy a hand.'

Between them they managed to get Pike into a sitting position. His head lolled back drunkenly.

'Hold him there!'

James got his arm round the dead man's back and tried to brace him from falling over again each time the ship rolled. There was not the strength left in his arm so he pulled Pike over, letting the corpse lean on his right shoulder. His cheek was against the dead man's left arm.

6

'Welcome back, Mr Pike,' Fitzhenry said. 'We missed you.'

The dead man's face was streaked with slime and his eyes wide and staring. He had been unlovely in life, and death had not changed him. His cheeks had sunk into his face so far that his lips were pulled back over his teeth, revealing the black blood and bruising of scurvy.

'Brace him hard, boy,' Royal said.

Faintly, above the noise of the ship James could hear the sound of the mess tin. At first they had had their own mess captain to fetch the food. That had been Somerwell, who died before Pike. But since they had been confined to quarters the marines had taken over mess duties as well. James could hardly recall Somerwell now. He had died one day when the ship lay idle in the doldrums. One moment he had been sprawled dazed and supine in the heat, squeezed in between Royal and Fitzhenry, and the next he was dragging against his chains like a madman. In one frenzied effort he had managed to pull the ringbolt from the bulkhead and then he had collapsed in the filthy straw, blood pouring from his mouth and nose. That was all he could remember of Somerwell; that and the fact that he had told the second mate, Rance, to clear out when he'd come looking for James. He could remember Rance all right; he could remember him standing there in the low doorway, the light glistening on his moist lower lip. He could even remember seeing his own teeth marks in Rance's arm. Then Somerwell, who spoke in a slow Dorset voice, had told Rance to clear out and Royal had said: 'If you want the boy, mister, it'll cost you half a hogshead of claret.' Rance had stood in the doorway licking his bottom lip uncertainly for a moment and then he had turned away. The crew were never comfortable in the 'tween deck holds: sometimes accidents happened to them.

James felt the dead body of Pike strain away from him as the ship took a big sea. He hung on with all his strength and slowly the corpse came upright.

At that moment the door opened and the mess party brought in the great pot of stew. Since all the meals were the same now, James had no way of knowing what time of day it was. A corporal in scarlet served the thin stew into bowls and a private added half a pound of bread per man.

'Four, it is?' said the marine.

'Five,' said Royal softly.

The corporal looked at him and then quickly away. His eyes swung briefly round the cell. They stopped on Pike for a moment and then went on. 'I didn't see the boy,' he said.

'He's there all right, mister.'

'Aye, I can see that now.'

'Helping Mr Pike. He's feeling poorly.'

'Aye.'

'I'll hold Mr Pike's till he's ready.'

The private looked uncertainly at the corporal. 'Give it to him,' the corporal said.

James ate slowly. Every time he chewed, his mouth hurt; each tooth seemed to exist in a separate agony. He dipped the bread in the stew to soften it but even that did not help.

Weeks before it would have mattered to him, and to them all, that they were getting less than their rations. There had been some talk of shaved weights in the galleys; it was said that the master was saving all the beef he could to fetch fancy prices in New South Wales. Now he found he was too ill to eat. Only Royal seemed unaffected, and since he lived on dead men's rations there was no complaint. Even Ogle's great body had shrunk.

'Give half to the boy,' Fitzhenry said.

Royal looked up at him from under thick eyebrows. 'Again?'

'Again.'

Royal studied him thoughtfully.

'I don't want it,' James said.

'You'll take it,' Fitzhenry replied, 'or it'll be your ration next he'll be gulping.'

'Not his,' Royal said. 'Not his.'

Ogle laughed.

'Hold out your bowl,' Fitzhenry said to James.

James leant forward and Royal poured half the greasy stew into his bowl.

'Now eat it,' Fitzhenry said.

James swallowed without chewing. He felt the warmth of it in his belly and glanced over at Fitzhenry in a moment of brief and uncharacteristic gratitude. He noticed the flash of the knife as Fitzhenry put it away.

Royal had tried twice to get the knife. The first time Fitzhenry had woken suddenly and Royal had taken the blade in the upper arm. The second time James, without thinking, had shouted a warning. That had been three days ago and he'd been aware of Royal's smouldering anger ever since.

He placed the empty bowl on his lap, just out of reach of the water and lay back against the wood. Fitzhenry began to cough again.

One of the first things James remembered about the *Babylon* was Fitzhenry's rattling cough. He had heard it the day he came aboard, and had seen the blood on his lips. That was in the beginning when you could notice blood as a special colour on his thin, white face. Now it was blotched with scurvy bruises and his lips were covered by beard.

But there were other memories before he had ever seen or heard of the *Babylon*. There was the journey from Scotland which had taken nearly a month in bitter winter weather. James could remember the weight of his leg-irons in the snow near Dalwhinnie as they got down to push; he could remember them digging the grave for a boy about his own age somewhere in the North Riding; he could remember that they had been in twenty gaols but could not separate them in his mind. He could remember being cold and hungry – but then he could remember little else.

Other pictures sometimes rose in front of his eyes; the triumph on Loxton's face as they dragged James away, the waxy texture of his mother's skin when the village wives came to lay her out, Mr McCrae at the Academy holding the birch up for him to see before using it on his back and legs, his father's outstretched arms and his drunken face, the lips moving 'Suffer the little children to come unto me'. But where had *he* been when he was needed most?

The farther south they had travelled from Scotland the

9

bigger grew the column until, as the carts creaked over the Portsmouth cobbles, the town shut its shops and the people lined the streets. He could remember that all right: a wind whipping up the Solent, the blur of faces; some incurious, some pleased, some weeping. And then they were being packed into the lighters, chains a-clank like some regiment in armour, and the black hulk of the *Babylon* tugging at her moorings in the freezing grey water of the Motherbank.

Briefly, before he was ordered below, he had gazed about him: to the Isle of Wight, its fields still covered in rime, down the Solent, across Southampton Water to where the East Indiamen rode high at anchor. He had felt no pang that this was the last he would see of his homeland, no tremor of instantaneous nostalgia, no ache above his heart. He had stood in the icy wind for a moment, a thin, dark boy, on the small side for sixteen years, hating what he saw. Then he was pushed roughly forward and the companionway gaped before him.

His was the last batch to come aboard. Most of the others had been there for a month or more, brought down from London or the Essex hulks, ironed and chained, already smelling of death and corruption. The stench struck him like a blow. He was manhandled to one of the partitioned cells. Vaguely he heard the irons being made fast to the ringbolt. He felt dizzy. Cold sweat had broken out on his face and body. In the far distance he heard a rattling, throaty cough, then he was violently ill over someone's legs. He barely felt the blow from Ogle that sent him crashing down on the straw.

'Edward Charles Winstead Beauchamp Fitzhenry. Uncommon fine names for an uncommon fine convict.'

Ogle had sniggered. Somerwell had somehow got his hands on a Bible and was reading softly to himself, spelling out the words. Pike was asleep. Royal was withdrawn, staring moodily at his hands. James remembered his hands: big and rawboned, split over the knuckles by the cold.

Fitzhenry paused for a moment before continuing. 'The usual reply is either good morning or good day or a pleasant inquiry about one's health or a nod or a shake, a smile or a wink would do, a touch of the forelock, finger against nose, thumb up, thumb down, even a twitch of the shoulder. Known as courtesy, salutation, what you will.'

'My name is James Fraser Black.'

'Capital, it speaks. And where, Lord James Fraser Black, do you hail from? Wales would it be? Or Ireland?'

Puzzled, James looked up at Fitzhenry. His white, wasted face made his age difficult to guess. It could have been anywhere between thirty and fifty. James realized he was laughing at him.

'From Scotland,' he said in a surly voice.

'One would never have guessed.'

That had been the beginning of it.

All that night the wind poured out of the north-west driving the *Babylon* before it. There was no question of heaving to or running out a sea anchor because the vessel was on a lee shore and with the wind in that quarter and the set of the current it would have been only a matter of hours before she was on the rocks.

In Table Bay shipwreck had already occurred. The previous day, when the coming gale was still just a puff of wind and a falling glass, three Indiamen, the *Earl of Dutton*, the *Surrey* and the *Lord Barkley* had hastily weighed anchor and put out for St Helena. The master of the Royal Swedish East Indiaman, *City of Uppsala*, then revictualling, decided to ride out the storm at his moorings. Less than twelve hours later the *City of Uppsala* had been blown half-way across Table Bay and had gone aground near the mouth of the Salt River. A detachment of dragoons had galloped hurriedly from the Castle, at the request of the Swedish vice-consul, to guard the scattered cargo against looters.

The gale was beginning to take its toll. In a back room of a building on the Kaisersgracht a Malay slave called Doman was putting the finishing touches to a yellow-wood table which had been ordered by one of the boarding-houses, when a wall collapsed and crushed him to death. At Paradise a Hottentot child, who had accompanied his mother to collect fire-wood, was killed by a falling branch. A mare, fourteen cows and more than thirty sheep were drowned when the Berg River burst its banks near Waggonmaker's Valley. A Buhsman family was struck dead by lightning in the Rye Mountains and a grazier was swept to his death when the dry bed of a Karoo stream suddenly became the channel for a wall of water three feet high.

The storm was also taking its toll in the *Babylon*. The death rate among the prisoners, which had slackened slightly as the ship reached cooler latitudes, now went above the daily average for the first time since the fevers of the doldrums. Between noon and midnight the dead man, Pike, was joined by nine companions. Lying face down in more than a foot of water, he was unaware of his good fortune.

James had long since allowed the heavy, waterlogged body to slide down to its original position and he knew that not even an order from Royal could put enough strength in his arm to hoist him up again. He tried to doze but the pain in his gums and teeth kept him awake. At times the swinging lamp seemed to hypnotize him, to lull him into a state where death seemed a welcome friend.

But he was not going to die . . . he was not going to die . . . He repeated the phrase over and over and shook himself awake and tried to fix his thoughts on anything that would make the brink of that friendly abyss recede. He cast about for some memory to sustain him. He tried to recall the few times he had been really happy, summer picnics with his mother on the banks of the Nairn, bird-nesting in the heather above Daviot, wandering alone over the moors of Drummossie. But there was no strength in these memories, they flickered weakly then faded, snuffed out by later and harsher events. He found himself hating again. It seemed to give him strength; it seemed, unlike his other emotions, to have a future.

He was dozing fitfully when the cell door opened cautiously. He caught the flash of a scarlet jacket. It was the Marine corporal from the mess party, a shifty-eyed cockney called Nollitts. He stepped carefully over Fitzhenry's sleeping body, his boots making small splashes in the scummy water, and squatted down next to Royal. From the beginning of the voyage some sort of relationship had been established between the two of them, as though they had known each other before. Once or twice he had brought Royal extra rations and would never have questioned, even silently, the dead body of Pike if the private had not been present. In the past week his visits had been almost regular. He would squat next to Royal for ten or fifteen minutes and the voices would mumble softly. James imagined that it had something to do with food.

He watched them incuriously and once saw Royal nod across to Ogle. Nollitts looked round and James noticed that his eyes were frightened.

He turned back to Royal and shook his head. Royal stared at him angrily for a moment and then said something further. Nollitts shrugged, nodded, and after a few more minutes rose to his feet and left as silently as he'd arrived.

It had grown colder. The icy water of the Benguela Current swept over the decks and through the seams bringing a chill to the air and frost to the breath. Lying in the 'tween deck holds, awash now to a depth of nearly two feet, some of the men began to get violent attacks of cramp. James felt the cold steal about him like a freezing blanket. His teeth began to chatter. He tried to keep his body from trembling but seemed to have no control over it. At first the rattling of the handcuff chain was slight, but then as his trembling increased it became more pronounced. Soon, he knew, Ogle would jerk on the chain and it would cut into his wrist, or he might hit him in the face as he had done twice before and James knew that if that happened now he would lose his teeth; already their moorings in his gums felt spongy. He wondered if he would ever be able to bite again, really bite, the way he had bitten Rance.

Rance, the second mate, must have seen James when he was first brought aboard because within a few hours of being locked in with the others a seaman arrived with a message that he was wanted on deck. He had with him a hammer and spike and struck the pins from the leg-irons. For the first time in four months James took a tentative step without the weight of the iron. He had difficulty keeping his balance.

'What do they want *him* for?' Ogle said.

The seaman shrugged.

'Mutiny!' Fitzhenry said. 'Only here five minutes and already an insurrectionist.' James said nothing. So many things had happened to him in the past few months that he had long since stopped inquiring into reasons.

'Nay, don't joke over summat like that,' the seaman said dourly. 'Orders from t' second mate. Strike they bazzels he says and bring t' boy aloft.'

James found himself looking down at the cadaverous face of Royal. The mouth opened in a cruel smile showing green stumps of teeth. 'You'll not look far for the answer, boy,' Royal said gratingly, and then he laughed.

Rance was waiting in his cabin. He was a man of medium height and plumpish. The pink skin of his scalp showed through his thin blond hair. He was perspiring slightly, in spite of the cold, and his heavy lower lip was moist.

'Seeton,' he said, addressing the sailor, 'take them irons to Mr Miles in Number two. He's a pair short.'

'Aye, aye, sir.'

The seaman turned away and James watched the leg-irons disappear with him. He felt a sudden surge of hope.

'What's your name, boy?'

James turned to face Rance who had seated himself on the low bunk. He noticed that the man's hands were trembling slightly.

'James Fraser Black, sir.'

'Age?'

'Sixteen.'

'Sir!'

'Sir.'

'That's better.' Rance smiled at him. There was something about the smile he disliked, but couldn't tell what.

'Are you cold, James?'

'No, sir.'

Rance's hand shot out and grasped him by the wrist. James recoiled at the touch of the warm flesh.

'Stand still, James.'

'Yes, sir.'

Rance dropped his arm. 'You feel cold, James. Very cold.'

'Yes, sir.'

'See that chest?' Rance said pointing to a brass-bound sea chest against the bulkhead.

'Indeed, sir.'

'Open it, James.'

He knelt down on the deck and pushed the lid. Rance leant forward and put a hand on James's shoulder. On top of the clothing lay a heavy seaman's jersey. 'Put it on, James.'

The jersey was too large but with the cuffs rolled up it was comfortable. James immediately began to feel warmer than he had for a long time.

'Now drink this down.'

He paused for a moment as the fumes of the grog suddenly recalled his father's breath.

'Drink it, James.'

He lifted the tin mug and drank it in a gulp. His throat burned, his eyes watered and the back of his nose stung but he kept the liquid down.

'Better?'

'Yes, sir.'

'You and me are going to be friends, James.'

'Yes, sir.'

'I've got my duties to attend to, but I'll be back, and then we can continue our talk. I like a talk, don't you, James?'

'Indeed, sir.'

Rance patted him on the shoulder and went out of the cabin, closing the door.

James stood in the small space, uncertain what to do. He had not been told to leave; on the contrary Rance had said he would be back, therefore he had to stay where he was. He sat down on the edge of the bunk. He could still feel the effects of the liquor in his head and suddenly he was overtaken by tiredness. His eyelids felt heavy. He pulled his legs onto the bunk and lay down in a deep sleep.

He came awake suddenly and found himself looking up into Rance's face. There was something different about it. It seemed to have thickened and coarsened; there was a strange look in the eyes.

15

James started to his feet. 'I'm sorry, sir. I didn't mean . . .'

He was flung back on the bunk. At first he thought Rance had pushed him, then he realized that the ship was in motion. Rance stood above him, swaying to the roll of the ship.

'Get up, boy,' he said harshly.

James sprang up again, this time holding onto the edge of the bunk.

'D'you think you're a damn passenger?'

'Indeed no, sir.'

'Indeed no! Get that jersey off!'

James pulled it over his head.

'Fold it and put it away!'

He did as he was ordered.

'Seeton!' Rance bellowed. The seaman appeared in the doorway. 'Take the boy below.'

Bewildered, James found himself being pulled and pushed along the deck. He felt doubly cold without the jersey. He stumbled down the companionway trying to keep his balance, but already his head was spinning with the pitch and roll as the *Babylon* passed The Needles and began to take the big seas of the Channel.

The smell in the steerage-hold was worse than ever. Most of the prisoners were sea-sick and in that foetid atmosphere it was only a matter of minutes before James joined them.

The following day, during the afternoon watch, Seeton came for him again; and again he was taken to Rance's cabin. Everything appeared to be normal. 'Well, boy,' the second mate said, when the door had been fastened shut. 'Found your sea-legs yet?'

James watched him carefully. 'I think so, sir.'

'Are you cold, James?'

'No, sir.'

'Get the jersey out.'

When James had put it on again Rance half filled the tin mug with grog and passed it to him. 'It'll do you good.'

'It made me sleepy, sir.'

'Drink it.' He watched James drain the mug. 'I don't like people taking advantage of me, James.'

'No, sir.'

'You took advantage of me yesterday.'

'How d'you mean, sir?'

'I was kind to you, wasn't I?'

'Yes, sir.'

'I said we should be friends?'

'Yes, sir.'

'I don't like people sleeping in my bunk, James. I don't like them putting their heads on my . . . on my . . . Not without my say so. Do you understand, James?'

'It was the grog, sir, it made me . . .'

'Do you understand?' Rance shouted.

'I understand, sir.'

'I'm glad.'

He paused for a few seconds, staring at James. The anger had left his eyes and they were moist and friendly. 'Can you sew, James?'

'I never learnt, sir.'

'But you watched your mother?'

'Yes, sir.' He could remember the many evenings they had spent alone together when his father went down the glens, the Bible clutched to his breast and the whisky roaring in his head. He could remember the flames from the peat fire playing on her hands as the needle flew in and out. He felt a prickling sensation behind his eyes and a stab of pain over his heart. 'Yes, sir. I remember.'

Rance left him with a white silk shirt, ruffled at the sleeves, with orders to mend a small tear in the shoulder. It was an expensive garment, rich and soft to the touch, much better than anything he had handled before. One day, he told himself, he would have clothes like this.

He was clumsy with the needle and after an hour the tear seemed somehow to be worse instead of better, but Rance hardly glanced at it when he came in. He appeared to have forgotten James was there.

That night James lay on the damp straw in the steerage-hold thinking of the warm, dry cabin, the thick jersey, and the soft silk shirt. The comparison made his present situation seem more unbearable than ever. So when, on the following day, Rance said he would make James his

17

servant for the remainder of the voyage, his heart was high. His duties were light enough: washing and mending (Rance taught him the rudiments of needlework), cleaning, making the bed. Seeton had brought in a mattress and James slept on the floor. For the first three days the weather was stormy and he hardly saw Rance. The second mate spent the off-watch hours asleep on his bunk and James had little to do.

He never went on deck, never even went to the galley for his food – this was brought by Seeton, who smiled at James in a meaningful but quite incomprehensible way – and the cabin became more and more a fortress to be held against the outside world. It became his private place and sometimes he would even find himself resenting the intrusion of Rance.

But as the *Babylon* ran down the Channel the wind began to lessen and the skies cleared. The Bay of Biscay was like a sheet of blue glass.

Still James kept to the cabin. The convicts were exercised once a day now and he could hear the clanking of the leg-irons as they shuffled round the deck, each man chained to the one ahead.

One night, when Finisterre was the nearest land to port, when the glass was high, and the *Babylon* was sailing herself, Rance came to the cabin earlier than usual. He had a bottle of rum in one hand and two mugs in the other. James could smell the grog on his breath.

'We haven't seen much of each other, James,' he said, pouring the liquor into the mugs.

'No, sir.'

Rance drank deeply and motioned for James to follow his example.

'But much better here, isn't it? I mean better than in them cells.'

'Indeed, yes,' James said fervently.

'Warmer and drier, more comfortable, better food, better clothing.'

James fingered the thick wool of the jersey. 'Much better, sir.'

'Thomas. When we're here together you can call me Thomas.'

James stared at him.

'Say it!'

'Thomas.'

Rance smiled wetly at him. 'That's better.' He began to drink in earnest, and then he began to talk. He told James of voyages to the Mediterranean, the Baltic, the Low Countries, the East Indies. He told about India and Ceylon, Madagascar and Mauritius, and then he began to speak of his childhood in his mother's boarding-house in Southsea.

'I hope you always respected your mother, James.'

'Yes, sir.'

'I said to call me Thomas.'

'Yes, Thomas.' The grog had gone to his head and he was having to concentrate on focusing his eyes.

'Drink up,' Rance said, slopping more grog into his mug.

'I don't think I . . .'

'You'll drink it!' Rance said. He put his own grog to his lips and drank deeply. 'My mother,' he said in a voice maudlin with drunken reverence, 'was the greatest mother a man could want. D'you hear that, James? The greatest.' He nodded to himself. 'Too late . . . we only know too late.'

The bottle was empty and he flung it with a crash into the corner. Then he rose unsteadily to his feet and shrugged into his thick jacket. 'I'll be back,' he said, more to himself than James. 'I'll be back.'

Later that night James had wakened to find Rance looming over him. He was dressed in his white silk shirt with a red cummerbund around his waist. His face was flushed and his lower lip glinted in the lamplight. He had taken one of James's hands in his own and was fondling it. 'James, my dear,' he said. 'I'm back.'

For a second James's mind was too fuddled to take in what was happening, then with a roar of rage he sank his teeth into Rance's arm and held on like a pit-dog even when the second mate's fists smashed down on him and Seeton caught him by the waist.

As a punishment he was stapled to the deck for three days without food or water. The convicts who shuffled past him on their daily exercise at first looked at him in sympathy but then, when salt from the damp sea breeze rimed his lips and eyebrows and when his skin began to crack and bleed, they averted their eyes. Their own conditions were bad enough without identifying themselves with something worse.

During that time he experienced moments of lucidness and long spells when his mind was lost to him. Rance had said he would teach him a lesson, and indeed he learnt one. When they finally took him below and manacled him to Ogle he was not the same person who had come aboard.

'James!' The name was a hiss in his ear. He came out of the doze fearful and panting. 'Lie still!' He tried to wrench over to see who it was but a long pale hand, surprisingly strong, was pinning him to the wet straw.

'Quietly,' Fitzhenry said, so close that his lips were almost touching James's ear. 'Make a noise and we're done for.'

James straightened his body slowly so there should be no tug on the chain. Royal was sprawled against the corner bulkhead in sleep and above the noise of the ship he could make out the rasping snore of Ogle.

'What d'you want?' he whispered.

'Not what you're thinking, my pretty.'

He felt a heartbeat of anger and, as though in anticipation of it, Fitzhenry strengthened his grip. 'If you want to die here then make a sound. We'll die together, all of us. Take that for a fact. It's all or none.'

'How did you get here?' James said, nodding slightly at the ringbolt that Fitzhenry was holding in his hands.

'It's been loose for weeks,' he whispered back. 'Now listen. Tomorrow or the day after, we put into the Cape. I know because I've heard them . . .' His body began to shake with silent coughing.

'Who?'

Fitzhenry lay against James till the coughing subsided. 'Nollitts and Royal, of course. They think I've been asleep. They're going to make a run for it. And Ogle with them, though he doesn't know it himself yet.'

'But . . .'

'Don't talk! I'll do the talking!' He lay still again, gathering the strength to continue. 'Listen carefully. Nollitts knows the Cape. He was there in '96 or '97 when she was ours. Royal was once a corporal of Marines and he and Nollitts knew each other before though Royal never served abroad. They aim to get away from the settlement and into the interior till the ship's well away.'

'And if they're caught?'

'Why should they be caught? The Dutch authorities are sympathetic to deserters – or so Nollitts says anyway.'

'Why should they take us?'

'They don't know they *are* yet.'

'But Nollitts isn't a convict,' James said doubtfully. 'Why would he go?'

Fitzhenry paused. 'Same reason as ours – he's afraid of dying.'

Ogle groaned in his sleep and turned over. The chain rattled slightly and James quickly turned with him, stretching out his arm so the handcuff wouldn't wake Ogle. He lay still for a moment wondering why Fitzhenry was including him. He felt suspicious and at the same time frightened. But anything was better than this.

'What's your plan?' he whispered finally.

'None yet. We'll plan things as they fall. Maybe it'll be the end of us but it'll be a better end than rotting to nothing down here.' He nodded towards the waterlogged body of Pike.

'I'm not afraid.'

'That would not have been my first thought. Keep yourself ready. Follow my lead. Do you understand?'

James nodded. 'I understand . . .'

Fitzhenry loosened his hold and with infinite care began to ease himself through the black, straw-covered scum, to his place. He wedged the end of the ringbolt back into the bulkhead and let himself lean against it. He began to cough again, this time more violently.

The storm slackened off. By noon on the following day the

21

wind had dropped to twenty knots and patches of blue began to appear in the sky. Each spell of watery sunshine was followed by a bank of dark cloud, heavy with rain. The cold front now stretched across half the Colony, from the Rye Mountains in the north-west to the Outeniquas in the south-east. The first frosts of winter had appeared in the Snowy Mountains and farther north, in the dark and forbidding interior, snow had fallen on the Dragon Mountains. Over the Great and Little Karoos the skies were leaden and a cold wind blew dust clouds across the endless plains almost as far as the Great River.

At precisely 6.17 pm in a rain-sodden dusk the *Babylon* slid softly into the sheltered waters of Simon's Bay and came to anchor two cable-lengths from shore.

It was a forbidding coast-line; ridge-back hills rising almost straight from the sea, black and gaunt against the evening sky. Near the small jetty was the Resident's house – unoccupied for another month – the small stone hospital, a warehouse and, farther along to the right, the slaughter house. All were in darkness. It was still too early in the year for business. The Government had laid down that May 14th was the official start of winter. From that date ships would anchor at Simon's Bay to avoid the north-westerly gales which made Table Bay a graveyard, not before; if they did they could fend for themselves. Not even the inn, which had been built in the '70s, showed a light. Its owner had died the week before and his body had been taken twenty-five miles to Cape Town for burial. The little port, which nestled in the great arms of the False Bay, was utterly deserted.

And then, quite suddenly, small pinpoints of light appeared on the side of the hill. The lights winked and jigged in the deepening darkness as they descended to a small white beach. A group of Hottentots began to run the shallow boats down to the water's edge. They were joined by their womenfolk with baskets of fish and bread, oranges, lemons, tangerines, dried snoek, gourds of goat's milk, leathern wine-skins of muscadel, parcels of Hottentot figs and *uintjies*.

The bum-boats were launched through the surf and the rowers strained on the oars. They were laughing and

22

chattering among themselves. Four hundred yards away the black masts of the *Babylon* moved threateningly against the horizon as she pulled at her anchors. To a watcher on the shore she would have appeared black and menacing; to the Hottentots in the boats she was like a gift from a kindly spirit.

They surged round her like a school of porpoises playing round a whale. One of the boatmen put a fish-horn to his lips and its mournful notes began to sound across the dark water. There were cries of 'Master, master,' and thumps and bumps as the swells raised the boats and brought them scraping down the *Babylon's* sides.

There was an immediate response from the deck. 'Mr Miles! Mr Miles! Keep those heathen off! Keep them off, I say.'

'Aye, aye, sir! Guard! Where's the damn guard? Where're the muskets? Fire over their heads! Over their heads!'

But the scurvy-ridden crew had already seen the fruit in the boats. Someone had thrown a line, others were trying to get the nets out. The Marines were helping. Everything was in total confusion. Within a minute of the boats arriving the first Hottentot was on deck.

Oranges and lemons began to roll underfoot. Men fought for half a squashed tangerine, tearing it out of each other's hands, licking the juice from their fingers, swearing and shouting. The officers were no better. Everyone on board was suffering to some degree from scurvy.

More baskets and more Hottentots came over the rails until the heathen were all over the ship, in the cabins, in the mess and galleys, in the fo'c'sle hold and the 'tween deck prisons. The loaded cannons had been forgotten in the rush for fruit. Someone fired a pistol but the roar of the shot was hardly heard above the din of bargaining and fighting. In any case, in the mood the men were in, the shot sounded more like a triumphant celebration than an attempt at discipline.

Below, the prisoners listened to the whoops and shouts in bewilderment. At first a rumour sped round the cells that they had been boarded by pirates from St Augustine's Bay and they lay in their chains knowing that if the ship was taken their throats would be summarily cut and their bodies heaved into the sea. No one was going to ransom *them*. So they lay quietly in their chains hoping, for the first time since the voyage began, that they would be left where they were. But then a Hottentot burst down the companionway with half a basket of fruit and the real reason became apparent.

To the ear-splitting din on deck was now added the frightful moaning and chain-rattling on the holds. It was at this moment that Nollitts went below.

Like all the other prisoners, those in James's cell had first been apprehensive, but when they realized what was happening they had lain quite still, taking their cue from Royal. He was sitting up straight, his bony face turned towards the door. Fitzhenry watched him from the corner of his eye.

The door opened and Nollitts entered. Then things happened so quickly that even later, when he tried to recall the events in their proper sequence, James was conscious of a blurring. The Marine corporal had a spike and hammer in his hands. He stepped over Fitzhenry to get to Royal and as he did so Fitzhenry flung his arms around Nollitt's waist and pressed the point of his knife into his stomach. The Marine swung round with an oath, raising the hammer shoulder high.

'Don't try it,' Fitzhenry said, 'or you'll get six inches of steel through your liver.'

'What do you want?' Nollitts gasped.

Fitzhenry ignored him, turning to Royal. 'Did you think to leave us, you poor fool? Did you think to let us rot in here while you escaped?'

'Escaped?' Ogle said, his coarse face puckering in a frown.

Royal turned swiftly to Ogle. 'You were coming, mister. Never fear that.'

'Don't lie to us,' Fitzhenry said. 'No one was leaving here except you.'

'By damn!' Ogle shouted, lunging across the cell at Royal, but brought up short by the chain. 'You'd a done me in! Just like them!'

'I told you,' Royal grated at him. 'You were coming. Ask Nollitts.'

24

The Marine, shaking with fright, could only nod.

'Don't you believe him,' Fitzhenry said maliciously. 'He'd have left us here to die as soon as blink. And with smallpox aboard. That's correct, isn't it, Nollitts? Smallpox.'

'I swear I'm not sure!' Nollitts whispered. 'It's what I heard . . . two cases in the fo'c'sle . . .'

'And that's why you're so anxious to desert, isn't it, my friend?'

'We'd never get there!' Nollitts shouted. 'Don't you understand? None of us!'

'Give the tools to the boy,' Fitzhenry ordered. 'And you, Royal and you, Ogle, when those leg-irons are struck, just remember that he,' he indicated Nollitts, 'is your only chance. He's the only one who knows the country. One move from either of you and he gets the knife.'

'What about yourself?' Royal said. 'You can't like *our* company so much.'

'That would be an understatement. However, at the beginning at least, we shall have to put up with it.'

Royal turned away to watch Ogle's legs come free, then he said to Nollitts: 'Did you get the keys for the cuffs?'

The Marine shook his head. 'There was no time to look.'

'That's steel,' Royal said. 'We'll never hammer that loose.'

'We'll find something ashore.'

Ogle had taken the tools now and with a few swift strokes had struck the irons from Royal and Fitzhenry. They moved about the cell for a few moments chafing their weakened legs, then Fitzhenry said: 'You lead, Nollitts, and remember – through the liver!'

The noise from the deck was prodigious. The wine-bladders had been broached and the men were screaming and singing. They danced with each other, fought and fell down laughing on a deck slimy with squashed fruit and fish. Any sign of authority had vanished. Late-comers were scraping up orange peel and squashed pulp from the deck seams and stuffing it into their mouths. Hottentots, wild with excitement and their own wine-skins, poured into every part of the ship parading their glistening naked bodies with ornaments of pots, pans, kerchiefs, buttons, jackboots –

anything they could lay their hands on – and all the time the black rain poured down, thunder rumbled over the mountains and, every now and then, streaks of jagged fork-lightning split the eastern sky. Occasionally a voice, louder than the rest, called for order, but it was quickly drowned in the roar of rejoicing. No one either saw or cared when Nollitts led the four prisoners onto the seething deck.

James was utterly bewildered. He paused at the top of the companionway, suddenly afraid of an outside world that seemed to have gone mad, then he was jerked forward on the chain as Ogle saw an orange lying unnoticed in the scuppers. He dived forward, scooped it up and stuffed it whole into his mouth. The juice ran down his beard and he sucked at the hair, licking as far round his mouth as his tongue would reach.

James knew that if they stopped now they might be lost and desperately he tugged at the chain, forcing Ogle to come, keeping his eyes on the bobbing patch of Nollitt's scarlet coat as he forced his way through the throng. He saw one of the Hottentots grab at the coat, then the tall figure of Royal loomed above him and the Hottentot disappeared under the heaving bodies.

They reached the comparative calm of the wheel-house and James paused for a second to get his breath.

'Come on, damn ye!' Ogle said, pulling at the cuff. At that moment James looked deeper into the wheel-house shadow – into the eyes of Rance. They were frightened eyes, wide and white in the darkness. He was crouched in the lee of the bulkhead well clear of the rioting men, as though he knew what old scores could be paid off on a night like this. In his hands he clutched an axe.

'You!' he cried. 'You young bastard!' He straightened up and raised the axe. 'I'll finish you now!' As he swung his feet slipped on the slimy deck and he came down on one knee. That was enough for Ogle. He raised his terrible right hand and smashed it down on Rance's neck. James was aware of his own left hand being jerked skywards and then down again in the force of Ogle's blow and then Ogle hit again and again and James felt the shock of the blows through his wrist as his own hand, quite out of control, collided time and again with Rance's neck. He had not the slightest doubt that they were killing Rance nor could he do anything to stop it, nor perhaps would he have done anything if he could. What he did do was scoop up the axe from the dead man's hand and follow Ogle as he surged forward to the rail.

And then came a shriek that froze the blood in James's veins. 'Murder!' the voice cried, 'Murder!' He looked back over his shoulder. Seeton was standing over Rance's body and pointing a trembling finger at James. 'Murder!' he shrieked again. In James's ears the voice was loud enough to wake the dead but in the general bedlam, in the hissing rain and rumbling thunder, it was insignificant and lost.

The next thing James remembered was sitting hunched in the boat as Royal and Fitzhenry pulled erratically on the oars. No one seemed to have noticed their escape but they knew it would be only a matter of time before the search would begin and the red coats of the Marines would dot the heath-clad shoulders of the hills.

They were almost dead with exhaustion. It was nearly midnight and they had been rowing for four hours in the pitch darkness with only a lightning flash every now and then to guide them. First they had found the little beach of the Hottentots. The lights still twinkled on the sand as the women waited for their men to return. Ogle was for beaching the craft there and taking a chance but Fitzhenry shook his head. He had long since given up the oar to Nollitts and now sat in the bow, coughing intermittently.

'Use what passes for a brain,' he said. 'They'd tear us to pieces if we came ashore in one of their boats.'

'He's right,' Nollitts said. 'I'd rather trust myself with the men than the women.'

So they veered to starboard and rowed parallel with the coast going farther and farther into the jaws of the False Bay. They took it in turns on the oars, James squatting face to face with Ogle when the big man's turn came to row, pushing as the other pulled. In Simon's Bay itself, sheltered by the surrounding mountains, the sea had been unnaturally calm, but as they moved slowly up the coast the swells became bigger and they began to ship water. Those who were not rowing bailed with their hands but it soon became obvious they were not going to keep up. In desperation they rowed as close to the shore as possible, straining their eyes in the darkness. But all they could hear was the hollow groaning of deep swells surging against rocks.

James was dizzy with the effort but each time Ogle took an oar he was forced to join him in the thwarts. And each time he did so he put the axe carefully between his knees, its leather-bound shaft ready at his free right hand. In his dazed state the axe was his only contact with reality. He seemed to have formed a special relationship with it. When he was not rowing he clenched it in his hand. Perhaps it was because he had seen Royal's covetous glance that it had taken on added importance, perhaps it was simply because it was the only real thing he possessed of his own, or had possessed all these months. He no longer thought of it as Rance's axe, that was now only a dim memory; it was *his*. The intensity of his feelings must have communicated themselves to Royal for he made no move to grab it even though there were times when he might have tried.

Intermittently the skies cleared and the bright, newly washed stars looked down on the slow-moving boat. But before anyone could make use of the additional light, dark clouds, which followed each other like regiments, covered the sky once more and the rain poured down. The boat was slowly filling with water.

'We've got to try it,' Nollitts gasped.

'I can't swim,' Ogle said.

'There's no other way!'

'Bail, blast you,' Royal shouted, heaving on the oars.

'I tell you it's no use!'

Suddenly Fitzhenry's voice croaked from the bow: 'Be quiet! Stop rowing!' The creaking and splashing of the oars ceased abruptly. 'Listen!' In the sudden silence there was a faint hissing noise. 'Shingle! I tell you it's shingle!'

Royal grunted. 'You'd better be right, mister.' He bent his

long back over the oars. The boat moved sluggishly forward, crab-wise on to the swells.

'Surf!' Fitzhenry shouted with all that was left of his lungs. 'Surf!'

The combers were small but sharp, curling abruptly to the beach in the face of the wind blowing directly off the land. There was no chance of swinging the boat round to ride them, it was far too low in the water.

James had the impression of being suddenly raised from the seat of his trousers, his stomach left somewhere in the bottom of the boat, then the sky tilted and foaming water closed over his head. Salt water stung his eyes and gurgled in his throat, his arm scraped on something abrasive, pain shot up through his left wrist as his body turned on the chain; he was unable to tell top from bottom. Then with a wrench he was brought up short to find himself standing knee deep in water moored safely to Ogle. The big man was blowing like a whale. He was aware of holding on to something as though his life depended on it and when he looked down he saw the bright blade of the axe.

Royal and Nollitts were already trudging up the beach when James saw the body of Fitzhenry lying at the tide's edge.

'Come on,' Ogle said, jerking at the chain and starting in the direction of the others.

'No. We've got to help him.' There was something in the way James said it, backed by the axe, that would have made a refusal dangerous. Between them they got Fitzhenry onto his feet but he was so weak he could hardly stand. James was tempted to drop him again where he'd lain. What, he asked himself, did *he* care? But since they had expended the energy to get him up, leaving him would be pointless. They caught up with the others in the lee of some sea-weed covered rocks.

The wind tugged at their wet clothes, howling down at them through a gap in the hills. The entire top layer of sand on the beach seemed to be moving and it struck them on the face and hands, stinging viciously. It was not a cold wind but in their present condition it cut at them like a blizzard.

They stood for a moment, looking at each other with weary desperation. All their energy had been used up in the escape and now they were uncertain and frightened.

'Which way?' said Royal at last, turning to Nollitts. 'You're the one who knows.'

The deserter was crouched against the sheltered side of the rocks, his scarlet coat black with water. Slowly he came to his feet. 'I've never been this far along. I thought we'd be going into Table Bay.'

'Well, do you know *where* we are?' Royal asked angrily.

'I saw a map once . . .'

'Well?'

'I'm trying to remember.'

'Remember quickly, mister, we can't stay here.'

'If we can get to the beach below Mouse Mountain that should do us. We can hide there for a while.'

'Where is this beach, then?'

'That way,' Nollitts said, pointing into the darkness. 'It must be that way.'

At that moment the sound of a cannon was heard over the water. The men paused, holding their breath. But there was only one shot.

'What's that mean?' Ogle asked.

'Could be a signal.'

'Come on then!'

James was never afterwards able to remember that walk with any clarity, only fragments remained: the moment when Nollitts slid down a slime-covered rock and was almost swept away, the troop of frightened baboons that fled screaming up onto the slopes of the hill and then began to pelt them with stones, the moment the axe slipped from his fingers. That had been one of the bad moments, for Royal had heard it chink on stone and had scrambled back to find it. James had only grasped it in time and, crouching there, had waited for Royal to make up his mind. Eventually he had turned away. It had been lucky that Ogle was still resenting Royal at that time, since between them they would have had no difficulty at all.

From the point where they had landed on the cluster of

rocks that marked the western end of the beach below Mouse Mountain they walked six miles and it took them the same number of hours. Where they could they tramped through the tide fringe to obliterate their footmarks, where they couldn't they clambered over wet and slippery rock.

For the first mile Fitzhenry had managed to push himself along but then he had lagged farther and farther behind until eventually, after one of their rests, he was unable to get up.

No one actually suggested leaving him, they were too far gone to talk, they simply made no effort to help. They walked away, leaving him huddled in a niche in the rocks. For a minute or so they heard his coughing, and then even that was lost in the night.

In spite of the dizziness that kept his mind whirling, James was conscious of Fitzhenry's nagging absence. He told himself that he had never liked the man! Never liked his urbanity, his polish or his cruel tongue. In any case, Fitzhenry was not his responsibility. Dragging along at the end of Ogle's chain, he felt a childish and fretful anger at Fitzhenry. There *was* nothing he could do. He couldn't stop Ogle. They couldn't go back . . . His thoughts were swallowed up in the painful process of trying to survive. It was only later he realized, with a sudden sense of desolation, that being with Royal, Ogle and Nollitts was worse than being with no one at all. With loneliness came fear, and his fingers closed more tightly on the handle of the axe.

Dawn – a strange unexpected dawn of windless clear skies, yellow sunlight and wet, sparkling landscape – found them huddled below Mouse Mountain. Before them was the gigantic white scimitar of the beach that ran as far as the eye could see, to their right was the blue water of False Bay, its inlets and promontories hiding the *Babylon*, and to their left the brush-covered dunes that hid the twelve-mile track to Cape Town. In all that great sweep of land and sea nothing moved.

· The sun was rising directly ahead of them and as it cleared the peaks of the Hottentots Holland they began to feel its warmth. For the first time in months they looked at each other in full daylight and what they saw made them uneasy.

Their issue clothing was torn, stained and rotten; their beards – the dark cast of James's face was already darker with young stubble – were filthy and unkempt, not so much hiding as accentuating the hollow cheeks and the staring eyes. Even Nollitts seemed to have suffered from the privations of the voyage. They looked at each other briefly and then kept their eyes away.

'We've got to move,' Royal said.

James found himself saying: 'What about Fitzhenry?'

'What about him?'

'Are we just to leave him then?'

Royal's eyes were devoid of interest. 'He had his chance,' he said briefly, then, turning to Nollitts: 'D'you know your way *now*?'

James tried again: 'They'll find him when they come looking for us. They'll know we came this way.'

'The boy's right,' Ogle said.

Royal looked at Ogle: 'Will you go back for him then?'

Ogle met his eyes and looked away: 'If I didn't have these cuffs . . .'

'Aye, if you didn't.'

Nollitts said: 'We've got to get food. We can't go back.'

Royal nodded. 'Now listen to me: we didn't sink the gig and they'll find that easily enough. And then they'll find our tracks; make no mistake. So it doesn't matter at all what Fitzhenry tells them. That's if he can speak, if he's even alive by the time they reach him.'

'I want these cuffs off,' Ogle said, jerking at the chain.

'You'll have to wait.'

They huddled for a while in silence, unwilling to break warm cover and then, from the fringe of the dunes, James saw a group of four or five people make their way down to the beach.

'Look!' he whispered. The others followed his arm.

Royal turned to Nollitts. 'Who are they?'

The deserter watched the group put down their baskets and scatter over the sand. They were about two hundred yards away and it was plain they were picking up something on the beach and storing it in bags.

32

'Shell-burners,' he said. 'For building lime.'

'Hottentots?'

'Probably. A lot of them live among the dunes. I had to come out this way once to search for a gang of runaways.'

They waited in the rocks and watched. Four of the Hottentots picked up the shells, a fifth had dragged a small dead tree from the fringe of the dunes and, after breaking off the lighter branches for kindling, set it on fire. The smoke rose in a steady vertical column gradually spreading out into a light grey haze.

'Those baskets,' Royal said. 'Food?'

'Too many,' Nollitts replied. 'They'll carry the lime back in some.'

'But in the others?'

'They come out for the day.'

'What do they speak?'

'Dutch. A little English from the Occupation.'

'All right, you're going down there.'

'Me?'

'Yes. You still look like a soldier. Enough for them anyway.'

'But they'll know I'm not Dutch. What'll I tell them?'

'Tell them anything you like. Tell them you're off an English ship. There's no law against that.'

'I don't like it. We're leaving a track a mile wide.'

'It doesn't matter what you like, mister, you'll go down.'

Nollitts was about to say something further, decided against it, and rose to his feet. They watched him pick his way down through the rocks and walk out over the smooth white sand to the Hottentots. His scarlet coat, torn and scuffed though it was, had almost dried and it made a splash of colour against the white beach and dun-coloured dunes. The Hottentots watched him come towards them. They hesitated for a few moments and then, when they saw he was alone, allowed their curiosity to get the better of them and gathered round him.

There were two men, two women and a boy of about nine. Living close to the settlement at Cape Town, they no longer wore the sheepksin kaross of the tribes in the interior, but the

cast-off clothing of the Christians. The four adults wore
coloured kerchiefs tied round their heads. The men had torn
shirts above knee-length trousers. On their feet they wore
soft leather sandals. The women were dressed in dirty white
shifts which covered their huge buttocks like table cloths.
The boy wore nothing at all. They formed a circle round
Nollitts and stared at him expectantly out of smoke-yellowed
eyes.

From their cover in the rocks Ogle said: 'What if they kill
him?'

'Then we'll know how friendly they are,' Royal answered
briefly.

In spite of the sun's warmth, James shivered at the
matter-of-fact tone.

'He's talking to them,' Ogle said.

They watched for ten minutes, then Nollitts turned away
from the group and, shambling through the sand towards the
rocks, began to shout and beckon.

'Damn him!' Royal said viciously. 'He's given us away.'
He straightened up. 'Give me the axe.'

'No,' James said.

'We might need it.'

'No.'

Royal stood staring down at him for a second. 'You'll pay
dearly, boy,' he said, and then stepped out onto the beach.
The others followed. Nollitts could barely speak when he
reached them. His breath was coming in spurts and his eyes
were terrified. 'We're lost!' he said. 'Lost!'

'Get hold of yourself!' Royal snapped.

'I tell you we're lost!'

'I thought you knew the country.'

Nollitts was shaking his head from side to side. 'No! No!
Not that. Listen, the Cape's fallen.'

'What d'you mean?'

'It's no longer Dutch. It's ours! Four months ago!'

He waited for the news to sink in.

Ogle, misjudging the case entirely, said: 'Why, damn,
that's good, isn't it?'

Royal turned on him: 'You fool! Don't you understand? It belongs to the King. If we're convicts in England then we're convicts here and they'll hunt us down till they find us.' He turned to Nollitts once more. 'What else did they say?'

The deserter could hardly speak. His hands were trembling and his body shaking. 'There's a troop of dragoons out. They passed near here this morning.'

'Looking for us?'

'They don't know. I didn't tell them who we were. Said we'd been shipwrecked farther up the Bay. Thought they might have been after a pack of runaway slaves. A farmer was killed at Stone Mountain yesterday.'

'Just our damn luck,' Royal said savagely. 'Have they got any food?'

Nollitts nodded. 'But they won't part with it unless . . .'

'Unless what?'

'Unless I give them this coat.'

'You'll give it then.'

'It's the only covering I've got.'

While they argued the Hottentots had been warily approaching. They stood in a group some ten yards away and now the men held assegais in their hands. Without enthusiasm Nollitts removed his coat and was about to hand it over when Royal reached forward and took it. The Hottentots moved backwards and for a moment it seemed they might either launch their assegais or run.

'Not before we know what we're bargaining for,' Royal said. He spoke to the Hottentots. 'Let's see the vittles first. The food.' One of the men nodded and trotted off down the beach. The others followed, crunching their way across the loose sand.

What they had was pitifully inadequate: a few handfuls of pulse, some dried fish and two pieces of boiled meat, each about the size of a fist. But there was also a single orange and, with a cry, both Nollitts and Ogle dived for it. The deserter had been a few paces ahead of Ogle and reached the fruit first. He cradled it in his hands as though it were a jewel. The sudden activity had caused the Hottentots to scatter but now,

35

when they saw the Christian making a fool of himself over a single piece of fruit, they chattered and laughed and re-grouped themselves.

'Give it to me,' Royal said.

'It's my coat you're bargaining with.'

Royal bent down and pulled the orange from Nollitts's hands. It was over-ripe and partly squashed. He handed it to Ogle. 'Eat it,' he said. The big man stuffed it into his mouth. Before Nollitts could complain further, Royal said: 'We'll need his strength yet.'

James, who had been partly jerked off his feet by Ogle's movement, felt his own jaws ache with longing as the juice dribbled down Ogle's chin. Every tooth in his head was ringing like a bell.

'Good?' Royal asked.

It was such an unexpected thing for him to say that James glanced swiftly up at Ogle as he said: 'Aye, but we need more.'

'We'll get more.' Royal turned to Nollitts. 'Ask them if they've got more. We don't want this,' he indicated the pieces of meat and fish that were now covered with a sprinkling of sand. 'We want more fruit.'

The Hottentots, who by this time had lost all fear of the Christians, were fingering the red coat and the shiny buttons. 'Tell them they can have the coat but we've got to have more fruit.' By means of signs, a few Dutch words he had picked up ten years before and the fact that one of the Hottentot men was able to understand the odd word in English, Nollitts managed to convey his meaning. One of the men nodded and pointed with his assegai towards the dunes.

'He says there's more where they live,' Nollitts explained unnecessarily.

'Let's get it then. The farther we go into those dunes the safer we'll be.'

The dunes rose sharply from the beach. On the seaward side they were bare and arid, but after a few miles they changed to gentler slopes. These were covered in mesembryanthemums and hakea. As they flattened out, the soil became a mixture of sand and earth and the bush grew denser, giving way every now and then to a shallow pan filled with the rain of the past few days. There was bird life everywhere: snipe, grebes, herons, flamingoes, wild duck, sandpipers, wagtails, dikkops. It was as though the rain had germinated a hundred different species. The air was filled with the drowsy *koer-koer* of turtle doves and the gabbling rattle of guinea fowl. Partridges and quail rose in whirring brown blurs, trees and bushes were heavy with finches' nests. Overhead, swallows and swifts chased each other in endless streaks of black. Deep in this tangle of bush was a stretch of water called Sea Cow Marsh which had been named after the hippopotami that had once inhabited it and which had long since fallen to musket balls. Around the lake, hidden carefully in the bush, was a cluster of huts. It was to this small village that the Christians were brought.

Some of the huts were nothing more than shelters against the south-easter; simple constructions of branches and reeds woven together. Others were bigger, with mud walls and rough, thatched roofs. There had been no attempt made to group the huts round any central feature and they straggled along the edges of the marsh, some facing one way, some the other, as though built by a people who had lost any feeling of community. There were about fifteen of them and only one could have been described as permanent. It was much larger than the rest, its walls were built of stone and lime, its thatched roof neatly trimmed and an attempt had been made to whitewash the outer walls. Sitting on the top step in the bright morning sunlight was an elderly Negress. She was the first black person James had ever seen, and in spite of his weariness and the pain in his gums he looked at her in awe. She was dressed much the same as the Hottentot women but her clothes were neater and cleaner. She sat there, puffing on a short pipe made of a hollowed bone, a look of mild interest on her face, as though she knew that by just sitting patiently life would come to her. At one side of the house an old Malay was boiling pitch over an open fire and carefully caulking the seams of a frail marsh boat which he used to tend his wildfowl traps. When he saw Royal and the others he straightened up and began to shuffle painfully towards them.

He came round to the front and stopped next to the Negress.

One by one they were joined by other villagers; some were Hottentots, some Malays and some appeared to be a mixture of the two. Soon there were about thirty men, women and children in a loose group about the white men. They chattered occasionally among themselves but their faces were apathetic and dull. Only the four adults who had led the Christians from the beach, and who had a proprietorial interest in the scarlet coat, seemed the least bit animated. They were talking excitedly to the Negress.

The sun was high in the noon sky. Already it seemed to have sucked up any moisture from the Flats and the thin sandy soil was hot to the touch. James could feel the heat beating down on his head and shoulders. The villagers had been moving closer to hear what the Hottentots were saying and their bodies seemed to cut off all coolness. James found himself in the centre of a hot press. The walk from the beach, although it had only been a few miles, had been through deep sand most of the way and the exertion, with that of the night before, had made him light-headed. His legs felt rubbery and weak. More than anything he wanted a drink of cool water. He opened his mouth and tried to ask for it but his tongue seemed clamped to his palate. He had a sudden sensation of things whirling round him. Yellow bodies, wrinkled faces, staring eyes, and then he was falling into darkness.

When he came to he was lying in the cool interior of the house and the old Negro woman was bending over him wiping his temples with a wet cloth and crooning to herself.

'Little master is awake,' she announced. 'Old Lena knows. Old Lena knows how these things are.' She stopped bathing his face and unhooked a leather skin from a peg on the brown mud wall. She held it near James's mouth. 'Master must drink,' she said. He craned forward and placed his lips on the unstoppered opening and Old Lena slowly raised the sack. The milk was acid and cold.

He looked about him. The interior of the house was one large room. Reed matting hung on the doorway. In the cool, dim light he could make out the others; Royal and Nollitts asleep on the floor opposite, Ogle snoring at his side. For the remainder of that day and night and for most of the following day James was unconscious. There were times every few hours, when he came close to the surface of sleep, occasionally even waking, and each time Old Lena was somewhere near. She seemed to have a sixth sense which told her when he woke and she would appear next to him, her pipe clamped firmly in her mouth, the sack of milk in her hands.

When, late on the second day, he came out of his semi-conscious state, feeling weak and drowsy, the first thing that registered was that Royal had the axe.

The three men were sitting on stumps around a low table. It had been moved across the room almost on top of James so that Ogle could sit with the chain on his lap. They were talking in low voices. The axe was propped between Royal's legs, the blade had been shined and the light-brown leather of the handle had been cleaned.

'So you're awake, are you?' Ogle was looking down at him.

'What's that?' Royal said.

'The boy. He's awake.'

'Then you'll be wanting your axe back. I cleaned and honed it for you while you were resting.'

Nollitts laughed briefly. James noticed he was still wearing the scarlet coat.

The matting over the door was abruptly pushed aside and Old Lena came into the room. 'Is the little master awake?'

'The little master . . . the little master . . . That's all we've heard,' Ogle said. He pulled on the chain, jerking it against the raw wound on James's wrist. 'Are you awake, little master?'

Old Lena looked at him fiercely. 'And you a Christian!'

'Aye, I'm a Christian all right, when it suits me, and it don't suit me in these chains.' He held up his great arm for the woman to see.

'Leave her be,' Nollitts said. 'If it wasn't for the boy they wouldn't be helping us.'

'Do we know they are?'

'I told you, the old man's gone to fetch tools.'

'That's what he *said*. Someone gets a split skull if we're played false,' Royal said. 'You told them that, Nollitts?'

'Aye. I said we'd kill the boy.'

'They should have sent someone else,' Ogle said. 'The old man's a cripple.'

Old Lena, who had been bathing James's head and neck, turned to Ogle. 'The Christians make him a cripple,' she said flatly.

As she spoke the light streaming through the doorway was suddenly cut off. The three at the table whirled round to face a newcomer, the axe sprang as if by magic into Royal's hand.

'Vreetman!' Old Lena spat out. 'You not welcome in this place.'

'Be quiet, old woman. I come to see the Christians.'

Vreetman moved into the room. He was a very big man. His skin was the colour of mahogany and the wide nostrils and flattened nose indicated that somewhere in his back-ground there was Hottentot blood. He was dressed in a long black watch-coat, leather trousers, soft leather shoes with silver buckles, and a black hat, topped by a pure white ostrich feather. In his right hand he carried a musket, in his left a heavy wine-skin. He stood looking down at the four of them for a moment and then he said in his deep voice: 'I too am a Christian. I have brought wine.'

Royal said suspiciously: 'What do you want with us?'

Vreetman had pulled a stump across to the table and was sitting down. The musket lay handily across his knees.

'You need help,' he said. 'I can give help. We can make a bargain.'

Old Lena, hunched on the floor at James's side, said: 'If Jacob was here you would not enter.'

'That old fool. He takes two paces back for each one forward.' He unstoppered the wine-skin. 'Have no fear,' he said to Royal. 'I have no love for the Governor.'

'What are you?' Royal said.

'A hunter who knows the way beyond the mountains.'

'Are you a Bastaard?' Nollitts said.

The other nodded with pride. 'You know of me?'

Nollitts shook his head. 'I was here before. In the Occupation.'

'Then you know I am a Christian like yourselves. Not like these heathen.' He indicated Old Lena. 'She was a slave. She and old Jacob.'

Royal interrupted impatiently: 'You said you knew the way into the interior.'

'Like my hand.'

'Can you guide us?'

'Perhaps. First let us drink the wine.'

James watched the bulging skin go round the table. When it reached Ogle he put it to his mouth and James could hear the liquid running down his throat as though into a bottle.

'The boy?' Vreetman said when the skin was passed back to him.

'He's not of us,' Ogle said. 'The old man has gone for tools. These cuffs'll soon be off.'

Vreetman nodded. 'The mountains are no place for children.'

'He's yours if you want him,' Royal said. 'He killed a man. Second mate on the ship. There'd be a reward.'

Vreetman looked down at James. 'Yes – that may be so –'

He passed the wine-skin round the table again and they all drank deeply. The red muscadel dripped down their beards. As James slid once more into darkness the wine stained his restless dreams like blood.

The next time he woke it was night. The great shadows of the others were flung onto the opposite wall by the feeble glow of a rushlight. Old Lena was crouched nearby, the whites of her eyes shining in the gloom. She had been watching him and when she saw his eyes open she crossed to him carrying an earthenware vessel in her hands. She knelt by his side and brought his head up to drink. It was an infusion of some sort and tasted of bitter herbs.

In a few moments he felt stronger and was able to sit up. He saw that the wine-skin was empty and had been flung to the mud floor. Vreetman was no longer at the table.

'I tell you I don't trust him,' Ogle was saying in a loud

drunken voice. 'A red coat, an axe, a few buttons. Why should he guide us for trinkets?'

'You don't know these people,' Nollitts said. 'They'd sell their mothers for a brass button.'

'And why did he have to leave? Why couldn't he have taken us then?'

'Would you go into the bush without enough powder and ball?'

They were shouting hoarsely at each other. Royal suddenly lurched to his feet and stood swaying over them. 'Hold your noise,' he said roughly. Then he turned to Lena. 'You,' he said. 'Where's that man of yours?'

She was looking past Royal. She paused for a moment and the others turned to follow her gaze. 'He is here,' she said. Almost immediately the matting was pulled aside and the old Malay, Jacob, shuffled through the door. He paused for a moment accustoming his eyes to the weak light and then began to move painfully towards Lena. His clothes were dark with his own sweat.

'Nothing!' Ogle shouted, and rose unsteadily to his feet pulling James after him. 'He's got nothing!'

'The files!' Nollitts said. 'Did you bring the files?'

In two strides Royal was across the room and had gripped the Malay by the shoulder. He swung the old man round to face him. 'What are ye up to? Tell me or I'll split your face!'

The Malay was trembling so much with fear and exhaustion that the first words to come pouring out were in Dutch.

'Use English, you heathen!'

With an unearthly shriek Old Lena launched herself at Royal from the floor. She fastened onto his right arm like an animal. Royal stumbled backwards, momentarily flung off balance, but then Ogle reached forward and plucked Lena into the air like a piece of white cloth. In the same movement he flung her into the far corner. She lay still for a second, then began to wail.

'Now,' Royal said, holding the axe in front of Jacob's face. 'Tell me!'

'Master must know the soldiers are out,' the old man

whispered. 'The soldiers on horseback. They are all over the Flats.'

'Dragoons!' Nollitts said. 'They're looking for us!'

'Be quiet,' Royal said. 'How do we know it's *us* they want? What do you say to that, old man?'

'It is true, master. They come this way.'

Royal stood in the centre of the room looking from side to side like a trapped animal. 'Someone must have told them,' he said savagely.

'Those Hottentots this morning,' Ogle said. 'We should have kept our bargain!'

'Master must know it was no one from here.' He glanced over at James. 'We knew what would happen.'

Old Lena had stopped her wailing and now she uttered the one word: 'Vreetman!'

Jacob swung round to face her. 'He was with the soldiers! He was talking to them!'

'He was here,' Old Lena said.

Royal turned swiftly to Nollitts. 'D'you know the way to those mountains?'

'Aye.' The deserter was troubled. 'But we'll never reach there with the boy.'

'That's not what I'm proposing,' Royal replied. 'We'll use the axe on these chains. Ogle, you stretch the chain on the stump. You, boy, hold your hand on the side and brace as hard as you can.'

James had seen and heard everything in a daze. He knew now that he was very ill; that they were right, he would never make the mountains. Obediently he knelt on one side of the stump and braced his left hand on the side. He was aware more of Royal's shadow than of the man himself as he towered above him. He watched the shadow-axe rise against the far wall and then felt the shudder as the blow coursed up the chains. It came again and again.

'I tell you it's no use,' Ogle shouted.

Royal only grunted. He struck again. James was bracing with all his strength, pulling against Ogle on the other side.

'The links are sinking into the wood!' Ogle cried. 'You'll never do it that way!'

'Then it'll have to be the other!' Royal shouted, and brought the axe down with a terrible blow. James felt himself suddenly released, as though he had been shot from a cannon. His body was flung backwards. The chain was no longer at his wrist. He heard a dreadful scream and wondered what was happening to Old Lena. And then he realized that the scream was coming from his own throat and that he no longer had a left hand.

The silent, shimmering days of autumn had arrived; the most beautiful time of the year. In the Constantia valley the leaves on the vines had turned ox-blood and gold; the grapes had been trodden and the madeira barrelled. In the Land of Waveren, seventy miles north of Cape Town, the horses and mules had performed their endless chore on the circular threshing-floors and the grain was in store against the winter. Under Table Mountain the oak leaves were turning. The summer fish had left False Bay and the snoek were beginning to arrive. Wild duck were flighting, testing their wings for the long haul to the Scheldt and the Pripet Marshes; the swallows were leaving. In the Hantam the wood-piles were being replenished; in the Snowy Mountains the graziers were bringing their flocks down to winter in the Karoo.

In Cape Town itself the long summer's dust had been washed away and the stream down the Heerengracht sparkled in the autumn sunlight. People came out of doors more, pretty girls were seen in open carriages; there were race meetings at Mouille Point, balls at the Castle and picnics on Table Mountain. The town had settled down again to the second coming of the British and in general things were looking up. Butchers no longer threw their offal into the streets to be fought over by packs of savage dogs. The streets themselves were cleaner. The houses gleamed whitely in their new coats of wash. In the taverns the wine had improved beyond measure and while one drank a glass of Pontac or Moselle one could listen to a fiddler or even dance a jig.

Of course there was still the occasional execution at the Christian gallows under Signal Hill but they were infrequent. On the other hand, if one wanted some fun, there was the

44

heathen gibbet at the mouth of the Salt River reserved especially for slaves and Hottentots. There the activity was more lively with the chance that a slave might first be broken on the wheel.

There was still no bookshop in the town, nor a library, nor a real school, but people didn't have too much time for reading – and anyway there was always the Bible. For relaxation they had music. Taken all in all, the Cape of Good Hope in the early months of 1806 was as sophisticated a community as any place six thousand miles from Europe was likely to be.

Autumn at the Cape is a time of expectancy, the noon air seems to tremble with portent. The skies are windless, the sunshine has a burnt ochre tinge and the nights are cool. It is a time of Indian Summer days merging imperceptibly one into the next; a vacuum awaiting winter's onrush.

During those soft autumn weeks James struggled for his life. Sometimes the coma was deep, sometimes shallow. The dream came regularly. He dreamed he was lying in a warm still room. Bars of mote-filled sunlight patterned the shadowy corners. It no longer seemed to be an eastern palace and there was no throne and no beautiful woman. But he couldn't be quite sure because everything was hazy, as though his eyes were out of focus. Somewhere in the dream was a face. Intermittently it swam before him; a young face it seemed to him, but whether a boy's or girl's he couldn't tell.

It was there now, floating on the edge of the dream like a pale cloud, all its outlines blurred. It had eluded him so often that now he made a special effort to concentrate. The outlines hardened slightly. It grew smaller. Abruptly he found himself staring into the grave and anxious eyes of a young girl.

'Where am I?' he whispered weakly.

'At Paradise,' she said automatically. He stared at her in confused wonder for a few moments and then she picked up her skirts and ran from the room, shouting: 'Uncle! Uncle!' down the long corridors of the house.

Suddenly there were other faces. One, round and cherubic, wore gold-rimmed spectacles and the sunlight flashed on the glass as though on the ripples of a pool; and another, thin and white, a stranger's face until he heard the rattling cough. It struck a dim chord in his memory. The young face again with the grave grey eyes; and black faces and yellow faces, smiling and laughing; a sea of multi-coloured faces, swimming together on the edge of his vision.

'Welcome back, Sir Jamie,' the thin, white face said. 'You've had us a trifle vexed.'

The next time he awoke it was night. For the rest of his life he would remember those few precious moments when he first came to real consciousness: the quiet hush of the room, the luxury of the white sheets, the dream-like quality of security and the absence of memory. For seconds he was suspended in time and place. He would remember always the pattern of the carpet on the floor and the soft reflection of the lamplight on the polished stinkwood furniture.

He heard the scratching noise of a quill on paper and knew he was not alone. He turned to see who was in the room and with the movement came a sharp stab of pain from his left hand that brought sweat out on his brow. He tried to touch it but instead he felt the coarse bandages. With the pain came memory and he groaned aloud.

There was the sound of a chair being pushed back and James found himself looking up into the round, smiling face with the gold-rimmed glasses. 'Well, well, well,' said a high, cheerful voice. 'Are you back with us for good? Yes, of course you are. Now give me your hand, sir, and first I'll take the pulse and then I'll shake it – the hand, that is, not the pulse. Sometimes wondered if I ever would. All wondered, even the maids. Tears and laughter, tears and laughter. Floods.' While this rapid-fire speech poured over James the other had taken his wrist between his fingers. 'Um . . . um . . . um,' he said. 'Mesembryanthemum. Very difficult word to spell. Can you spell it? No reason why you should. Pulse all right.' He patted the hand between his own. 'And who am I, you ask? Quite right, I know you. You don't know me. No reason why you should. Henry Goodsir, physician, at your service.'

He gave a quick nod of his bald, pink head and formally shook James's hand. 'Welcome to Paradise.'

'Paradise?'

'As close as many of us will come,' said Dr Goodsir cheerfully. 'The house, sir, the house. Place is called Paradise, house is called Paradise. Not my choice. Called that when I bought it. Wouldn't have called it that myself. Tempting fate. Let's see your tongue.'

While talking Dr Goodsir had been carrying out a swift and professional examination of his patient. As he did so James was able to study him more closely. The doctor was about sixty, a little on the short side with a pink and well-scrubbed complexion. His head, which appeared at first sight to be too big for his body, was bald on top and fringed by a circlet of grey hair. He was dressed in dark blue broadcloth, white breeches and hose, yellow silk waistcoat and a grey cravat. The clothes were very tight on his rotund figure. Behind the gold-rimmed spectacles his eyes were bright and restless like a bird's, but there was a depth to them that contradicted his cheerful and eccentric manner. James lay back on the pillow, tense and suspicious.

Dr Goodsir peered down at him thoughtfully. 'Finished your inspection? Small, fat man who talks too much, eh? Well, never mind, never mind. Questions: how are you? What happened to you? How did you come here? And where is *here*? Answers: to the first you'll do. Answers to the rest later. Plenty of time. Know something about you, learn more later. Desperate criminal. Whole house full of desperadoes. Never thought it would come to this.' His eyes twinkled down at James. 'Don't hold with transportation. Never have. Don't hold with scurvy, dysentery, missing hands.' He paused to see what effect his words were having, then he said in a different tone: 'You're safe here, my boy. Safe. D'you understand that?'

'Yes, sir,' James said, speaking with reluctance. 'I understand.'

Dr Goodsir nodded then crossed to the table at which he had been writing. He picked up a little silver bell and tinkled it. Almost immediately the door opened and a coloured maid entered. She was middle-aged and moved as silently as a shadow on her bare feet.

'Doctor rang,' she said.

'Doctor rang, right enough. Take a look there, Maria,' he indicated James. 'James, say good evening to Maria. 'Knows more about you than any woman except your mother, or at least I hope she does. Been washing you every day for three weeks.'

Maria was suddenly embarrassed. 'Good evening, master.'

'Good evening,' James said.

'All right, Maria, a bowl of hot broth to start him on his way. You've got some ready, I've no doubt.'

'The doctor knows I make it every day for Mr Fitz.' She gave a curious little bob of the head to James and disappeared as silently as she'd come.

'You'd think with seven of her own she'd have had enough. Quite wrong. Been fussing over you like a hen.'

'Uncle?' The voice came from the doorway and Dr Goodsir turned.

'Now, what are you doing out of bed?' he said in a mock-serious tone.

'I heard voices.'

'Come in then, come in.'

As she came towards the bed, and while her face was still in shadow, James knew that this had been the face of his dreams, the one that had seemed to float always just out of focus.

'We've been very worried,' the girl said in a grave voice. 'All of us.'

She was slightly younger than James and her golden hair was rumpled from sleep. She wore only a light blue shift. The lamplight gilded and burnished her hair, bringing it alive in a ball of golden fire. Her face was narrow and her chin firm, and there was a sprinkling of freckles on the bridge of her sunburnt nose. She was still so closely identified with his subconscious that for a moment he was not certain that she was real.

'This is Frances,' said Dr Goodsir. 'Beware of her. She'll

stand no nonsense from me or anyone else. Isn't that so, my dear?' Talking to her, his voice had changed. It was softer and the faint edge of mockery had disappeared.

'How do you do,' James said.

'How do you do,' Frances replied solemnly. 'You mustn't believe everything Uncle Henry says.'

At that moment Maria arrived with a bowl of steaming broth and he became aware that the doorway had filled with faces. He could make out shining white teeth and eyes. He felt a momentary pang. Was it pleasure? Nostalgia? Gratitude? He reached out his hands to take the soup but Maria held back. There was a sudden deathly stillness in the room as though even the furniture was holding its breath, and then, as his eyes lighted on the bandages of the stump the waves of pain came flowing up his arm and exploded in his brain. There were tears on Maria's cheeks.

At the beginning of his convalescence he alternated between periods of lucidity and times when his mind wandered. He would find himself back on the hills above Daviot or in the crowded classroom of the Academy. He would see Rance's face above him or feel again the weight of Pike's waterlogged body; Somerwell, dying of heat-stroke in the tropics; Loxton writhing in the heather with James's bodkin at his throat. Fragments of memory chased each other through his troubled sleep and when he awoke, usually in a fit of deep depression, he was unable, for a time, to tell which was real.

But there was always someone at his bedside to help him reorientate himself, either Frances, or Maria or Dr Goodsir himself, working away at the table under the lamp.

At first, when Maria had come with the bowl of warm water and the towel, he had attempted to wash himself, but in trying to manipulate the bowl with a left hand that was not there, he had spilled the water over the bedclothes. No one had said anything. The linen was changed, the bedclothes taken to the kitchen to dry and a new set brought.

After that Maria had no more trouble. As she washed him she would gossip. James learnt a lot about Maria and her three husbands – he was never quite clear whether they shared her or whether they had followed each other in natural progression – and her seven children. And he learnt a lot about Dr Goodsir; chiefly that his servants loved him with the amused affection small children would have for an eccentric benefactor.

When she wasn't gossiping she was nagging. 'Master James's bones stick out like an old horse,' she would say. Or, 'Master James didn't eat his food yesterday.' And if it wasn't Maria, it was Frances. She would sit quietly in the chair by his bed, hour after hour, as he slept; watching him twist and turn, moan and grind his teeth. She was always there with a damp cloth to bathe his head when the pain was bad, or tuck the blankets under his chin when he began to shiver. Often, when he woke, the first things he saw were her grey eyes and he would give a shudder of relief.

Then she would begin to talk; Lettie, the cook, had cut her finger that afternoon; old Moos, the gardener, had found a baby squirrel in one of the oaks; one of the maids was going to have a baby and no one knew who the father was; her uncle had taken the carriage and gone into the town for supplies; he'd found a new plant for his collection; Fitzhenry's cough was worse than the day before, or it was better than the day before, or it had rained in the night or it hadn't. She related the day's minutiae in a solemn, slightly breathless voice.

The squirrel died, the cut healed up, the maid wasn't going to have a baby after all. In spite of himself James began to get caught up in the daily serial.

At other times he would lie alone with his thoughts and managed to piece together some sort of patch-work. He could recall the *Babylon* and even the escape. He could remember them scrambling up the beach and crouching in the lee of the sea-weed covered rocks. And then . . . nothing. Only a grey blankness until he awoke in Dr Goodsir's house.

He knew that at some point in the blank patch he had lost a hand. He did not know how or why and in his early weakness and lassitude he was incurious. He was also aware, though he could not remember what, that something had happened between Fitzhenry and himself and occasionally, without any warning, he would feel a flash of anger towards the other man.

So when either Maria, when she was washing him, or Frances, when she was reporting the activities of the house, touched on Fitzhenry, his lips tightened and he lay back in silence. This passed unnoticed because in all the weeks at Paradise he had, in any case, hardly spoken a dozen words.

He knew Fitzhenry was very ill but that hardly touched him at all. What did bother him was that Frances seemed to find Fitzhenry amusing, or at least she was always reporting what he'd said. Once she told him how brave Fitzhenry thought he was, and instead of being pleased he had taken this as a gibe and felt a black anger spread through him at the thought of Fitzhenry and Frances discussing him.

'I wish you wouldn't talk about me,' he had said to her.

For a few seconds she made no reply, and then she said: 'You mustn't hate *everyone*, James.'

Frances, James found as the weeks passed, was like that. She said unexpected, baffling things. Sometimes they were embarrassingly frank. Like the time he asked for a pitcher of water and she turned on him saying tartly: 'It's time you learnt to say please!' He was wary of her for a day or two after that.

It soon became apparent that, young though she was, Frances was the keystone on which Paradise was founded. Without her the big house would have run down and come to a halt. Food would never have arrived, beds would have gone unmade, supplies would never have been fetched. Dr Goodsir lived in a botanical and zoological fairyland of his own, in which the ordinary things of every day were simply an intrusion. Not that he neglected his patients or his niece; he spent part of each day with James and another part with Fitzhenry. He was kind and considerate. He would play endless games of chess with Fitzhenry or tell James about the new specimens he was cataloguing; it was just that he took life's organization for granted.

There was something else that James was to learn as he lay in the big bedroom and watched the raindrops course down the panes: he was Frances's property. She had found him, she had brought him in. Nothing was said, but he could feel a tacit acceptance among other members of the household.

But how she found him, or why or when were part of the blankness and he had no strength left over for curiosity. He did learn other things about her: that her father had been Assistant Secretary at the Cape in the First British Occupation, and that he had been killed in a hunting accident near Swellendam two years after her mother had died of fever. Dr Goodsir, who had been at the Cape for eleven years, first as Surgeon with John Company and then, when he had received his inheritance, as a private physician, had become her guardian. He discovered these facts without any conscious effort, his brain simply piecing them together from things he heard. He never encouraged people to talk to him, nor did he discourage them; he lay between the linen sheets like a vegetable.

Winter arrived and with it a change came to the house. Day after day the north-west wind raced across the stormy Atlantic, driving the black cloud-regiments before it. They marched across the sky until they met the great crags of Table Mountain squarely in their path and then released their loads. Paradise lay on the wet side of Table Mountain and from James's bedroom he could look up to the shoulder of the mountain, half hidden by traceries of mist, and see the silver streaks of waterfalls slashing the black rocks. After each storm there would be a period of calm, of bright rain-washed days and daffodil-yellow sunshine; again there would be that feeling of expectancy in the air. He became good at predicting when each storm would come. He found that a day or so before one was due, the mountain seemed to move much closer to his window. He could make out separate cliffs and rocks that were normally only a grey blur. Then he would hear a rustle, like that of stiffened petticoats, as the dry oak leaves were blown lightly on the flagstoned verandah. The rustle would become a rush of air in the leafless-oaks, then a shard of mist would coyly appear on the top of the mountain and it would only be a matter of hours before the mist gave way to rain-clouds.

Watching the changing landscape with what interest he could muster, it was some time before he realized the change in the house. Sounds which he had come to associate with the pattern of the day now seemed muted. He no longer heard laughter from the kitchen or the clattering of china; footsteps in the corridor were softer, as though people were walking on tip-toe. Maria had stopped her gossip. He was washed less frequently and then by Dr Goodsir. Much of the sparkle seemed to have left the doctor's eyes and even Frances's face was more solemn than usual. But all this hardly impinged upon him until one day, waking suddenly from sleep, he saw Dr Goodsir and Frances standing together by the window. He heard her say: 'But what can we *do*, uncle? There must be something!'

'Do? Do! Quite right. Something must be done. But what? Done everything, tried everything. Here,' Dr Goodsir said tapping his head, 'and here,' he pointed to his chest. 'That's where the trouble is. No physic for what ails him. Seen too much, done too much, experienced too much. More than body and mind can stand.'

'If only he . . .' Frances began. 'I've tried to tell him.'

'Both have. No good. Slips away into another world. Ears close, mind closes. No effect.'

'If he knew, do you think . . .?'

'Perhaps. Kill or cure. Must do something!'

James knew then that Fitzhenry was on the very edge of death and instead of leaving him unmoved, as he might have expected, he felt a strange touch of apprehension, as though Fitzhenry's passing would remove for ever a landmark in his life.

Later, when Dr Goodsir was changing the dressing on his arm, James asked after Fitzhenry. Dr Goodsir looked down at him in surprise. 'Fighting,' he replied. 'Fighting.'

It was only later that James discovered it was *his* life that had hung in the balance.

Sunshine followed rain, rain followed sunshine. The winter weather conformed to its annual pattern. He was no longer interested. And then, on a day in August, when the mountain was covered in heavy cloud and a dying gale soughed in the trees, the door of his bedroom was pushed slowly open. In the half-light of the dismal day two dark figures entered; one held onto the other's arm as he shuffled painfully forward.

James was vaguely aware that he was not alone. He assumed, for he could now hardly tell one part of the day from another, that it must be time for his plate of broth, and he half turned in the blankets. The two figures had reached the foot of the bed and there they stopped, their black faces merging with the darkness of the room. They were a ghostly couple; faceless, disembodied, messengers of death. He stared at them for a second, then his heart began to flutter and beat irregularly. He pushed himself up in the big bed trying to get as far away from them as possible, and all the time horror was mounting inside him like the chill of an open grave. And then one of the figures spoke. 'Little master,' it said. 'Little master, it is I . . .'

But that was all James heard. He gave a frightened cry and leapt out of bed. His legs buckled beneath him and he crashed forward senseless on the floor.

It was debatable as to who had been the more frightened, James or Old Lena. But there was no time for hysterics because Dr Goodsir, who had been waiting in the shadows near the door, hurried into the room.

'Help me. Back into bed,' he said. They lifted James and put him between the covers. 'Brandy,' Dr Goodsir said and poured a good measure into a wine glass. 'Head up. Hold him!' Old Lena got her strong, wiry arms under his back and lifted his frail body as though it were an empty leather bag. At first the brandy spilled down his lips and chin, but little by little Dr Goodsir forced it between his teeth and watched as he swallowed. His breathing became easier, his eyes flickered once or twice and then opened. He found himself staring into Old Lena's anxious white orbs. For a moment the terror swept back and then something seemed to move in his brain, as though a knot was loosening itself, and all the fear drained out of his body. He smiled.

Dr Goodsir mopped his brow. 'Desperate measures!' he said in a shaking voice. 'Desperate measures!' But by that time James had slipped into a quiet, untroubled sleep. It was his seventeenth birthday.

Within a week of Dr Goodsir's experiment he was showing signs of improvement. As the newly cut keys unlocked the doors of his memory, the days that followed were of great intensity. He found he could remember almost everything, and with Dr Goodsir's patient prompting he thought he could even recall what had happened after 'the accident'. This was Dr Goodsir's phrase and would never be his; never as long as he lived. But how much was memory and how much the result of what he learnt he wasn't sure. Could he *really* remember being helped out of Lena's house by the two old people after Royal and the others had fled? Had he been conscious, even for a fraction of a moment, when they had plunged the bleeding stump of his arm into the cauldron of hot pitch? And what of Fitzhenry, almost dead with exhaustion, who had stumbled on their hiding place in the bush as the searching dragoons shouted to each other in the darkness?

At times he thought he could remember these incidents with great clarity, at others they seemed to have happened to someone else. He knew they had made a litter and carried him six miles to Paradise, but that was all. He could not remember the journey though he could appreciate how dreadful it must have been, not only for himself, but for the two old people who carried him through the night. Nor could he remember their arrival; the sleeping house that suddenly came awake to the wishes of a young girl. But at least if he could not be sure of his memory he was sure of the facts and that suddenly mattered a great deal to him. On the facts depended the later payments and he was quite certain that payments would be made.

He was conscious too that luck had played its part and since his life, up to then, had been utterly devoid of it, there was some crumb of reassurance to be taken for the future. It was more than luck, it was coincidence, that Lena and Jacob had once been bought and freed by Dr Goodsir; it was lucky too, in a dreadful way, that when he was younger old Jacob had had the Achilles tendons of both ankles cut after trying to escape, since it was his very slowness that had discovered Vreetman's treachery. James knew there was a great deal to be thankful for and a great deal to regret, but if Rance had taught him one thing it was that it was better for others to do the regretting. One day it would be Royal's turn to regret, and Ogle's and Nollitts's! This he promised himself.

Winter gave way to spring; filaments of green hung from the oaks in the garden, pink and white blossom covered the peach and apricot trees, grass sprang up everywhere, even from the thatch of the roof. As the season strengthened so did James. He was still withdrawn, but that was part of his nature now, more of a quiet reserve than an emotional blank. He began to put on weight and though no colour came to his dark, saturnine face, his eyes were clear and healthy. Much of the pain had gone from his arm except for the occasional twinge in a hand that wasn't there. With his improvement the house returned to its normal and cheerful business. Dr Goodsir was busier than ever with his collection and James saw less of him than before but the physician still made it a practice to visit him every day. There was talk of a tutor being engaged for Frances, Maria was going to have another baby and James was mildly shocked that someone of her age could still indulge in such extravagant pursuits.

Lying in bed he began to feel restless. He was not conscious that with his returning strength he was getting ready to face life again, all he knew was that he was tired of being confined to one room.

'I'm better now,' he said to Dr Goodsir for the tenth time in a week. 'I want to get up.'

'Want, want, want. That's the voice of health all right,' Dr Goodsir had replied with asperity. 'Same story. Never fails. Always know better than the doctor.' But Dr Goodsir was aware of his improvement and when Frances, who was equally restless for James to be up so she could show him her world, also began to nag him, he relented to the point of allowing him to sit on the verandah for a few hours every day.

At first he had to be carried by the servants but after a few days his legs began to grow stronger and he could usually manage to totter out on the arm of Frances or one of the maids. For a while his new mobility was the most exciting thing in his life. Old Moos, the gardener, cut down a poplar sapling and trimmed the bark off it to make him a stick and soon it became adequate enough for his short, fragile steps. With mobility came discovery and for the first time he was able to explore the house and grounds.

Paradise had been built at the beginning of the first British Occupation of the Cape by a cavalry officer for his bride. Within two days of her arrival from London she had announced her intention never to live in so isolated a spot and had boarded the next Indiaman and sailed away. For a number of years the house had stood empty, almost completely hidden from the world by poplar thickets and groves of silver trees. Then Dr Goodsir had bought it not for any aesthetic reason but simply because 'specimens' grew at Paradise in great profusion. His delight at finding *lythrum hyssopfilolia*, which he still maintained must have been accidentally introduced from Europe, was worth every penny piece he'd paid. The house had been built in the Dutch style, with graceful gables, dark thatch, and crisp white walls. The great door, opening out onto the verandah, was painted dark green to match the shutters. The floors of all the rooms were large square red flags, which made Paradise a chilly place in winter but cool in summer. It was not as elegant as the farms at Constantia or the country houses at Rondebosch but Dr Goodsir had had no thoughts of elegance when he bought it. The gallery was a simple affair with a yellowwood dining table and chairs at one end, and at the other, where the slave benches would have been – Dr Goodsir did not hold with slavery – a fire-place had been built ranged round with leather-thonged chairs.

Most of the furniture in the house was made of stinkwood or yellow-wood and with the constant waxing and polishing it gave a depth to the rooms, its soft reflections lighting dark corners. Corridors branched off from each side of the gallery, onto which the bedrooms let, and behind it was the territory ruled over by Frances: the small *dispens* where the linen, table-ware and provisions were kept, and, behind, the kitchen.

With the house had come three acres of land which was covered in oaks, poplars and silver trees. On shady banks periwinkle spread in green profusion, geraniums and irises grew wild. In this jungle Old Moos cultivated lettuces, beans, peas, onions, cabbages, carrots and potatoes for the kitchen. At the back of the house, beyond the stables, Frances nurtured a flock of tame guinea fowl which arrived singly or in pairs, roasted or stewed, on the dining-room table. Dr Goodsir, who identified himself a little too closely with the local fauna, was wise enough not to ask questions. He dearly loved a prime bird. Occasionally, too, there were quail and partridge, and pieces of venison – gifts from the Malays and Hottentots who were his infrequent patients. For the rest, supplies of poor beef, flour, maize, butter, lamp oil, vinegar and spices were brought from the town. They never needed to buy soap or candles, which came as gifts from Dr Goodsir's grazier friends in the interior of the Colony.

Paradise lay under the shoulder of Table Mountain with the Devil's Mountain on one flank and the Wine Hills on the other. It was two miles off the main carriage road to Cape Town and in wet winters, when the mountain rills rushed down to fill the Liesbeek River the track from Paradise was often impassable. At those times the flock of guinea fowl diminished rapidly.

As far as James was concerned its isolation was its strength. Together he and Frances wandered the surrounding woods. Sometimes they would pick flowers and grasses for Dr Goodsir's collection and at others they would venture down to the outskirts of the villa gardens at Rondebosch and watch the carriages pass to and fro on their way to the town. Their world was bounded by the settled areas; Rondebosch, the Governor's summer home at Newlands and the wine farms of Constantia. At first, when he was able to get about with more ease, James found an added spice in exploring the perimeter of his prison – a feeling shared equally by Frances – and they would lie for hours in the warm spring sunshine, hidden in thickets overlooking the unsuspecting gardens of the wealthy burghers. It was exciting to watch the slaves hoeing and weeding, to hear the children at play, and to watch the slow, pompous daily life of the adults unfold before their secret eyes, but as he grew stronger he realized that large as his prison was, it was still a prison and he was still a prisoner.

For a long time the fact that he was a branded criminal and the memory of his arrest and trial, were buried beneath all that had happened later. He forgot there was an added dimension to his existence and the sudden realization of his situation came as a shock. It was brought home to him when Major Paxted came to dinner.

James had been feeding the guinea fowl behind the stables in the late afternoon, holding the bowl of crushed maize under his left arm and flinging the grains in a semi-circle with his right, when he heard the sound of a horse on the hard-baked clay of the yard. He watched incuriously as the stranger dismounted with a jingling of harness and spurs. At that moment the yard was completely deserted, and, quite naturally, he put down the bowl of maize, and started forward to greet the officer. There was no thought in his mind other than that he must welcome the stranger and take his horse when suddenly the Major, who had been looking vaguely about him for some sign of life, saw him.

'Halloa there,' he called. 'Is there anyone at home?'

James froze. In the dim recesses of his mind the voice, or perhaps not so much the voice as the *kind* of voice, struck a chord. He was plunged back abruptly to the hiding place in the bush with Old Lena and Jacob pressing on both sides of him, invisible in the dense black shadows; and all round the clash of harness and spurs and the voices of the Dragoons shouting to each other; voices like this one.

'You there, sir,' Major Paxted said, puzzled. 'Esteem it a favour if . . .'

James heard no more. In a moment he had sprung behind the stable wall and was racing through the underbush into the heart of the thicket.

Hours later Dr Goodsir found him crouched amid a tangle of vines and blackberries half-way to the foot of Table

Mountain. He was holding a heavy oak branch in one hand and his lips were drawn back over his teeth in a snarl. In the bright moonlight he looked like a trapped animal.

'Get back!' he hissed.

Dr Goodsir looked down at him thoughtfully and finally said: 'No business of mine. Only wanted to say Frances is worried.' He turned on his heel and disappeared through the trees. It was after midnight when James slipped silently through the dappled moon shadows to the safety of his room. Nothing was ever said.

The second time his security was threatened he tried to kill a Hottentot. It was summer by then and the south-easters were raging. By this time Dr Goodsir had fitted a steel hook to his left stump and he found he was able to climb trees again and start an egg collection. He was half-way up a wild fig tree, searching for nests in the thick foliage, when he looked down and saw something white waving in the wind.

It was an unfamiliar movement and he gently lowered himself from branch to branch until the leaves cleared and he could get an unimpeded view. He found himself staring down on the crown of a black hat topped by a tall white ostrich feather. The owner of the hat was sitting with his back to the tree, his musket a yard from his right hand. He wore a black watch-coat, leather trousers, black hose and soft leather shoes with metal buckles. One name burnt itself into James's brain: 'Vreetman!' Without thinking he launched himself from the lower branches and before the terrified Hottentot knew what had happened he was on his back and a madman with a steel claw was about to tear out his windpipe.

'Master!' the Hottentot managed to call out. 'No, master!'

Then, through a red mist, James saw that the man wasn't Vreetman at all. He leapt to his feet and ran headlong into the trees.

He was away two days that time, living on unripe blackberries in the kloofs of Table Mountain. When he came to his senses and realized that his clothes were in shreds and that he was starving, he made his way back to Paradise. Again nothing was said and this was eventually to worry him more than his actions. Apart from the anxious frown on

Frances's solemn face and Dr Goodsir's remark that unripe blackberries were bad for the digestion, it was as though nothing had happened and it gave him a feeling of unreality. For several days he kept to his room and during that time the true nature of his own relationship with Paradise dawned on him. He had simply accepted the place and the people as another unplanned step in his life. This was where the mistake lay.

Dr Goodsir and Frances belonged to a different world, one that went beyond the confines of Paradise. They could move in it freely, their only restrictions being Fitzhenry and himself. Almost immediately he found himself resenting them and their unspoken demands that he look at himself and his future. His future? He had never given it a thought. Why should he, since there was always the chance it would be worse than the present. It was true that occasionally he felt restless and constricted, but that was offset by comfort, kindness and security. When he realized this a cold hand seemed to grip him round the heart. There would be a time when he must go, when he would be alone again. For hours he wrestled with the thought, wondering, with a mixture of self-pity and apprehension, what he would do in a strange land by himself where every man's hand would be turned against him.

He went to Fitzhenry. He had visited him several times since he grew strong enough to leave his bed but on each occasion it had been either with Dr Goodsir or Frances. And even when Fitzhenry had begun to improve and his bed was taken onto the verandah on fine days, James had avoided that side of the house unless he knew that Fitzhenry, or Mister Fitz as Maria had named him, was not alone. Among his never-to-be-forgotten memories was Fitzhenry's cough, fading in the distance, as they left him on the beach.

Why he went to see him now, he wasn't sure, unless it was an instinctive feeling that their futures were somehow linked. The visit was not successful.

A black south-easter was howling across the isthmus and Fitzhenry was confined to his room. James found him propped up on the pillows, a volume of Linnaeus, from Dr Goodsir's library, lying face down on the covers.

Although the past months had done a great deal for Fitzhenry it was not apparent to a casual inspection. His hands were still white and almost transparent, his cheeks, now clean shaven, were marked by two blotches of colour, his hair was long and silky, coming down almost to his neck. There was something feminine about his fragility until one saw his eyes, bright and glittering.

'Well, well,' he said, greeting James. 'If it isn't the laird himself.'

The waspish tone stung. James's anger lay very near the surface these days. He fought down an impulse to counter with an acid reply, knowing very well that a verbal engagement with Fitzhenry would leave him floundering, and announced instead: 'I've come to see you.'

'An excellent observation,' Fitzhenry mocked. 'Linnaeus would be proud of you.' He tapped the cover of the book. 'Very precise on facts is our friend Linnaeus. But . . . I'm forgetting myself. Make yourself comfortable.' He waved limply at a chair.

James shook his head and wandered to the window, watching the oaks lash at themselves in the wind. 'How are you feeling?' he finally asked.

'In fine fettle,' Fitzhenry said with a smile. 'If it wasn't for this slight indisposition I'd be shinning up and down the crags like a clansman. No need to ask the same of you. Quite apparent. With that hook you look more like a pirate every day. Putting on weight too. Disgustingly healthy.'

James took a deep breath. 'I want to thank you,' he said.

'Whatever for?'

'For helping . . . when they brought me here.'

'Don't be ridiculous. I could hardly walk myself. I simply followed my nose. No thanks due at all and anyway it should really be the other way round. You could have left me to drown.'

James looked away in embarrassment and the subject of the beach, which might, if he had suddenly taken his courage in both hands, have been demolished for ever, seemed to increase as a barrier between them. The words of regret were almost in his mouth but would not emerge. His brain clamped down on them: *let someone else regret.*

'Dr Goodsir's going on a journey soon . . .' James tried again.

'And you think we should go with him?'

'Well, we can't stay here for ever.'

'We? Oh, yes, I see what you mean, forgive me. The criminal element. Well, you know, Jamie, my boy, I've almost forgotten about that.'

'Forgotten!'

'You see my criminality is so . . . so slight, compared with some others.' He was smiling mockingly at James. 'After all, my only transgression was statutory — though they tried to call it treason. No,' he continued reflectively. 'I don't think I shall be any trouble. Now you, on the other hand . . . Ah. Very different proposition. Real desperado. It must be that Highland blood. Fancy attacking a school fellow. It simply isn't done, you know.'

'*Who told you?*'

'You did. Babbled your head off when we first brought you in. Loxton, I think you called him.'

James felt his world tilt slightly.

Fitzhenry was still talking. 'You see I've no conscience, Sir James. None whatsoever. Here I am and here I stay, and very comfortable thank you.'

Loxton! He turned to the door.

'The trouble with you, dear boy,' Fitzhenry said irritably, 'is that you lack a sense of humour. You're as solemn as an owl. I shall have to tell Frances about you.'

James whirled on him. 'Leave her alone, damn you!'

Later in the day, when his anger had cooled somewhat, he met Dr Goodsir coming from Fitzhenry's room. For the first time the doctor was looking less than his usual cheerful self. 'You've been annoying Mr Fitz,' he said severely . . . 'I won't have it.'

'He baits me,' James said sulkily. 'He always has.'

'Has it not occurred to you that if it hadn't been for his baiting as you call it, you might never have survived the voyage? The only value hatred has is that it creates a will to live. Now go out and see if you can find me some *asparagus scandens.*'

It was one of the longest consecutive speeches James had ever heard him make.

He lay on a bed of dry pine needles high up the slope of Table Mountain. Away on his right he could see the Stone Mountain and then Mouse Mountain and the long curving beach below it where they had first met the Hottentot shellburners. Ahead of him were the wind-swept Flats and beyond them the mountain barrier of the Hottentots Holland. The black south-easter had moderated but the windclouds still lay heavy between the peaks.

He turned to Frances, who was lying at his side. 'Why didn't you tell me?' he asked.

Frances's face was pink with exertion and her blonde hair hung about her cheeks in damp wisps. 'There wasn't much.'

'I trusted you.'

She put a hand out and touched his mutilated arm. 'It wasn't important.'

'You all knew. You and your uncle, even Fitzhenry.'

'You don't like him, do you?'

James dug his hook into the soft pine needles. 'No. I don't.'

'He's fond of you. Does that surprise you?'

'Very much. The way he talks you wouldn't think so.'

'He'll stop when he gets stronger. You'll see. Did you know that for the first three days he hardly left your side? Uncle Henry had to order him to bed. He said he was killing himself.'

James shifted uncomfortably on the slope. 'I don't want to talk about him,' he said suddenly. 'We always talk about him.'

'The trouble with you, James Fraser Black,' she said crossly, 'is that you have no humility.'

'I'm hearing a great deal about the trouble with me this day,' James said. 'First it's no sense of humour then it's no humility.' He rolled over on his back and began to pick his teeth with a dry pine needle.

'Why do you follow me around,' he said at length, 'if you don't like me?'

'Follow you around! Why I'll . . .' In a moment she had scooped up two handfuls of pine needles and had rubbed them into his hair and down his shirt front. It was done half in anger and half in childish high spirits but the effect on James was alarming. He had grabbed her, thrown her down and had the hook raised – all before she could move or say another word. The laughter in her eyes vanished.

'Frances!' he said, holding her now as though she were made of fragile porcelain. 'Frances, I'm sorry!' He brushed the pine needles from her skirt and helped her to sit upright. Then he passed a trembling hand over his forehead. 'Something happens,' he said. 'Something just happens and I don't know what it is.'

She was kneeling at his side and stroking his arm. 'It's all right,' she said soothingly. 'It's all right!'

'One minute I'm — And the next! Frances, I get so frightened!'

'It's all right. It's all right.'

'Don't you see, someday I'm going to . . .' His body began to tremble more violently.

'Is this how it happened with Loxton?' she said.

He nodded.

'Tell me,' she said. 'It'll help.'

There are some stages of one's life which don't seem to start anywhere definitely and which end, almost without trace, simply merging with the next. It was not this way with Loxton. He was a separate unit, an enclosed area of time. James could even remember precisely the moment he had first heard of Loxton. It was on the day he went to the Academy; a cold, damp day with a bitter north-easter blowing in across the Moray Firth. Because it was his first day at the Academy he knew no one and he stood alone in the yard at the dinner hour, eating the oatcakes his mother had wrapped. One wall of the school house was sheltered from the north-easter but since it was already packed with twenty or thirty boys there was no room for James and he stood about fifteen paces away, pretending to be unaware of the situation. He could not, however, help hearing the remarks.

'My father says there's black blood in the Frasers . . .' 'Mine says they're double-faced . . .' 'Mine says they love the English. . . .' 'Mine says ye can never trust them. . . .' At each sally the boys laughed excitedly among themselves. Most of them were Mackintoshes and McCraes.

James turned his back on them. He had a sudden feeling of acute loneliness and unconsciously his feet took a pace towards the gate in the wall. Then he checked himself. He was not going to run away for all the Mackintoshes and McCraes in the world.

There was an abrupt silence among the pack, then an outbreak of whispering and a voice, suppressed with excitement, said, 'Go on, Hamish!'

He heard steps behind him and he half turned to face a small fat boy with a round cocky face. James transferred a half-eaten oatcake to his left hand. The fat boy looked him up and down and then at last he said: 'Are you afraid of Loxton?'

James stared back at him. His lips were tight. 'No, I'm not!' he said.

A look of puzzled surprise came into the fat boy's eyes, then it changed to one of anticipation. 'Am I to tell him that?' he asked.

'Tell him what you please.'

That's how it had begun. For two days they had left him alone, non-plussed at so intransigent and unfamiliar an attitude; wary of the thin dark boy with the bleak eyes. Then, on the third day, he was standing alone once again in the yard when someone kicked him from behind. He whirled round and faced a sandy-haired boy half a head taller than himself and with a good breadth of shoulder. He knew he was looking at Loxton.

'Are ye feared now?' Loxton said menacingly.

James swallowed. 'No!' he said.

There was a patter of feet behind him and he felt another kick. At the same time Loxton pushed him roughly on the shoulder. He was kicked again. They seemed to be all round him, laughing and shrieking. He tried to hit out but there was always someone behind him. He flailed his arms, broke through the pack and reached the wall. There he turned at bay and caught the fat boy, Hamish, a clout on the side of the head that produced a scream like a dying pig. He saw Loxton in front of him and tried to swing with his other fist but the bigger boy simply knocked it aside and grabbed James by the front of his coat. The others were onto him like terriers and he sank under the weight. Blows were raining down but he hardly felt them. His face was rubbed in the dirt, someone was kicking his thigh. Then abruptly the blows stopped. There was a scramble to get away. He lay there panting, his eyes half closed. When his vision cleared he found himself staring up at the severe black figure of Mr McCrae.

'Get up, ye filthy wee beast!' Mr McCrae shouted angrily. 'Not here five minutes and there's rioting.' He had an ashplant in his hand and struck James between the shoulder blades. 'Get up, dom ye!'

After that he had been a marked man. In the classroom there was Mr McCrae with his bony fists and his birch; outside there was Loxton.

Loxton's persecution had no subtlety and very little variation. He was a dull boy, the son of a well-to-do tradesman in the town, and his bullying was the casual thoughtless kind that might simply have passed as a phase had it not been for the small, fat Hamish. He never forgot the blow James had landed; nor the indifference in James's voice when he had first spoken to him. His relationship with Loxton, as James was to discover many years later, was that of jackal to lion.

But if Loxton was hardly aware of his own careless violence the same could not be said of James. Much of the spirit had gone out of him after the first fight. A stage was quickly reached when there was no point in fighting since the odds, even if he had caught Loxton a lucky blow, were too great. Ironically Loxton was not hated by the rest of the boys for his bullying. He was the strongest in the school and they needed a hero. Provided he concentrated on James and kept his fists off everyone else, then a hero he would remain.

James took to arriving at school at the last possible moment and leaving as late as he could; he preferred the occasional blow from Mr McCrae to the ambush outside. What made it worse was that he never knew whether or not, somewhere along the path home, they would be waiting for him.

There were many times that first winter when he lay awake at night, shivering with cold and the anticipation of what might happen the following day. He tried to tell himself that one day all this would be forgotten, or if remembered, something to joke about, but it made no difference. And there were other times when he wrestled alone with arguments he would present to his mother, but they always came to nothing because he knew how much store she set by education. 'I've saved the money, Jamie. I've saved it all these years.'

When he came home late, with his jacket torn or his face bruised, he would blame it on bird-nesting, a fall from a tree; and since his mother wished to believe this, she believed. Occasionally his father was home to greet him; back from some long, mad journey of the mind, sober, sick, his face waxy on the pillow. There were times when James even thought of going to *him* but as soon as he got into the loft bedroom and smelt the awful smell of sickness and stale liquor and heard the mumbling lips praying, praying, he would steal quietly away. His mother had once told him he was not to judge his father too harshly; as a six-year-old child at the time of Culloden he had seen his parents slaughtered at their own fireside by the Duke's men. But knowing, even understanding, was no substitute.

James grew thinner. He slept badly and when he did sleep his dreams were troubled. He was always tired. He could not remember his lessons. Because he could not remember his lessons he was punished. It was a vicious circle.

One spring Sunday, about two years after he had first gone to the Academy he was out birdnesting in the trees on the edge of Loch Ruthven. It was a lovely soft day of fluffy clouds in a pale blue sky. The early heather was green against the hillside and the light breeze that blew up the valley smelt of new grass and flowers. For the first time for many months he was rash enough to feel happy. He hadn't gone far when he saw the osprey's nest, a bundle of black sticks against the sky, high up in the branches of an old pine tree. From the ground he could not tell whether it was an old nest nor was he able to detect whether a bird was sitting. But his collection was conspicuously devoid of an osprey's egg and there was only one way to find out. He began to climb. Half-way up he heard the thump of big wings. The female had moved from the nest and was perched on a slender branch about five feet away from it. She was slowly moving her wings to keep her balance and craning her neck down angrily at him. He paused and looked around but the male was nowhere to be seen. Warily he started climbing again.

The osprey launched itself from the branch and began to circle round the nest. James could hear the hiss of the wing feathers. As he reached the topmost branches the osprey came for him, beak open, claws wide, wings thudding on the air. But she was a young bird and lacked confidence. She jerked away at the last moment and went rushing past his head. He held onto the trunk and covered his head with his other arm. Before she could turn and come again he had reached the nest and slipped one of the three large eggs into his shirt. He sheltered under his arm again as she raced towards him. Again she sheered off. Hurriedly he began the descent.

When he reached the ground his legs were shaking from the effort. He sat down with his back to the trunk and carefully brought out the egg. It was a beautiful egg, larger than a hen's egg, its creamy shell marked by red-brown blotches. It was still warm from the nest and from his own body. For a few seconds he looked at it in wonder and admiration then he took out a sharp bodkin and carefully pierced the ends. He put his lips to one end and was about to blow when a shadow fell across him and he looked up. Loxton and Hamish were standing in front of him. They had been rabbiting and Loxton's hands and clothes were covered in dried blood.

Hamish was the first to react. 'It's an osprey's egg!'

James tried to cover the egg with his hands but it was too late.

Hamish turned to Loxton: 'You've always wanted one.'

'Aye!'

James rose quickly to his feet. 'There's more in the nest,' he said breathlessly.

'He wants that one,' Hamish said.

'I'll just take that one,' Loxton repeated. 'And if there's more in the nest you'll just shin up again.'

James felt the tree at his back and it gave him confidence. 'You'll not have this,' he said. 'Fetch your own.'

'Give it here!' Loxton tried to grab it but James was too quick. He pulled his hand away. In doing so his fingers closed too tightly round the egg and he felt the sudden stickiness of the yolk as it broke in his palm. He opened his hand and stared down at the mess. Hamish laughed. It was at that point something seemed to give in James's head. He threw himself headlong at Loxton, the bodkin in his raised hand. He heard Hamish give a startled cry and that was all he heard or saw or even remembered until they pulled him off Loxton sometime later.

At his trial the Sheriff of Inverness professed himself appalled. He called James an animal and Mr McCrae was there to give chapter and verse. They said he had attempted to kill Loxton and for all he knew this might have been true. He didn't care. Even as the sentence of transportation was read out, his thoughts were somewhere else. He was remembering the small graveyard under the hill at Daviot where they had buried his mother. The physician who attended her death said she died of a sudden fever but on the faces of the villagers who saw him in chains at the graveside, the reason was plain enough: she had died of a broken heart.

It was early evening when James and Frances came down through the silver trees towards Paradise. He was quiet now.

'Why didn't you tell me before?' Frances said.

'I don't know. It never seemed the right time.'

'I would have understood.'

'I know.'

What she had just said was nothing less than the truth. He had a feeling she would understand almost anything he did. All he would have to do was tell her. And he realized then, if only dimly, that she was the only person he *would* ever tell things to. He wanted to tell her this, too, but found himself incapable. Instead he reached for her hand and felt the answering squeeze.

'I suppose,' he said at length, 'it was because of your uncle. Why ever did he take us in? Why ever did he keep us?'

She didn't answer for some moments and then she said: 'About three years ago a transport called at Table Bay. There was smallpox on board and Uncle Henry was asked to help. He was away for a week and when he came back we could hardly recognize him. He didn't smile or laugh again for a long time.' Then she stopped and, turning to face him, said fiercely: 'It's over now, it's over. Nothing like that will ever happen to you again.'

But she was wrong.

Midsummer arrived, bringing hot, drowsy days. A great weariness seemed to come over the land and at Paradise the Hottentot servants disappeared for hours on end to sleep away the afternoons. Some slept where they sat, too lazy to move from the hot kitchen, others chose the corridors or shady nooks on the wide verandah.

'Two things our friend the Hottentot loves,' said Dr Goodsir, who had nearly measured his full length over the recumbent form of Maria. 'Sleep and food. The former more than the latter. No question.'

The noon sun shrivelled the grass and the south-easter which pushed across the isthmus every afternoon, blew the brown stems away. The countryside became dry and crackling. James was more restless than ever. Twice more he had gone in alone to see Fitzhenry without getting anything concrete. The older man seemed content to lie where he was, fussed over by Frances and Maria and even Dr Goodsir. Or was he content? James could never tell whether he was being serious or not. What made it worse was that Fitzhenry had now taken over Frances's tuition, with the result that James

71

was more frequently thrown on his own company. He spent hours lying among the pine needles on Table Mountain or swimming lazily in a pool he had discovered at the watershed of the Liesbeek River.

The only person who was really busy was Dr Goodsir. He seemed impervious to heat, wind or drought. It was as though James had been placed in a vacuum while everyone waited for him to make up his mind. But make it up to do what?

And then one morning after breakfast Dr Goodsir said: 'Must start getting the wagon ready,' and James knew that something was happening at last.

'Need your help, of course,' Dr Goodsir said. 'Great deal to be done.'

He felt a curious fluttering in his stomach, a mixture of apprehension and excitement. 'Will I . . .? I mean, are you . . .?'

Dr Goodsir laughed at the solemn tone. 'Well, I'm not. Eventually get found out. Friends all over the country. One particular. Needs someone to help with the stock.'

So that was it! Dr Goodsir had been planning it all along.

'New life. New people. New home. Wonderful opportunity. Grow with the country. Great future. What d'you say?'

'I'm ready,' James said with a slight tremor in his voice.

Dr Goodsir laughed at the solemn tone. 'Well I'm not. Great deal of hard work yet.'

There was indeed. Every two years Dr Goodsir made one of his long journeys into the interior of the Colony collecting plants, animal skins, bones, pieces of lyddite, samples of rock – anything that might have some significance. He kept a voluminous diary which one day he hoped would be published. It was now nearly twenty-four months since his last journey and all his equipment had to be overhauled. The wagon was brought out of the stables where the guinea fowl had been using it for a roost and Dr Goodsir and James made a thorough inspection. The sail-cloth had rotted and would have to be replaced, the *disselboom* had warped and split, the *onderstel* needed re-pitching, the fellies had shrunk during the dry weather, the leather *strops* had hardened and some of

72

the bamboos in the frame would have to come out. It was going to be a long job.

James went to it with a will. He and Old Moos cut and fitted a new *disselboom*, replaced the tire-bands, fitted the sail-cloth which Dr Goodsir had brought from Cape Town and cut new leather thongs for the ox halter and the yokes. Sleepy Hottentots were pressed into service to fashion the rush mats that went under the sail-cloth and even old Jacob arrived to fit the inside of the wagon with chests for Dr Goodsir's mass of apparatus.

It was hot, sweaty work but after a week James began to feel the muscles in his back and arms tighten with unfamiliar strength and he threw himself into it with increasing energy. There was only one occasion when he walked from the yard and left Old Moos to work alone, and that was when the time came for painting the undercarriage with pitch. The smell of the hot tar made him uneasy.

In the midst of all this activity Dr Goodsir's pile of necessities was growing. Almost every day he took the carriage into Cape Town, returning late at night with more and more supplies. They began to pile up in untidy heaps all over the house. There were gifts for tribal chiefs and goods for bartering: black, white and red porcelain beads, gilt rings, brass rings, blue check handkerchiefs, plain, gilt and ornamented buttons, lengths of tobacco, snuff, knives, pocket tinderboxes and steels, looking-glasses, brass wire, sheets of copper and tin, spike nails and blankets. In another room there were six muskets and powder horns, a fowling-piece and shot-belt, a large rifle which could fire a two-ounce ball, two cases of pistols, a cutlass, four barrels of gunpowder, bags of shot, gun flints, bullet moulds, lead and tin in bars. There were bags of rice, bread and biscuit, flour and wheat, barrels of wine, rum and brandy, water casks, books on zoology, mineralogy, natural philosophy, medicine; there were saws, hammers and hatchets, a Portuguese dictionary and a Dutch dictionary, fish hooks and lines, a set of nautical almanacs – and the English colours which, Dr Goodsir said, he always raised and lowered at sunset no matter where he was.

Fitzhenry remarked that it seemed Dr Goodsir was either going to buy the country or conquer it by force of arms. James said he could not imagine where everything was to go and Old Moos shook his head gloomily and estimated it would take a hundred oxen to move the wagon out of the yard, let alone drag it up hills.

The only person who seemed left out of the general activity was Frances. She hardly saw James now. She spent her mornings learning Latin and Greek, arithmetic and English literature from Fitzhenry and in the afternoons, when she was free to roam the woods and slopes with James as they had done a month before, he was unavailable. Sometimes she would come out into the yard and gaze thoughtfully at the work, but after a few minutes would turn aside and go off by herself.

One Sunday in early March they found themselves together for the first time in several weeks high up the slopes of the mountain on the bed of pine needles which had, by this time, become their special place. They had lain there for hours in silence watching the south-easter clouds begin their shy envelopment of Mouse Mountain, content to be together. At length she said gravely: 'You're going away.'

He nodded. They hadn't spoken about it before, both seemingly reluctant to touch on the subject.

'Will you remember us?'

He turned over on his side to face her. 'Of course I'll remember you. What nonsense is this? I'm not going away for ever. Dr Goodsir says that in a year or so all this will have been forgotten. You'll see, I'll be back. And anyway, you'll be able to visit me. You can come with your uncle.'

'He won't take me yet,' she said. 'Not till I'm older.'

'Well then, I'll come and see you. Now don't fret.'

'I don't like things changing,' she said.

'Everything has to change, forbye there's nothing for me here, nothing I can do. I've no trade and no degree. It's better this way.'

'I suppose so.'

'And if . . . I mean when . . . when I've . . .'

'Yes?' she said gently.

'Well, you know, if all goes well . . . in a year or two . . .'
He felt himself covered by a hot flush. Once again the words
were eluding him.

'Yes?' she prompted again.

'You know what I mean!'

'No, I don't. Tell me.'

He pushed himself restlessly onto his stomach. 'Well, a
man's got to make a mark somehow. You understand that.'

'I understand.'

'And when I've made it . . . When I've got something.
Why . . . then I'll come for you.' The last sentence came out
in a rush.

'Will you, Jamie? Do you promise?'

'I said so,' he said crossly.

'I'll wait then. I'll be here waiting.'

'Don't say it like that,' he said ungraciously. 'I told you I'll
be here to see you.'

'I know. But I'll wait anyway.'

'I don't want you to talk that way!' He had a sudden
confused feeling that she was making him responsible for her
happiness.

'All right,' she said soothingly. 'We won't talk about it any
more.'

After a few moments he mumbled ashamedly: 'I'm sorry,
Fran. I'm no good at talking.'

'I know. I know.'

They were silent again for a while, both with their own
thoughts and then Frances said, 'You don't have to worry.
When you go, I mean, I won't fuss. I won't cry.' She reached
out and touched his bad arm. With anyone else he would have
jerked away in anger but Frances was different. The arm had
never been any embarrassment between them. 'Remember
when Uncle Henry . . .?'

'Yes. Yes.' Remember? Would he ever forget when the last
of the tar on the stump had had to come off.

'*You* cried then.'

'I did not! Men don't cry.'

'You're not a man yet. Anyway men *do* cry. Uncle Henry
cried when he came back from the convict ship.'

He moved again restlessly. 'What's the matter with you? What's all this talk of crying?'

'I like to talk about things.'

'Well, I don't. Not about things like that anyway.'

'And then when I've talked about them they're never so bad when they happen.'

'I'm different,' he said abruptly.

The gentle south-easter sighed in the branches above them moving the tops of the trees against the sky. Frances was lying on her back. 'I wish there were big clouds,' she said dreamily. 'I like to see them sailing on the wind.'

'I can smell smoke,' he said.

'And then if I half close my eyes I can pretend the whole world is sailing with them. Jamie?' Her voice had changed.

'Yes?'

'Hold my hand and then we can sail together. Far away over the mountains and the rivers, and we'll be together *always*.'

'Someday,' he said. 'I promise you that, Fran,' and he leant over and kissed the golden blonde hair that smelt of sunshine and grass and now, strangely, of woodsmoke. He sat up abruptly.

'There's a fire somewhere,' he said, getting to his feet.

'I hope the bush hasn't caught. Two years ago Paradise was nearly burnt down.'

He gazed down onto the shimmering valleys below. 'There it is,' he said, pointing in the direction of the Wine Hills. They could see the thin spirals of smoke. 'And people.' He couldn't make out whether or not they were trying to put out the fire. Then, faintly, came the noise of banging.

'It's a wolf hunt,' Frances said excitedly. 'They've fired the bush to drive them out. I wish Uncle Henry knew, he's always wanted a hyena skin.'

'Hyena?'

'They call them wolves here.'

The smoke was coming from a large circle and James could see the hunters waiting on the perimeter. Every now and then the sunlight glinted on a musket.

'Let's go down,' he said.

76

'We can't. They'll see us.'

'Come on, we'll hide. No one'll know. We may even see a hyena.'

'All right,' she said doubtfully. 'But what if it attacks us?'

'Don't be silly. They're the most frightened things in the country. Your uncle has said so often enough. Anyway I'll be there to protect you.'

'Take my hand then, and don't run too fast.' Together they scrambled down the slope. The pines gave way to silver trees and scrub oak. Sometimes they trotted and sometimes slowed to a fast walk. It was very hot under the shoulder of the mountain. They crossed the dry bed of a small rill and began scrambling up the farther slopes. The smell of smoke had grown much stronger and they began to hear the voices of the hunters and the noise of the Hottentot beaters.

The Wine Hills ran down from the great buttress of the mountain in a series of gentle rises and it was on the side of one slope that the hunt was now reaching its climax. The beaters had moved in a great semi-circle driving what game there was into a tangled mass of reeds, wild bamboo, wild olives and thorn bush. It was too dense for the hunters to penetrate and the edges had been set alight. The flames crackled and sparked, moving towards the centre of the big circle in a series of leaps. Every few seconds a clump of dry reeds went up with a whoosh.

James and Frances made a wide circle and came out on top of a small knoll. There, hidden in a thicket of scrub oak, they could look down on the hunt. It was very confusing. The hunters were a mixture of farmers from the Constantia Valley, two or three soldiers from the Castle, Hottentot servants, Hottentot marksmen, a well-dressed burgher from Rondebosch and the occasional black slave carrying a second musket for his master. The smoke grew thicker as the flames chewed into the new growth. It swirled round the hunters, blown here and there on eddies of wind; the air was filled with feathery ash. James, looking down and hearing the orders bellowed in English or Dutch, or a mixture of the two, thought the scene was like a battle painting: the sweating, shouting men, the smoke – and now the thunder of guns.

Small game began to break through the circle of flame. Duikers, their coats singed and burning, were shot down as they paused to get their bearings; cobras and puff-adders who found a chink in the wall of flame, were beaten to death; a porcupine climbed slowly towards James, the tips of its quills alight, and then it fell over on its side.

'Oh, look!' Frances's voice was horrified. 'It's still alive.'

The porcupine's legs were moving spasmodically. 'I'll kill it,' James said and reached for a length of dead branch.

'No! Don't kill it!'

'D'you want it to die slowly?'

'N – o –'

The porcupine lay in a small clearing and James moved stealthily out of his cover towards it. It was making a pathetic squeaking noise. He raised the branch to put it out of its misery when he heard a rustle in the bush close by. He checked the blow and turned. He found himself looking into the berserk eyes of a large animal. It was less than five yards from him, a fully grown spotted hyena pushed over the limits of its natural cowardice into courage. The heavy mane of hair on its shoulders was covered in tendrils of smoke, its huge head hung forward. Foam dripped from the massive jaws. Its upper lips were drawn back from its teeth in an hysterical snarl. The head was slowly moving from side to side.

James stood like a rock. If he had slowly moved aside, allowing the hyena passage through the thicket, he might have been all right: as it was he stood fast. Behind the hyena was the sound of the hunt, the flames and smoke; ahead a single figure. The hyena came at James in a pattering rush.

James swung the branch and felt it knocked aside. He had one split-second smell of the hyena's rank breath and then the great beast's weight was on top of him. His scream was drowned by the roar of a musket. He felt the hyena lurch away from him as it took the heavy ball in its shoulder. It thrashed about next to James sending up a shower of small sticks and leaves, snarling and moaning as it tried to bite the bullet hole. Then gradually it subsided and death came to it in a series of convulsive twitches.

James looked up at the hunter in gratitude and found

himself staring into the eyes of Vreetman. The Bastaard had finished reloading and was holding the musket at James's chest. He said thoughtfully: 'It is better hunting than I expected.'

James rose shakily to his feet. 'What d'you want of me?' he said.

'Money,' Vreetman said simply. 'Bills were posted on you.'

'I'll give you money!' James said.

Vreetman laughed. 'I'll get more than a few stuivers for you, Englishman.' He kept the musket pointed and felt around in the leather bag that hung at his waist. He brought out a length of leather thong. 'The first time I saw you,' he said, 'you were chained; now you'll be tied and this time you'll stay tied unless you've another hand to lose.' He looped the thong round James's right wrist and pulled it tight.

'Yes,' he went on, 'the bills say you killed a sailor, an officer. There'll be plenty of dollars for the sight of *you*.'

Behind Vreetman James caught the flash of Frances's dress as she rose in the bushes. She had a heavy stone in her right hand. James prayed wildly that she wouldn't involve herself. The arm went back at a childish angle. He opened his mouth to shout at her. Then the rock rose in a slow parabola and came lobbing into the clearing. It struck Vreetman harmlessly on his right leg. He spun round snapping the musket to his shoulder. As he did so James swung the hook. The point slashed into Vreetman's neck and James saw a fountain of blood. The Bastaard reeled away, falling over his own legs. He collapsed near the twitching hyena. 'I tried to throw!' Frances was shrilling. 'I tried to . . .' James grabbed her by the wrist and they fled through the scrub following the same wide circle that had brought them there. But instead of going up the slopes of the mountain they cut along its base and approached Paradise from the other side.

Six hours later, under a hazy moon that bathed the Flats in silver, James galloped along the post road to the interior of the Colony. He wore a heavy watch coat that buttoned to his neck, a brace of pistols in his waistband and a black tricorne on his head. In a money belt worn next to his skin he carried twelve golden sovereigns and a hasty note from Dr Goodsir to Mynheer Hendrik van Roye, whose farm Bitterfountain lay more than ten days' hard riding to the north, in the area known as the Snowy Mountains. At his side thundered Juli, one of the servants, to guide him on his way.

Everything had happened so quickly that there had been no time for farewells or recriminations. He kept on telling himself as he galloped through the night, that he was leaving the past behind. But the grim mountains rearing skywards ahead of him, their ragged teeth touched here and there with ghostly white, were like omens of what was still to come.

Book Two

THE PLACE OF SLAUGHTER

People were those who
Broke for me the string.
Therefore,
The place became like this to me,
On account of it,
Because the string was that which broke for me.
Therefore,
The place does not feel to me,
As the place used to feel to me,
On account of it.
For,
The place feels as if it stood open before me,
Because the string has broken for me.
Therefore,
The place does not feel pleasant to me,
On account of it.

Bushman lament,
translated by BLEEK AND LLOYD

The snowy mountains spread over a thousand square miles in a tangled wilderness of kloofs, hollows, tablelands, peaks and shoulders. They rose from the surrounding land like a great volcanic island and a traveller, creaking in his ox-wagon over the flat and arid Karoo, would have been aware of them first as a series of hazy peaks seeming to grow out of nothing. Then, as he began the slow climb of the Camdeboo, the green uplands, the great treeless range would have swelled to the skies. In winter, when the snow lay feet deep on the peaks and the bitter east wind was blowing, he would have found the area almost deserted for, as the weather grew colder, the graziers moved down to the Camdeboo with their flocks and finally down to the Karoo itself. In spring the flow was reversed and by summer the same traveller might have seen a whole land restless with the movements of sheep, cattle and horses.

The Snowy Mountains were like another sort of island. Lying 400 miles to the north-east of the Cape of Good Hope they formed a remote bastion on the very fringes of the Colony with all those miles of semi-desert between them and British authority. Certainly, there was some sort of authority at the settlement of Graaf-Reiner which was not too far away, but the village had always been a hot-bed of Jacobinism and a haven for the disaffected.

The graziers of the Snowy Mountains were their own masters and solved their own problems in their own ways. What they wanted was land and more land, flocks and bigger flocks, water and more water. They *liked* their community cut off from the world and, individually, liked to be cut off from the community itself. They were loners, solitaries, each family with its servants and, in some cases, slaves, formed its own society within the society and a farmer whose nearest neighbour was less than twenty miles away felt crowded. This was *their* land for *their* animals; *they* had taken it, *they* would keep it. They wanted no help from the British Governor at the Cape – and no hindrance either as their hunger urged them farther and farther into the unknown. To the north, north-west and north-east lay the whole of Africa, untamed and open, waiting for God's chosen people.

Until that time the Bushmen might well have considered that since they were some of the first people ever to inhabit southern Africa, God might have meant it for *them*. They would have been wrong. This race of diminutive Stone-Age hunters who knew nothing of cultivation or husbandry and who held their freedom too dear to follow either, had existed for centuries on the trapping and killing of game; at the same time fitting perfectly into nature's balance. Now they were becoming the expendable 'third party' in the mounting pressure created by northward-moving Christians and southward-moving Bantu.

At first they tried to go on living their traditional lives, but for every one antelope killed by their arrows for food a hundred were falling to Christian muskets. Where once vast herds of eland and springbok, ostriches and quagga roamed, the land now pastured sheep and cattle. The Bushmen were being driven from the plains into the wild mountain caves to live on roots, lizards, locusts and tubers; once they had fed on wildebeests and zebra.

So when the herds and flocks followed them into ever more remote areas they might have been forgiven for assuming that God had sent them a new food supply. Again they were wrong; and to prove on whose side God really was, both Christians and Bantu were exterminating them on sight.

A partial genocide had already cleared many of them from the land, the only evidence of their existence being a legacy of beautiful sculpture and rock painting. What had once been one of the happiest and most benign races on earth had now been shattered into small bands, starving and vengeful, who were hunted down like jackals. There were few to mourn their passing.

In the Snowy Mountains the spring of 1811 was late and treacherous. James, as usual for the past three years, had spent the winter months tending the flocks on the Karoo. By the first days of September the water holes were dry, the bush was dark brown and the noon temperatures trembled in the eighties. The stock, already weak from two seasons of drought, began to die. Then had come a message from Hendrik van Roye – Uncle Hendrik, as he now called him – that the spring flowers were out on the mountains and the season was early. James started the drive up to the Camdeboo and within another week the flocks were safely in the hidden valleys and high plateaux of the Snowy Mountains. Almost at once, as the lambing began, the weather changed. Iron-coloured clouds built up from the north-east, night temperatures fell below freezing. Few lambs survived. The same thing was happening on other farms and, since sheep and cattle were a grazier's bank-account, slaughtering for the table was kept to the minimum.

The faces of the farmers changed to the sullen colour of the sky as they watched their flocks diminish. For years many of them had given an annual present of meat – sometimes as many as thirty or forty head of cattle each – to the Bushman clans of the remote glens and fastnesses and in this way they had bought their friendship. They had almost forgotten what marauding bands were like. The Bushmen had honoured the agreement. Some farmers, in lean years, would even hand over an entire flock to a small party of Bushmen who would graze them in distant valleys and return them at the end of the season sleek and fat, their numbers increased.

Now the gifts abruptly stopped and since much of the game had been cleared so that domestic stock could prosper, the Bushmen were left with nothing – except the herds of cattle and sheep. When they needed meat, they killed: their appetites were added to the weather.

'They have to eat, too,' Hendrik van Roye said one day, after he and James had found a shortfall of nearly a hundred ewes in the south pastureland. 'But, man, it's a bitter thing. Every day less and less. It's like crossing a desert with a handful of water and watching it trickle through the fingers. There is no way to stop it.'

'We could ride out and shoot a few,' James said matter-of-factly. 'Teach the others a lesson.'

The old Dutchman shook his head. 'You can't shoot a man because he's hungry.'

But there were others in the Snowy Mountains who took a different view, the Muller family in particular.

Some weeks earlier, when the graziers had trekked from the mountains, to take their three-monthly communion at Graaf-Reinet, the Mullers had been active. Otto Muller, head of a family of six sons, each of whom was a head taller than his father and who lived in constant fear of him, went from one wagon camp to the next preaching the need for more room, more land, more water and the inevitable corollary that the

Bushmen must be exterminated so that, in flagrant disregard of official policy, the graziers could expand their lands by moving beyond the frontiers of the Colony.

Otto Muller was a bitter, dried-up bantam of a man whose father had first come to the Cape with a regiment of Hessian mercenaries and had deserted soon afterwards.

'We shoot wild dogs,' he said, over and over again. 'We shoot leopards and jackals, and all of them put together are less harmful than the Bushman. And remember our women and children. Who will look after them when we get a poisoned arrow in the back? The English Governor? The English soldiers?'

The graziers, solemn in their black church clothing, would nod in agreement or turn away from the bitter tirade, embarrassed at this talk of slaughter at a time when their slow thoughts were on God.

For the latter, Otto Muller had a different approach: 'If God had not meant us to prosper He would not have put us here, and we cannot prosper if our cattle and sheep are to be killed around us. It says in the Book: "If a man shall steal an ox or a sheep, and kill it, or sell it; he shall restore five oxen for an ox and four sheep for a sheep." Have we ever received such payments? Have we received even one ox or one sheep? I tell you it also says in the Book: "Eye for eye, tooth for tooth, hand for hand, foot for foot, burning for burning, stripe for stripe." The Bushmen are no better than animals, therefore they must pay like animals.'

Except for Hendrik van Roye, Otto Muller was the biggest grazier in the area and few people openly opposed him. Many shared his feelings, but there were others whose lust for land was not quite so keen, who were content to be left alone with what they had, to live in peace with their neighbours and the Bushmen. Van Roye was one of these. Not that he had always been a man for compromises. He had had his share of fighting. As far back as he could remember, in his grandfather's day, there had been raids and counter-raids, and even farther back, before he was born, his family had fought Hottentot cattle thieves near the Cape. It could be said that what he owned he owed to his gun and to the guns of his two sons, swept to their deaths in the flooded Sundays River, themselves giving chase to a Bushman raiding party. But that had been many years ago and after the first incoherent anger, in which he could only think of revenge, Uncle Hendrik had finally asked himself why God had visited such a tragedy on his house, and had been momentarily stunned at the answer.

After that it was he who had organized the gifts of cattle and sheep; pleading, cajoling and brow-beating his neighbours until there was such peace as few of them could recall.

Now, for reasons which were beyond his power to rectify, the peace was in the balance.

Such was the situation on the frontier of the Cape Colony in the treacherous spring of 1811 when James Black rode into a cold morning wind in search of game, his Bushman servant, Stone-Axe, running easily beside him.

He was greatly changed since that day nearly five years before when he had ridden a spent horse into the Snowy Mountains. Physically he was a man; as supple and tough as tanned ox-hide. He had need to be, for the Frontier was no place for weaklings; they died off early. His mind had undergone the same process. Living as close to nature's disasters as he did, there was no room for sentiment or softness; the Frontier had simply finished off the process started so long ago by Mr McCrae and Loxton and Rance.

With the growth of his body and the tightening of his muscles had come new confidence in himself. He no longer flew into sudden rages. What was the point in being angry with a sheep or a cow or even a Bushman? In his mind they were all animals and losing one's temper with an animal was only a waste of energy. Controlling his anger gave him a new freedom. It was there within him, honed and refined to knife-blade sharpness; not to be squandered without reason but ready when needed. Like the day nearly two years before when he had first seen Stone-Axe.

He had been out looking for strays in a melancholy glen called Dark Valley, a lowering place of scree and shale, often damp with mountain mist, when he turned the shoulder of a rise and suddenly came upon a man flogging a Bushman. He was unaware of James. He had a rhino-hide *sjambok* in his hand, the handle of which was a four-plait over wood. The three-foot tongue had been shod with a steel tip and every time he struck it drew blood. The Bushman was taking the beating as though made of stone.

If James had pulled Violin to a halt and watched for a few moments he would have recognized the man for what he was, a poor-white nomad, one of a score of down-at-heel vagabonds who roamed the mountains with their small flocks, sleeping rough and stealing what they could.

But he did not wait. He jammed his spurs into the mare's sides and she sprang at the couple as though shot from a catapult, knocking them aside like bales of straw. In a second he was out of the saddle and standing over the half-stunned herder.

'In God's name,' the man cried. 'Who *are* you?'

The Bushman was crouching in the long-stemmed grass, the deep cuts on his body oozing with blood, and James felt a rising sense of disgust. One didn't even treat an animal *that* way.

He scooped up the *sjambok* and lashed down at the man. The tongue bit into the leather trousers, slicing them to ribbons, laying bare the white flesh underneath. He hit again and again until the man was howling for mercy, then he pulled out his big Hereneuter knife, cut the *sjambok* to pieces and threw them down to the ground. His anger was spent.

'Don't let me ever see you here again, my friend,' he said. 'The next time you may not be so lucky.'

The Bushman had disappeared, but a mile farther down the slope James became aware of movement on his left; the Bushman's bobbing head was level with the stirrup-iron. It was a sight with which he was now so familiar he would have felt naked without it. He asked no questions, the Bushman proffered no statement. He guessed he might have escaped from some farmer to whom he was indentured but it made no matter. From then on Stone-Axe lived so close to James he might have been his shadow. Wherever he went, Stone-Axe was by his side; if he visited a neighbour the Bushman would wait through the long hours outside the house, occasionally coming to a window to make sure he had not been harmed.

When he went to sleep on a sunny mountain slope the first thing he always saw on waking was the squatting figure of the Bushman keeping watch. One of the few times they were separated by more than a couple of feet was at meals and Stone-Axe would lurk in the shadows across the room watching his master with anxious eyes.

'You know,' Uncle Hendrik said with a smile one evening, 'if you ever choked on a chop-bone I think he'd kill us all. So chew slowly.'

James laughed. 'He's like a good dog.'

'You're wrong. Don't underrate these people. I remember once an old fellow telling me that though the Bushman had to kill game for food they had a great love for the animals. In a way they worship them – the animal-person inside each. Perhaps that's where his bond is with you, with your soul, with the James-person inside you.'

'I suppose when he eats me you'll say he loves me all the more.'

Aunt Hannah looked across with mock alarm. 'How can you say such things? And at the table, too.'

'Well, you've got to admit he smells like he's been rolling in midden.'

'Yes,' Uncle Hendrik said thoughtfully. 'But you must always look for a reason. If we walked naked in the world as they do we would also rub our skins with fat. The sun can do terrible things to a man's body.'

James smiled, unconvinced.

'Wait until you see one of their paintings before you laugh at them,' Uncle Hendrik said, shortly. 'I saw one once, a beautiful thing of leaping springbok. It was in a cave west of here. One whole wall was covered in drawings. I remember there was a huge eland, too. Wonderful drawing. But they say there are few painters left. The art is being lost. If we start our troubles again there will be no Bushmen left to learn.' He brooded silently for a moment, then added: 'In many ways they are like us. What they want is freedom. Freedom above everything; even above life itself.'

But in his new-found overlordship James paid little attention. It amused him to have Stone-Axe follow him like a hound; it gave him a sense of power. He allowed him to make a bow and quiver-full of arrows, even allowed him to tip them with poison, to the alarm and indignation of the neighbours. To James he was purely a superb hunting animal and he wanted him suitably equipped. He continued to treat him like a dog, a pedigree dog that must be loved and well cared-for, to be sure, but a dog nevertheless. And like a dog Stone-Axe slept on the floor at the foot of his master's bed.

However, in many ways Stone-Axe was better than a dog, James reasoned. He was more company, for instance, and he could do clever things like making fire by whirling one stick in the groove of another. By using thin leather strips he could sew the ox-hide soles of their *veldschoen* onto the goatskin uppers so neatly the seams could scarcely be seen. Occasionally when they went to the Sundays River he made fish traps; he supplied the house with wild honey; he could find Aunt Hannah the canna roots she needed to boil up with mutton fat for soap – though he would never use it; he could tell how many springbok were in a herd by looking at the spoor and also say how long it was since they had passed; with a stick and a bunch of leaves he could imitate an ostrich and work his way into a herd of quagga and get off two arrows before they even sensed the deception.

Without consciously trying or even being aware of what was happening to him, James was learning the bushlore of Africa from one of its great specialists.

Uncle Hendrik watched the growing bond between them reflectively. 'Don't expect to keep him always,' he said on one occasion. 'You may be disappointed.'

'He'll never leave here.'

'I wouldn't be too sure. They're funny creatures. One day he may suddenly get an urge to return to his clan and there's nothing anyone can do to stop him.'

'Where do you think he came from?'

'Difficult to say. I'd guess from farther north, up the Great River way. Years ago we used to light bonfires on the mountain tops as a signal to the Bushmen. Then they'd come down for their presents of cattle and sheep. He might have been one of them. Many stayed. Unfortunately, many were forced to stay. But one thing's certain; in their present mood they'd kill him if he went back. Tame Bushmen are always suspect.'

'But what about the Reverend Harmsworth? He's got scores round the mission.'

'That's not quite the same. They came as a clan. If they go back to the mountains they remain a clan.'

After that James saw Stone-Axe through slightly different eyes. He found himself faintly resentful that one day the little Bushman might leave him.

But there was little time for introspection. Life itself was too crowded. There were occasions when he remembered Paradise with nostalgia, recalling with intense clarity the smells of the house and garden, the drowsy *koer-koer* of the turtle doves. He saw himself again hand in hand with Frances or watching Dr Goodsir losing a chess game to Fitzhenry and at these times he would feel an odd sensation over his heart. The time before Paradise seemed utterly remote and the mists of his memory closed about it, drawing it farther and farther away.

In the first months he had been achingly homesick for Paradise and had watched the horizon daily for Dr Goodsir's wagon, but it had never come. Occasionally he would hear news of his expeditions, but they were either far to the west or north of the Snowy Mountains. And then even that had faded as the love of Aunt Hannah and the real affection of Uncle Hendrik had drawn him into the gap left by their sons until finally he became one of them, treating them with the casual affection of any growing youth for his parents.

There was one other significant change in him: he was no longer embarrassed about his arm. On the contrary, the Frontier was a place where men wore their scars with pride and a slight limp from an encounter with a buffalo or a face gouged by a wounded leopard were badges of rank. From the first his hook had drawn stares of open admiration and envy, not so much from the fact that he had lost a hand, but because he had gained so fine a weapon. Youths of his own age had been very reluctant to test his temper so long as it swung by his side. To Stone-Axe it had an almost mystical quality.

Since the Bushman had never seen anything like it before he simply put it down to wizardry. At first James had revelled in the feeling of power it gave him but after his encounter with the drover he realized its potential danger and got Stone-Axe, much to the little Bushman's dismay, to fashion a buckskin sheath for it with a wooden peg at the end. He kept the sheath soft and pliable and after a little practice he could whip it off in a matter of seconds and lay bare the gleaming polished claw. He knew now how important those seconds could be.

He lay hidden in the patch of tall reeds which grew like a tuft of bristle from the bank of the dry mountain stream. He held the rifle tight against his cheek, sighting down the long barrel. His muscles were aching with the sustained effort and the tip of the barrel began to move in a slight, trembling circle. He could feel his eyes smarting as the wind drove flurries of snow into his face. He shook his head slightly, released his breath in a long sigh and allowed his body to relax. He let the butt of the rifle rest on the ground and rubbed his eyes. It was no use, they were too far. At his side he felt the faintest of movements as Stone-Axe turned to look at him inquiringly.

'Too far,' he whispered. 'Too damn far.'

Stone-Axe looked down the valley again. James put the fingers of his right hand in his mouth and blew on them; they were white with cold.

Four hundred yards down the valley to his left the small herd of springbok huddled against the wind; obscured every few seconds as the snow flurries hissed down the mountain slopes. There were three rams and eight does and he wanted at least two. But the buck were nervous. Every now and then one would take a few steps forward, scent the air, move its head up and down, from side to side, start, stop, and then with tripping steps rejoin the others, stirring them into movement.

Half an hour ago, as the first light of morning had streaked the snow-capped mountains, he had thought he was in the perfect position. The buck had been down to the spring at the bottom of the valley and were slowly making their way up to the heights. He had left his horse behind a small knoll and taken up his position in the reeds. The wind was behind the buck and in the normal course they would have had to pass him. There was no way up the slopes opposite because not even a springbok could get up the steeply overhanging cliffs. They would have to pass him at the narrowest point before swinging away to the right up the only outlet to the valley. He had been counting on getting them bunched side-on and sending one ball through three or four animals, the way Uncle Hendrik had taught him. This was the way the Frontier graziers saved powder and ball – and, in hard times, fed their families. And times were hard now and fresh meat was a priority and James knew that even if the springbok walked to within twenty feet of him and stood in an obliging bunch he might still come away with nothing. Lying up in melting snow was not the best way of keeping one's powder dry.

The buck had begun to drift uneasily. Some of the does had turned and were allowing their steps to take them further down the valley. The snow flurries had eased slightly but every few minutes one came off the top of the hills and obscured the herd like spattering raindrops on a window-pane. There were two avenues of escape for them: they could either go back down the valley or break up the slope behind James.

He felt a touch on his arm and looked down into the Bushman's almond-shaped face. In the leaden light his skin was the colour of an old lion, his slanted Mongolian eyes as soft as a kudu doe's.

James was suddenly aware of his acrid smell and wished he was lying up-wind of him. The first day he had acquired Stone-Axe he had taken him down to the spring and scrubbed him, to the Bushman's horror, but the smell remained. It was a compound of ochre and rancid mutton fat, eland fat, axle-grease, dagga, wood-smoke and the strong herbal smell of the bush.

Now the little Bushman made a curving motion with his hands. He indicated the slope up which the buck could break away and then brought his hand round to indicate a position behind them. James nodded. It might work.

Stone-Axe carefully cut a dozen thin reeds from the clump, trimming the soft tops. Then he dived into the leather bag that hung from his neck and brought out a handful of old red flannel off-cuts. He tied a piece of flannel to the top of each reed as James watched expectantly. He had heard of this, but never seen it done. Stone-Axe finished the work to his satisfaction, slung his stiffened-leather quiver of arrows down his back, scooped up his bow, folded the sheep-skin kaross more tightly round his body and slipped between the reeds like a grey shadow.

James watched him flit from bush to bush, pausing, moving, using the ground to its best advantage. Within fifty yards he was only visible as a puff of wind is visible, gently stirring the long grass. James turned to watch the bare shoulder of the hill with blurring vision. The cold was piercing and there was rime on his eyebrows. The barrel of the rifle burnt his hand. Now that Stone-Axe had gone he seemed, apart from the buck, the only living thing in a wilderness of jagged hills and white winter grass. Then he saw the first of the reeds – and then another – and another. They seemed to appear by magic on the slope until the full dozen, each surmounted by its tattered ensign of red flannel, marched in a long straggling line into the misty morning.

The buck had seen them too. The leading ram raised its head and snorted. It jumped straight up in the air and sprang down the slope, stopped, sniffed, took a dozen more pattering paces and stopped again.

By this time, he knew that Stone-Axe had got behind the herd and his scent was coming to them on the wind. They began to bunch and move. The does broke for the slope then saw the flannel-topped reeds, paused in fright and wheeled up the valley. He raised the rifle. The herd was still uncertain. They couldn't go right because of the strange phenomenon which had appeared on the slope; they couldn't go back because the smell of man was drifting up the valley to them. Suddenly they broke up the valley in a series of long, springing jumps, their hooves cracking on the frosthard ground. A hundred yards short of James they slowed again, wary now, but not in immediate danger. A doe lagged, the herd strung out and then in fright she raced to catch up, bumping the others and bouncing them again. They were less than thirty yards from James when he fired.

The roar of the rifle was like a thunderclap in the silence. Its echoes crashed from peak to peak. A bird shrieked in fright. By the time the smoke cleared from his eyes the herd was only a distant memory, a drumming sound as it left the head of the valley. On the ground in front of him a ram and a doe were kicking out what remained of their lives.

He picked himself up and ran forward. The ram had thrashed itself onto its forelegs and was trying to rise. There was no time to reload and he scooped up a heavy rock and smashed it onto the white blaze-mark in the centre of its forehead. It jerked convulsively. He hit again. A film spread over the eyes and the ram subsided. He ran on the doe. Blood was pouring from a great hole in her side and she was coughing gouts of it onto the thin white layer of snow. He pulled out his knife and swiftly cut her throat, feeling the blood pour warmly over his hand. He wiped the blade on a tuft of grass and returned it to its sheath.

There was a pattering of feet as Stone-Axe arrived. His eyes were alive with excitement and delight. He stopped short and then came forward in a stiff, exaggerated strut. 'Behold us!' he shouted to the grey sky. 'The hunters! Look on us, the killers of Elephants and Mighty Bulls! Behold us the Big Elephants! The Lions! Look on us! Admire and confess, you worthless people, that we are the Great Bull Calves!'

James smiled. It was always the same after a difficult kill.

'Claw and Axe of Stone!' the Bushman shouted into the wind was cold. 'Fetch the horse.'

'All right,' James said, and indicated the antelope. The warmth of anticipation and action was fading fast and the wind was cold. 'Fetch the horse.'

He slit open both paunches, carefully removed the stomach and the gall bladder from each and filled the cavities

94

with grass. Stone-Axe came down the slope with Violin trotting behind him and James slung one buck ahead of the saddle and one aft. He looped their legs with thin strips of leather *reimpie* and drew them tight under Violin's belly. The mare's nostrils were flexing nervously from the smell of blood but she knew her business and stood quietly as the job was finished.

Suddenly the Bushman stiffened and turned. 'Someone comes,' he said.

James turned to look down the valley in the direction he was pointing. He could see and hear nothing. Then, after a few moments, he heard the thud of hooves. He reached for his rifle, loaded quickly, and swung into the saddle. As he did so he heard a wordless shout of rage echo from the cliffs. He looked round for Stone-Axe but he was no longer at the mare's head and only a slight quiver in the reed patch gave his presence away. James knew that by this time he would already have an arrow tight against the bow-string.

The rider emerged from a swirl of mist and was on top of James almost before he saw him. He hauled back cruelly on the reins and brought his foam-flecked stallion to a slightering halt. James recognized him at once. It was Hans Muller of the Clan Muller of the farm Clearwater and James did not like him one little bit.

They eyed each other in silent antagonism for a brief moment then Muller, who was almost speechless with anger, shouted: 'You have taken my meat!'

'What are you talking about?'

'Meat!' He indicated the carcasses. 'My meat!' He was nearly choking.

'That's where you've made a mistake, laddie,' James answered. 'And don't point that thing at me. It might go off, and scare the horse.'

They were both big men and the heavy brown corduroy of the Frontier graziers which they wore over waistcoats of soft, dappled calf-skin made them look bigger still. Muller was built like an ox, with great shoulders and heavy limbs. He wore a full sandy beard which gave him a shaggy, unkempt appearance. At first sight he seemed substantially the bigger of the two, but a closer look would have given a better picture. James at twenty-two was just over six feet in his goatskin shoes, with powerful, sloping shoulders that rose into a long, tensile neck. His dark, Celtic face was clean-shaven and had been flayed by wind and sun so the skin was tight over the cheekbones, drawing his mouth into what seemed a thin smile, but above it his blue eyes were cold and bleak. By the constant use of his right arm the muscles had developed out of proportion and his right shoulder rode slightly higher than his left. Muller gave the impression of being built from granite blocks, massive and brittle; James was like a tree growing in the desert, fibrous, springy and tough.

'Now,' he said, in fluent Dutch, 'perhaps we can talk like reasonable men.'

'I haven't come to reason,' Muller said. 'I've come to get what's mine.'

'Oh? And why do you reckon that two buck shot with my gun and by me not thirty minutes ago suddenly turn out to be killed by your gun and you? It's something I'd be interested to hear.'

'I was following them,' Muller said heatedly. 'From dawn this morning. I picked up their spoor not two hundred yards from the spring and I've been watching them for an hour.'

'You had your chance. You should have taken it.'

'I could have shot that ram two miles from here,' Muller said, indicating one of the carcasses.

'Why didn't you, then? Oh aye, you needn't bother to answer. I know very well. You wanted more, the whole damn lot with one ball. That's the trouble with you. You've been doing that for years, that's why in the hard times we're up all night and riding through the day for bits and pieces when the land should be crawling with game.' The smile that wasn't a smile gave the words a quality of disdain. Muller flushed.

'Look here, Englishman . . .' he began.

'Scotsman.'

'What . . .?'

'There's a difference,' James said, coldly.

The German paused and then said slowly: 'I'm warning

you. There's going to be trouble. There are some here who don't like strangers.'

'Some? Why don't you come out with it, man. You mean the Clan Muller. Well, you listen to me, there are some here I'm not overfond of either and you can take that any way you like.'

'I could shoot you down now,' Muller said, 'and there would be few to ask questions.'

'Aye, so you could. But I think you're misreading the facts. I'm no stranger here any longer, five years have seen to that. And as for shooting me down, well now, you just might. But . . . man, you wouldn't last a quarter-hour with an arrow in your back.'

Muller turned in his saddle and swept the surrounding veld with his eyes. It was empty. He paused at the reed bed.

'Just so,' James nodded. 'Just so. Stone-Axe, come out of there and say good morning.'

There was no answering quiver in the reeds. The German looked puzzled, then swung back to James. 'You're making jokes,' he said. And then, from a tuft of grass no bigger than a table and less than twenty feet from the two horsemen, the little bushman suddenly rose. His bow was held slackly in his left hand, the arrow-head pointing to the ground. He was quite composed.

'Now,' said James pleasantly. 'You've got your choice. Shoot me and the first thing he'll do is kill your horse. That way he'll make certain; then he'll hunt you down like a jackal. Or else you can shoot him – you've had enough practice in that kind of thing – but then I'll blow your head off.'

Muller lowered the heavy rifle onto his pommel. 'So you've still got him.'

'As you see.'

'He should be exterminated with the rest. They're nothing but animals! We've lost more stock this year than ever before.'

'Exterminated! Aye, so you can make slaves of their women and children. That's a fine Christian attitude for folk who are always ranting about the Lord. And as for the stock, you know as well as I that three dry summers and a late spring have accounted for most of the loss. Now then, make up your mind.'

'Look,' Muller said, after a pause. 'I'm a fair man. Give me one of those buck and I'll repay you in two days.'

'No.'

'Man, you know what my father's like. I can't go home with nothing . . . And anyway, there are only the three of you. With us, it's different.'

'I'm not taking these home. They're going to the mission.'

'The mission! But they'll just feed them to the Bushmen.'

'Probably.'

'You'd take the food out of Christian mouths and give it to heathen?'

'I'm not taking food out of Christian mouths and I'm not giving it to any heathen. I'm doing what Uncle Hendrik told me to do and that's that!'

'Uncle Hendrik! My father will be interested to know that.'

'That's your affair.' He turned to Stone-Axe. 'We're going.' The Bushman nodded and took up his place by the left stirrup.

'One thing more,' Muller said. 'Lisé is back.'

'I know.'

'I'm going to marry her.'

'Perhaps,' James said. 'Perhaps.' He dug his heels into the mare's sides and cantered off up the valley, Stone-Axe running easily at his side.

The wind still blew cold but the clouds began to break up and the sun rose above the shell-pink peaks. The springbok carcasses had stiffened and rubbed uncomfortably on the mare's back. They had come eight miles and there were another eight to go before reaching the mission station. James was cold, hungry and tired, but most of all hungry; he wanted food and coffee, perhaps with a little brandy in it to take the numbness from his bones.

They were passing in the lee of a slight hillock when he first saw the vultures and felt Stone-Axe pull gently on the stirrup.

It was a sight he was all too familiar with, but since they were on Bitterfountain land each incident had to be investigated. He had no doubt what he would find: the dead body of a cow or sheep. What he had to know was how it had died: from the cold, from an encounter with a lion or leopard, or wild dogs, or jackals; or had it been killed by Bushmen?

He turned Violin's head and made for the hillock. Because of the early low cloud and snow only a few vultures had arrived and had hardly begun their grisly work. Even so, what he saw came as a shock.

Four freshly killed heifers lay on a patch of bloody ground. Nearby were the remains of a fire. They had been hamstrung and then their throats had been cut. There were long slits in their bellies, from which the vultures had half drawn the entrails. He knew no animals had done this. The vultures flapped away, croaking balefully, and James and Stone-Axe were left alone with the carcasses. It was even too cold for flies. The Bushman went to the fire and put his hand into the ashes.

'How long?'

'T'oa-t'oa-t'oa.' Stone-Axe said, holding up two fingers three times. Everything beyond two was made up in additions of two.

'Six hours,' James said to himself. Perhaps longer. Sometime late last night. 'Bushmen?'

Stone-Axe shook his head vigorously. 'O Claw,' he said, 'these killings are by Christians.'

'Christians? That's rubbish. Who would kill four beasts when one would do? This has been done by a Bushman clan, it sticks out a mile.'

Stone-Axe watched his master's face impassively. 'You know everything, O Claw,' he said.

'Oh come on, then,' James said irritably. 'Don't get all bloody pious. If it wasn't Bushmen, who the hell was it?'

'People.'

'People! You'll have to do a lot better than that, laddie.'

Without the least embarrassment Stone-Axe took him by the hand and led him closer to the carcasses.

He explained what had happened much as he might have done to a child of his own race, his voice faintly querulous as though explanation were superfluous.

When he had finished James nodded. 'Maybe,' he said slowly. 'Maybe. We'll hear what Uncle Hendrik has to say about it.' The Bushman moved towards the open belly of one of the heifers. 'No, no,' James checked him before he could get his hands on the entrails. 'Leave them be, you little heathen. We've work to do.' They moved off down the slope and the vultures flapped heavily back to their meal.

As is often the case in the high places of Africa, the weather was capricious. The clouds sailed away over the horizon, the wind gradually lessened until there was only a slight breeze bending the knee-high grass and the sun beat down more confidently. What snow was left melted into runnels giving the hills a sparkling look. Larks sang in the blue sky, swallows and swifts dipped and raced, kestrels hung on blurring wings, tick-birds flighted, hares broke cover, a *lammervanger* sailed by. James could almost feel the bursting life-force renewing itself around him.

'Are you hungry?' he said to the tireless Stone-Axe.

'I am hungry.'

He was tempted. High Valley, the de Blaize's farm, lay only a few miles off his road. It would be nearly breakfast time.

And, of course, there would also be Lisé.

'All right, then,' he said. 'We'll find some food.'

By the time they reached the homestead, tucked away in the shelter of a ridge, the wind had dropped and the blue smoke from the chimney was rising in an unbroken column. The house was typical of the Snowy Mountains: low-roofed and long, its walls built of mountain-stone and mud, the roof thatched with reeds, the floor a mixture of dung and ox-blood which shone dully when cleaned. The middle section was one huge room in which the cooking and living was done. At one end, around the stove, the Hottentot servants spent the days in warm shadow, at the other was the sparse furniture: the brass-bound wagon chests, the rocking chairs and the settles with leather-thonged seats. The sleeping-chambers were simply tacked onto the end of the house so that a large family would have a longer house than a small one. The servants slept in a lean-to at the back.

It was a house of the utmost simplicity, but on a sunny spring morning a place of cheerful comfort after a hard ride.

Blom, a Bushman servant, came round to take James's bridle. He was an old man with a withered left hand which had given him a special relationship with James.

'Morning, little master,' he said, as James towered over him. 'Has the little master brought the hand of iron?'

It was an old joke between them. 'I've told you, Blom, the price is sixteen virgins. When you bring them we can talk.'

Old Blom chuckled to himself. 'Sixteen!' he said and shook his head. 'Little master would have nothing left but *reimpie*.'

There was a gurgle of laughter from Stone-Axe at the coarse allusion. Smiling, James walked to the house.

Aunt Hester was comfortably settled in one of the rockers, her bare feet on the warm foot-stove, when he came through the low doorway. The house was filled with cooking smells.

'Ach, James, but this is nice,' she said.

'Hello, Aunt Hester.' He bent down and kissed her on the cheek. The rocking-chair groaned with pleasure under her huge bottom.

'Lisé,' she called. 'Come and see who's here and set another place for breakfast.'

Lisé de Blaize came out of the bedroom on the left and greeted him with reserve.

'Come on, James,' Aunt Hester said, and her laugh caused little tremors up and down her body. 'You don't have to be shy.'

'Didn't want to make you jealous,' he said as he bent forward and kissed Lisé with elaborate casualness on the cheek. 'You know you've always been my first love.'

Aunt Hester laughed until the tears rolled down her fat cheeks and the breath wheezed in her lungs. 'Jamie, you're a sight for tired eyes,' she said. 'No one can make me laugh like you. First love, indeed!' Once again she shook gently.

In a momentary flash of memory he heard again Fitzhenry telling him he had no sense of humour.

'Come, sit down by me,' Aunt Hester said. 'Uncle Frans isn't in yet, but he won't be long and then we'll eat. Are you hungry?'

'A little. Just a little.'

'Lord in Heaven!' she said. 'I know that little appetite of yours.' She turned to the far side of the room. 'Bring water.'

A Hottentot servant brought a basin of warm water and a coarse towel. James removed his *veldschoen* and eased his feet into the water. 'That's better. It was cold early on,' he said.

As they talked he watched Lisé moving about the table. This was the first time he had seen her since her return from Graaff-Reinet a week ago and he could hardly believe she was the same little girl who had been sent to the minister's house there four years ago to learn reading, writing and counting.

He guessed she must be seventeen or eighteen now, already well into marriageable age on the Frontier. She had hair as blue-black as a rifle barrel, the long tresses caught in a green bow at the nape of her neck. Her skin was the creamy light brown of weak coffee and her mouth was wide.

Her eyes, which were almost black, were hidden by long lashes and held demurely down but there was nothing demure about the swell of her breasts which pushed against the tight cotton dress or the line of her buttocks as she leant across the table to arrange a plate or knife. The de Blaizes were French Huguenot stock and it was said that Lisé's maternal great-grandmother had been a freed Madagascan slave – though no one said it to Uncle Fran's face.

Over the years co-habitation between black and white or yellow and white had been frequent and then casual and few Frontier families did not have some heathen blood in their veins. In Lisé the mixture had reached a perfection rarely seen and James, sitting listening to Aunt Hester, found himself excited by her beauty. He himself took a servant girl when and where he needed to but that was purely functional. Most other bachelors – and sometimes married men – did the same. And in spite of the religious fervour which governed much of the Frontier life such behaviour was silently condoned as long as it was not paraded.

James remembered another occasion when he had visited High Valley before Lisé had gone off for her schooling. Uncle Frans had been out on the hills and Aunt Hester was in bed with rheumatism. He and Lisé had gone together to search for guinea-fowl eggs.

It was a warm day in mid-summer. The search was perfunctory and yielded nothing and when they found themselves by the side of a mountain brook running through a secluded kloof, Lisé had said she was tired and wanted to sit for a while. He had flung himself down beside her and, strangely, the wide landscape was too small to hold them. They seemed to touch every time one of them moved; to rub or bump, and the more they moved the more restless each became until James found himself kissing her with awkward passion. Her response was immediate and violent and in the next hour he found out more about the female form than he cared at that time to know.

For three days afterwards he had lived in a state of profound self-disgust. He washed his hands a great deal and even prayed to a long-forgotten God for forgiveness. He promised that if nothing cataclysmic happened to him he would never touch another woman as long as he lived. But as the weeks passed with no noticeable change in him, the promise was pushed into the back of his mind and he began to recall the incident with pleasure. By the time he was ready to experience it again Lisé had left for Graaff-Reinet and there were only the Hottentot girls with which to probe the mysteries.

Now, as he watched her setting the table, he wondered what memory, if any, she still retained of that day. Probably nothing, erased by the pious atmosphere of the Minister's house. Certainly she was a different person from the hot-blooded, barefoot girl he had known who could ride a horse without a saddle and load and fire a rifle with commendable speed and accuracy.

Uncle Frans came through the door. He was as lean as a strip of *biltong*, with a sense of humour as subdued as Aunt Hester's was loud.

'I thought so,' he said, coming forward to greet James. 'When I saw the little chap outside I knew you couldn't be far away.'

He turned to kiss his wife and she patted him affectionately on the hand. 'Lucky you came when you did,' she said. 'Jamie has been paying me too many compliments.'

'Before breakfast, too? I admire your spirit,' Frans de Blaize said. He washed his face, neck and hands in a fresh bowl of warm water and rubbed them dry.

'That little Bushman of yours, what d'you call him . . .?'

'Stone-Axe.'

'That's right. Man, with those arrows and that bow in his hands I get a prickling sensation in my back whenever it's turned towards him.'

James laughed. 'Uncle Frans, he'd no more shoot at you than at me.'

Uncle Frans smiled. 'I know, I know. That's what I keep telling myself. I still feel prickly.' He turned to Aunt Hester. 'What about the food, woman? Or has your head been turned completely?' As they rose to go to the table he put his arm around Lisé and kissed her on the top of the head and James felt a surge of envy.

While he sat through the long grace he watched her under his eyelids and felt a spasm in his stomach as he realized he was being as closely scrutinized.

They ate big plates of sheep's innards cooked in mutton fat, hot mealie bread and bowls of fresh milk. The sun was warm on the verandah as they moved out of doors to drink their coffee.

Frans de Blaize filled his pipe with slow deliberation and passed the length of tobacco to James. When they were both smoking comfortably he nodded to the sun-baked veld and said: 'If this holds I'll save a quarter of my lambs. Yesterday I didn't think it possible.'

'I know. Uncle Hendrik felt the same.'

'I told Hester no more slaughtering after tomorrow. I would have taken the rifle and gone after game.' He pointed with his curved pipe-stem at the springbok carcasses. 'Hendrik was wiser than I.'

'They're not for us. I'm taking them to the mission.'

'For the Bushmen?'

'It's Uncle Hendrik's idea, not mine.'

'He's a good man, but I think he's misguided. The more you feed them the more they'll want and the more will come. Like bees to honey. There'll be trouble yet.'

James shrugged. He was not really interested.

'You take the Reverend Harmsworth,' Uncle Frans continued slowly. 'He's another good man. Lives by the Book. Saintly, if you like, but he's creating a situation he won't be able to control. Where will he get the food to feed them now? At times like this no one has anything to spare, we turn in on ourselves; live close and hard. Even game is scarce, as you know. Well . . . I mean, you can't take a Bushman out of the mountains one day and tell him you'll feed him if he leads a Christian life and the next say you're sorry but the food's run out. Where must he turn to but our flocks?'

He pointed again, this time at Blom who was squatting next to Stone-Axe sharing a pipe with him. 'Old Blom there. He's been with us, I don't know, six, seven years – and now suddenly he wants to get baptized. Baptized! He's got no more notion of baptism than a porcupine! He hears stories, that's all. He hears that if you get water sprinkled over you it means a full belly of meat for the rest of your life.'

They talked on in a desultory fashion. The sun was warm on James's body and the food and the pipe had given him a feeling of sleek well-being. His thoughts turned idly on other things and he glanced across at Lisé. She was sitting on the top step bending over a piece of sewing.

'Well, this won't get the work done,' Frans de Blaize said, rising and stretching. He patted James on the shoulder. 'Come and see us soon. You don't visit us often enough.' He walked around the side of the house, shouting for a Hottentot servant.

Aunt Hester was already dozing in her chair. James said softly to Lisé: 'I'd best be on my way.' She nodded without speaking. 'Will you walk down the valley a little?'

'If you like.' She put down her sewing and kicked off her shoes. Her naked feet stretched in the sun and for a moment he felt she was exposing herself to him. He gave Stone-Axe the mare's bridle and told him to wait on the far side of the rise. The Bushman, whose eyes had never left his master, looked slightly anxious but James brusquely motioned him on and he leapt nimbly into the saddle and took the mare down the valley at a canter.

Now James was alone with Lisé he discovered that his confidence had vanished. They walked slowly down the dusty track keeping a good three feet between them. Once, to avoid an ant-bear hole, he stepped to the side and brushed against her dress. 'I'm sorry,' he said confused.

At length he said, 'Are you glad to be back?'

She shrugged. 'It makes no difference.'

'We missed you.'

'We?'

'Well – I did. We all did.'

'That's nice.'

'And – we – *I* – thought of you often.'

'I'm glad. I thought of you, too.'

'Did you?'

She stopped suddenly and faced him. 'Yes, often. In the beginning, that is, while I waited for you to visit me. Oh yes, I thought of you a lot. And then when you didn't come I didn't think of you so much.' Her black eyes glinted with anger.

'Lisé, you know how it is,' he began. 'I can't get away from the farm. Then in winter I was on the Karoo for months on end.'

'I know how it is. But you came in for communion. You came in every three months in the summer. I know that because I asked father.'

He could not explain that, with memories of his own father, nothing on earth would have induced him to cross the threshold of a preacher's house again. 'I'm sorry,' he said. 'I'll try to make up for it.'

106

'Save your sympathy for the mission,' she said flatly.

They walked on in silence for a moment, then he said: 'I saw Hans Muller this morning.'

'Oh?'

'He said he was going to marry you.'

'Did he?'

'Is it true?'

'Perhaps,' she said.

'You're not serious!'

'Why not?'

He took her by the tops of her arms and pulled her towards him. 'You couldn't marry a clod like that.'

'Let me go!'

'Please . . .'

She tried to pull away and his foot came forward against a tussock of grass. He half stumbled and brought them both down. She was under him and he pressed down on her, kissing her neck and arms and finally finding her mouth. The saliva was warm and pungent.

She twisted her mouth from under his and glared up at him. 'D'you want to put your hand up my dress?' she asked viciously.

'What?'

'That's what the minister wanted. All the time. He said it would bring us closer to God. Is that what you want, too? To get closer to God?'

The words struck him like a sheep-whip. He drew away from her as she straightened her clothing. 'I'm sorry,' he muttered, getting to his feet and brushing dust and dry grass from his corduroys. 'I didn't mean —'

She faced him, the swell of her breasts rising and falling with anger and exertion. 'Have I shocked you? Don't you like to know these things?'

'It's not that. It's just . . .'

'It's just that it makes me sound like one of your Hottentot maids! Isn't that the reason?'

'Don't talk rubbish!'

'Servants gossip,' she said. 'Or didn't you know?'

'If you listen to that sort of talk, there's nothing more to say,' he said, with an attempt at dignity. He turned on his heel and walked swiftly up the rise. He felt shaken and angry. He knew that Stone-Axe would have watched the entire scene and if there was so much as the faintest trace of a smirk on his face he'd wipe it off with his fist. But the Bushman was not there. Violin was tied to a thorn bush at the bottom of a narrow gully but there was no sign of Stone-Axe at all.

'God damn you!' he said savagely. 'Where the hell have you got to now?'

He untied the mare and moved down the gully. 'Stone-Axe!' he shouted. 'Where are you, blast it!'

There was a faint answering cry and he made out the Bushman's tiny figure coming down a heavily bushed *krantz* about four hundred yards away with the speed of a baboon. He mounted Violin and rode to meet him.

Stone-Axe's face was almost completely hidden behind a mask of dark wild honey. It dripped from his cheeks and great lumps of comb, honey and white grubs oozed between his fingers as he gulped mouthfuls from his cupped hands. He was in a state of ecstasy.

He held up his hands in offering but James shook his head in disgust. He was tempted to teach him a lesson there and then but he knew that nothing on earth would stop a Bushman once he saw a honeybird and began to follow it. He watched Stone-Axe gorging himself for a few seconds and then heard the ominous hum of a wild bee and knew it wouldn't be long before the maddened swarm found them.

Stone-Axe looked up. 'The little people will be here soon, Claw.'

'Come on, then.' He dug his heels into Violin's sides and they set off at a sprint down the gully.

They came down the track to Bitterfountain in the chill of evening. The last of the sun had bathed the peaks in purple and the valleys were hidden in a dark blue haze. The homestead crouched in a hollow and smoke from its cooking fires drifted about in a gauzy layers. The smell of the dung fires, acid and herby, spread out across the veldt to meet them.

108

James was saddle-sore and tired. The mare, scenting her home, quickened her walk to a triple and Stone-Axe effortlessly increased his stride, his feet making the slightest *poff poff poff* in the dust at her side.

'I'm back,' James called as he reached the front of the porch. He dismounted stiffly. A young Hottentot boy, Apie, the son of Clara, one of the maids, came from the back of the house and took Violin's bridle.

'Rub her well,' he said.

'Yes, master.'

He gave his rifle, powder-horn and bandolier to Stone-Axe. There was no need for further instructions; the rifle would be cleaned, the powder-horn filled and the empty pockets of the bandolier replenished with moulded slugs, part tin, part lead, which Stone-Axe would sew into tiny greased-leather bags for swift loading.

The house was similar in construction to High Valley but bigger. It contained much the same furniture, though of better quality. Hendrik and Hannah van Roye were seated in the rocking-chairs near the oil-lamp.

In the right-hand corner of the room the cooking fire flickered, causing shadows to dance and jump. The light from the flames played on the faces of the heathen servants, touching their high cheek-bones and flat, wide noses, and made their eyes seem large and white.

Except for the faint chink of crockery and tin they were silent as they listened to the voice of Hendrik van Roye reading from the big clasped Bible. He read slowly and resonantly, holding the heavy book close to the lamp. '*And the Lord said, I have surely seen the affliction of my people which are in Egypt, and have heard their cry by reason of their taskmasters; for I know their sorrows . . .*'

He paused as James quietly settled himself in one of the chairs and then went on: '*And I am come down to deliver them out of the land of the Egyptians and to bring them up out of that land unto a good land and a large, unto a land flowing with milk and honey; unto the place of the Canaanites and the Hittites, and the Amorites, and the Perizzites, and the Hivites and the Jebusites. Come now therefore . . .*' James let the words wash over his tired body. It was strange that he had never minded Uncle Hendrik reading from the Book or saying grace or conducting the singing in the morning from *Willem Sluiter's Gesagen* even though the Dutch was difficult to follow. Perhaps it was because it *was* all in Dutch that it was different here on the Frontier. He never thought about his father at all.

Uncle Hendrik was looking old. His hair was still thick but it was now completely white. His sparse beard was stained yellow from his pipe. Once he had been a huge man but age was beginning to shrink him, a process that had been accelerated by an accident which had crippled him. He gave the impression of a big tree that had been struck by lightning. Aunt Hannah was a good ten years younger. At times her face seemed almost youthful, but her body was beginning to spread and sag. She had wide hazel eyes, soft and kind, with a far-off sadness in them.

She was good with the servants; they both were, although Uncle Hendrik was the stricter. They had built up a paternal relationship over the years and the servants now looked upon themselves as children of the house. It was a good arrangement and one which the van Royes fostered.

'They're only children, after all,' was one of Aunt Hannah's most frequent comments when something went wrong.

'I know, Hannah, I know,' Uncle Hendrick would say. 'But they have to learn and it is we who must teach them.' It was Uncle Hendrik who kept the balance between spoiling them and crushing them, and they respected him for it.

It was typical of his sense of justice that the only time James had ever clashed with him had been over the servants. It had been several years before when he was going through a period in which he thought servants had been placed on earth especially for him.

One afternoon he had found Clara hoeing weeds between rows of newly-planted vines which Uncle Hendrik was growing as an experiment. It had taken him months to get the cuttings and since he wasn't sure whether they would survive the cold winters he was treating them with the care of a nervous bridegroom.

James had ordered Clara out of the garden to help him plait the handle of a stock-whip. Four-plaiting was complicated and almost impossible with only one hand.

'Master can see I'm busy,' Clara had protested.

'Don't answer me back!'

Unwillingly she had followed him to the barn behind the house and had spent the next three hours teaching him the intricacies of leather work. It was almost evening when she got back into the garden. She had been told to finish the hoeing that day and began to work with reckless speed. Inevitably, she cut two of the vines.

When Uncle Hendrik came to inspect the work and saw what had happened he gave a great roar of rage. Clara flung down her hoe. He picked up a heavy stone and hurled it at her head as she fled through the bushes. If it had connected, it would have felled her.

Later, after his temper had cooled, he found out from the other servants what had happened. He sat down in his chair and waited for James. The atmosphere in the house was electric. The servants huddled together like frightened children, muttering under their breaths, already sorry for what was about to happen. Aunt Hannah sat by her husband's side and tried to sew, but after she had pricked her finger two or three times, she put the sewing down and turned on him. It didn't happen very often, but when it did it made an impact.

'Hendrik,' she said quietly. 'He is only a baby.'

'He's almost a grown man!'

'Now you listen to me. He has come to us like a gift from the Lord. He is in our trust. He is still unfamiliar with our customs and our life. He is like a young tree suddenly growing in every direction at once. I say to you now that you will not raise a hand to him. You have already lost your temper once today. What would have happened to Clara if your aim had been good? You would have killed her. And for no reason! You will do nothing!'

She sat back, hands folded adamantly on her lap, lips pressed tightly together.

Uncle Hendrik said nothing. The servants shuffled uneasily in their corner.

When James came into the room he was greeted by utter silence. He stood with the new whip hanging idly from his right hand and stared about in bewilderment. Slowly Hendrik van Roye got to his feet. Aunt Hannah said only one word: 'Hendrik!' It burst the silence with the force of a small explosion.

He stood facing James. 'Give me that whip,' he said.

James held it out with a frown. Uncle Hendrik walked down the room and threw it into the fire. Then he turned. 'When you want help to make another one,' he said, 'come to me.'

Nothing more was said, but lessons were learnt all round.

'. . . *When thou hast brought forth the people out of Egypt,*' Uncle Hendrik's voice went on, *'ye shall serve God upon this mountain.'* He closed the Bible. 'Amen.' Aunt Hannah and James echoed the word and they heard the muttered 'Amens' from the servants.

In a new voice, Uncle Hendrik pondered: 'A land flowing with milk and honey. That's what we have always been looking for. They say it's to the north.' He stretched and rubbed at his twisted leg. 'Always to the north.'

They ate a meal of stewed mutton, turnips, mealies which had been ground, soaked in water and boiled, and finished with a bowl of fresh milk each. Afterwards, while Aunt Hannah portioned out the food for the servants, James and Uncle Hendrik took their pipes into the lamplight and, in what had now become an established custom, reviewed the events of the day and planned those of the next.

'I didn't know there were so many,' James was saying of the mission Bushmen. 'The Reverend Harmsworth must have about eighty or ninety now and he says a few more come every day. Two springbok won't go far among those people.'

Uncle Hendrick pulled slowly on his pipe. 'We do what we can,' he said. 'If others did the same there would be no problem.'

'Uncle Frans thinks it's a mistake.'

'Oh, so you were over at High Valley.'

'I called in for breakfast.'

'Ah, yes, breakfast. I understand Lisé is back.'

'Yes.'

'And that makes breakfast taste all the better.' Uncle Hendrik smiled.

James found himself flushing unnaturally. Aunt Hannah, who was moving around the table, said: 'Don't tease the boy, Hendrik, you can see he's tired.'

'Yes, yes, of course. It's a long ride for breakfast.'

'It was on my way,' James said. 'I got the buck down near the south boundary.'

'That was a bit of luck.'

He was not in the mood for banter and swiftly changed the subject. 'We found four dead heifers down there.' Hendrik van Roye's face became grave. 'Heifers! It wasn't cold enough for *that*.'

'They'd been slaughtered for food.'

Uncle Hendrik shifted angrily in his chair. He opened his mouth to say something, then seemed to get a grip on himself. Finally he said mildly: 'You see, if you don't give them food they take it and you can't control what they take. If they had come to me they could have had a few sheep, but they're frightened now so they steal – and I lose four good heifers. Rather ten sheep than one heifer.'

'Stone-Axe says it wasn't Bushmen.'

'That's nonsense. Who else?'

'That's what I said. But he's certain and I think he may be right.'

'He's turned your head, that one.'

James looked across the room into the shadows. The other servants were already curled up on their mats near the fire but Stone-Axe still sat with his back to the far wall; his eyes on James, watchful and brooding. James felt a quick spasm of affection for the little man.

'I must say it looked that way at first,' he said. 'But then he showed me one or two things. You know how Bushmen love the entrails?'

Uncle Hendrik nodded.

'Well, none had been touched. Only the liver and kidneys had been taken. They hadn't even cut meat from the buttocks. And the fire-place they built was much bigger than a Bushman's. And anyway, they slept there afterwards.'

'That's unusual,' Uncle Hendrik agreed. 'They certainly would have cut off as much as they could carry away. Unless they'd been scared off.'

'No, the fire was almost cold. Stone-Axe said about six hours. And why kill them there? They could have driven them into the mountains and no one would have been any the wiser. They were strays.'

'I've never seen a Bushman leave the entrails,' Uncle Hendrik said. 'That's certain. They dry them for necklaces. How many does your little man think there were?'

'Four.'

'A heifer each! It doesn't sound like Bushmen.'

'But that still leaves us with the question: if not Bushmen, who else?'

Uncle Hendrik remained silent for a few minutes, then said: 'About ten years ago something similar happened. A gang of reivers hid out in the mountains for months. They usually live to the east of here on the borders of Kaffirland; rotten people who call themselves Christians: deserters, murderers, thieves. They steal cattle from the Colonists, who blame the Kaffirs, and then steal from the Kaffirs, who blame the Colonists. As long as one side blames the other, they can go on stealing in the confusion. But after a hard winter the Kaffirs sometimes come over the border to look for their cattle and these people get out of the district for a while till the trouble's over. Then they drift this way.'

'What happened to them?'

'At that time we were friendly with the Bushmen and told them that as long as the reivers were in the mountains there would be no presents for them. They cleared them out fast enough. Two killed in one day and the others went off north towards the Great River. I'm told they're still up that way somewhere.'

'Couldn't we try the same thing again? With the Bushmen, I mean.'

'Why should they do anything to help us now?'

James was suddenly irritated. 'Bushmen! That's all I hear. Why don't we get up a commando and drive them out of the mountains – all of them, the reivers as well. Uncle Frans says the way things are going there'll only be trouble, and I think he's right.'

Uncle Hendrik looked at him gravely. 'I hoped I'd never hear you say that, son,' he said. 'I tried to teach you to be different.'

Later that night as James lay awake between the rough blankets listening to the light breathing of Stone-Axe from the floor at his feet, he forgot all about the Bushmen. He was tasting again the inside of Lisé's mouth, feeling her body in his hands, remembering the first time.

Summer came to the Snowy Mountains. Soft winds blew in from the Indian Ocean and fleecy thunderheads sailed across deep blue skies, often building up to a storm in the afternoon and leaving the veld sparkling with raindrops in the early evening sun. Where the winter grass had been burnt the land blushed green. Wild flowers patterned the valleys. In the sheltered kloofs weeping willows bent to the mountain streams, poplars shed their velvet, mimosas rose in crowns of yellow, their branches oozing gum which Stone-Axe ate with relish. Cobras and puff-adders dropped their skins, mouse-birds flopped in the trees waiting for the garden fruit to ripen. The land began to burgeon.

A traveller passing through the mountains at that time might have thought it was one of the world's most fortunate places, but he would have been wrong. The summer rains were a little *too* good, the grass grew a little *too* lushly, and in some parts, where it was damply warm to the touch under the noon sun, insect life was also thriving. Ticks hung on the cattle like bunches of purple grapes, blow-flies attacked the anal folds of the sheep, maggots ate into the living flesh. The animals, weak after the severe winter, were unable to cope with the very richness of the new season. Two of Uncle Hendrik's prize Spanish rams, which he had ordered at great cost, died of stomach worms. The whole household watched in anguish as they wasted away, becoming dropsical and pot-bellied, razor-backed and bottle-jawed. In the marshy hollows the sheep developed foot rot. There was talk in the district of a general murrain and words like anthrax and rinderpest were whispered. Even some of the horses, which were almost free of disease in the high mountains, contracted the fatal distemper which was known as *paardeziekte*.

The graziers waited and prayed; there was little else they could do.

Game was scarcer than it had been for years. In a dry summer, when there were few places buck could drink – and those well known to the hunters – larders were filled with venison and biltong. But in wet summers, when water was plentiful, the game drifted across the face of the countryside, moving towards ever more remote places where the sound of rifles had never broken the stillness.

The Bushmen raids grew more pronounced. There was no game for them either.

When farmers met the talk gradually focused on three things: their flocks, the extermination of the Bushmen; the closing of the Reverend Harmsworth's mission.

Towards Christmas one of the small graziers who had suffered most from stock thefts and sickness, a man called Redder, shot his wife and four small children, two Hottentot servants, a breeding-ram, his best stallion and then put the barrel of an elephant gun in his mouth and pulled the trigger with his toe. He blew the top of his head through the reed-thatched roof and was only identifiable by his clothing.

Others who had suffered almost as badly, drifted down to Graaff-Reinet, where they spent the last of their money on strong spirits and moved off towards Kaffirland looking for easy pickings.

At Bitterfountain Uncle Hendrik worked with grim determination. He seemed to be everywhere at once, limping along on his twisted leg as fast as he could. One moment he was helping James shear away maggoty wool, the next he was

116

in the barn with one of the mares, rubbing and drying, changing sweat-sodden blankets at midnight.

His temper became short, his cheeks sunken and his eyes unnaturally bright. 'God has visited a pestilence upon us,' he said as he hurried from task to task. And then he would mutter to himself and the servants would eye him strangely. Ever since the wagon had fallen on the old master's leg they had feared something like this would happen – and now it had.

The change in him affected Aunt Hannah. For the first time since her sons died she snapped at the servants. She was never satisfied, never still.

In the midst of it all James lived partially in another world. He worked as hard as anyone on the farm, but his thoughts were on Lisé.

Every Sunday he rode the fourteen miles to High Valley to see her. At first he tried to shoot a springbok to furnish himself with a pretext but the time taken to find the game cut so much into his few leisure hours that he finally gave it up and simply presented himself at the house. Since Sunday was the only day on which the farmers did no work he had half expected to find Hans Muller already in attendance but he learnt that the Mullers had trekked down to the plains in their wagons to shoot eland and quagga and so he had High Valley to himself.

The barrier between Lisé and himself gradually diminished. In the Snowy Mountains, like any other enclosed and remote community, feuds were not uncommon, but they usually broke out over boundary rights or water and involved whole families, not single individuals. Lisé was a young and beautiful woman, ripe to the point of bursting; James was the nearest man for forty miles not old enough to be her father; and Lisé was bored. She would probably have denied it if asked, especially in front of her parents – it would have had a flavour of ungodliness and even ingratitude about it – but nevertheless, her days were so predictable, following each other in such a perfect pattern of ordinariness, that they seemed to be lived in a listless vacuum.

She rose early, before her mother, and supervised the

lighting of the fire and the brewing of coffee. Her father would drink his, standing near the door and looking out over the hills, summing up the day silently to himself. Then he would disappear and she would be left alone with her toilet. In the primitiveness of her room she could have completed it in a few minutes but she had brought a looking-glass with her from Graaff-Reinet and in the revealing light of early morning she would examine herself minutely, sometimes undressing again to look at her dusky body, pinching the near-black nipples into rigidity, brushing and combing her long dark hair.

This could take her as long as two hours; time that slipped away in sensual daydreams. Then her father would return, her mother would be dressed, the servants would gather and, after a short prayer, they would sing together from *Willem Sluiter's Gesagen*.

Apart from laying the table – Aunt Hester did not like the servants to touch the cutlery – there was little else for her to do for the rest of the day except her sewing, and even that was done better by one of the maids.

Sometimes she wished she were back in Graaff-Reinet treading the dangerous path between God and the minister; at least it had been interesting.

The warm days of summer passed her in an endless stream, grouping themselves into time sequences that divided one Sunday from the next. Sundays became important to her for James came visiting on Sundays. Her attitude towards him was ambivalent. She liked to shock him as she had done after her return, because she knew it irritated him and at the same time excited him. But she also sensed the latent violence in him and knew that too much irritation could turn into anger, too much excitement into loss of control. Sometimes, in those grey early dawns, when her limbs were heavy and warm, she would try to picture what loss of control might mean and she would find herself tensed by a mixture of dread and anticipation.

Sundays took on their own pattern. Lunch was always the week's most important meal and Aunt Hester, with a zeal quite unlike her normal self, would personally attend to its details. They might have chicken broth seasoned with red pepper and ginger, and flavoured with cucumbers and tamarinds, then plates of cauliflower and beans flavoured with vinegar, and chicken-and-pigeon pasties. And all the while, at least on hot summer days when the flies were bad, the servants would stand behind their chairs and gently fan the air with ostrich feathers.

In the afternoons, when Aunt Hester and Uncle Frans were overtaken by torpor, James and Lisé would slip away into the hills and find a shady place by a stream and lie on the soft green grass that grows under mimosa trees.

On those drowsy afternoons James's hand would stalk the contours of her body like a Bushman might stalk game. Her reactions differed from Sunday to Sunday as though she were putting into action plans conceived during the previous six days. Sometimes she would allow him to caress her but at others, when he was as tense as a drawn bow, she would say flatly: 'I don't want you to put your hand there,' or 'Please don't do that,' and he would recoil as though slapped in the face. And sometimes she would not even allow him to start and he would turn away sullenly, telling himself it had something to do with the dim mysteries of the female being but remaining unsatisfied by the rationalisation. At these times he felt humbled and he resented it. He told himself that one day he would take her whether she wanted him to or not, and that would be that. But when it did happen, it wasn't like that at all.

On a hot January day, the very kernel of summer, when the land lay still and shimmering under the glaring dome of the sky, they decided to go farther afield than usual to the cool gorge of the Crow River. It was fed by springs in the high mountains and even in the direst weather there was usually a trickle of water. Now it ran half full over a slate bottom, twisting and turning, tumbling over slight falls, deepening into slow pools. They lay on a ledge, shaded from the afternoon sun and trailed their hands in the water.

Lisé had been quiet, almost reserved, as they walked to the

stream and he had decided to remain cool and detached as a warning that she was not the only one whose behaviour could be unpredictable. She didn't seem to notice.

She leant forward towards the water, cupping her hands below the surface and bringing them up to drink. Drops of water beaded her upper lip.

At last she said: 'Hans Muller is back. He came over yesterday.'

'Oh?' he said coldly. 'That must have been nice. You'll be making plans for the wedding then.'

She looked sideways at him under heavy lids, a half-smile on her face. 'What wedding?'

'I assumed you had it arranged.'

'So did Hans, I think.'

'Well, you have my felicitations when you do decide.' He rolled over on his stomach and flicked a pebble into the pool.

'You must admit he's a good catch.'

'I admit nothing of the sort. He's a loutish clod.'

'D'you think when Uncle Otto dies he'll inherit Clearwater?'

'They'll probably follow the old custom and split up the land and flocks between the sons. And don't forget he's got five brothers.'

'I've wondered about that,' she said thoughtfully.

'I'd wonder a bit more if I were you. If it's lands and flocks you want, find an only son.'

They lay in silence for a while, letting the warm afternoon envelop them. 'James?'

'Yes?'

'What's going to happen to *you?*'

He laughed harshly. 'D'you mean if you marry Muller? I shouldn't let that worry you. Forbye there are always the Hottentot maids – as you yourself reminded me.'

'No not that. I mean what are you going to do?'

'Do? I'm going to do exactly what I'm doing now. What do you mean, *do?*'

'I just wondered, that's all.'

When James first came to the Snowy Mountains it had been given out that he was living at Bitterfountain for health

120

reasons and that he had been sent there by a doctor at the Cape of Good Hope. It was a simple and effective label and had been readily accepted by the graziers who had enlarged endlessly on the virtue of pure mountain air.

'I'm needed at Bitterfountain,' he said, quietly. 'I belong there now.'

'I've often thought that one day you would simply go away as suddenly as you came.'

'I couldn't, even if I wanted to, which I don't.'

'But what happens to you when Uncle Hendrik dies?'

'I've told you, nothing. It's been arranged. There is no other family except some cousins at the Cape. Bitterfountain comes to me. They both want it so.'

'So you'll be the king one day.'

'I'd rather not discuss it any further,' he said shortly.

The expression on her face became petulant and she turned away. After a few moments she said: 'It's hot.'

He nodded.

'It's the hottest day of the summer.'

'Perhaps.'

'I like swimming.'

'Here?'

'Sometimes I come here by myself but I've always been afraid to go in. With you here it's different.' She turned her back on him and said: 'Please help me with the fastenings. I can't manage.'

'You're not really –'

'Why not?'

With stumbling fingers he began to loosen the clips at the back of her dress. She leant against his knees. As each fastening came undone the opening of the dress stretched wider and James saw she was not wearing anything underneath it. He undid the last fastening at her waist and the dress fell away, revealing her naked back. She held the front against her breasts.

'Now you,' she said.

'I can't swim,' he said, and his mouth was dry.

'It's not deep. Look, I'll show you.' She stood up, let the dress fall to her ankles and stepped out of the shadow into the sunlight. Her body was the colour of an apricot and James had never seen anything so beautiful. He watched her lower herself into the water. She splashed a handful at him. 'Come,' she said. 'Come in.'

He paused fractionally. Very few people had ever seen him without his hook and she had not been one of them. But she was below the surface of the water now and her breasts were pale blobs in the pool. He wrenched at his clothing and then swiftly began to untie the thongs which laced the leather cuff to the top of his left forearm. The hook fell away leaving the pale pink stump uncovered. They were both utterly naked now.

Lisé was standing on the rocky bottom of the pool, her shoulders out of the water, staring at his arm. James looked up and flushed, the blood making his dark face even darker.

'It's nothing,' she said in a tone of slight wonder, more to herself than to him. 'It's only an arm.'

'What did you think it was?' he said angrily.

'I didn't know – I couldn't even guess –'

He made a move to draw on the black leather cuff but she came towards him and put her hands on the stump. They were wet and cool and the first hands, other than his own or Dr Goodsir's, ever to touch the scars. An animal feeling of complete abandonment shivered through his body.

'You're hot,' she whispered. 'Come in with me.'

He opened his mouth to speak but it was so dry that no words came. He was poised on the edge of the rock. Seconds passed as they stared at each other; then suddenly he leant forward with his right arm and lifted her out of the water. She locked her hands behind his neck and pressed herself, wet and slippery, against his boiling skin. His lungs deflated in a groan and he savaged her lips and gums. Then he took her there on the hard ledge, her body cold beneath his own.

The violence of it left them drained and shaken.

Later they splashed together in the pool and it was a long time before he even noticed the hook lying on the rock, forsaken and bereft. When he did, a feeling of strange vulnerability came over him.

★   ★   ★

As the summer wore on the stock thefts became more serious. Most were of the usual Bushman pattern: the driving off of a part of a herd or flock, the chase by a group of hastily summoned neighbours, the wilful slaughter of the animals that couldn't be driven into the mountain fastnesses, the frustration and anger of the graziers at the wanton destruction of their animals.

And interspersed with these raids came reports of another sort: of heifers and young lambs killed and eaten by the side of big open fires, their entrails left intact.

Most farmers did not think further than the Bushmen but Uncle Hendrik was disturbed. He was certain now that there was a band of reivers in the district, reaping the benefits of the undeclared war between Bushman and grazier.

'In the end they are even worse,' he said to James. 'They kill only the best.'

A change came over the Frontier. Farmers who were delighted if they only saw a neighbour at three-monthly communion began to meet at each other's homes on Sundays to make speeches about the will of God and the extermination of the Bushmen. Chief among them was Otto Muller who, with his six sons, had almost cleared the eland and quagga from the plains and had returned with four wagon-loads of *biltong* which he had sold at a splendid profit throughout the district.

The talk finally settled on one topic, a punitive commando that would ride into the mountains, equipped to remain away from home for a fortnight. During that time it would hunt down the bands of Bushmen in their caves, smoke them out and end the whole business once and for all. But the organization of a commando, considering the wide area on which it would draw, was an unwieldy affair. Each grazier had his own ideas on when and how it could best be employed and had the right to say so.

Late one evening after a sultry day of black thunderheads and charged air, the Reverend Harmsworth arrived at Bitterfountain. His horse was foam-flecked and almost spent, its wild eyes rolling.

Uncle Hendrik was already drowsing over his last pipe of

the evening. Aunt Hannah was at her sewing and James was cutting a criss-cross pattern on the ironwood stock of a new whip, when the clatter of hooves brought them all up together in sharp anxiety. Aunt Hannah looked quickly at the two men.

On the far side of the room the Hottentot servants stirred uneasily and a dark shadow detached itself from the wall and glided across the room. Stone-Axe crouched down beside James, handing him the cleaned and loaded rifle.

'Trouble,' Uncle Hendrik said. 'It's trouble.' And after the mounting tension of the past weeks he was simply voicing all their thoughts.

James crossed to the window and held the rifle loosely at the ready.

'Hendrik van Roye,' a voice called from the darkness outside. 'I must speak with you.' It was a high voice with the hint of a quaver in it.

'That's the Reverend,' Uncle Hendrik said, pushing himself out of his chair and limping across to the door. 'Let him in, James. Let him in.'

The Reverend Harmsworth came into the room, blinking at the yellow light of the single lamp. He was a thin man of medium height with a sensitive almost pretty face and light wavy hair.

He had first come to the Cape four years before as a representative of the London Missionary Society and had worked among the Hottentots of the south-east. Gradually he had come to see that the problem of the Bushmen was more immediate, that their final extinction would not be too long delayed unless something was done. He had left the Society and moved to the borders of the Colony – even beyond – wherever his flock might need him. This had given the authorities at the Cape cause for great annoyance for they had expressly forbidden proselytizing north of the Frontier. The LMS quickly denied any connexion with him.

After reaching the Snowy Mountains he had tried to spread his evangelical net wide enough to cover the graziers as well as the Bushmen, but the farmers, desperate as they were for a resident clergyman to save them the long journey to

Graaff-Reinet, held back in suspicion. They watched and waited and eventually their fears were realized: not only was he not of their religion but he seemed to hold the Bushmen as equals. Within a month of his arrival they were chuckling over a rumour that he was really a woman dressed in male clothing.

The result had been that he grew closer to the Bushmen and began to identify his own isolation with theirs. It was natural that he should move a few miles over the border, where a beautiful spring of water coursed gently through a narrow valley, and found his mission station.

Not all the farmers were against him. They saw what he was trying to do, saw his thin body grow thinner and his long white hands grow ugly and calloused with the work; they saw the stubborn passion in his eyes grow stronger and, grudgingly, they admired him. Uncle Hendrik was the first to send him food and after that rarely a week went by without one or two sheep being driven across the hills to Silverfountain, as he had named the mission. The gifts were largely anonymous; few graziers wanted to advertise their generosity.

When the Bushmen began shyly arriving from their secret places Albert Harmsworth knew that God had heard his prayers.

'Come in, come in,' Uncle Hendrik was saying. 'Come and take a seat. Man, you look all in.'

The missionary was covered in dust from his long ride and the whites of his eyes were a hazy red. 'Thank you,' he said.

James, who always reacted to his delicacy with subdued anger, turned away and lowered the rifle.

Aunt Hannah clapped her hands and called for coffee and one of the servants added more dung to the fire and pumped up the flames with a leather bellows.

'It's not often you give us the pleasure of a visit,' she said, frowning in pity at the sight of his wasted face.

'Pleasure,' Albert Harmsworth said vaguely, peering about as though to re-orientate himself after the ride. 'Pleasure . . . no . . . not often . . . not often . . .'

'Here,' Uncle Hendrik said as the strong black coffee was

125

brought from the fire, 'you'll need something to go with that,' and he reached behind him and brought out a bottle of Cape brandy, adding a stiff measure to the coffee.

Mr Harmsworth drank it, barely conscious of the addition of the spirit, and in a few minutes the colour returned to his cheeks. 'Hendrik van Roye,' he said, 'you are the only man I can turn to, the only one with the courage and influence to stop it.' The pompous phrases delivered in a high voice sounded odd and at another time James might have had to hide a smile.

'Tell us what we have to stop,' Uncle Hendrik said, shifting on his chair.

For a moment it seemed that the Reverend Harmsworth might break down. His eyes were shiny with tears and a tremor affected his chin. He closed his eyes, made an effort to control himself, held on tightly and a few seconds later opened his eyes. 'Forgive me,' he said. 'When I first came here, you were good to me. I thank you for that.'

'We did what we could.'

'It was a start. It gave me a start.' He looked down at his pale hands, scarred and cracked from manual work. 'I thought that was all I needed.' He was talking more to himself than the others. 'I thought that if I showed my will, if I made my own will the will of God, eventually victory would come. I tried. You *know* I tried –'

'No one could have tried harder,' Uncle Hendrik said.

'I built the mission with my own hands. I went into the mountains in search of my flock.' He glanced up. 'Do you know the verse from Isaiah 8 "He shall feed his flock like a shepherd: he shall gather the lambs with his arm . . ."?'

' ". . . and carry them in his bosom, and shall gently lead those that are with young",' Uncle Hendrik finished.

The Reverend Harmsworth nodded slowly. 'I found my flock. Now it is gone.'

'All of them?' James said, surprised.

'Gone – or going. By tomorrow they will all have gone, nearly two hundred of them. All except two, a man and his son; you will find their bodies staked out on the side of the track to Clearwater. The white-necked crows have al-

126

ready eaten their eyes and the jackals their tongues; tonight the hyenas will be cracking their leg bones and tomorrow the vultures will finish the work. Finally there will only be enough left for the ants. You may well look surprised. They were shot down by one of the Mullers yesterday afternoon as a lesson to the Bushmen and to myself. When I saw Otto Muller he told me they were wild Bushmen caught raiding his sheep; but he lied. I had baptized the man less than six weeks ago. His son was only twelve years old.'

'Are you sure of this?' Uncle Hendrik asked.

'Positive. I've seen their bodies. Not pretty things now.'

'My God, but that was a savage thing to do.'

'I'll wager it was Hans who did the work. It has his smell about it,' James said.

The Reverend Harmsworth turned to him as though seeing him for the first time. 'You brought me some venison once when we were starving. Did I thank you then?'

'Thank Uncle Hendrik.'

'I am too much in his debt already.'

Aunt Hannah said: 'They'll come back to you. You'll see. This will blow over.'

'And be killed by the first gun that finds them?'

'No,' Uncle Hendrik said fiercely. 'We'll stop that. We are not all barbarians.'

The Reverend Harmsworth shrugged. 'By that time there will be nothing left to return to.'

'You can stay here until they return to the mission,' Aunt Hannah said. 'Then you can go back. I don't want to think of you living there alone.'

'It's kind of you. But perhaps I haven't made myself clear. The mission is finished. God's will has been done. By tomorrow or the day after it will have ceased to exist.' He saw the look of accusation in Uncle Hendrik's eyes. 'Didn't you know that the Mullers are taking the land? Their flocks are already on the way. That's why I sent my people to the mountains. I'm not willing to let them fall into bondage.'

'I don't believe it,' Uncle Hendrik said, shaking his head as though to convince himself.

'Then ask your neighbour, Frans de Blaize. It was he who sent me word.'

'But your land is over the Frontier.'

'D'you think that really matters to a man like Muller? He has wanted the spring ever since I built there.'

'But why now? There's enough water this summer for everyone. Too much.'

'That's it. In a dry summer he wouldn't dare, everyone would be watching. Now, water is almost an embarrassment. People's minds are on other things.'

Uncle Hendrik nodded slowly. 'We *have* been too much engaged with ourselves.'

'And ridding the district of two hundred savages; wouldn't that make Otto Muller a hero?'

'Two hundred more in the mountains! My God, what won't they do to our stock?' Uncle Hendrik said.

'That's not quite what I meant. But I take your point.'

'This must be stopped quickly. Reverend, you will sleep here tonight. It's late and we can do nothing now. Tomorrow morning we will visit Clearwater.'

The Reverend Harmsworth nodded. 'That is why I came to you.'

The three of them rode in silence. The dawn air was soft and cool on their faces. Occasionally a covey of partridges whirred out from under the horses' hooves in startled clatter. The only other sounds were the creak of saddlery and the jingling of bridles. They had taken coffee and rusks in darkness and had left Bitterfountain even before the palest milk showed in the sky.

James rode with his own thoughts. Every now and then he glanced down to his left stirrup to where the small round head of Stone-Axe should have been bobbing. Without the Bushman he felt strangely forlorn, but Uncle Hendrik had been adamant. 'It'll only provoke them,' he said. 'You know how Muller feels about him.' So, for the first time, Stone-Axe had been left behind, his face, as he stood on the verandah, a study in anguish and uncertainty.

The track was narrow and twisting. Uncle Hendrik went

first, then the Reverend Harmsworth, who sat straighter in the saddle and rode with shorter stirrups than the Frontier farmers, and then came James, the rifle lying ready in the curve of his hook.

He noticed that Uncle Hendrik was already sitting slightly lopsided, letting his weight fall onto his good leg. It was the first time the old man had ridden a horse since the accident.

Suddenly the grazier raised his hand and they stopped. He fought his stallion briefly and the horse side-stepped from the track, making space for the others.

In the early light the bodies, or what was left of them, looked pathetically small. The Bushmen had been staked out at the side of the path by wrists and ankles. There was little left of either face and the soft flesh round the neck had gone. The boy was missing both arms and the man had lost a leg below the knee. Both their bellies were distended to twice the normal size. The three men looked down in silence and then the boy's yellow body writhed momentarily and gas erupted through the anus in a hissing fart.

'His name was Caama,' the Reverend Harmsworth said, dismounting.

'What are you doing?' Uncle Hendrik said.

'I'm going to bury them.'

'No, no, there's no time!'

'We can't leave them here to rot!'

'Cover them with stones, then. There's no time to dig. James, help the Reverend.'

James slid from the saddle and began collecting boulders which they packed over the bodies.

'At least the animals won't get them now,' the missionary said, dusting his hands on his trousers. Uncle Hendrik had watched the work in silence. There was a pinched look about his mouth.

By the time they reached the Clearwater homestead the sun was well up and the morning mist had been burnt away. They sat their horses in a semi-circle at the front of the house and looked around.

'There's no one here,' James said. 'They've left.'

'Otto!' Uncle Hendrik shouted. 'Otto Muller!'

'I saw a movement at one of the windows,' the Reverend Harmsworth said.

'Perhaps they're at breakfast,' Uncle Hendrik said, without conviction.

Then the front door opened and a woman came out onto the verandah in front of them. She wore a faded print dress and her lank hair hung untidily about her careworn face. There was a look of defeat and utter hopelessness in her eyes. 'What do you want?' she said.

'Freda, it is I, Hendrik van Roye.'

'I can see that. What d'you want?' Otto Muller's wife answered.

'We wish to speak with Otto,' the old man said, frowning with displeasure.

'He said you might be here; you and the Reverend.'

'We wish to speak with him.'

'You're too late.'

'One of the boys, then.'

'Have you ever known Otto Muller without his sons?' She smiled, a secretive and bitter twisting of the lips.

'Do you know why we are here?' the Reverend Harmsworth said.

'Oh, yes. I may look like one of the servants but sometimes they tell me things. And I have ears, of course.'

'Freda, don't talk like that,' Uncle Hendrik said.

'Yes,' she said, ignoring him. 'I know why you are here and you are too late. Though what you could have done earlier I don't know. Do you think you could have stopped them?'

'God willing, yes.'

'God,' she repeated, and laughed out loud. 'God has never heard of the Snowy Mountains.'

'That's a blasphemous thing to say,' Uncle Hendrik said.

'Yes. If Otto was here he'd thrash me for it. And yet at this very moment he is taking the Reverend's land. It will take more than God's name to stop him.'

James had been watching in silence. He had only seen Aunt Freda two or three times in his life and then in company with her family, when she had remained as silent as a stone. The rumours were that the Mullers treated her with less respect than a Hottentot servant. Having been served by Otto Muller to the total of six loutish sons, her value to him was at an end. It was even said that they no longer shared the same room and that Muller often took a maid into the marriage bed. James looked at her with a mixture of sympathy and disgust; she wore her martyrdom like a badge.

'There are ways to stop them,' he said.

She turned to look at him. After a few seconds she said: 'Yes, you perhaps. You have grown well, James. You're a man now. But what can you do alone?'

'I'm not alone.'

Turning again to Uncle Hendrik she said: 'You are fooling the boy, Hendrik. Once, yes, you might have stopped them. I can remember when a word from you would have been enough. But that was years ago. You're an old man now. Look at you, you can hardly sit a horse. One good leg and one bad. *Crookback*. That's what they call you now, Hendrik; did you know that? *Crookback!*'

'You speak to me like that. After all these years,' Uncle Hendrik said, his voice lowered almost to a whisper.

'Yes, and I'll say something more. You have brought this on yourself. Two sons already dead because of the Bushmen. Do you want to risk another?'

She turned away from them and entered the house, closing the door behind her.

James was watching Uncle Hendrik. His face had taken on an ashen pallor and he looked older than his years.

'We're wasting time,' James said.

Uncle Hendrik did not appear to hear.

'You're not going to pay heed to her?'

'James is right,' Mr Harmsworth said. 'Pay no heed to her.' He gathered up his reins. 'Where now, Hendrik?'

The old man looked up slowly. 'I don't know. I don't know.'

'You're not giving up, are you?'

He seemed to pull himself together. 'No, no. We need help. She's right, we can't go after them by ourselves.'

'But by that time they'll be grazing the mission lands,' James said. 'Look, I'm not sure whether this is the right thing to do, taking sides with Bushmen against Christians – though I don't hold the Mullers high in Christianity – but since we've started, let's finish it.'

But Hendrik van Roye had already turned his stallion towards the track. 'We must get help,' he said loudly. 'I have friends all over the district. They have been my friends for years. I've given them counsel! I've helped them in the bad times. Now I have only to ask. You'll see, you'll see.'

He urged his horse forward, his big, angular body hanging more to the one side than ever.

They rode for a week, sleeping each night at a different farm. They rode through rich valleys and over rocky shoulders, they pushed their way through heavily bushed ravines and crossed plateaux of high, waving grass. They rode until they were so saddle-sore they could hardly sit. Each day James expected Uncle Hendrik to topple out of his saddle as his crouching, sideways seat grew more pronounced. Each day the lines of pain on his face grew more sharply etched; the glitter in his eyes more naked, but he went on. By the end of seven days it was apparent they had achieved nothing, and never would.

At first the graziers had greeted them courteously enough but then word had got around the district and opinion had hardened. Wherever they went they were met with stories of Bushman depredations, most of which were exaggerated, some nothing more than rumours; but each was given an immediacy by farmers suffering a general anxiety. Even Frans de Blaize had been infected.

They were received in the living-room at High Valley as though they were tax-collectors. Even Aunt Hester was not her usual self and Lisé was bristling with hostility towards the missionary. James told himself that this was to be expected.

At first de Blaize had been conciliatory but then as Uncle Hendrik brushed his excuses angrily aside he had turned sullen.

'What you ask is impossible,' he said shortly. 'No one will stop the Mullers. Why should they? The mission is beyond the Frontier, the Government itself specifically forbade missionaries moving there. With respect, Reverend, the land does not belong to you or to anyone. If the Mullers have claimed it, nothing can be done.'

'Even if it is a blatant case of theft?' Mr Harmsworth said angrily.

'But theft from whom? I have heard you say more than once that all the land really belongs to the Bushmen. Then you must have taken it from them. Muller is taking it from you.'

'That's sophistry. You know I did not *take* the land. I *kept* it for them.'

'But you sent them away!'

'Only because there would have been trouble and because it became impossible to feed them.'

'Reverend, do you realize what you've done? You've endangered the whole Frontier. I knew this would happen. I told James months ago. Isn't that right?' James nodded wearily.

Suddenly old Hendrik van Roye lurched to his feet. 'Cowards,' he cried. 'Cowards!' He staggered to the door and James ran to him and took his arm. He helped him mount his horse and the three rode slowly away from the farmhouse.

They had not gone more than half a mile before Uncle Hendrik fell forward in his saddle and lay limply along the stallion's neck.

'I've got to get him home,' James said.

The missionary nodded. 'Yes, there's nothing more he can do now.'

'And you?'

'I must go where I'm needed.'

'To the mission?'

The Reverend Harmsworth shook his head. 'The mission no longer exists, not physically, anyway. Now it exists only as an idea and ideas are stronger than bricks and mortar. No, James, there is no longer a mission station at Silverfountain. Perhaps that was my mistake. Instead of bringing them to me I should have gone to them.'

'You're not going into the mountains now?'

'Of course.'

'Look, come back with us. Stay for a few weeks. You know

how pleased Aunt Hannah will be. When things quieten down we can make new plans.'

At that moment Uncle Hendrik raised himself upright in the saddle. 'Come,' he said. 'We must go on. I have friends. They'll help, you'll see. Friends . . .'

'Take him home, James. Take him home.'

'Come with us, then.'

But the missionary had already turned and was riding slowly towards the Bushman country.

Uncle Hendrik was muttering to himself. Drops of spittle oozed from the corners of his lips. James took the stallion's reins and urged Violin forward. 'We're going home,' he said, but Uncle Hendrik did not seem to hear.

It was late afternoon before they reached Bitterfountain. The heat had gone out of the day and evening was approaching. In later years, with the memory of that evening still vivid in his mind, the one thing James could not recall was whether or not he had had a premonition of disaster.

They came down the track through the valley. He was still leading the stallion and the first thing he saw was the smoke as a dark smudge against the evening sky. There was something odd about it, quite unlike the blue-grey drift from the cooking fire. This was thick and dark and there was too much of it.

'Uncle Hendrik!'

The grazier's head came up slowly and James found himself looking into vacant eyes. 'There's a fire near the house.'

'Fire?'

'Near the house. Can you ride? I'll go on.'

'Yes – yes – fire, you say?' He stared down at the smoke. 'My God, James,' he said. 'That's the house!'

They went down the slope of the valley at a wild gallop and reached Bitterfountain together. The smoke, thick and oily, was rising from the two great roof beams of yellowwood which had fallen into the living-room, bringing down the thatch. Everything else had already burnt and the rooms were naked to the sky.

Near where the front door had been, Aunt Hannah's body

lay on its side. She had been stripped of her clothing and her large breasts, in life a comforting and ample bosom, hung pathetically down into the ash and dust. It was quite plain that she had been raped and then her throat had been cut. Thirty feet from her lay the body of the maid Clara. She had died in the same way. Later, James found the bodies of two other servants near the back of the house. It seemed they had been caught trying to run. The backs of their heads were pulpy and covered with flies. And that was all. There was not another living thing at Bitterfountain.

Later, when James's mind cleared partially he realized that Stone-Axe's body was not among the dead.

'But the Lord is with me as a mighty terrible one: therefore my persecutors shall stumble, and they shall not prevail: they shall be greatly ashamed; for they shall not prosper: their everlasting confusion shall never be forgotten . . .'

The voice went on and on and it was the first thing James heard when he opened his eyes. He was stiff from lying on the ground and wet with dew. The voice had been going on hour after hour, ever since about midnight when Uncle Hendrik had discovered the half-charred Bible among the ruins of the house. There was not much of the big book left but what there was he read out loud.

'. . . But I will punish you according to the fruit of your doings, saith the Lord: and I will kindle a fire in the forest thereof, and it shall devour all things round about it.'

The dreadful blood curses from the Book of Jeremiah rolled off his tongue, filling the still morning air with noise and thunder.

They had buried Aunt Hannah and the servants the night before and then there was nothing they could do until morning. James had lain down in his blankets on the far side of the house and watched the figure of Uncle Hendrik crooning among the ruins, lit garishly by the flames of a new fire he had built as the old one died away.

'Everything, everything!' he had muttered, piling the half-burnt chairs and tables on the flames. Then he had found the Bible.

135

Now, in the early light, his dusty figure was hunched above the smouldering farmhouse like a great vulture. *'Behold, a whirlwind of the Lord is gone forth in fury, even a grievous whirlwind: it shall fall grievously on the head of the wicked . . .'*

A light dawn breeze wreathed his body in smoke but he did not seem to notice; nor that the half-burnt pages of the Bible flicked over in his fingers. He read, without comprehension, the words which presented themselves: *'Howl, ye shepherds, and cry; and wallow yourselves in the ashes . . .'*

They had hardly spoken to each other. They had done what was needed, the old man calling on some deep-held reserves of strength. He had not broken down until later and by that time James had his own feelings in ice-cold control. At first he had been too stunned to take in what had happened. He had reacted automatically, first gathering Aunt Hannah's body in his saddle blanket and carrying it out of sight. He was in a state of numbness – or so he thought in the beginning – but the numbness did not pass.

'Blow ye the cornet in Gibeah, and the trumpet in Ramah: cry aloud at Beth-aven, after thee, O Benjamin . . .'

He regarded Aunt Hannah much as he would have done the body of a stranger. His first true reaction came with the thought that he would have to rebuild the homestead and that he would do so with his own comfort in mind. But first there was the matter of Stone-Axe. He lay there with the imprint of a cold smile on his lips. He had no doubt that Bushmen had wrought the present havoc and Stone-Axe was ultimately a Bushman before anything else – or why was his body not among the rest? One day he would find him and discover the reason.

'Blow ye the trumpet in Zion, and sound an alarm in my holy mountain: let all the inhabitants of the land tremble: for the day of the Lord cometh, for it is nigh at hand . . .'

James climbed out of his blankets and went over to the old man. He looked at him dispassionately seeing, not so much a kindly uncle who had taken him in, but a ranting stranger.

'Come,' he said. 'We'll go to High Valley. Uncle Frans will look after you for a while.'

Hendrik van Roye went on reading as though he had not heard. His hair and beard were covered in grey ash and his face was chalky. Only his eyes were alive and glittering.

'*Multitudes, multitudes in the valley of decision: for the day of the Lord is near in the valley of decision . . .*'

James picked him up as though he weighed no more than a child and carried him to his horse. Uncle Hendrik grasped the Bible, fearful that it might be taken away from him. They rode slowly out of the valley, James leading the stallion as he had done the day before.

The sun was up and the dew was sparkling on the grass. Birds were singing. It was a beautiful autumn morning. Across the veld boomed the hoarse voice: '. . . *he that fleeth of them shall not flee away, and he that escapeth of them shall not be delivered. Though they dig into hell, thence shall mine hand take them; though they climb up to heaven, thence will I bring them down . . .*'

James lay on a stretch of green, downy grass and stared up through the fronds of a mimosa tree into the warm autumn sky. He was aware of Lisé lying next to him and that in the past few minutes she had moved slightly so that her body was just touching his. It was an open invitation; all he had to do was stretch out his arm and she would move willingly into its crook. He lay perfectly still.

In the past month he had become sated with Lisé. The excitement of the first time, on the banks of the Crow River, had vanished into the limbo of familiarity. For the first few days at High Valley it had been intoxicating to live so closely to her and amusing to share a secret unknown to the others, but it had quickly palled in the cloying constriction of the family. He soon found that if Aunt Hester did not share their secret entirely she knew some of it at least and her sly coyness, which he had once found beguiling, became elephantine and boring. He became the recipient of little favours like the best cuts of meats, his clothes were fussily inspected for tears, then mended with a flourish, he soon had his own chair – 'Bring James's chair closer' – his words took on an unnatural significance – 'James says' or 'James thinks'

– and through it all Aunt Hester managed to keep up a barrage of winks, nudges and chuckles that he found almost unbearable.

To escape he would take Lisé to the Crow River and there on its sunny banks he would explore her body and forget the burnt-out farm and Aunt Hannah's brutalized corpse, and he would also try to forget the arch behaviour of Aunt Hester and the lost, brooding figure hunched near the fire which had once been Uncle Hendrik.

It was unfair, he supposed, to blame Lisé for her mother but at the same time she seemed willing to connive in the winsomeness. It was apparent that their attitudes had crystallized into one of pre-marital expectancy. Two months before, James had seriously thought about marrying Lisé. On the Frontier the choice was, at best, limited. But now he pushed the thought away. He knew, without any doubt, that to marry Lisé would mean to marry, by association, her mother, and he was equally aware that between the two of them he would be gobbled up, digested and reproduced as someone different; recreated into a form that *they* wanted a husband and son-in-law to be. None of this was apparent to Frans de Blaize, who spent each day riding the boundaries of his land and waited with a sort of dull anticipation for the Bushman hordes to pour down from the hills and ruin him; nor to Uncle Hendrik who mooned over his Bible, nursing it guardedly like a child who fears a toy will be taken away.

After the first week at High Valley James had begun to feel restless. He assumed this was a natural result of being cooped up with strangers so he went out alone on Violin and rode until he was tired. He remained unsatisfied. He supposed it was time to go back and begin the rebuilding of Bitterfountain but the thought of the work involved to create a big new house only for himself and Uncle Hendrik made the effort seem unsatisfactory. In fact, he could think of nothing he really wanted except to go out and – The thought had first come to him like a physical extension of sensation in his hand, a prickling at the edge of his scalp, an excess of saliva in his mouth . . .

He wanted to kill something. He wanted to feel something

soft and beat it and beat it until it became spongy. At these times he would think of Stone-Axe.

And then, as if in answer to his needs, came the news that at last a commando was to be formed against the Bushmen.

Ever since Aunt Hannah's death neighbours had been riding to and fro from High Valley to commiserate with Uncle Hendrik. Some, knowing his attitude towards the Bushmen, had waited tentatively for a change in him, for a return to a civilized state of mind. They hoped to find a smouldering powder barrel which would explode them all into action. Instead they found a mumbling old man who preferred the pages of his ruined Bible to their most piously-phrased attentions. It was natural that they should misconstrue his attitude. Frans de Blaize told James one evening that Otto Muller was openly calling Uncle Hendrik a coward, and a deranged one at that.

James shrugged it off. He had almost succeeded in forgetting what had happened. He wanted no part of the regrets; he wanted to be left alone. But he was not left alone. There was always Aunt Hester or Lisé or both so that when Uncle Hendrik suddenly said one day, in a moment of abrupt lucidity: 'There is a commando. We will ride!' he had felt a sense of elation that life was about to move on.

His feelings were mirrored in Uncle Hendrik. As the silt in the old man's mind cleared slightly he gave up his place near the fire and spent the days on the stoep in the autumn sunlight cleaning his rifle and moulding the lead slugs. He worked without speaking, coldly and purposefully, like some ancient patriarch about to seek his vengeance.

James felt a tickle in his left ear. Automatically, he brushed the fly away and then realized that it was not a fly but one of Lisé's little games.

'Stop it,' he said.

'Stop what?'

'Oh God, let's not go into all that again.' He had endured this game several times. Lisé would pick a grass stem, tickle his ear and then deny it. The first few times he had smiled dutifully but then it had begun to pall.

'Into what again?'

139

'I just don't feel like playing today.'

'What's the matter, Jamie? What's wrong with you?'

'Nothing, nothing.' He sat up and put his arms around his knees.

'This is our last afternoon,' she said.

'I know.'

'You might act as though you're enjoying it.'

'I'm sorry.'

'Jamie, do you still love me?'

'Can't we talk –'

'No, we can't. I want to know.'

'Yes, of course.'

'Of course what?'

He jerked to his feet and stood looking down at her. 'Stop it! Stop it!'

She stared up at him, wide-eyed, then demurely lowered her lids. 'All right,' she said softly. 'I know you must be worried.'

Suddenly contrite he squatted down next to her, taking a strand of her black hair between his fingers. 'It'll only be a week or so,' he said. 'Perhaps less.'

'But you might be killed.'

'Nonsense. What are a few Bushmen? It's Uncle Hendrik I'm thinking about. He's too old for this sort of thing.'

'You'll be careful, won't you, Jamie?'

'Yes, I'll be careful.'

'Come, lie down again.' She patted the grass beside her.

He took up his original position. 'I can't stay long. We're leaving at sunset,' he said.

She leant over and kissed him. 'We've got long enough.' She began to unlace the cuff of his hook. Since the first time she had always insisted he remove the hook before they made love. He reached to stop her, then checked himself. What did it matter, he would be leaving soon, anyway.

Afterwards he quickly strapped on his hook and felt better. Instead of the drowsy sensation of repletion which normally drugged his limbs he seemed more restless than ever. He wanted to spring to his feet and march briskly away. After a while Lisé said: 'What happens when you come back?'

He leant forward to hold his knees again and chewed on a grass stem. 'We've got to rebuild Bitterfountain.'

'We?'

'Uncle Hendrik and I – though I'm not sure what *he* can do now.' He turned towards her and said, half-ashamedly: 'We won't be able to see each other so often. I mean, you know – not as often –'

He stopped when the expression on her face turned cold. She said: 'But we'll have *some* time together, won't we, Jamie?'

'Of course, of course.'

'And there'll be time to go to Graaff-Reinet, won't there?'

'What on earth do you want to go there for?'

'To get married.'

He felt a chill hand on his heart. 'Married?'

'I'm going to get married,' she said, and her face was stony.

'To whom?' he said in a whisper.

'To you, Jamie. I'm carrying your child and it's going to have a Christian father.'

It was as though a hill had collapsed on him. 'Are you certain? I mean –'

'Of course I am,' she said, irritated. 'Do you think I wouldn't know a thing like that?'

'No, no, I mean are you certain I'm –' He stopped as the inference became plain.

The irritation in her eyes gave way to anger. 'I think you'd better go now,' she said, 'before you say anything more. And while you're gone you'd better do some thinking.' Her tone turned savage. 'Remember Hans Muller would hunt you down like a jackal if he knew.'

A cold night wind was blowing over the mountain-tops carrying the first damp taste of winter. James stood as close to the big bonfire as he could and let the warmth from the growing flames seep into his body. Uncle Hendrik was impervious to everything but the job in hand, which was feeding the fire.

They were high up on the north side of Deception Peak and from his place near the fire James could look out over the range of the Snowy Mountains and see the pinpoints of light on five of the surrounding peaks, which meant the other fires were burning well. If he could see them, so could the Bushmen.

The fires had been Uncle Hendrik's idea. 'They'll think we're offering gifts,' he had told the others. 'Like we did in the old days.' There had been some objections because of the shortage of wood, but finally, after Uncle Hendrik had offered one of his own wagons for breaking up, they had agreed to search for what wood there was.

Their plan was simple: the fires would draw some of the Bushmen from the mountains to the hundred head of cattle lowing faintly in the valley below. They would be free to take the herd and drive it back to their village; not one of the forty members of the commando, hidden in a nearby kloof, would stop them. This was Otto Muller's refinement on Uncle Hendrik's suggestion. They would let them get right away, give them two days to get back to their village, two days of feasting and dancing, and then the graziers would fall on them like wolves. This time it would be a clean sweep. Only the women and children were to be allowed their lives, and these would be spent in service to their new masters. It seemed an excellent plan all round.

James felt himself shiver slightly. It was a feeling of anticipation rather than apprehension; he felt himself ready for what was to happen. Perhaps, he thought, he might even find Stone-Axe. He would have to remind the others that the privilege of dealing with the little Bushman was his alone.

'Bring some of that wood round this side,' Uncle Hendrik said, and he dragged what had once been part of the *disselboom* of the wagon to the sheltered side of the fire. They had spent most of the sweaty day dragging the wood up the slope and now, leaving the warmth of the flames, he shivered again as the perspiration dried damply on his body.

'What if they don't come?' he said, heaving the length of rounded timber onto the fire in a gust of sparks.

'They'll come,' Uncle Hendrik muttered briefly. 'They've always come.'

They hardly spoke at all now, except in short exchanges.

142

Sometimes the old man would relapse into one of his long moody silences and pull the Bible from his saddle-bag and mouth the Old Testament verses. At others he would withdraw into himself, his eyes glittering like chips of agate.

The fire grew like a huge orange flower until flames were leaping up through the dry wood and sparks were flitting into the windy darkness.

'That's enough,' Uncle Hendrik said. 'Fetch the horses.'

They picked their way carefully down the mountainside, letting the horses find their own path. As they drew closer to the valley the herd's lowing became louder.

The others were already in the ravine when they arrived. In the light of the small cooking fires James could make out the Mullers – Otto and his sons Jacob, Fritz, Cornelius, Heinrich and Karl – and he knew that Hans would be somewhere close. Then there were the Smit brothers from Windy Corner and old man Fischer from Brakwater and the Cloetses, father and three sons, and Lessing, who had once been an Army officer, and Celliers and De Villiers from over Blue Cliff way, and there were more fires farther up and he could not see who their owners were. There was a smell of roasting meat in the air and the sound of jingling bridles.

'Have you watered the horses?' Uncle Hendrik said.

'I'll cook first.'

'Leave that to me.'

He led the horses down to the small brook that trickled through the ravine. He felt the air damp on his face and wondered if there was rain on the wind. He stood between Violin and the stallion and let their heads sink down to the water and then became aware that another rider was already at the stream. In the darkness he could only make out the man's bulk, but as the moon broke through the cloud-layer for a moment he found he was looking at Hans Muller.

For the past two days they had been circling each other like two young buffalo bulls, neither anxious to get too close to the other.

'Well, now,' said Muller. 'The Scotchman.'

'You've got it wrong again,' James said, 'but no matter.'

'I've wanted to talk to you but whenever I looked for you it seemed you were not there.' The German's heavy irony was not lost on James.

'D'you say so? Now that's a strange thing, I was thinking the same myself. Mullers underfoot everywhere but never the eldest son and heir. Very strange indeed.'

Muller pursued his own train of thought: 'I said to myself the Scotchman can shoot springbok all right but when the springbok shoot back, that's another matter.'

James let the horses' heads come up from the stream. They paused, chewing on the bit, and then began to drink again, sipping delicately at the surface of the water. Muller's horse had finished, but he made no move to go.

'You know, Muller,' James said mildly. 'You're a very aggravating man. It's a wonder someone hasn't dealt with you before. But just at the moment I'm hungry for my supper so if you've got anything to say to me, then have done with it.'

The big German led his horse closer. 'This is what I've got to say,' he said in a voice dangerously controlled. 'You've been seeing Lisé.'

'Man, your information's out of date. I've been staying with her this past month.'

'I know that. But now you're going back to Bitterfountain isn't that so?'

'Correct.'

'Keep clear of her then, I'm warning you.'

'Dearie me, what a great big bloody blethering bore you are, Muller,' James said. 'I'm not one of your brainless brothers, laddie, to be warned and threatened and spoken at like some heathen servant. Now you listen to me. I'm tired of hearing that silly voice of yours, so take a word of advice: if you don't stop flapping your mouth open at me I'll reach down your throat and have your tongue up by the roots.'

The German dropped the bridle as though he had been stung and stepped towards him. 'You speak to me like that!'

He lunged forward and gripped James by the lapels of his heavy corduroy coat. At that moment Otto Muller's voice came through the darkness. 'Hans! I want you! Come here!' Muller stiffened. His fingers seemed to lose their strength and his hands dropped away. For the first time he saw the naked hook shining like silver fire in the dark. They stood there facing each other, the German's heavy breathing the only sound.

'That was daddy,' James said in an icy voice. 'You'd better run along.'

Muller nodded his head slowly. 'There's always another time,' he said.

'Aye, well, you know where to find me.'

'And you won't have your little Bushman hiding in the grass. Maybe we'll even find him. I'll make you a present of his head.'

'Remember this, Muller – and you can tell your clan as well. Stone-Axe is mine to deal with. Touch him and you can start to worry about your own head.'

'Hans!' Otto Muller's voice was angry. 'Where are you?'

'Coming!'

'Bear it in mind,' James said as he slid the leather guard back over his hook. 'Just you bear it in mind.'

The German turned away, dragging his horse after him.

The Bushmen came at dawn. At first light James, Uncle Hendrik, Otto and Hans Muller had rounded up the grazing herd and then waited at the head of the valley. The remainder of the commando stayed hidden. They saw the Bushmen first as a series of bobbing dots on the far horizon. As they grew closer James counted twelve men. They were running with the effortless ease of hunters and he knew that they had kept up the same pace throughout the night.

About two hundred yards away they slackened their pace and came forward more warily. Each had a bow in his right hand and a quiver of arrows slung down his back. Apart from that they were naked. They were wretchedly thin. In the chilly dawn wind and under the racing grey clouds their bodies were a sickly yellow, the skin hanging slackly in leathery folds. Their eyes were sunk into their heads and their rib bones stood out to be counted. James glanced briefly at Uncle Hendrik and saw the fire burning in his eyes. He hoped he would control himself; he had no desire to feel an arrow-head in his throat.

Otto Muller, perched like a bantam cock on the broad back of a 17-hand bay, said briefly: 'Leave this to me!' He urged the horse forward to meet the hunters. As he moved the Bushmen stopped and fanned out in a semi-circle. They were about thirty yards away.

'Who speaks for you?' Otto Muller said.

They remained silent, looking up at him uneasily. Muller went forward a few more paces. Away to his right the herd moved restlessly.

'Have you not ears? I am Otto Muller! I ask again, who speaks for you?'

Again there was no answer. Before James could stop him, Uncle Hendrik trotted forward. Muller looked around in surprise but the old man ignored him. He brought the stallion to a halt ten yards from the Bushmen. 'Do you know me?' he asked coldly.

One of the hunters, slightly older than the rest, stepped forward. 'We know you, O Greybeard.'

'Have you known me for many years?'

'For many years.'

'Have you trusted me?'

'We have trusted you.'

'Have I made you gifts of meat?'

'Before, yes, you gave us meat.'

'Before, did you rob us of meat?'

'Before, you gave us meat.'

'Before, did we not live in friendship?'

'Before, we were friends. You gave us meat.'

'Are the Bushmen people hungry for meat?'

'We are hungry for meat.'

Uncle Hendrik pointed to the herd. 'Do you see the meat?'

'We see the meat, O Greybeard!'

'Take the meat then for the Bushmen people and leave us in peace.'

'We will take the meat. We were hungry and you gave us meat. Greybeard has filled our bellies with peace.'

As one, the Bushmen raised their bows in salute and then began to run towards the herd with shrill shouts of joy. Uncle

Hendrik turned his horse and rode past the others. James noticed that his face was bleak as a rock.

All that day the graziers sat by their fires drinking black coffee and smoking their pipes. The wind gradually grew stronger and by nightfall was blowing half a gale. When James opened his eyes the following morning his blankets were stiff with cold and the whole world white with snow.

Some of the others were already up and he could hear their voices. Otto Muller was the centre of a group. One of the Smit brothers was saying: 'We'll never find them in this wilderness! The tracks are gone, everything's wiped out. What's the point of going on?'

Otto Muller said hotly: 'The point? The point is we've come this far and we're not going back empty-handed!'

Another said: 'We didn't bargain for snow. I'm needed on the farm in this weather.'

'You fool, unless we get rid of these people you won't have a farm.'

'We know why you want to go on, Muller. You want the women and children.'

'That's my business! We agreed to ride together and no one's going to back out now. Good God, man, they've got a present of a hundred head!'

'They'll probably leave us in peace then.'

'Don't talk nonsense. They'll have half finished them by now. You know how a Bushman eats.'

Lessing, the ex-Army officer, said: 'There's no point in arguing. The facts are simply: the snow has wiped out the tracks and we can't follow them. Do we stay here until it melts or do we go home? That's the question to be settled.'

Uncle Hendrik had been standing nearby, but whether he had been listening or not, James could not tell. He might well have been a tree growing out of the snowy ground. He turned to the group and said: 'There is a way. Let ten or a dozen ride in different directions. Let them watch the sky. The first to see vultures has found the village. Then come back here and tell us.'

There was another snow-shower about noon which added a

new surface to the old, but apart from that the skies remained clear. The wind died and the ground froze hard. By evening the first of the riders were returning. They had spent all day in the saddle and were bone weary. James himself had ridden upwards of forty miles without seeing anything other than jumbled valleys and peaks stretching away on each side.

It was already dark when Hans Muller rode in. His beard and eyebrows were still rimed from the earlier fall. He dismounted stiffly and stood warming himself over the nearest fire while he told them about the vultures. He had ridden, he said, for more than thirty miles before he saw them and it was a view that had lifted his heart.

Seventeen hours later, after riding most of the night, the commando found itself on the heights overlooking the Bushman village. Vultures wheeled sluggishly in the air above them. Below was a scene of carnage few could even have imagined.

'My God,' Otto Muller said to no one in particular, 'and you call these people human!'

The village lay in a natural cul-de-sac. The huts, thirty or forty of them, were dotted about without any plan at the top of a steep-sided valley. Behind them, great bush-covered cliffs rose up like the walls of a Spanish castle. The huts themselves were no more than small shelters against the weather. Each was made of reeds covered in skins and, from a distance, they looked like black beehives against the snow. In the open spaces between them dung fires were burning, but the smoke was lost against the greyness of the cliffs and sky. Looking down from the heights James could see very few Bushmen. Those who were visible hunched near the fires, roasting meat. The remainder, he assumed, had eaten as much as their bodies could hold and were sleeping like glutted pythons in their huts. It was a peaceful, almost idyllic scene.

But then his eyes took in what the others had already seen and he felt a ball of sickness and anger in his stomach.

The corpses of the cattle lay on the edge of the village. They had been slaughtered in their dozens and the snow was clogged with blood. Some beasts were still alive, sunk down

148

on their hamstrung haunches, bellowing piteously. Others, already dead, lay stiff in the snow, their ripped paunches streaming entrails like wet red necklaces on the white ground.

There had been an orgy of killing; a fantastic, primeval ritual of slaughter. It was easy for James to imagine what had happened: the hacking and stabbing, the thrusting of spears, the slicing open of still live bellies to paw and pull at the warm viscera, the arms red with blood to the shoulders. He did not think of the starving Bushmen bodies he had seen two days before; he was aware only of the present, of the savagery of the scene, and he was caught in his own savage and trembling emotion.

The man next to him had been looking at the feasting through a military telescope and now he passed it to James. The brass tube was as cold as a rifle barrel. He put it to his eye and immediately the picture separated into its several parts, each becoming close and clear as he moved the glass. He kept it on one family group, watching as they picked up lumps of meat from the noisome ground, thrust them onto the sharpened ends of thin sticks and toasted them over the fires. Although, from the number of slaughtered beasts, every Bushman in the village must have eaten prodigiously, the group he was watching snatched the gobbets of meat from the fire before they were barely warm and stuffed them into their mouths. They ate so ravenously that every now and then one would walk away from the fire and vomit.

He let the glass wander from one group to the next. Most of the Bushmen wore heavy sheepskin karosses pulled right around their shoulders, but some seemed, in their gluttony, to be impervious to the cold and strutted between the fires, their semi-erect members pointing the way as though exercising themselves between bouts of feasting.

He held the glass steady. Something had seemed familiar. He swept it back to a group on the far side. Yes! There it was again. The Bushman was sitting in profile. There was something about him . . . a look of . . . Stone-Axe. But was it? The face was in shadow; it was too far to be sure. James strained his eye until it began to blur with water. He transferred the glass to his other eye. But the Bushman turned to crouch over the fire and he could only make out the back of his head.

'Seen enough?' the man next to him said, reaching for the glass.

He nodded. 'Enough to last me the rest of my life.'

As they waited, the gluttonous orgy continued. Bushmen left the fires to sleep in the huts and others emerged to take their places. One walked casually to a hamstrung cow and cut a piece of buttock meat. Then, as casually, he returned to the fire, carrying the dripping lump in his hands. Somewhere behind him James heard a farmer retching.

And all around the village were the vultures: swooping and settling, fighting among themselves, pecking at dead eyes, thrusting beaks up a still-warm anus, burying their heads neckdeep in a torn belly. The Bushmen ignored the birds as they would have ignored a swarm of greedy flies.

There was enough for everyone: enough for the Bushmen and for the vultures, enough for the hyenas and the jackals who would come in the night. There had never been so much meat, dead and half-dead, in the combined tribal memory of the Snowy Mountain Bushmen.

James felt himself begin to shake with rage at the terrible and wasteful debauch. In a way it was worse than what had happened to Aunt Hannah. He could dimly understand the atavism inherent in man's barbarity to other men but what he saw now, the wanton destruction of a hundred head of cattle, their mutilated corpses flung together in piles of discarded flesh, touched the deep spring of Frontier philosophy that had unconsciously grown within him. There was no room in his mind just then for the fact that these beasts had been willingly sacrificed so the graziers could, in their turn, slaughter the Bushmen: if ever he, or anyone else, needed a reason to sanction their annihilation and to take part in it, it was there, spread out before him.

He could feel his rage, loosed of all restrictions, breaking through the self-imposed barriers. 'What are we waiting for?' he shouted harshly. 'Haven't we seen enough!'

150

'Keep your voice down,' Uncle Hendrik cut in sharply. 'Let them finish their meal.'

For a further two hours the commando lay hidden on the heights. It wasn't until mid-afternoon that the fires were allowed to die down and the last Bushman crawled into his hut. The village slept – not even a guard was left.

'It is time,' Hendrik van Roye said. By now, without any discussion, it was tacitly accepted that he was leading the raid. 'But first let us ask God to visit our venture with success.'

They stood in the lee of some boulders out of sight of the village and listened to Uncle Hendrik's words. Above them vultures flushed around the sky cawing balefully at this new intrusion. The horses blew and stamped. Surreptitiously the graziers were looking to their priming. James slipped the soft leather guard from his hook.

Hendrik van Roye's voice rolled over them, resonant with passion as he pleaded their cause. The wind had come up again on the high mountains and his beard blew half across his face. It was a strange scene, enough to make the strongest of them shiver.

He finished the prayer and opened the charred Bible. And then he raised his eyes to the sky and repeated the verses from Jeremiah without needing to look at the text.

'Behold the whirlwind of the Lord goeth forth, a continuing whirlwind: it shall fall with pain upon the head of the wicked . . .'

The last phrase came out as a shout and the commando, filled with the fire and smoke of the Old Testament, wheeled their horses to the slope and thundered down on the stupefied village.

James could feel the cold wind on his face as Violin slithered down the slope and he could hear the sound of the hooves on the frozen ground, but after that the sounds became mixed with the screams of dying Bushmen, the roar of the heavy guns, the smashing noise of rifle butt meeting skull and over it all and through the drifting smoke of the black powder, the bellowing of the hamstrung cattle and

151

his own voice undulating with lust.

The graziers swept through the village like a cavalry squadron at the height of its charge. They broke down the huts as though they were made of paper, fired point blank at the writhing yellow bodies, used the butt twice, three times, and then their impetus carried them beyond the village to reload.

Twice more they charged before the Bushmen even had time to realize what was happening to them and by then the corpses were staining the snow alongside the beasts.

James rode with the ferocity of a Mameluke. He fired from the saddle and then bent low on Violin's left side using the hook as one might use a lance for pig-sticking. Within minutes his arm was dripping blood to the elbow.

Someone had overturned a hut onto one of the fires and the reeds had caught alight and now they were being used to fire other huts. Soon the village was a blazing shambles. Women and children, panic-stricken and bewildered, ran screaming in all directions, some under the horses' flying hooves.

From out of the milling figures he caught a glimpse of the one he had been searching for. Just a movement of the body, a flick of the kaross as the little Bushman ducked and weaved through the pack. James whirled Violin round on her hind legs and raced after him. He was certain now that the figure had been Stone-Axe. He rode Violin at a woman with a baby on her back and felt the thud of their falling bodies transmitted up the horse's forelegs. He was past and gone before the scream died on her lips.

He galloped Violin out of the blazing huts, always keeping his eye on the figure that darted ahead. Suddenly he was almost at the base of the cliffs, and the Bushman stopped, casting about for some way either to left or right, but there was none. He whirled to face his pursuer and for the first time James saw the bow in his hand. In that second Violin slipped on the icy ground, shooting him forward in the saddle. For a moment he was completely defenceless. The musket hung at an angle from his right hand as he clung wildly to Violin's mane. He tensed himself for the biting pain of the arrow. But it didn't come. He righted himself and swung the musket to his shoulder in one movement and found himself looking into the face of old Blom, who had once been Frans de Blaize's servant.

Blom's eyes, wide and terror-stricken, softened with recognition. 'Little master, it is I – Blo . . .'

But the pattern of action was too advanced, the trigger already too far back. The rifle exploded with a crash and old Blom snapped down like a jack-knife, his hands shooting automatically to the area that had once been his stomach. He would never bring the sixteen virgins now or get an iron hand in return. James jammed his spurs into Violin's flanks and raced back to the slaughter.

He was half-demented with the orgy of killing. He could still hear his own voice yelling for blood but its timbre had become so hoarse he hardly recognized it. He rode, fired, clubbed, hooked – all with the deadly economy of a fighting machine. There was a feeling of exultation in everything he did; it was as though he was acting naturally for the first time in his life.

Their very success split the commando into small units and when James heard Uncle Hendrik's booming voice calling for them to regroup he was on the far side of the village and the first arrows were whistling through the air. He decided to stay where he was. He knew what the tactics would be now: ride in to rifle range, fire, retire to load, advance to fire, retire to load – this made possible by the fact that the Bushmen were on foot and they were mounted. It would be a matter of picking off the male Bushmen now until none was left.

He fired from the saddle, saw the ball take an old man in the chest, its velocity knocking him back several yards, then he turned Violin's head and galloped down the slope to an outcrop of rock where he could reload in safety. His hand was trembling so much with excitement that it took him longer than usual.

He had just finished when another rider came galloping round the massive boulders. He looked up, ready to smile in triumph, when he saw the man was Hans Muller and that his horse seemed to be dragging some sort of black bundle at the end of a long leather thong.

'Hey, Scotchman!' the big German shouted boisterously. 'I was wrong about you! Man, you're a real fighter!'

In spite of himself, James felt a sensation of pleasure. He was about to say something in return when the dark bundle at the end of the thong gave a retching moan. He looked down and thought at first that it consisted of loosely-tied skins, but then he looked closer. He was staring down at what was left of the Reverend Harmsworth. The missionary had been tied by the wrists and dragged along behind the horse for a distance of about eight hundred yards. The clothing on the left-hand side of his body had been shorn away and his hip and shoulder bones stuck out through the worn flesh. His face was pitted with holes where the galloping horse had kicked up stones and one eye hung down onto his cheek. A large stone must have struck him in the mouth for his teeth were smashed to stumps and the blood dripped down onto what was left of his waistcoat.

Every detail of the scene, the blood-stained body, his own bloody arm, the exalted expression on Hans Muller's face, the panting horses, seemed to set solid in James's mind. In that fraction of a second when past, present and future met he experienced a feeling of revulsion so great that bile filled his mouth and he began to choke.

Another sound came from the dying missionary and this time it was more of a whisper. James saw him again riding, riding, riding, trying to save his mission and his Bushmen. Again he heard him say, as he turned his horse's head towards Buhsman country: 'I must go where I'm needed.' And now this.

He jumped from Violin's back and ran to him. He drew his knife and slashed at the thong. The missionary collapsed into the snow.

'Reverend!' James said. 'Reverend!'

'The Lord is my shepherd; I shall not want . . . the Lord is my shepherd; I shall not want . . .'

'Reverend, it's me, James Black.'

Out of the mouth, which was simply a red hole in his broken face, the first verse of the 23rd Psalm was endlessly repeated.

James turned and faced Muller. The German's eyes were frantic with triumph. 'He was living in the village! Can you believe it! And he tried to stop us. He said, let's talk, so I said all right let's talk and so I brought him *here* to talk.'

'The Lord is my shepherd; I shall not want . . . the Lord is my shepherd . . .'

James looked up at Muller for a long moment and saw himself and felt sick. 'Go away, Muller,' he said finally. 'Go away.'

'But . . .' The German was looking at him oddly.

'Just go away,' he repeated slowly. 'If I ever see you again I'll kill you. I want you to know that, I want you to understand.'

The voice was unlike his own. It was hollow and infinitely sad; there was an anguish in it that seemed to come from beyond the grave.

'The Lord is my shepherd; I shall not want . . .'

He turned back to the missionary. He was aware of the German's horse leaving the place almost on tip-toe.

The missionary's one eye stared fixedly at him and slowly the mouth moved. 'You will never be forgiven for this day!'

James felt a cold and irrevocable finger touch his heart. 'I know,' he said.

The Reverend Harmsworth moaned again. He lay in the grip of the spasm for a few moments, his head cradled on James's arm. Finally he whispered again. 'James . . .'

'Yes.'

'For the love of Almighty God finish it. I cannot bear it longer.'

'Yes.'

He eased the missionary's head down onto a pad of snow and fetched his rifle.

'The Lord is my shepherd; I shall not want. He maketh me to lie down . . .'

James put the barrel next to his temple and pulled the trigger. Then he buried him under a pile of stones just as the two of them had buried the Bushmen.

He lingered near the grave for a long time as though waiting for an impossible absolution, then he mounted Violin and rode back to the ruined village. Except for the dead it was completely deserted, but he heard sporadic firing coming from the cliffs and he turned towards them.

The commando had dismounted and seemed, at first, to be firing into the air, but as he drew nearer James could make out what had happened. He stood about 100 yards short and watched.

Those women and children who survived sat in a dejected huddle near the horses under the watchful eyes of a grazier. The males had taken to the cliffs and were trying to escape up their sheer sides like a troop of baboons. It was at these climbing figures that the commando was firing.

It had become a contest. They were taking it in turns to shoot at selected targets and wagers of sheep and cattle were being laid. James heard Hans Muller's voice, now strangely brittle, as though his enjoyment was partly forced, boasting about his marksmanship. After almost every shot the men waited to see the body fall.

The end was predictable. The cliffs were too sheer even for the Bushmen and at last the few survivors were pinned on a ledge about half-way up. Above them a slight overhang made further climbing impossible; below them were the guns. In desperation they began hurling stones.

James was unable to watch their final stand. It was pathetic and at the same time magnificent and he could not bear to see them die.

He turned Violin again and rode back to the village. He made his way in and out of the burnt huts staring down at the bodies. He spent ten minutes there before he realized he was looking for Stone-Axe. If he *had* been in the village he wanted to bury him away from the vultures and hyenas: it wouldn't be much, but at least it would be a symbol.

'James!'

He looked up and saw Lessing riding towards him. The ex-Army officer looked angry and depressed.

'They call that sport,' he said, indicating the cliffs. 'I call it butchery! If your uncle was there he'd stop it soon enough!'

'My uncle?' James remembered then that he hadn't seen him with the others. 'What's happened to my uncle?'

'Didn't you know, then? I'm sorry, James. His body is over there.'

They went to the outskirts of the village and he saw Uncle Hendrik lying on his back, the arrow still sticking from his neck. The poison had already blackened the skin around the wound and had almost covered his face. In his hands he gripped the broken Bible.

'Will you help me?' James said. 'There's an outcrop of rocks down below.'

They buried him near Mr Harmsworth, building a cairn of stones over the body to keep the jackals away. When they had finished, James looked around for the Bible, since it seemed necessary to mark the death with scriptural solace, but he realized they had buried it as well. There was nothing to do except stand in the late afternoon cold and pretend to a sadness he did not feel. There were no emotions left.

The firing had stopped and he knew the end had come. What now? Would the men take their pleasure with the Bushmen women?

Suddenly he had a great urge to quit the place forever. 'I'm going to ride,' he said to Lessing.

The ex-officer nodded. 'I've had enough, too,' he said. 'I'll go with you.'

They turned their backs on the place of slaughter and rode slowly down the valley.

Book Three

THE ROAD TO LITAKUN

'Daylight the next morning brought to view a desolate, wild and singular landscape. From our station on the top of a deep descent, the mountains . . . appeared before us. The only colour we beheld was a sterile brown, softened into azure or purple in the distance: the eye sought in vain for some tint of verdure; nothing but rocks and stones lay scattered every where around.'

Travels in the Interior of Southern Africa,
by W. J. BURCHELL.

A hot, dry wind blew out of the north-west. It had begun the day before, gradually increasing in strength, until now the whole surface of the brown semi-desert seemed to move with it. James pulled the kerchief tighter over his mouth and brought the wide brim of his hat farther down over his bloodshot eyes. He leant into the wind pulling Violin behind him. Like her master she held her head low and moved slowly, picking her way over the burning, rock-strewn surface. Her black coat was covered with dust and her bones stood out like knuckles; sand frosted the corners of her eyes.

They were climbing the slope of a small hill and James felt the weary tug on the reins as her pace slackened. He jerked cruelly at the bit. 'Come on, damn you!' he muttered. The mare stumbled forward and for a few paces almost caught up with him but then she lagged again as the incline grew steeper. He bent his head lower and pushed on up the slope against the stinging gale.

His mouth was as dry as the ground he trod. Earlier he had put a small pebble under his tongue the way the Bushmen did but even that could not produce saliva for ever and now it felt the size of a boulder and rasped whenever he moved his tongue. His lips were dry and cracking and his eyebrows were stiff with grit. There was still about a pint of water left in his leather water-bag and he had promised himself a mouthful when he reached the summit. Until then he would go on as he was. Through the haze of flying dust the noon sun bore down pitilessly.

Half-way up the hill the surface deteriorated further. Patches of hard-baked earth, over which they had been able to pick their way near the bottom, changed to bands of micaschist which glittered angrily in the sunshine. Violin stumbled, slithered, righted herself and then stumbled again. James stopped. He was about to feel for the *sjambok* which hung at the side of the saddle when he realized that not even a beating would do much good now. Or if it did, and she got to the top, the effort could well be her last and he would have no chance of regaining the wagon. How far, he wondered, would they have got, these past two years of wandering, without her? He dropped the reins, knowing she would stand without moving, and struggled on up the slope, one hand in front of his face. If anything, the wind seemed stronger. There was something eerie about it, coming as it did from clear blue skies; perhaps this was not uncommon in the Bushman country near the Great River. That's if they *were* near the Great River. They *had* to be. North . . . north . . . north . . . always north. And that's where the Great River lay. To the north.

He was using his hook now to pull himself along, digging the point into cracks in the rock and then hauling. The leather scabbard had long since disintegrated and the steel had become scarred and worn, like James himself.

The brittle rock sliced at the soft *veldschoen* on his feet. They were far too thin for this sort of work and he thought he had better get Keyser, the Hottentot stockman, to fashion him a new pair. Not that he was very deft – nothing like Stone-Axe had been. You could have given the little Bushman a piece of river-horse skin and eventually he would have worked it into something soft and snug. And then he remembered that Keyser was no longer with them: gone, vanished, disappeared, two days ago after they l ad eaten the last of the sheep. He had taken with him the spare rifle, a bullet mould, two water-bags and eight pounds of lead. No, there was no Keyser any longer. Nor Andries, nor Stuurman nor Dikkop: they had all deserted weeks ago, even before things had got really bad.

He held his hand before his eyes and stared ahead through the slit in his fingers. The wind was like a moving wall, solid and resistant. He got down on his hands and knees and crawled the remaining distance to the summit. He lay down in the shelter of some rocks and closed his eyes, resting them for a few moments before looking out over the landscape that spread before him.

The hill he had climbed was like a miniature volcano. The sides rose symmetrically, cone-shaped, but then, just as they were closing towards their apex they stopped abruptly as though a scythe had neatly sliced off the peak.

He saw that he was on the edge of a vast plain. It stretched as far as the horizon, glinting here and there as the sunlight struck the mirror surface of the mica. It was perfectly flat except for wart-like eruptions that were hills almost exactly similar to the one on which he lay. It was as if, in some past, two of the hills had coupled, producing a thousand identical offspring.

His practised eyes swept the landscape for three things; water, game and Bushmen. But there were no trees to hint at a secret spring; no signs of life, animal or human. In all that great expanse of country nothing moved except the tumbleweed, rolling on its endless journey wherever the wind might send it.

He experienced a feeling of utter desolation and hopelessness. His head dropped onto his good hand and he closed his eyes. How many hills had he climbed, how many times had his searching eyes looked out over the scenes like this, how often had he come back to the wagon, spent almost to the point of collapse? On each occasion he had retained a spark of confidence and hope. 'Tomorrow,' he would say to Lisé as they lay in the darkness of the tented wagon, listening to the sleepy snufflings of the child. 'Tomorrow we'll find a spring. You'll see.' He had stopped repeating that the Great River was just over the next rise.

She had believed because she wanted to believe, but eventually hope had become as scarce as the water in their leather bottles. And now, for him, it seemed to have run out.

He turned to look back the way he had come. Somewhere in the vast wilderness of stone and hookthorn was the wagon. He wondered if they were all right. For a second he considered leaving them where they were; simply ploughing on into the wind, giving himself up to the elements and the harsh land, moving into a sort of mindless limbo where death would swiftly take him; but it was only for a moment. His brain cleared and he thought of his son Robert and his wife, waiting for him in the tearing wind, and there was no question then of doing anything other than what had to be done.

How long he lay on top of the hill he didn't know, but when he raised his head the first thing he saw was the hyrax. It must have come out of its rock burrow while he was resting, for it did not seem to be aware of him. It sat in the sun on the sloping rock not more than fifteen feet from him, a small brown creature, like an earless rabbit, its fur blowing in the wind.

And his rifle was in his saddle holster.

He wanted the rock-rabbit. He wanted its skin to make shoes for Robbie, he wanted its carcase to stew. If they were careful it would make enough for two meals. He could smell the stew already cooking in the pot; he could see the look on Robbie's pinched face. After the endless meals of drammach the thought of it was almost too much to bear.

But if he went to get his rifle he knew there would only be bare rock by the time he got back. One sudden movement and there would be a brown blur and he might wait all day for

161

the animal to return. Slowly he felt about on the ground with his right hand. He rejected, without seeing them, four or five small rocks. Then he touched something bigger. Its edges were jagged and it almost filled his palm. His fingers closed over it and carefully he moved it into view. It seemed ideal. Heavy, coarse and sharp. He knew from experience how tough a hyrax could be so his aim would have to be exact. There was no point in hitting it anywhere but the head.

The rock-rabbit crouched side on to him, unsuspecting. With infinite care he began the long process of getting himself into a more comfortable throwing position.

He began to move his legs. His *veldschoen* grated on the schist and he stopped. Then he realized that not even the keen hearing of an animal would pick out such faint sounds in the overwhelming noise of the gale. He moved again and after a few minutes his legs were tucked under his body and he began to raise himself on his knees. He balanced the weight of the stone in his hand. He had to be right first time for there would not be another. He took his weight on his knees and the points of his feet and slowly brought his arm back. Not too hard . . . not too hard . . . he had to strike it right . . .

In that second he saw the snake.

It had issued from the boulders about the hyrax, a python about eight feet long, its mottled body covered in the brown dust of the desert. He slowly lowered his arm and watched. In spite of his exhaustion he found himself drawn to the scene. Here was the real hunter, fully equipped.

The snake stopped about six feet from the rock-rabbit, gathering its coils in a bunch. Something must have warned the hyrax because it suddenly darted its head from side to side. In that moment the python struck. Its head, which was held about four inches above the rock, shot forward, mouth agape.

It caught the hyrax near the rump and the animal leapt into the air with a petrified scream. The fangs could not have penetrated very deeply because the rock-rabbit seemed to shake loose. It fell on its side, feet churning to get a grip on the rock. One, then two loops of the python's body slipped around it but the snake had no anchor for its tail and was

162

unable to exert the pressure needed to kill. They rolled on the slippery surface for a moment then began sliding downwards. The snake was thrashing about and the rock-rabbit was screaming and James suddenly realized that their long slide would take them to a series of holes in which they would be completely lost to him. He sprang to his feet, flinging the rock as hard as he could at the coiling bundle, and leapt after it. He hacked at the mess of coils and fur, feeling the hook go in. Then something seemed to explode. He had caught the python. He felt as though his arm was being pulled out of its socket. He was wrenched off his feet. As he fell he grabbed up another rock and brought it smashing down near the snake's head. He hit again and again. He was almost lying on top of it and he felt the head burst under the blows. The coils jerked once or twice and were still. The hyrax gave a bleat from the centre of the bundle and he finished it off with a single blow. He stood back and surveyed the mess, seeing not the snake's pulpy head or the limp brown body of the hyrax, or the blood-covered stone in his hand, but a week's supply of meat.

His legs were trembling so much he was forced to sit down and it was almost an hour before he tucked the hyrax's bloody body into his belt and managed to drag the snake down to where Violin stood. The mare smelt the snake and when he reached up to her for the water bottle she started nervously.

'Whoa!' he muttered. 'Whoa!'

He tried to grab the reins but she jerked her head. 'Stand still!'

At that moment the snake coiled and uncoiled in a post-death spasm. Violin gave a snort of terror and sprang sideways. Her hooves slipped on the schist, she reared upright for a second and then she was down in a cloud of dust, her legs kicking wildly in the air. James stumbled forward. Before he could reach her she had regained her feet and was slithering down the slope.

'Stop!' James shouted. 'Stop!'

She reached the bottom of the slope and stood watching him. As he approached she retreated across the plain in the direction they had come. He felt tears of frustration and rage behind his eyes. He began to run. After twenty or thirty yards he knew she would never stand for him. Slowly he turned and began climbing the slope again. The hydrax's body bumped on his thigh.

The snake was lying where he had left it. Occasionally the muscles quivered. He wrenched his knife from its sheath and sawed off the head. 'Blast you!' he shouted. 'Die!'

He stood in the burning wind for a few moments with the snake's head in one hand and the knife in the other. Then he flung the head away, grasped the snake by the tail and began the long trek back to the wagon.

He walked for hours, often tripping and stumbling, pushed on by the gale that blew at his back. Somewhere along the way he realized that the rock-rabbit had slipped from his belt and was lost, but the fact made little impression on him other than to make him tighten his grip on the snake. He had the tail over his right shoulder and had sunk his hook into the firm flesh, holding the steel shank with his other hand. The snake was heavy and his back muscles began to ache.

After a time he lost all sense of direction. He staggered on with his head down, pulling the heavy snake, aware only that if he kept the wind at his back he must reach the wagon. Briefly, and at long intervals, he saw Violin against the skyline. She would wait until he drew near before trotting away ahead of him again to be lost in the folds of the ground. Sometimes his eyesight would play tricks on him and she would appear to be standing upside down in a shimmering lake. He did not want her to be upside down because he knew his rifle would fall from its scabbard and he would lose it. But there didn't seem to be anything he could do to stop her.

At other times, when the air trembled around her, she would seem like a great eland bull and he would hurry forward, forgetting he no longer had his gun. An eland! They would have meat for weeks if only he could shoot an eland. He had wanted to; he had spent whole days searching for the big antelope – but there were no eland. They had vanished off the face of the earth with all the other game. Bushmen, he thought.

Bushmen. The word struck at his subconscious, bringing

him to a sudden stop. His senses cleared slightly. He had only meant to leave the wagon for an hour and he realized it was now nearly dusk. And they were in Bushman country. He took a renewed grip on the snake and battled forward.

Two months earlier an elephant-hunter on his way back to the Colony with a wagon-load of elephants' teeth had told them of trouble near the Great River.

'Even a hyena will turn if you press him hard enough,' he said. 'The Bushmen have been shot at, starved, hounded; their clans have been broken up – man, they're at the end of their tether. In the south we pick them off like baboons whenever we see them; in the north, beyond the Great River, the Bachapins kill them for sport; my advice to you is to go softly.'

But James hadn't really listened. 'Tell me about the Bachapins.'

The elephant hunter had smiled.

'Is that where you're making for, Litakun?'

'Yes, Litakun.'

'Have you got anything to barter with?'

James nodded. 'Sheep and cattle.'

'You really think you'll drive flocks that far?'

'Why not?'

The old hunter, who was called Hartmann, shrugged his shoulders. 'My friend, I've just told you. Don't forget, the Bushmen are hungry. And if you get past them there are the Islanders.'

'The Islanders?'

'You haven't heard of them?'

'No, I don't think so.'

'You'd know if you had. They live on an island in the river: cut-throats, bandits, Christian, heathen, all mixed up. Murderers and robbers – and they've got appetites too. So my advice to you is to go softly.'

That had been eight weeks ago and with four armed Hottentot servants James had felt safe enough. Now Hartmann's words came back to him.

He pressed on across the plain, fear lending energy to his muscles.

It was almost dark when he reached the wagon. Lisé was lying between the back wheels, holding the heavy fowling-piece between the spokes. He tried to say something to her but he could no longer move his tongue. He dropped the heavy body of the snake and sank down on the ground next to her. She flinched away from his blood-stained hand and forearm.

'I thought you were dead,' she said fearfully. 'When Violin came back I thought you were dead.'

He could only shake his head. He wanted water desperately but first he dragged the snake's body towards her, like a child offering a gift. She looked at it in horror. 'Oh, my God,' she said. 'What have you brought us?'

At that moment Robbie began to cry from his bed in the wagon.

James raised the tin cup and let the water roll over his tongue and down his throat, then he put the cup away so he would not be tempted to drink any more. There was only half a bag left.

He watched Lisé as she mixed a plate of drammach – cold meal and water – and began to feed Robbie. He felt his stomach heave at the sight of the food. They had been living this way for days now, too fearful to light a fire in case it attracted Bushmen. The boy was fretful and turned his head away from the tasteless mess, but his mother held him more closely and forced the spoon into his mouth.

The wind had suddenly died with nightfall and now a yellow moon rode high in the heavens. By its light he watched the boy. Robbie was as thin as a winter lamb. He had his mother's eyes, wide and bottomless brown in his father's sallow face. They were all thin. Lisé's face had fined down, the thinness giving her an added, almost waxy beauty and the bones of her cheeks cast slanting shadows to her mouth. Her wrists were like slender reeds. But the greatest change had occurred in James. His clothes, poor leather garments like those worn by drovers, hung loosely on him and flapped whenever he moved. They were torn and stained with dried blood. His cheeks were hollow and covered with stubble; his

166

hair was lank and uncombed. Only his eyes were alive; glittering bleakly in the moonlight.

The boy should be getting better victuals than drammach, he thought. It was weakening food; no strength in it. They should have chanced a fire and cooked the python. What did it matter if it was snake? The Bushmen ate snakes, lizards, grubs, caterpillars, locusts, anything they could lay their hands on. *They* didn't think food was unclean. Food was food. But Lisé had been adamant and he had pulled the snake away from the wagon and flung it into a nearby donga. He didn't feel resentful, he didn't feel anything at all, he was almost beyond feeling. He lay back on his kaross and tried to remember the taste of the water.

Later, when Robbie had eaten all he was going to eat and had been put in his blankets in the back of the wagon, he felt Lisé move into her kaross by his side. She did so without quite touching him and he wondered if he was also classed in her mind now as unclean. Not that it mattered much; they had not had intercourse for weeks. He had a feeling that this was a time, when two people were worried and desperate, that their bodies could give each other solace and comfort; a time when love and courage could be transferred physically, but he made no move to touch her. Since they had married he had fulfilled his obligations to the point of satiety. There was little pleasure in it for him and coupling with her became another habit, like shaving. He had come to believe that he would never ultimately satisfy her and this had depressed and humiliated him for a time, but then he had begun to feel that it was perhaps not himself that was at fault and that the same thing might happen to any man. Still, it was a small price to pay for his son. And really, in many ways, Lisé was a good wife. It wasn't her fault that she had no home to build, no settled way of life. She was good with the boy and that's what mattered now.

'James.' Her voice came out of the darkness beside him. The tone was low so as not to wake Robbie but there was a hardness in it that he had come to expect. 'James.' He pretended to be asleep. He felt her hand on his arm and suddenly she shook him roughly. 'James, wake up!'

He felt a flash of anger. Damn her! Couldn't she let a man rest!

'James,' she said again. 'We must turn back! We can't go on!'

Didn't she understand anything? Didn't she realize that they had come beyond the point of no return; that if there was no water behind them they *had* to go on?

'James, listen to me!'

He shook her hand off roughly. 'Leave me alone,' he said.

She began to sob. It was the first time he had ever heard her cry. He lay on his back and stared up at the stars listening to her unhappiness, feeling nothing at all. Turn back, she had said; but there was no way back for him, not even if a fresh-water lake appeared every mile of the way.

After a while the sobbing diminished and she fell asleep and he was left with his thoughts. He wished there was some brandy left in the barrel; he wanted to be anaesthetized; his thoughts always led back to the same point.

There could never be a way back. He might just have been able to live with the death of the Reverend Harmsworth and the slaughter of the Bushmen – just. Eventually the memories and the guilt would have been distorted by mental adjustment, possibly even by an easy compromise made without conscious effort. Time would have taken care of it. But it was only some days after he had ridden away in sick disgust from the ruined village that he had learnt the truth, and that was what made it so hard.

He had been drawn back to the ashes of Bitterfountain. The old homestead was as he remembered it, a pile of blackened rock and burnt wood. For two days he had camped nearby doing little else than sitting on the hillside staring out across the veld trying to make some sense out of what had happened. Slowly the house reconstructed itself in his thoughts and Aunt Hannah became less a naked corpse in the dust than a living person who had offered him love and affection; Uncle Hendrik changed back from a deranged old man calling the Bible to help in his rage, to a teacher and a guide. Chinks appeared in the walls he had built around himself. He felt vulnerable and, strangely, he didn't seem to care. He wanted the memories.

Hour after hour he sat and brooded until finally the thought came to him that he would rebuild Bitterfountain as it had been. He would marry Lisé and their children would grow up there, as he had grown up. He realized with bitterness that this was the only real home he had ever had and how important it had become to him – too late. He did not want that to happen to *his* children.

Lisé would make him a good wife. Not, perhaps, the wife he would have chosen but then what right had he to free choice after what had happened? *Some* payment was due.

The thought of what had to be done seemed to renew him. He began to plan. He scrambled to his feet and went down the hill and examined the ruined house with more care. Much of the stonework was intact. The foundations were still there and parts of the walls. He would need wood for beams and joists and this he could get in Graaff-Reinet. He would use reeds for the roof and the floors would be dung and ox-blood. Furniture was a problem but the de Blaizes would probably be able to lend him a few necessities in the beginning and he would make the rest himself. He would build two bedrooms, one for himself and Lisé and the other for the baby. And a hut for the servants. A decent hut with sound walls and a good roof.

Gradually his enthusiasm grew. Here he would build a rainwater tank, there a swing for the child. He'd put a porch on the front and build a verandah, much wider than the old stoep so they could sit there in the warm evenings and look out over the orchard to the mountains beyond.

And he would plant trees. Plum trees and peaches, apples and apricots, and he'd have a lemon tree growing near the front of the house because he loved the smell of the blossom. They'd grow lettuces and turnips, potatoes and carrots. And beyond the orchard a patch of mealies.

He paused. Water. Trees needed water. Well, he would irrigate. In the hills about a mile from the house there was a small spring. Uncle Hendrik had often talked about diverting it past the house but somehow they had never got around to it.

He'd do it! He'd dam it at some likely point and then lead the water off through a series of furrows. If he had enough water he could plant other trees as well, and his thoughts went back to the lovely oaks and pines near Paradise. Why not? He could *try* them. He might even build a small reservoir so they could swim in the hot weather. With a constant water supply the possibilities were endless.

He felt restless. He wanted to begin at once, but there was little he could do. He couldn't start building, he couldn't even begin to clear. But he could go and find the best place to build the small dam. He strode off across the face of the hills feeling the blood pumping in his veins. He'd do the thing systematically, starting right at the top about three miles away where the spring bubbled out of the hillside and work his way down its watershed, where other springs joined it, until he reached the nearest point to the house.

It wasn't as easy as it seemed, for the spring, which started as a trickle, gradually grew into a burn about three feet wide, overgrown by wild brambles and acacia. After an hour of forcing his way through the spiky thorns some of his enthusiasm waned. He came to understand why Uncle Hendrik had postponed the operation for so long. But he went on, hacking at the thorn bushes with his hook, splashing down the centre of the stream where he could, bent almost double in the green tunnel.

He had come more than two miles downstream when something in the thick bush caught his eye. He stopped and looked carefully. Whatever it was, it seemed to shine dully. The bush was badly matted and in deep shade. He went forward cautiously. Gradually his eyes grew used to the darkness. The object seemed to wink at him and at first he thought it was the eye of a wild-cat or perhaps even a lion cub. He stopped and craned forward. It couldn't be an animal because it didn't move. Then he saw that a narrow shaft of sunlight was falling through the tangled bush and this was causing the twinkling effect. He went forward another two paces, pulling away the branches of a thorn tree to get a better view. He found himself looking down on what was left of a man. The body was badly decomposed. Columns of black ants were moving in and out of the empty eye sockets. It was clothed in an old torn coat which had once been scarlet and the sunbeam was shining down directly on one of its brass buttons. In the centre of the coat and still deeply embedded in the body was the head of a Bushman arrow.

James knew he was looking at a thing which had once been Corporal Nollitts.

Lying there in the wagon on the edge of the Great Thirstland, listening to Lisé's soft breathing and the boy's occasional snufflings, he felt again the shock at finding Nollitts's body. It had come not so much from the actual discovery as the realization of what the discovery meant.

He had almost succeeded in forgetting Royal and Ogle, but now they were suddenly and terrifyingly real again. It did not take much imagination to reconstruct what had happened. Like any other band of wanted men they must have worked their way to the fringes of the Colony to join the bands of freebooters on the borders of Kaffirland away to the east. After raiding on both sides of the border until a dangerous situation arose they would have drifted westward to the Snowy Mountains, as their predecessors had done. But the pickings in a settled area must eventually have become too risky and they had moved slowly north until they had come across the defenceless homestead.

James tried to visualize them lying up on the slope above the farmhouse, watching and waiting; hungry perhaps, needing clothes and ammunition. He tried to recall their faces but found that this was impossible; he could only imagine a collective menace. And were there only three of them? Or had they gathered others like them?

And then had come the attack, with only an elderly woman and some heathen servants to fight them off. They must also have guessed the feelings of the district: that the Bushmen would be blamed – and they had been right.

How was it he had never even considered the attack on Bitterfountain in terms of Christians? There had been evidence enough; the unexplained killing of the heifers, Uncle Hendrik's talk of reivers. No, they had simply accepted that Aunt Hannah had been killed by Bushmen. *Bushmen!* The very lymph in his bones seemed to freeze in horror at the thought of what they had done to the Bushman village.

And Stone-Axe! Where was he? No doubt lying dead somewhere in the veld with a ball through his brain, his body already devoured by animals. And yet it was Stone-Axe, a Bushman, who had been the only line of defence. James was quite certain the arrow-head in Nollitts's body had come from Stone-Axe's quiver.

All the plans vanished from his mind. He could not have stayed on at Bitterfountain now there was no question of an easy compromise with himself.

He had considered, in spite of the obvious danger to himself, telling the others how wrong they had been but then he realized that he had been as much to blame; he had been as certain as anyone that the Bushmen were at fault. It would be no good telling them now, nor would they want to hear.

Within a week he and Lisé were married; within two, despite Aunt Hester's hysteria and the morbid warnings of Frans de Blaize, they had started their wanderings, grazing the flocks wherever there was water and grass, living in the wagon or in sod-built bothies; never staying in one place for very long except when the Grigua woman delivered Robbie. They had stayed for five months then.

In his aimless trek, searching for some place or some *thing* – uncertain yet of what – they drifted westward, then eastward and then westward again – and always slightly to the north. Always to the north. What was it Uncle Hendrik had said: a land flowing with milk and honey? Didn't it always lie to the north?

And all the time, as they travelled through a land parched and stunned by drought, he had watched for signs; used fireplaces, dead animals, unfamiliar tracks, anything that might point to the presence of Royal and Ogle. Without a reckoning the milk would sour, the honey turn bitter.

* * *

Palest grey was showing in the eastern sky when he woke. His body ached from the effort of the day before and his skin felt hot and dry. His tongue was still swollen, rasping angrily on his palate whenever he moved it. He *had* to have a mouthful of water. He slid from the kaross and stepped down onto the sandy floor. In the windless, early dawn the desert was hushed. Without the burning sun all its contours were softened and even the wart-like hills, which dotted its surface as far as the eye could see, had a strange bleak beauty which would fade as the day grew stronger. But James saw nothing but a waterless waste stretching on all sides of him.

The water-bag hung high up in the wagon tent and he felt for it. There wasn't much left. He frowned. Lisé must have been extravagant with it; perhaps Robbie had needed some in the night. Whatever the reason, he was certain the skin had been almost a quarter full after the drammach was mixed and after he had had his own ration.

Then he remembered the bag on the horse. Violin was still unsaddled and he walked around to where she was standing on the other side of the wagon. The first thing he saw was the long cut in the water-bag, which must have happened when she fell. It was quite empty and he felt the flutterings of panic.

He stood uncertainly for a moment, then he raised his eyes and searched the sky for cloud, but as far as he could see the air was clear as glass. The feeling of panic left him and was replaced by a dull apathy. There was nothing to do but go on. He began to inspan the oxen.

When they had first started out the wagon had been drawn by a span of sixteen prime bullocks; now the number was down to eight. If he had to, he would kill them one by one and feed the blood to Robbie. They were his last line of defence, but he knew that once he began the killing he would already have started to die.

The animals were thin and exhausted. They had last watered the day before at a stinking hole in a dry river bed and he knew that unless they found water that day, or at the latest the day after, there would be no need to kill them. First he yoked Rooiland and Vosberg, the two great rear oxen, and then went up the line with Bleskop and Doring – he usually acted up in the morning but came to the yoke now with head low and eyes almost closed – right to the lead couple, loosening the thongs under their throats to give them as much comfort as possible.

This was usually one of the more pleasant times of the day. Often, if they were near a stream, he would wade out to the middle, hold onto a boulder and let the rushing water wash over his body. Then he would eat a big plate of liver and kidneys and drink a mug of black coffee before yoking the oxen for the day's trek. But now he tied Violin to the back of the wagon and pulled out the long bullock whip and sent the lash cracking through the air. 'Huk-yeah!' he called. 'Huk-yeah!' The oxen leant forward against the yokes and the wagons began to move. He had heard no sounds from the inside but he knew Lisé must be awake. He didn't want to face her. Let her lie there. At least it wouldn't make her thirsty.

The sun came up. It seemed to race over the horizon as though frantic to reach its zenith and the first rays struck him with the heat of a branding iron. He pulled his hat lower on his face. He was up front now, leading the oxen. Between the hills the desert floor was flat, a perfect road-bed, but the oxen were almost dead on their feet and he knew that if he wasn't in front to lead them they would slow down and stop. He pulled on the leather *riem*, dragging them along behind him.

All his actions now were those of a sleepwalker. He knew only one thing: *they must go north*. He kept the morning sun on his right and plodded on into the wilderness.

In the part of his mind that was not numb with heat and exhaustion he knew what he was doing was wrong. They should be lying-up during the day and travelling only at night. You didn't get as thirsty that way and you had more chance of remaining unobserved. But it was too late for caution.

The wagon creaked painfully behind him, the hooves of the bullocks scraped on the rocky surface, the sun rose higher in the clear blue sky.

Without any warning at all he heard a thud behind him and

felt a jerk on the leather thong. Everything stopped. He turned and saw that Doring had collapsed. The bullock lay with its neck outstretched and its nose half-buried in the sand. It was trembling. James took the heavy bamboo whip stock and smashed it into the bullock's ribs. 'Get up,' he said hoarsely. Doring jerked and blew. He thumped the butt into her again. 'Come on, come *on!*'

'What's wrong?' Lisé called from the wagon.

He didn't bother to reply. He caught up the ox's tail, bent it almost double and sank his teeth into it. Doring bellowed and tried to kick, then lay quietly. He took out his knife, placed the point near the join of tail and rump and pressed hard. Again the ox bellowed and kicked; again it refused to move.

'All right,' he said, savagely. 'All right.' He gathered some pieces of dry tumbleweed, crushed them together in his hands and placed them by the ox's belly. He took out his tinder box.

Lisé had come down off the wagon and was standing at his elbow. 'What are you going to do?'

'You'll see.'

The tinder caught and he held it out to the tumbleweed.

'Jamie!' she cried, trying to step between him and the animal.

'Get out of my way!' He caught her roughly and pulled her aside, sending her sprawling on the ground. He pushed the flaming tumbleweed against the bullock's belly. The beast bellowed with pain. Its back legs jerked as it tried to rise. Its hindquarters came off the ground. Its head still rested on the sand, mouth open, bellowing, then abruptly its body collapsed and it was dead.

'Oh, my God,' Lisé whispered. 'What have you done?'

He stood above the dead beast in a half crouch, willing it to get up, unable to accept that its life had slipped away. He turned to Lisé and saw her looking up at him and saw the horror in her eyes and then felt the horror flooding through himself as he realized what he had just done.

He glared down at her through blood-red eyes. 'Jamie,' she said. 'What's happened to you?'

He passed a trembling hand over his face and took two paces towards her. He was giddy and nauseous. The sun beat on his head and shoulders. 'I'm sorry, my dear,' he said. 'I'm so sorry.' Slowly his knees buckled and he fell forward onto the ground.

When he came to he was lying in the shade under the wagon and Lisé was bending over him wiping his face and wrists with a damp cloth.

'Don't talk,' she said. 'Here.' She held a cup of warm, brackish water to his lips and he drank in small swallows. The water seemed to disappear into the sides of his mouth like light rain on desert sand.

'Is that better?'

He nodded. He still felt giddy but the nausea had left him and he looked up at her in gratitude.

'I'm sorry,' he said again.

'It's all right. Lie still.' She held the cup to his lips and he sipped.

After a moment he said: 'It was a terrible thing to do.'

'You weren't yourself.'

'Even so . . .'

'Have some more.' She held the cup up again.

'No, save it. There's none left in my bag.'

'I know.'

'Well, save it. Robbie will need some, and yourself.'

She shook her head. 'You come first.'

'Me? After what I've done?'

'Yes.'

'But why?'

'Because you're my man,' she said simply.

He put out his hand and touched her arm. The very tenderness of the gesture was something entirely new between them. She took the hand and held it.

'Everything seems to have gone wrong,' he said. 'Everything. I'm not even sure what we're doing here except that I *had* to go on. I couldn't stay.'

'It's all right,' she said. 'You're not to think of that now. Don't blame yourself.'

'But I do blame myself. You could still have been at High

Valley, cared for, looked after; we might even have stayed at Bitterfountain and tried to make a go of it. Instead . . .'

'You don't understand, do you, Jamie? I love you. I want to be with you. Oh, there were times at first when I wondered and times, right in the beginning, when I thought of marrying the richest farmer I could find. You were right when you said I should find an only son. That's how my mind was working. But, oh Jamie, I was bored. I was bored at home, bored with the very thought of living like that. Sometimes I even thought the minister's house was better than High Valley. It was more exciting.'

She smiled and he smiled back at her. 'But perhaps a little more dangerous,' he said.

'I'm not sure about that. Look what happened to me at home.' She returned to her thoughts: 'No, it's only since I left that I've started to grow up. I was a child then, I'm not a child now.'

'No.'

'It's only since we left that I've begun to live. Really live.'

'You mean you've *enjoyed* it?'

'Is that so hard to understand? You're forgetting that this sort of life was in my blood.'

He nodded. 'I thought you were unhappy, dissatisfied – in more ways than one.' He looked up at her quickly. 'Were you?'

She flushed slightly then bent and put her head on his chest. 'I thought it was *you*,' she whispered. 'I thought *you* were unsatisfied and I didn't know what to do.'

'Oh, God, we should have spoken about it earlier,' he said. 'That's my fault. I never talk things out. I can't seem to find . . . I just don't know how to . . .'

'Sssh. Never mind. We know now, that's the important thing.'

'Yes,' he said sadly. 'We know now.'

She pushed herself up and looked into his eyes. 'Don't say it like that. We're not finished yet,' she said.

He came up on one elbow and kissed her gently on the mouth, then he held her close to his chest looking past her into the searing desert. He should be saying something strong and optimistic but once again the words would not come.

'Birds!' Robbie's voice came from the wagon tent. 'Birds!'

James, still holding Lisé tightly, said: 'What kind of birds, son?'

'Birds, birds.'

'They may be guinea fowl or quail,' James said. 'I'd better see.' He stood next to Robbie. 'Where, son?'

'Birds.' The boy pointed to a low hill about 400 yards to their left. Half a dozen white-necked carrion crows were circling on the other side.

James took up the rifle. 'You never know, a lion might have killed in the night,' he said. 'If he has he won't be far from water and I might be able to spoor him.'

She smiled. 'I told you it wasn't over yet.'

The sun smashed at him and he staggered slightly, but the water had helped and he went on.

The hill was like a thousand others, small and flat-topped. He could see the crows working on the other side and decided he'd walk around instead of over. A lion always drank after he had eaten, which meant he wouldn't want to go far for his water. James began to hope. But when he came round the other side of the hill he realized that whatever the birds were attacking was far too small to have interested a lion. As he drew closer he saw it was still alive. When the birds dived it moved from side to side, trying to avoid them. At first he thought it was a wounded porcupine, drawing itself up into a ball; but when he came up to it he saw . . .

'Stone-Axe!' he yelled.

The little Bushman was buried up to his neck in the sand of a dry donga. The white-necked crows had been trying to pick out his eyes and he had been moving his head back and forth to frighten them away. This was the movement James had seen. So far he had been successful. He retained his sight, but the rest of his face was a mask of blood where the sharp beaks had slashed and gouged. In another fifteen minutes he would have become too feeble to ward off the attacks. First, he would have lost his eyes and then the birds would have put their beaks into the empty sockets and pulled out his brain.

His tongue was black and swollen. The first thing James

did was urinate into his mouth, then he began to dig the sand away until he could pull the slight body from its living grave. The wrists and ankles were tied with thongs. James cut them away and Stone-Axe sprawled limply out onto the ground.

'You'll be all right,' James said. 'You'll be all right. You'll see. I won't let anything happen to you.' The words came pouring out. 'I'll look after you. I'll . . .'

The Bushman's eyes flickered open weakly. 'O Claw,' he whispered. 'The Great Bull Calf. The Lion's Son.'

'Yes, you wee devil,' James said through the tears that were blurring his eyes. 'It's the bull calf that's found you.' He picked him up as though he was a child and began to walk back to the wagon.

For the rest of the day he sat by the Bushman's side. They had made a palliasse of tumbleweed and skins and placed him on it in the shade. Every now and then James would squeeze drops of water from a soaking rag into his mouth. Their supply of Halle medicines was almost exhausted and James had treated the facial wounds with a mixture of urine and gunpowder in Hottentot fashion. At intervals during the afternoon Stone-Axe would blink his eyes awake and smile up into his face. From time to time he even managed a few words before he lapsed once again into an exhausted sleep and slowly James began piecing together a picture of what had happened.

Late in the afternoon, when the worst of the heat had passed, he cut the throat of the dead bullock's yoke-mate and drained the blood into a bowl. This he fed to Stone-Axe with a spoon. Then he cut out the heart and liver and grilled them over a small, smokeless fire, and they all ate.

Robbie had come down once or twice to stare with grave, worried eyes at Stone-Axe. Lisé had avoided him completely. By nightfall the Bushman was sleeping normally.

'He's come a long way.' Lisé said as they lay on top of their karosses in the darkness of the wagon.

'From beyond the Great River,' he said. 'It's not easy to make out what he's saying, but from what I can gather he's been some sort of prisoner of the Bachapins or he's with some

Christians who are being held there. I'm not quite clear about that. Anyway, they gave him a letter and sent him south to see if he could reach the Frontier and get some help. He didn't have much difficulty getting away from the Bachapins but once he'd crossed the Great River he ran into a clan of his own people, wild Bushmen. He travelled with them for a couple of days until one went through his things while he slept and found the letter. They didn't know what it said, of course, but they'd seen things like it before and that was enough to brand him a tame Bushman. So they burnt the letter and fastened his wrists and ankles and left him buried up to his neck in sand for the birds to do the rest.'

'James?'

'He'd have been dead in half an hour.'

'James?' she put out her hand to touch him. 'Why are you doing this for him? Why didn't you leave him?'

'God, what are you saying?'

'How do you know it wasn't Stone-Axe himself who killed Aunt Hannah?'

He lay in silence for a moment. Tomorrow they would use up the last of the water.

'There's something you should know,' he said. 'I should have told you earlier but it goes back a long way, a very long way.'

'Do you want to tell me?' she asked softly.

'Yes.'

He told her about himself from as far back as he could remember. Half-way through she slid over to join him, taking him in her arms. He could feel the wetness of tears on her cheeks. When he finished it seemed natural that she should say nothing, but that all their feelings and thoughts should be distilled into one act. They took each other; fusing at depths neither had ever thought possible, passionately yet tenderly gentle, and then they slept.

In the morning Stone-Axe was gone and so was the last of the water. James looked at the empty bag, unwilling to believe his eyes.

'Why?' Lisé said bitterly. 'Why?'

He shook his head. 'He must have had his reasons.' He

clung onto his belief in the Bushman, telling himself that he had doubted once and been wrong. They were preparing to move out when he saw a dark smudge against the skyline. It was Stone-Axe. In his arms he held six ostrich eggs, each one plugged at both ends. Carefully he laid them on the ground at James's feet. 'Drink well, O Claw,' he said. The shells were filled with water.

'I told you,' James said to Lisé.

Later in the day Stone-Axe, who seemed to have totally recovered and who had been scouting ahead and to the side of the trail, took James aside.

There were signs, he said, that a Bushman clan was in the area, perhaps the one which had left him to die. Soon they would discover that one of their water caches had been rifled, the most heinous crime that anyone could commit against them, and then they would search for the thieves. Why not shoot the bullocks, or even leave them where they were? No Bushman would pass up the chance of a feast. They could put the woman and child on the mare and travel light.

James was tempted. He looked back at the weary beasts leaning against the yokes. Certainly, with Violin alone they would travel much faster, but that would mean leaving the trade goods behind and without the means to barter there would be no chance of food, perhaps not even of help from the Bachapins if they were really holding Christians prisoner.

He shook his head. 'No, we'll go on as we are, for a while anyway. How many days to the Great River?' Stone-Axe held up three fingers. That was two days too many; even Violin wouldn't last that long.

About four in the afternoon they reached a dry river bed. Dusty thorn trees straggled along the low banks. 'We'll stop here for a few hours,' James said, 'and then push on at dark.'

Stone-Axe had picked up the big wagon-whip and was looking at the bamboo stock speculatively. He held it up to his eye as though it were a long, thin telescope and tried to look through it but the tube was blocked at each joint.

James helped Lisé and Robbie to the shade. The earlier confidence seemed to have drained from her and he was too exhausted to fill her with new hope.

'Claw,' Stone-Axe called from the wagon. 'Where is Black Lightning?' This was his name for the long-barrelled rifle.

Puzzled, James took the weapon down from its hooks in the tent.

'The long steel,' Stone-Axe said.

He drew out the ram-rod. 'You're not going to start cleaning it now?'

The Bushman shook his head. James watched as he kindled a fire from dead wood. When the coals were glowing he placed the ram-rod's tip in the heart of the fire and allowed it to become red hot. Then he pushed it down the bamboo stock, carefully burning out the woody joints. Smoke rose from the bamboo as the hot steel cut through it. Stone-Axe worked from both ends until at last he could hold the slender pole up to the sky and see light.

'Come,' he said. 'Bring the water-bags.'

They went down into the dry bed of the river and walked for about a quarter of a mile until they came to a place where the bed sloped down to a natural hole. Here Stone-Axe began to dig. First he dug the sand away with his hands and then he used the sharp point of the ram-rod, loosening the whiteish sand and bringing it up with his hands. He worked quickly and methodically. Soon the hole was too deep for him to reach the bottom. He took the long bamboo, placed it in the hole and began to work it round and round and side to side, bringing it up every few minutes to knock the impacted sand from the central columns. Slowly the bamboo sank into the river-bed. He worked at it bit by bit until only a foot of the pole stuck out. Then he motioned James to bring the water-bags. He placed his lips over the top of the bamboo as though about to blow some strange underground horn.

But he did not blow, he sucked. The effort was so great that within seconds his eyes were bulging from their sockets and blood was seeping from the wounds on his face. James watched with alarm. Stone-Axe was using his body as a living pump. His stomach was flattened against his backbone, his chest seemed to shrink, his legs began to tremble, his eyes began to water. He sucked with all his strength. Suddenly he gave a spluttering cough and James saw water begin to drip from his chin. Stone-Axe grabbed one of the water-bags and held it near his mouth. The water, which lay in the pocket under the river bed, surged up the pole into the Bushman's mouth. He scooped up a straight stick, held the end in the side of his mouth and placed the other end in the top of the waterbag. The water ran down the stick into the bag.

It came more easily now and his body began to resume its proper shape. It was steady and rhythmical pumping. The bag began to fill. James took his turn on the bamboo. He sucked until he thought his ribs might collapse but was only able to produce a mouthful of water. It tasted of natron and drew his mouth harshly and finally he gave way to Stone-Axe again. It took them nearly two hours to fill one bag completely and half the other.

When they could go on no longer Stone-Axe drew out the bamboo, filled in the hole and brushed away all traces of their presence. At nightfall they went forward again.

The Bushmen came in the night. They came suddenly, ten or a dozen of them, like dark shadows flitting across the desert. They had been expected for the past hour since Stone-Axe had come in from their flank and announced in a low voice: 'O Claw, the People are near.'

Lisé and Robbie were lying flat on the wagonbed, covered by skins. The boxes of trade goods had been piled around them. James had considered stopping but since there was only the one wagon they could not form a laager and there would be no advantage. They might as well keep on as long as they could. There was also the possibility that the Bushmen might not attack, though James admitted to himself this was remote. If for nothing else they would avenge the theft of their water.

The roar of the massive fowling-piece he had given Stone-Axe was the signal for the attack. He happened to be looking into the same area of darkness when the muzzle-flash lit up the heathen. He was wriggling along on his stomach within a dozen yards of the wagon when Stone-Axe fired, almost cutting him in half. A second later he heard the *yuk* of an arrow striking and then Rooiland's bellow as it jerked against the yoke.

In the corner of his eye he saw a shadow move and he swung and fired. He was not sure whether he had scored, but the shadow seemed to disappear. He flung himself onto Violin's back and raced away from the wagon. This was the old Frontier tactic against unmounted men and James used it without thinking. As long as he could remain free and mobile they had a chance.

There was another bellow from the oxen and he knew that a second one had been hit. It would only be a matter of time before the Bushmen picked them off. He reloaded and turned. The fowling-piece roared again and this time sparks from the muzzle set fire to a stand of tinder-dry grass. It went up with a whoosh. In its light he saw another Bushman scuttle for the cover of some rocks. He aimed and fired and the ball lifted the Bushman off his feet and slammed him to the ground. James wheeled away to reload. He stopped in the shadow of a small *lopje* and waited for a movement. At that moment the yellow moon slid over the rim of the earth and lit up the scene almost as bright as day. Nothing moved except the doomed bullocks thrashing at the yoke.

Then he saw Stone-Axe drop from the back of the wagon and come running towards him. 'Come, Claw,' he panted. 'The People are frightened.'

'They've gone?'

'Black Lightning has frightened the People.'

James spurred Violin down to the wagon. Stone-Axe raced beside him. 'We'll do as you say, little one,' James said. 'It may not be too late yet.' Four of the oxen were down, their bodies twitching as the poison worked its way towards the heart. 'Lisé', he called. 'Bring Robbie! We're moving!'

They put Lisé in the saddle and she held Robbie on the pommel in front of her. Stone-Axe took one water-bag and James the other. Each carried a gun. They did not pause to look back, they did not even stop to despatch the wounded beasts; they knew the Bushmen would return.

For the first hour they kept Violin at a trot, the two men holding onto the stirrup irons for support. Then they stopped

184

for ten minutes and James filled his hat with water, letting the mare drink.

They went on for another three hours, alternately walking and running and during that time they stopped twice more, each taking a mouthful of water and refilling the hat for the horse. Without her they might just as well have cut their throats.

As he stumbled along, clutching the stirrup, James felt no animosity towards the Bushmen. There was a certain justice in the fact that they, who had so often been the hunted, should now be the hunters. What was it Uncle Hendrik had once said? That they loved their freedom more than life itself. One had to admire a race of people, decimated and defeated, stripped of their ancestral lands, plundered of their game, living on nothing but roots and grubs where they should have been eating eland steaks; starving, dying and yet – and yet without the fatal flaw of civilized man: the knowledge of their own defeat. For they were The People. Not just people, but The People, inheritors of the land when the Old Race rose from the ground to become the stars.

James remembered Stone-Axe once describing to him that in the beginning there was a dim light over the earth and the Sun-armpit lay sleeping and two women of the Old Race ordered some children to pick up the Sun-armpit and they did this unawares and threw him into the sky and he became round and shone down on the earth giving it light and making it warm. That was before, in the long, long before of the Bushmen, when *they* were the Children.

At the next stopping-place Lisé could hardly dismount. James lifted Robbie from his position along Violin's neck and waited for her, but finally he had to lift her down as well. He found she could no longer stand and laid her gently on the ground. Her face was twisted with pain. She lay against his chest and he held the water-bag for her to drink. She stopped after one mouthful but he said, 'Go on, you need it.' Then he gave an extra share to Robbie. He and Stone-Axe took only one mouthful each and then he watered the mare.

Lisé said: 'Jamie, I can't go on.' For the first time he heard the utter defeat in her voice.

'Just for a little,' he said. 'We'll lie up as soon as it gets light.'

He sat down next to her and put his arm round her shoulders. She let her head fall on his chest. 'Oh God, Jamie, I'm tired.'

'I know. I can't think how you've held on this long; you and Robbie.'

'James, if anything should happen – to me, I mean – and if there's no hope for any of us . . .' She looked across at Robbie, who was lying on the ground in a state of unconscious exhaustion.

James nodded. 'Yes, but it won't come to that,' he said grimly. 'We can't be far from the Great River now. And the nearer we get the less chance there is of an attack.'

Lisé pressed his hand. 'You don't have to say things like that.'

Stone-Axe, who had been sitting on his haunches nearby, raised his head. 'It is the truth,' he said. 'The People no longer go to the Great River in these parts. The Bachapins hunt them. The Islanders hunt them. The People must go.'

James heard the sadness in his voice but at the same time he took heart from it.

'There, even Stone-Axe says so,' he said to Lisé.

She seemed about to say something but then her face wrenched with pain. 'It's all right,' she managed as James turned. 'It's only cramp from the saddle.' In a little while they went on.

'Claw!' The name penetrated James's subconscious and he jerked upright. For the past hour he had been hanging onto the stirrup, letting Violin drag him forward. The strength in his legs seemed to have drained away at last.

'What is it?'

Stone-Axe pointed to a patch of scrub about forty yards away. In the bright moonlight it looked white and ghostly. James raised the rifle but could see nothing except tangled branches. He blinked and rubbed his eyes. Stone-Axe was not given to extravagance. Suddenly, from the depths of the bush a figure rose, then another and another. Automatically he fired, the rifle and the fowling-piece blasting together. He ducked next to Violin's flank as the flight of arrows scythed over their heads. He fired again and then grabbed the mare's rein, pulling her into the safety of a rock. He heard the fowling-piece boom and then he was weaving in and out of the rocks. He paused, reloaded and circled the bush. He saw a movement and fired. Stone-Axe was circling from the far side and James prayed he wouldn't aim high. He was directly in the line. The fowling-piece fired again and he heard the whistle of shot. The patch of scrub was still. He moved towards it cautiously, holding the rifle at the ready. He heard a slight sound on his left and whirled. It was Stone-Axe coming up with him.

'T'ao,' Stone-Axe said, holding up two fingers.

'In one shot?'

The Bushman nodded without pride.

There were four bodies in the scrub. One of the Bushmen had had his side blown out. The heavy buck-shot charge had gone right through him, killing the man behind.

'Why only four?' James said, puzzled.

'Violin,' Stone-Axe said.

He understood. The others would be feasting on the slaughtered bullocks. These had come for the horse.

Stone-Axe said: 'It is nearly day.'

James returned to the mare. Lisé was crouched forward in the saddle, her body shielding the child's.

'It's all right,' James said. 'There were only four of them. We're going to rest up in a little while.' She was too exhausted to reply.

They went on for another hour, moving away from the track into low hills and gullies. Stone-Axe lead at a trot. Finally they reached a bushy kloof with cliffs on either side. The thorn trees formed a rough archway at the opening.

'You'll have to walk,' James said. 'I'll take Robbie.'

He reached up for the child but Lisé didn't move. Her body was leaning even farther forward. 'Lisé', he said. 'It's all right now. They've gone.' She didn't seem to hear him. 'Help me,' he said to Stone-Axe. 'She must have fainted.'

But they couldn't shift her. Her hands were twisted into Violin's mane and she had pushed her feet through the stirrups then twisted them round so they lodged between the leathers on top of the stirrup irons. James stood for a moment, moved by her courage, then he reached up and tried to pull her fingers from the thick hair. They were cold and stiff. He felt a prickle of apprehension. He tore at the twined hair until her hands were free. Stone-Axe loosened her feet, then they slid her body out of the saddle. Robbie slept along the mare's neck like a young marsupial.

'Bring the water,' James said, but Stone-Axe was already kneeling beside her. He looked up and his eyes were bright with tears. Then he pointed to the arrow-head in her side. Like all Bushman arrows the head had only been lightly fixed to the shaft so that when a wounded animal ran through the bush it might sweep away the shaft but the poisoned head would remain. Death had already stiffened Lisé's body and it was then that James realized this wound must have come in the first attack and that the poison had been in her for most of the night.

All that day he sat huddled in the cave holding Robbie between his knees. Even when the child wanted to pass water James made him do it there on the sandy floor and as soon as he was finished he scooped him back into the protection of his legs. That was almost the only movement he made. Across the floor Stone-Axe squatted. His eyes never left James's face.

They sat like this, hour after hour, and the only time the Bushman left him was to search for food. He ate automatically, taking the pieces of food from Stone-Axe, who was serving him as a Bushman woman would serve her man. Later, when he realized that the white, sweetish meat came from the roasted body of a puff-adder, he spewed it out.

In the grey dawn they had buried Lisé at the mouth of the kloof. James had watched the body slowly disappear under the sand and stones which Stone-Axe had gathered. He was stupefied with tiredness and grief. *It couldn't be happening.* But it *was* happening – it had happened. Many times he had watched the dying agonies of an antelope shot by Stone-Axe and a moan escaped his lips and sweat broke out on his brow

188

as he thought of what *Lisé* must have experienced. *I can't go on*, she had told him. But he'd made her go on. And all the time the poison was working through her tissues and the arrow-head was gouging deeper and deeper into her side.

When Stone-Axe had finished he had led James to the cave. He had tried to take Robbie in his arms but James had pushed him away, scooping up the sleeping child, holding his hook in front of him as a warning.

The little Bushman had seemed to understand. He had moved round to James's other side and taken him by the elbow. And during that day, whenever he passed, he would touch him, or stroke his arm. The gestures were quite unselfconscious.

The cave was dominated by a huge Bushman painting. It was a work of the greatest beauty and covered an entire wall. It consisted of six ostriches; four were black with white tail feathers, the other two were light blue. Their long, graceful necks twined in and out of one another. At any other time James would have been absorbed by it but now he did not even bother to look up, not even when Stone-Axe, trying to penetrate his grief, pointed out that the sixth ostrich was not a bird at all but a Bushman dressed in an ostrich skin who had infiltrated the flock and was about to use his arrows on the others.

Who was to blame? The questions went round and round in his mind. At first, when he realized how she had died, he had felt an almost overpowering urge to kill Stone-Axe; to smash his body to nothing. Then, as quickly as it came the feeling had left him. Stone-Axe wasn't to blame. The Bushmen? But hadn't he helped to slaughter a whole clan? Who then? He let his head fall onto his arm. Who? There had to be someone. His mind went back all the way to Inverness but not even he could lay Lisé's death at Loxton's door. He was left with himself.

As soon as darkness came Stone-Axe led them on. James no longer cared which way they travelled so long as his son was cared for. If the Bachapins were holding Christians prisoner, they were probably walking into a trap. He didn't care. The Bachapins would have milk and food. He had

189

nothing left to barter with except himself, but what he did now was no longer important. If he had to work for their keep he would; and Stone-Axe would too. It didn't matter . . . nothing mattered . . . only that Lisé had died rather than let the boy come to harm. He carried Robbie in his arms and stumbled after Stone-Axe and the desert swallowed them up once more.

His memory of the trek through the Great Thirstland stopped with Lisé's death. Afterwards he was never able to recall their arrival at the Great River with its yellow waters stretching for nearly a quarter of a mile. He did not notice the beautiful stones strewn near the banks; nor the lush green of the vegetation. He could only vaguely remember the secrecy of their crossing at dead of night, floating across on a raft which Stone-Axe had lashed together with acacia bark, unaware that they had made a detour to avoid the Islanders, of whom the Bushman was so afraid. He drank the water Stone-Axe gave him and ate the food. But always he saw that Robbie ate first.

They went on into the land of the Bachapins, the boy riding the mare, the two men walking at her side.

Book Four

THE NIGHT OF THE HYENA

'The old she Hyena,
The old she Hyena,
Was carrying off the old Woman from the old hut,
The old Woman in this manner,
She sprang aside,
She arose,
She beat the Hyena.
The Hyena, herself.
The Hyena killed the Hyena.'
                    'The Old Woman's Song' from *Specimens of
                    Bushman Folklore*
                            collected by BLEEK and LLOYD.

And so they came to Litakun. Their presence had been
marked at least ten miles before they reached the town.
James, walking with head bowed, hardly caring what lay
around him, felt Stone-Axe's touch on his arm. He followed
the Bushman's pointing finger and saw, briefly, the tall black
figure of the herdsman as he ducked behind a clump of
mokaal trees.

'He tells to the next; and the next to the next.'

James nodded. The sooner the Bachapins knew, the
sooner *they* would know. He looked to the priming of the
rifle.

Almost imperceptibly, as they drew nearer the town, they
were joined by warriors; first one, then three, then half a

dozen until about twenty young men were formed up loosely on their flanks. Each warrior carried a shield and two throwing assegais.

One shouted something and Stone-Axe answered. 'What did he say?' James asked.

'He remembers me, Claw. I gave him honey once.'

Another warrior called something across the intervening veld. 'I drew a thorn from his foot,' Stone-Axe said, raising the fowling-piece in greeting.

But these were the only two moments of friendliness. For the rest the warriors watched the three of them in detached silence and James, remembering what Hartmann had told him of the Bachapins' ruthlessness to the Bushmen, wondered what was in store for Stone-Axe, or for all of them.

As they came over the top of a rise the town of Litakun was spread out before him. He was suddenly brought out of his moody reverie by its very size.

It was built in a circle and consisted of row upon row of conical huts, each surrounded by a high guard fence made of saplings and reeds. Its diameter was about a mile and a half and it nestled under the shoulders of a series of low scrub-covered hills. As the scene became clearer he realized that the houses were built in small groups, separated from each other by hard trodden areas which, in Christian townships, would have been used as roads. These were simply open spaces covered here and there by karoo bush, and very occasionally a mokaal tree. Everything was neat and ordered. On the outskirts of the town a crowd had collected and as they saw the small party top the rise they moved across the plain to meet them.

Almost immediately James was swallowed up in the throng. He held Violin's bridle tightly in one hand and felt Stone-Axe grip his other arm. He moved forward through the heaving press of bodies feeling their fingers on his clothes, sometimes just touching, at others pinching through the leather jacket and finding flesh. He kept his eyes down and his temper under tight rein.

'*Muchuko! Muchuko!*'

He shouldered someone aside and tramped on steadily. 'It's all right, son,' he said to Robbie. 'They won't hurt you.' His voice lacked assurance and the boy looked down with a worried frown on his face.

'*Muchuko!*'

James shifted the weight of the rifle and the crowd quickly gave them more room. He noted the movement. Good, he thought, they're frightened of it. But within a few moments the bodies were packed as tightly as ever. Some were laughing, others gabbling in excited tones; they seemed amused, enthusiastic, like a gathering of expectant children who weren't sure what was about to happen but who were looking forward to it anyway.

He began to feel more optimistic. He smiled and his smile was greeted by an outburst of laughter from those nearest. He could still feel their fingers on his clothes and the occasional sharp nip as they gave him a friendly pinch, but he told himself that this must be some form of greeting or custom and he bore the twinges as good-naturedly as he could.

Through the babble of voices one word was repeated over and over again. '*Muchuko! Muchuko!*' It was taken up as a sort of chant.

'What does it mean?' James said.

'Tobacco. They want tobacco.'

'*Muchuko,*' James said. 'Tobacco.'

Those nearest heard him use the word and immediately set up a shrill chorus. '*Muchuko! Muchuko!*' nodding their heads vigorously and clapping their hands with delight at his understanding. They had been brought to a stop now as the crowd pressed round, palms outstretched for a gift of tobacco. Robbie, who had been getting increasingly frightened, now began to cry.

'It's all right, son,' James said quickly. 'They only want tobacco.'

'*Muchuko!*' the crowd roared.

James turned to them and shook his head. 'None!' he shouted. 'No *muchuko!*'

'*Muchuko!*' came the reply and now there was an undercurrent of annoyance.

James turned quickly to Stone-Axe. 'Tell them we haven't got any tobacco, or there'll be a riot.'

The Bushman shouted something to the Bachapins in their own language and almost at once they fell silent. And then one man, bigger than the rest, thrust his face into James's and shouted 'Muchuko!' in a loud voice. At the same time Robbie gave a slight cry. There was a flash of silver as James clubbed the man with the back of his hook. He sprawled in the dust. The effect on the crowd was magical. They had never seen a hook before. There was a stampede to get clear. Some ran all the way into the town, others paused after only a few paces and turned, awestruck, to confirm their earlier vision. James sensed that this was a vital moment. The man he had hit was still on the ground. He bent and helped him to his feet. He wobbled on his legs for a moment and then, with a rueful grin, began to rub his head. There was a howl of delight from the crowd. Even Stone-Axe was grinning. They pushed forward and the crowd let them through, joining up behind them at a slightly safer distance.

They entered the town. James could see now that the houses were not as symmetrically spaced as he had first thought. There was no regular plan at all; they were simply scattered about, in some places far apart, in others so close together that there was no space to walk between them.

As they passed down the open spaces families ran out for a sight of them; the women half-astonished, the children half-afraid. More joined the following throng until it seemed James was at the head of a triumphal procession.

There were mutterings of 'Muchuko!' from the newly-joined followers but these were quickly silenced by those who had seen the thing at the end of James's arm.

They came at last to a hut no bigger than the rest where the crowd stopped. James glanced at Stone-Axe. 'We are here, Claw. King Mateebe.'

As he spoke three men emerged from the doorway. They looked carefully at James, their eyes straying constantly to the hook about which they had already heard, then they peered at Robbie and Stone-Axe, and even gave Violin a long and close inspection. They spoke no word and no sound came from the crowd. James knew that this was the moment to offer a gift of some kind but he had nothing to give.

One of the men spoke. James looked swiftly at Stone-Axe for translation. 'King Mateebee speaks. He welcomes you.' James glanced up at the Chief. He was a man about medium height, strongly-muscled, with a shining black skin. His beard was worn longer than seemed fashionable at Litakun and his eyes were set close together and looked shrewd, almost cunning. He wore a leather cloak which hung down his back and round his neck was a thick necklace of twisted sinews and one string of large beads alternately white and purple. From one of the sinews hung a sheathed knife. Apart from these adornments he was naked. He wore nothing on his feet nor on his head, but his hair was plastered with a mixture of grease and a shining mineral powder called *siblio*. On his left arm, above the elbow, were five broad rings cut from an elephant's tooth. Standing next to him was an elderly man, wizened and with greying hair who, James was to learn later, was called Sekootu, the Chief Counsellor. Beyond Sekootu stood the vast bulk of the King's bodyguard. His name was Mollende and, like many strong men, he wore an expression of amused benevolence. He was staring at James's hook with unashamed interest.

The crowd had increased in size and was pressing round the hut, waiting expectantly. 'Thank the King for his welcome,' James said. 'Tell him that I bring greetings from the Christians across the Great River.'

James noticed Sekootu turn to the King and mutter something in his ear, then King Matebee addressed him through Stone-Axe.

'The King asks if the Christian brought anything else from beyond the Great River?'

'Tell the King I am truly sorry there is nothing else.'

'The King asks if the Christian has brought tobacco for him?'

'Tell the King I have not even tobacco for myself.'

'The King asks if the Christian has brought any snuff?'

'Tell the King I have no snuff.'

'The King asks if the Christian has any cloth?'

'No cloth either.'

'Tell the King I had a wagon-load of beads and other presents for him but the Bush –' James checked himself. 'The Islanders have plundered the wagon.' A slight muttering broke out among members of the crowd.

'The King says the Islanders are bad people.'

'Truly bad.'

'The King asks if the Christian has brass buttons.'

'The Islanders have also taken the brass buttons.'

There was a pause and the two groups watched each other in silence.

After a few moments Sekootu spoke again in the King's ear.

King Mateebe's eyes flicked back and forth as he listened. Then he spoke again.

'The King says how did the Bushman Stone-Axe bring the Christian to Litakun?'

James had been expecting the question. 'Tell the King that the Bushman Stone-Axe is the Christian's servant. Tell the King that the Bushman is like a hunting dog to the Christian. Tell him that the Christian brought up the Bushman from a puppy. Tell him that the Christian sent a message to the Bushman that he was coming to Litakun with gifts for the King and that he hoped to barter with the King for elephant's teeth.'

There was another pause as this piece of information was digested.

'The King asks how a message came to his kraal without him knowing?'

'Tell the King that the Christian has great powers.'

Sekootu spoke again hurriedly.

'The King does not believe in these powers. Christians have been here before and they had not great powers except their guns.'

James held out his hook so that everyone might see it. There was a murmur of awe from the crowd. 'Ask the King if he has ever seen a hand of iron before and then let him think again about my power.'

This seemed for the moment to be unanswerable and the

conversation languished. The crowd stood poised for the debate to continue.

At length the King spoke again. 'The King says he wishes to have the hand of iron.'

James shook his head. 'I cannot give the King something which belongs to my body.'

'The King says the Christian must show him then how to get a hand of iron for himself.'

'The King must first cut off one of his own hands to pay. Only a very brave man can have a hand of iron.' Again there was an expectant mutter and James realized he had gone too far. King Mateebe was looking at him angrily. He was losing face. Suddenly he turned to the huge bulk of Mollende and said: 'Here is the King's hand of iron.' The crowd chuckled at this neat piece of sophistry and the King's expression changed. James breathed again. He was finding it difficult to keep up with the swift changes in mood.

He had been keeping a wary eye on Robbie. At first the boy seemed to have been enjoying himself perched up on Violin's back but now the harsh sunlight and the dust which rose from so many feet made him feel faint and he swayed in the saddle.

James put an arm up to steady him and then lifted him down. 'Ask the King if he has milk for the Christian's son.'

King Mateebe had already begun to nod his reply when Sekootu once again whispered to him.

'The King says there is no milk.'

'What? In the whole of the town? Why, we saw hundreds of cattle on the way.'

'The King says the Bachapins need the milk.'

James glared angrily at Sekootu whose wizened face was pointed at him like a ferret.

'All right,' he said. 'Ask him what he wants.'

There was a hurried consultation. 'The King says he wants Black Lightning.'

James sucked in his breath and his grip tightened on the rifle. 'A gun for a bowl of milk! Tell the King not to joke.'

'The King says for the gun he will give food and milk to us all every day we are here. He will also give two oxen and one elephant's tooth.'

James looked about him uncertainly. Giving up his rifle was like giving up his life. But what other choice was there? Without food they would die anyway and Robbie *had* to have the fresh milk. He was as thin as a twig. But his rifle . . . He looked down at it. Every instinct inherited from the Frontier made him reject the thought. And yet . . .

'Tell the King he can have the other gun.' He pointed to the fowling-piece.

'The King says he knows such guns. They are full of wind and smoke and kill little birds. His enemies are not little birds but men.'

Robbie was leaning against James's legs and he could feel the boy begin to tremble with exhaustion. 'All right,' he said to Stone-Axe, 'tell the King I agree.'

'I don't think that will be necessary,' said a voice in English. It was a curiously pedantic, over-exaggerated accent. Deep down in James something stirred. He swung round and saw Fitzhenry pushing his way through the crowd towards him.

'Well met, Sir Jamie,' Fitzhenry said. 'Well met indeed.' He caught James by the shoulders and looked into his eyes and said in a gentler tone: 'It's good to see you, boy.'

The crowd had parted to let him through and now they closed round again, boiling with interest and wonder. James was experiencing similar feelings. 'Where in God's name have you sprung from?' he asked in amazement.

'Oh, here and there,' Fitzhenry said. 'Hither and yon.' He turned to smile at Stone-Axe. 'You show a rare turn of speed, little man.' The Bushman smiled back uncomprehending.

King Mateebe, who had been watching the events with equal bewilderment now turned to Fitzhenry and with ill-grace began to speak, but Fitzhenry raised an arm and replied in the same tongue.

The King listened, frowning. He seemed about to say something more, decided against it and turned back into the hut followed closely by Sekootu. Mollende remained where he was, still fascinated by James's iron claw.

Fitzhenry drew James away. He pointed to Robbie: 'The lad looks all in.'

Stone-Axe had picked Robbie up and was holding him in his arms.

James said bitterly: 'And they wouldn't even give him milk.'

'I know. They would've before but things have got complicated. Why on earth did you bring a boy on something like this?'

'I don't understand.'

'I would have thought –' Fitzhenry shrugged. 'Still, it's nothing to do with me. Where are the others?'

'Others?'

Fitzhenry turned to look at him. 'Yes, the others. The commando.'

'There are no others.'

'I see,' Fitzhenry said thoughtfully. 'Well that changes things.'

James frowned with irritation. 'Look, I'm not –'

Fitzhenry put up a hand. 'Later,' he said. 'First let's look after the lad.' He led them through the maze of huts. He had put on weight and seemed much stronger, though his body was still on the slender side. The sun had tanned his skin and James could see that he was nearer fifty than forty. His hair and beard were iron-grey.

'You speak their language?' James said.

'Enough. Told old Mateebe it wasn't Christian custom to do business on an empty stomach. Very keen on etiquette, these people.'

'I was about to hand over my rifle.'

'I know. Got there just in time. It might have been the end of all of us.'

They had reached the outskirts of the town and James saw a large stockade in front of them. It was the sort of enclosure meant for cattle. But over the top of the reeds he could make out the white canvas of two wagons. Even then he did not realize their signifance. Too much had happened to him, there was too much he did not understand. His brain was as tired as his body. He had not yet really assimilated the fact that it *was* Fitzhenry. They turned into the enclosure, and the first person he saw was Frances. He stopped dead. His

199

mind reeled away in a series of leaps and somersaults. From a great distance he heard Fitzhenry say: 'Yes, it's himself, James Fraser Black of Inverness come to pay us a visit,' and then he felt Frances's hands on his arms and heard her say: 'Oh, Jamie, Jamie,' as she pressed her head to his chest. What he didn't see was the watchful expression in Fitzhenry's eyes.

It was evening of the following day and they sat now in the lamplit interior of one of the wagons – James, Fitzhenry and Frances – grouped round the pallet on which Dr Goodsir lay. His sunken cheeks were yellow with fever and covered with a sheen of sweat. The skin on top of his bald head had tightened on his skull like damp parchment. James had got over the first shock of seeing him and now sat silently with the others, the flow of talk checked for the moment in deference to the sick man.

James himself was feeling better. He had slept, after watching Frances take over Robbie with all the old acceptance of responsibility, for nearly twenty-four hours. Then he had made a meal of boiled rice, raisins and a big bowl of sour milk. His muscles and bones were still sore from the journey and though his mind remained sluggish the thought patterns were beginning to arrange themselves once more.

He tried to piece together what he had heard. Dr Goodsir's party had left the Cape six months before on a journey that was to have taken them north to the Bechuanas and then in a great sweep to the south-east to investigate a strange new ruler called Chaka who, so the rumours gave it, was welding a group of lesser tribes into a formidable nation called the Zoolus. He was said to be friendly to the few Christians who had landed on that part of the coast and Dr Goodsir was anxious to add the habits of the Zoolus to the habits of other tribes he had investigated. Fitzhenry, who had accompanied Dr Goodsir on four previous expeditions and was compiling their accounts into a work of travel, had come, naturally enough, to gather further material. Frances had come simply because she was Frances.

She had spent six years with relatives in Gloucestershire,

trying not to assimilate the English education and manners for which she had been sent, and had said flatly on her return that Europe meant nothing to her and that if Dr Goodsir wished her to remain at the Cape while he explored the unknown parts of southern Africa he would first have to drug her and then bind her in chains and then have her thrown into the Castle dungeons. Her uncle had given in gracefully; and secretly he had been delighted. He had sent her to England against his own inclinations because he had not wished her to sacrifice the chance of becoming a cultivated woman. He himself had no wish ever to return and had been quietly pleased to find his impressions of Europe confirmed. There were too many people; life was too complex; freedom was limited by convention.

At first the expedition had gone well. They had journeyed to the Rye Mountains, then drifted across the Karoo expecting a reunion with James at Bitterfountain but when they found he had long since married and gone they did not linger. About a fortnight later, when they were on the edge of the great plains, Stone-Axe joined them. They woke one morning to find him sitting at the fire, hunched in his kaross, exhausted and hungry. They welcomed him as a guide.

It was while they were travelling through the Bushman country south of the Great River that the strain began to tell on Dr Goodsir. He was now in his sixties and, although he would admit it to no one else, he knew this would probably be his last expedition. At the Great River he went down with fever. This was not unexpected since he had had recurring bouts for a number of years but what was significant was that it did not leave him after a few days as it usually did.

They camped on the banks of the Great River for a fortnight while he regained some of his strength. Frances was for turning back to the bracing air of the Snowy Mountains where he could recuperate, but Dr Goodsir was adamant.

They had come this far; they would go on.

Two days short of Litakun the fever had overtaken him again. This time it was even worse and for days his brain seemed to be affected. They had now been at Litakun for more than a month.

'At first they seemed to like us,' Frances said, referring to the Bachapins.

'Greedy devils,' Fitzhenry said.

'But not at first – except for tobacco. *Muchuko*, that's all we heard.'

'I know,' James said dryly. 'They haven't lost the taste.'

'But they gave us milk and meat.'

'And now we have to pay,' Fitzhenry said. 'We pay for everything, even a bowl of milk. So many beads for this, so many buttons for that, so many spans of tobacco for the other. They're like a tribe of displaced Venetians.'

'Mustn't judge too harshly,' Dr Goodsir said weakly. 'Could have slit our throats weeks ago. Taken what they wanted.'

'They're as timid as rabbits,' Fitzhenry said.

'Children,' Dr Goodsir said. 'Not rabbits. Like shiny things; beads, buttons, copper wire – and tobacco. No other opportunity of getting them; don't really blame them.'

'It's old Sekootu. He's the Shylock.'

'What will they do,' Frances asked, 'when they find we've almost nothing left?'

'I think they know,' Fitzhenry said. 'Someone must have been at the chests. Sekootu was after me again this morning about a gun. Told him we needed an ox for slaughtering and the cheeky fellow said we hadn't enough beads left to buy one. I don't know whether he meant that the bead market was glutted, but there was a shrewd look in his eyes.'

'Why don't we let them have the gun,' Frances said. 'Then they won't worry us any longer and you'd have time to get well again?'

Dr Goodsir shook his head and James got the impression they had been over this ground time and again. He sympathized. A gun was power and it was best to keep power.

Dr Goodsir said: 'Once they escort us safely back across the Great River they can have one. Mateebe knows this. I've told him several times.'

'Yes,' Fitzhenry said, 'and he's said as often that if you're going to give him one then, why not now.' They lapsed into silence again. Then Fitzhenry turned to James. 'Stone-Axe was our last hope. We thought he might get through to the Colony with the letter.'

'And the only thing he found was me,' James said.

Frances put out a hand and touched him on the arm without saying anything. Fitzhenry caught the gesture and frowned. He's jealous, James thought, with a shock of surprise.

'We were hoping for a dozen like you,' Fitzhenry said.

'About the gun,' James said. 'I offered him my fowling-piece and he turned it down flat. Said it couldn't kill enemies.'

'The Islanders,' Dr Goodsir said. 'They plunder the herds. Got a dozen guns between them.'

'Well, what could one gun do?'

'When you've never owned a gun before even one is a hundred times better than none.'

'When they get one they'll want a second and then a third,' Fitzhenry said.

Dr Goodsir nodded. 'My feelings precisely.'

James had been brooding on the problem and now he spoke again. 'If we were able to help them clear the Islanders, then –'

'What with?' Fitzhenry said. 'Two men and a girl? I've told you, the Bachapins are as timid as rabbits.'

Dr Goodsir's eyes had closed and in the lamplight his flesh was waxy. They rose silently from their seats on the almost-empty chests and crept from the wagon.

Litakun slept. It was a clear cool night and overhead the glittering stars wheeled across the sky in their millions.

'I'll look in on Robert,' James said.

Frances had taken the boy into her wagon, James and Fitzhenry slept round the fire with the Hottentot servants. Fitzhenry stood watching them until they climbed under the canvas then turned to his kaross near the fire.

The boy was sleeping athwart the rear of the wagon. The lamp had been turned down to its lowest and the shadows almost hid the crouching body of Stone-Axe. In his hands he held the fowling-piece. As James and Frances entered he left his place and dropped noiselessly to the ground.

'He was there all last night,' Frances whispered. 'I don't think he slept at all.'

'If anyone wanted to harm either one of you – or me for that matter – they'd have to cut him to pieces first.'

They looked down at the sleeping child. The shadows seemed to make his pinched cheeks appear even thinner but the dark smudges of exhaustion under his eyes had vanished.

'He's gey thin,' James said.

'He won't be for long,' Frances said. 'He had two bowls of milk today and he'll have them every day if I've got to barter all the guns we've got.' She bent and pulled the coarse blanket up to his neck letting her fingers trail lightly across his cheeks. 'He's beautiful,' she said. 'In a way it's lucky he was so young. I mean, he won't remember much.'

'I hope not.'

Robbie stirred slightly and she stroked his hair and said softly: 'There, there, it's all right.' In his sleep the boy reached out with his hand feeling for her and she let it clasp round her fingers. 'He held onto me like this for hours last night,' she said.

'He's missing her.'

She nodded and after a while said: 'She must have been very lovely, Jamie.'

'Yes. She was.'

Frances looked up at him. 'Tell me about her.'

He had told them briefly of the journey through the Bushman country which ended with Lisé's death but had left out the details. His omissions were almost subconscious but now he felt a need to tell Frances. He kept nothing back. He told her everything he could remember about his relationship with Lisé from the beginning. It seemed that once he started he could not stop. At first he spoke slowly, searching for the right words, but then he began to breathe more quickly and sentences came tumbling out of his mouth with a rapidity unusual for him.

His tone rose and the boy turned in his sleep, troubled by the torrent of words. His hand gripped Frances more fiercely and she smoothed his hair in regular soothing sweeps. At no time did she try to stop James or interrupt him, sensing that this was a moment of catharsis.

It was only when he reached the last stages of their journey together that his narrative slowed and his voice grew anguished and when he had finished her cheeks were wet with tears and his own eyes were brimming.

They were silent for a long time before she spoke. 'She must have loved you very much.'

Missing the point of the remark, he nodded slowly and said: 'It was the bravest thing I've ever known.'

'And now you're blaming yourself.'

'I can't avoid it.' Then suddenly he said with bitter shame in his voice: 'I've tried to blame everyone else, you see.'

'I could say it's not your fault,' she said, 'and it would be true. But it wouldn't help at present. You'll live with it because you want to live with it but in spite of that it'll pass.'

But there were some things, he thought, that didn't pass. He remembered the dying words of the Reverend Harmsworth: *You will never be forgiven for this day*, and he felt something inside him cringe.

They sat with their own thoughts for a while and then he said softly: 'Do you love Fitzhenry?'

She looked up. 'Why?'

'I'd like to know.'

'I'm not sure.'

'That's strange for you – being uncertain, I mean. You always seemed so sure of everything at Paradise.'

'Perhaps one is at that age. I know what you mean, though. Someone had to be a tyrant, nothing would ever have got done otherwise, with Uncle Henry the way he was. But I didn't care for it. I'd rather have had someone to guide me.'

'Like Fitzhenry,' James said.

'Yes, like Fitzhenry. Remember how we used to call him Mr Fitz?'

He nodded. 'It seems a long time ago.'

'I think we misjudged Mr Fitz,' she said. 'That foppish manner only runs skin deep. Underneath it there's kindness and strength. Oh, there is. You'd be surprised. And sadness too – that above all.'

'He's in love with you.'

'Yes, I know. Before I left he was just a sort of friendly relative living at Paradise and then, when I got back, things seemed to change. He seemed nervous of me in a way I can't explain and that made *me* nervous.'

He studied her in the half-light, seeing the golden hair and the fine chiselling of the face, the slight swell of the breasts. No wonder, he thought, that things had changed.

'It was funny Mr Fitz being nervous,' she went on. 'Even the servants noticed it and when they saw us together they would smile behind their hands in an irritating way. It was only after a month or so I realized what they were smiling at.'

'Has he asked you to marry him?'

'Yes.'

'And?'

'I told him I'd give him my answer when we returned.'

'Do you think you will?'

'I think so. I think I can make him happy and that's what he needs more than anything. He's been desperately hard wounded.'

'How's that?'

She shook her head. 'He'll tell you if he wants you to know.'

He felt an abrupt spasm of jealousy. He and Frances had always been like brother and sister; but now *that* had changed too.

'You wouldn't marry him from pity,' he said.

She smiled gently at him. 'If I marry him the reasons'll be my own, Jamie.'

'I'm sorry. I shouldn't have said that.'

'Time has passed,' she said. 'People change.'

'I'm being mule-headed,' he said. 'For the past few days time seems to have turned tumble. But you're right. It's different.' He touched her hand with his fingers. 'Whatever you do I wish you to know I wish you well, Fran. It's just that . . . oh, I don't know . . . I wish sometimes that things could've been different . . .'

'I've wished that many times.'

They fell silent for a while and then he said: 'Where will you live?'

'At Paradise, I suppose. Though I'd rather live in the wilds somewhere, the real Africa. Life at the Cape is a little too much like England.'

'You didn't care for that?'

'I hated it.'

'Do you remember our place up on the mountain under the pines?'

She nodded. 'I used to go up there after you'd gone and lie in the wind and look out over the land and wonder what you were doing.'

'When did you last go there?'

'Just before we . . .' She flushed. 'That was unfair.'

'And did you take Fitzhenry with you?'

'No, I did not. And now I think it's time you were going. You're beginning to confuse me.'

He paused as he climbed down over the *disselboom* and looked back but she was already bending over the child.

Fitzhenry was still awake near the fire. 'Is the boy all right?' he asked.

'Yes.'

'I wondered; you took a long time.'

As the days passed James realized that what everyone was waiting for was some sign of change – either for better or worse – in Dr Goodsir. Even the Bachapins were waiting. There was a curious air of suspension.

The Christians were left severely alone and even the group of Bachapins, who used to stand around the wagons from early morning to afternoon waiting hopefully for gifts of tobacco, finally stopped coming. Each day Fitzhenry and James would take a couple of spans of tobacco or a few beads from the rapidly dwindling stock, and go into the town to barter for milk and beef.

'I suppose we've got something to be thankful for at least,' Fitzhenry remarked one morning as they brought back the meagre supplies to the silence of the camp.

'What's that?'

'Leaving us like lepers, I mean. At first when we bought a cow for slaughtering the whole of the Royal Household would descend on us to help eat it up. Expensive habit that.'

His remarks only served to heighten their feeling of isolation. Even the children shunned Robbie.

James had sensed early what the real trouble was. They were leaderless; they were waiting for something to happen. They were playing into King Mateebe's hands. Once the trade goods ran out there would only be the guns and even if the Bachapins kept their side of the bargain and delivered the oxen in exchange, how far south would they get without rifles? However, just knowing did not help and he was too apathetic to do much more than sit in the shade of the wagon and smoke his pipe.

Then, about two weeks after his arrival, something happened which precipitated action. One day after the midday meal King Mateebe arrived with his entourage.

James was in his usual place playing absentmindedly with Robbie when he heard Stone-Axe's low mutter. 'Claw. People.' The Bushman had kept a safe distance from the Bachapins since his return, only venturing out into the town with James. Bushmen were not highly regarded among the Bachapins who spent nearly as much energy as the Frontier graziers in hunting them down. James had already seen four or five slave-children haunting the streets like yellow ghosts and once had been offered, for a three-finger span of tobacco, a child so drawn, thin and pot-bellied that when he had pushed roughly past the owner he had hurried back to the wagons to stare down at the sleeping form of Robbie.

He rose to his feet and reached into the tented wagon for his rifle. Stone-Axe stood half a pace behind him. Fitzhenry was away trying to find game and he had seen Frances go into Dr Goodsir's wagon some time before. He stepped out and approached the King. King Mateebe was surrounded by nine or ten people and he could make out the inevitable Sekootu at his side. Behind him towered the benign figure of Mollende.

'Give my greetings and welcome to the King,' James said

to Stone-Axe. The Bushman stepped forward and then, perhaps because he sensed a moment of trial had been reached or perhaps because of the ghost-children he had seen in the streets, he drew himself up to his full diminutive height and delivered himself in the epic style. 'Behold!' he cried. 'The Lion speaks! The Great Bull Calf! The Eland's Son! Slayer of Python! Man of Men! It is Claw Iron-Hand who speaks!'

The King looked up in shocked amazement, Sekootu was staring at Stone-Axe with ill-concealed malevolence and the rest of the party glanced at each other nervously. Only Mollende's expression remained unchanged.

James had been almost as surprised as the others and now, with a tight half-smile on his face, he saw Stone-Axe start out on his stiff-legged strut to stop half a dozen paces from King Mateebe. 'Yeah!' he cried again. 'It is I, Axe of Stone, the mouth of Claw! What sayest thou?'

James felt something inside him stir; his heart began to beat more firmly, his muscles contracted, his back straightened, his apathy fell away like a cloak. Then his voice rang out. 'Ask the King why we merit the honour of a visit?' The question was courteously phrased but even though the Bachapins did not know what the words meant they felt their cutting edge.

The King seemed about to answer when Sekootu stepped to one side and made a beckoning motion behind him. There was a movement at the gate of the stockade and six red and white bullocks were driven through the gate. Then Sekootu turned to James once more and said: 'We have come for the gun. This was the price agreed.'

James ignored him, speaking directly at the King through Stone-Axe. 'The King knows full well the gun is to be handed over only once we are past the Great River. The King also knows that by bringing the oxen now he is trying to force us to go against our word. Tell the King I see this plan as clearly as the stones on the bottom of a mountain pool.'

This was duly delivered with all the majesty at Stone-Axe's command and James heard Mollende's loud laugh roll over the stockade. The King, ensnared in a mesh not of his own making, rounded angrily on Sekootu who seemed to be trying to lose himself among the others. Then King Mateebe, in a tone much subdued, turned to Stone-Axe. 'The King asks if he may just look at the gun, O Claw.'

James was about to open his mouth and issue a firm refusal when Dr Goodsir's weak voice called to him from the inside of the wagon.

'Tell the King,' James said, 'that Claw would speak with the Old One.'

He climbed under the tent where Frances was sponging Dr Goodsir's face and neck.

'You heard?' James said.

'Yes.'

'I'm going to say no. We've got them confused.'

'No, let him see it.'

'But . . .'

'It can't do any harm. Show them we're still friendly. Could wipe us all out in the night if they felt like it.'

'Yes, but. . .'

'They'll go away and brood. You made them lose face.'

'All right,' James said reluctantly. 'Which gun is it?'

'Mine,' Dr Goodsir said. 'So it won't make *that* much difference.'

James reached up and took the musket from its hooks and jumped down lightly from the wagon-tree. 'Tell the King the Old One says he may see the gun.'

There was an expectant chatter from the Bachapins as they crowded round. James noticed that the crestfallen expression had disappeared from Sekootu's face and his eyes were filled with shrewd satisfaction. Suddenly James found himself wondering why they only wanted to inspect the gun, something he was certain they had done on several occasions. And then, in a flash, he realized that they had played right into Sekootu's hands.

The King stepped forward and spoke again; there was nothing subdued in his voice this time.

'The King wishes to see the gun fired,' Stone-Axe said.

So that was it. If he refused now a great deal more face would have been lost, perhaps too much for their safety.

'All right,' James said. 'We will go to the edge of the town.'

He turned to Stone-Axe and spoke quickly in a low voice. The Bushman was clearly puzzled but he nodded his head and hopped swiftly into Dr Goodsir's wagon. In a few moments he was back, still clutching the fowling-piece which seemed as much a part of him now as his bow had ever done.

They moved off through the empty spaces of the town, gathering the inquisitive inhabitants as they went until, by the time they reached the bare veld on the outskirts, a fair-sized crowd had collected.

The King and his family and advisers stood on one side, the crowd on the other and James and Stone-Axe alone in the middle. There was a certain hesitancy among the Bachapins about getting too close to Christian weapons and for a moment they were restive as those at the back pressed forward while those in front dug in their heels and tried to stop themselves from being precipitated into the area of fire.

About a hundred paces away a gnarled mokaal tree struggled up from the earth and from one of its branches hung a bird's nest. It was at this that the King now pointed. He wanted James to fire at it. James was a better than average marksman but the nest was moving gently in the breeze and he knew that the chances of hitting it were slight.

'Tell the King,' he said aloofly, 'that as he rightly says this gun is not for shooting little birds, but let him watch closely and I will show him something that even the Christians wonder at.' He put his hand into his pocket and drew out a length of tobacco. There was an immediate stir of interest. It was about six inches long and resembled a piece of thick rope.

'The Bushman Stone-Axe will stand the same distance as the tree,' James continued, 'and he will hold the *muchuko* in his mouth. Then we shall see.' Stone-Axe, who had been freely translating James's phrases into the more elaborate epic language of the Bushman, suddenly stopped as he became aware of what he was saying. He turned to James, his yellow skin a shade paler. 'Claw,' he began, 'thou art certainly the Great Bull –'

'Silence!' James commanded.

King Mateebe was watching intently and the crowd as soon

as they realized what was about to happen, began to giggle in delight.

James caught Stone-Axe roughly by the shoulder and began to drag him across the veld. The little Bushman, wearing an expression of sad confusion, allowed himself to be pushed and pulled as though going to the gibbet.

As soon as they were out of earshot James talked softly out of the corner of his mouth and he felt Stone-Axe relax somewhat under his hand. He stood him in profile to the crowd and placed the length of tobacco between his lips, then marched back to his original position. He carefully loaded the rifle. Stone-Axe seemed no bigger than an ant-heap; the tobacco, sticking out sideways, only just visible.

James took careful aim and fired. The crowd, who had been watching every action in awed silence, now broke out into a roar as they saw something jerk from the Bushman's mouth and fall to the ground.

When the smoke cleared from James's head he could see Stone-Axe bending over. He suddenly straightened, held something aloft and began running towards them. James prayed that he'd understood.

Half the crowd ran across the veld to meet him, setting up a howl of triumph as they saw what he held. Stone-Axe came to a halt before James and handed him the tobacco. The ball had sheared it off about two-thirds of the way along, leaving the end torn and frayed. James handed the *muchuko* cere-moniously to King Mateebe.

The King had lost much of his regal dignity in the past few minutes. He had been almost as excited as his subjects and now, as he stared at the shattered target, his eyes opened wide in wonder.

Twice more James aimed at the target and twice more Stone-Axe returned with evidence of his remarkable accuracy.

Then Sekootu said: 'The King wishes to shoot the gun.'

'He'll kill the Bushman,' James said.

King Mateebe spoke again and James waited for Stone-Axe to translate. 'Well?' he said at last.

'The King says,' Stone-Axe muttered, 'that there are many Bushmen. He will find you another.'

'Ask the King where he will find another brave enough to stand with *muchuko* in his mouth?'

King Mateebe pondered this for a moment and then shrugged. 'The King says he will shoot into the skies.'

'All right.' James loaded the musket and handed it to the King. He took it gingerly and then, aping James, placed it to his shoulder, pointed the barrel skywards, closed his eyes and jerked on the trigger. The gun went off with a roar and for a moment the King was wreathed in black smoke. Then his grinning face emerged. James waited for the gun. But suddenly the King turned, handed the musket to Sekootu and stood with folded arms.

'The King says the gun is now his. He has paid the oxen and he has fired it.'

Ever since the exhibition had begun James had been expecting something on these lines. He reached for the fowling-piece.

'Tell the King we will now test the bird-gun. Tell him that unless the musket is returned I will make Sekootu sing like a bird.'

Sekootu had already become uneasy and had detached himself from the crowd. He was making his way towards the first line of huts.

King Mateebe did not move. He stood there with his arms folded, impassive, daring James to an open act of violence against one of his people. James knew that if he killed Sekootu their own lives would be over in a matter of minutes, but at the same time if he didn't fire, the carefully-created image of himself as a mysterious iron-clawed stranger who could outshoot anyone the Bachapins had ever seen, would disintegrate. Equally, if he fired to miss, Sekootu would simply go on and the gun would be lost – as the King and Sekootu obviously meant it to be. He had been watching Sekootu's movements, and now as he reached the limit of the weapon's range, James suddenly raised it to his shoulder and fired.

The result was spectacular. Sekootu who had been half-running half-walking seemed to be propelled abruptly forward. His legs churned, his body jerked, and then he was lying flat on his face screeching like a flock of crows.

No one had expected James to fire, least of all the King. His face became suffused with anger. He spoke once sharply and James felt his hook held in a powerful grip as Mollende's hands closed on it. There was nothing he could do; the giant Bachapin held him as though he were a child.

Several of the crowd had run towards Sekootu who was still screeching at the top of his voice. Then one turned and ran back, a puzzled look on his face. He said something to King Mateebe who hurried forward, beckoning Mollende to bring James.

They found themselves staring down at Sekootu's quivering black buttocks. Here and there blood was oozing from tiny holes, in other places the black skin was punctured by what looked like white crystals. The King bent down, picked up one of the larger crystals, looked at it carefully and then placed it on his tongue.

'Tell the King,' James said, 'that there is a saying among the Christians that if you wish to catch a bird, first put salt on its tail.'

There was a pause as the crowd digested this aphorism and then suddenly, as one, they burst into shriek after shriek of laughter. Even the King's face began to tremble and tears streamed down his cheeks and James could hear the great roar of Mollende's enjoyment in his ears and feel the delighted blows which the giant was raining on his back. And in each pause, as the crowd drew breath, the painful screeches of Sekootu added fuel to the humour until everyone was almost helpless with laughter.

For the first time James realized that sweat was dripping down the inside of his trouser legs.

'I don't like it,' Fitzhenry said for the second time.

He had returned from a fruitless chase after quagga and had entered Dr Goodsir's wagon in the early evening to find

James and Frances seated on the chests, James in the middle of his story of the events that had occurred. He had listened with the others in a fretful silence, caused half by his lack of success in finding meat and half for a reason he would have been hard put to define.

'I'm not asking you to like it,' James snapped. He had borne Fitzhenry's edginess with silence up to now and he was faintly surprised to hear the bleakness in his own tone.

Since his arrival at Litakun he had been fighting an unconscious battle inside himself against authority. Fitzhenry and even Dr Goodsir had taken up the same adult positions they had held in respect of James's youth at Paradise and this had confused him to the extent that he had waited for the older people to give him a lead and, finding none, had relapsed into a fatalistic apathy. But Stone-Axe had shown him the path that afternoon and he had taken it with all his old self-confidence.

'I beg your pardon?' Fitzhenry queried.

'I said I'm not asking you to like it.' This time his voice was lower but the authority remained and he was aware of Frances's eyes, worried and frowning, fixed on the two of them.

Dr Goodsir raised a weak hand. 'Let him be, let him be,' he said to Fitzhenry. 'Go on, James.'

'Well, when they found that Sekootu was yelling his head off and all he had was a backside full of rock salt, they almost fell down laughing, even the King – and that big fellow Mollende, the King's bodyguard, he laughed so much I thought he'd crack.'

Dr Goodsir was smiling. He was looking better than he had for days. 'Queer sense of humour these people have. Saw one of them get knocked about by a bullock one day. Rather badly too. Had to set an arm. You'd have thought it was the funniest thing they'd seen in years.'

James nodded. 'I was banking on it. Something similar happened when I arrived and it made me think. That's why I got Stone-Axe to load with salt. I had a feeling Sekootu would try something tricky.'

'You think it was only Sekootu?'

'Probably all in it. But when he got the worst of it they were happy enough to reject him.'

'They won't for long,' Fitzhenry said. 'They'll brood about it. He won't let them forget the real purpose of the demonstration.'

'I know,' said James. 'But it might take them a while – every time Sekootu forgets and tries to sit down they see the joke all over again. But the point is they think I'm a hell of a fine fellow at the moment – iron hand, remarkable shot, servant with the courage of a lion, expert at debate, brilliant exponent of humorous rough justice. Oh yes, they were filling me up with beer and Mollende was trying to buy my hook and old Sekootu was standing on the other side of the hut looking at me as though he'd like to wear my entrails round his neck.'

'And you say,' Dr Goodsir interposed, 'that Stone-Axe really thought you were going to shoot the tobacco from his mouth.'

'I swear he went three shades lighter,' James said and Dr Goodsir chuckled to himself.

'But you loaded with ball, didn't you?'

'Yes, but I fired wide. Then as he heard the shot he spat out the tobacco, bent to pick it up, forced a twig through it, broke off one end and fretted it a bit and then came running back. He played up wonderfully when he knew he wasn't going to get a ball through the head.'

'All I can say is you're damn lucky,' Fitzhenry put in.

'Perhaps you're right,' James said, 'but you never know how lucky you are until you try.'

'And now?' Dr Goodsir said.

'Now I'm going to try the Island. At the moment the Bachapins think I'm some sort of wizard so I've made an agreement –'

'*You've* made an agreement,' Fitzhenry said angrily.

'Please,' Frances said. 'Let James finish.'

'We clear out the Islanders and they give us forty bullocks and twelve elephants' teeth and see us safely on our way through the Bushman country.'

'And you say the Bachapins agreed to go on the expedition.'

'Well,' James said. 'Not exactly. But I think I can . . .'

'Ah,' Fitzhenry said heavily.

James felt anger flick at him. He was about to turn to Fitzhenry when he saw the appeal in Frances's eyes and he held himself in and turned back to Dr Goodsir. 'I think I know how to make it work,' he said, 'but first tell me all you know about the Islanders.'

'Well, it's only hearsay,' Dr Goodsir began. 'Originally the part of the Great River nearest here was infested with a gang of bandits called the Jäger Hottentots. At one time they used to live much nearer the Cape, but during the first British Occupation, a rumour went round that all Hottentots were going to be forcibly conscripted into the Army. Nonsense of course but the Jägers believed it and they followed their leader, Africaander, out of the Colony. Set up camp on the banks of the Great River and plundered wherever they wished. Reduced some smaller tribes to starvation. Wiped out others. Camp became a home for every wandering cut-throat and thief in the land.

'When they'd plundered the countryside they moved off into the country of the Namaquas to the west. But a dozen or so remained on an island. Christians mainly, or people who called themselves Christians – army deserters, murderers, riff-raff. All of them well-armed.'

'That's not as many as I thought,' James said.

'But too many,' Fitzhenry put it. 'Twelve armed men on horseback could route five hundred spears on foot. Specially if they got 'em in open country.'

'That's true,' James said. 'But the object would be not to be caught on open ground.'

'You mean an assault on the Island itself?' Dr Goodsir asked.

'Why not?'

'Because no one's found a way of reaching it,' Fitzhenry said.

'You mean no one's tried,' James said flatly.

At that moment there was noise of a commotion outside the

wagon and he could hear Stone-Axe's voice. He reached for his rifle and jumped down onto the ground. The darkness was broken by a dozen flickering torches. He could make out King Mateebe and members of his bodyguard and then he saw Mollende. The giant was holding something in his arms and when James saw what it was he felt each hair on his body stiffen. It was the dead body of a Bachapin. His genitals had been hacked off, his entrails hung out of his stomach in glistening tresses and his face was so badly damaged as to be unrecognizable.

No one spoke until at last James said: 'What is it? What's happened?'

The King spoke to Stone-Axe and he had no need of translation to hear the accusatory tone.

What had happened was quite simple, almost stark in the telling. The mutilated body had once been a Bachapin herdsman. He had been found tied to a tree, already dead. The method of his dying had been devised by the Islanders, of that no one seemed in any doubt, since its very viciousness was meant to induce terror into the tribe. After killing the herdsman the Islanders had driven off more than a hundred head of cattle.

The King motioned to Mollende who let the body drop at James's feet. Then he spoke again.

Stone-Axe said: 'The King says if the Bachapins had guns this would not have happened, O Claw. The death rests with the Christians.'

James was suddenly angry. 'Tell the King,' he shouted, 'that with his help we will rid him of the Islanders. Tell him that's what I've been trying to explain. Tell him that if the Bachapins had more courage they could have wiped out the Islanders themselves a long time ago.'

But King Mateebe had already turned on his heel and he and his entourage moved slowly from the stockade, leaving the body of the herdsman. Later James and Stone-Axe dragged it to the outskirts of the town and covered it with stones.

The following day there was an ominous silence in Litakun. When James and Fitzhenry went out to barter for food they found the streets empty and the huts closed to them. The few people they did meet shook their heads and said there was no milk, no maize, no beef. They made do with a little boiled rice and a handful of raisins each.

Fitzhenry said: 'A week of this and the guns will be here for the taking.'

Dr Goodsir had weakened during the night and Frances was now continually at his side. Most of the time Fitzhenry stayed with her.

James felt curiously left out and he returned to his place in the shade of the wagon and tried to make some sense of what had happened. And then, in the middle of the afternoon he had a visitor.

Sekootu came hobbling into the stockade and James remembered that he had not been amongst the King's party the night before. Sekootu raised his hand. 'Greeting, Iron-Claw,' he said. James raised his own hand. He said to Stone-Axe: 'Tell Sekootu I am glad to see him in good health.'

The wily old Bachapin managed a sickly smile.

'Ask him if he will not sit? It is surely more comfortable than standing in the sun.'

'Sekootu says he is used to the sun,' Stone-Axe translated, grinning widely.

James shrugged. 'As he wishes. Ask Sekootu to what we owe the pleasure of his visit? Has he come to bring us food? Does he know that the people will no longer barter with us?'

'Sekootu knows. It is not his wish, but the King's.'

So Sekootu was no longer the King's trusted adviser. James stored this piece of information away.

'Ask Sekootu what we can do for him?'

'He wishes to know how Claw will attack the Islanders?'

James looked at him carefully. 'Tell Sekootu that without help there can be no attack.'

'But if help is given?'

'Can he arrange such a thing?'

'It is possible, Claw.'

'Ask him why he does this now? Why not before?'

Sekootu remained silent for some moments and then said: 'Because of the King's cattle.'

Things suddenly began to fall into place. This was part of the King's personal herd which had been stolen. The murder of the herdsman had meant little or nothing, it was the cattle that were important. And Sekootu knew it. If he could come up with a plan which could restore the cattle and only risk the lives of the strangers and perhaps a few Bachapins he'd be back to his old position, stronger than ever before. And, of course, if the Islanders and the strangers slaughtered each other their weapons would be there for the taking.

'How many men would the King send?' James asked.

Sekootu shrugged. 'That would be for the King to say.'

'Tell the King I will think about it,' James said. 'I will give him my answer tonight.'

It was well after midnight when he returned to the wagons. He was tired and frustrated after hours of arguing with King Mateebe. Frances was still with Dr Goodsir and James climbed inside the wagon-tent. The strain of the Doctor's illness was beginning to tell on her and in the soft lamplight her face looked tense and drawn. James felt the weight of renewed and great responsibility. There was not only Robbie to worry about but Frances and Dr Goodsir and, if it came to that, Fitzhenry.

He looked down with pity at the old man. Each day now he seemed to shrink still further.

'I've had to change his blankets twice tonight,' Frances said wearily.

Dr Goodsir was dripping wet. It was as though all the lifeforce in his body was escaping through his pores and eventually only a dried-up husk would be left. She gently wiped away the sweat from his face and neck and he moaned and twisted as a new spasm shook his body.

After a while James said: 'The King's agreed.'

'Does that matter now?'

Sensing her desperation he nodded at Dr Goodsir and said: 'You couldn't move him anyway. It would take a month to get to high ground and he'd be dead long before that.'

'How do you *know*? You can't tell. It may be his only chance!'

'Don't you think I feel the same way about Robbie?' he said bitterly. 'But how far do you think we'd get without our weapons. And don't make any mistake, that would be the price of our leaving.'

Wrangling with King Mateebe who, when the final moment came seemed to have neither the power nor the wish to commit his warriors to battle and had stood fast on a figure of ten spears with Mollende to command them, James had felt tempted to sacrifice the guns. But then he had remembered the slave-children, scavenging among the dogs for food. Was that where Robbie might end? From talks with Dr Goodsir he had learnt that the Bachapins were basically a peaceful and rather timid people. He knew that in the past other, more warlike tribes had poured out of the north and decimated them. Even the present Litakun was a make-shift capital, a temporary resting place after the sacking of their former kraal. Only guns could secure its future safety. But whose need was greatest?

'Stone-Axe could guide us through the worst,' Frances said.

'You're forgetting,' he said gently. 'Stone-Axe nearly died going through alone. How much less of a chance would we all have?'

'Oh God,' she said, tears showing brightly in her eyes. 'I can't *stand* it any longer. Not for myself, but for Uncle Henry. Every day there seems less and less of him. Jamie, we've got to *do* something.'

He nodded. 'We are going to do something. The King has agreed to ten warriors and Mollende. And then there'll be myself and Stone-Axe and . . . and Fitzhenry.' He looked swiftly up to her. 'I'm sorry, Fran. We'll need him.'

'Yes, I know.'

'But I'll bring him back, don't worry. We'll all be back soon.' He added flatly: 'I have a talent for killing in safety.'

'I want you both back,' she whispered.

He let the significance of the remark slip past him. He was unwilling to step onto the dangerous ground it would lead to.

He remembered a different feeling and a different scene before he left Lisé to go on the commando. This time he was not going on a light-hearted mission of reprisal. He wanted no complications to cloud his thinking. He knew that his mind would have to be as clear and cold as ice.

'We'll be back,' he said. 'But if . . .' he saw the immediate flicker of alarm in her eyes and knew she was not thinking about herself. He reached out and took her hand, feeling again the almost-forgotten response. 'But just in case, there's a mission station near the Great River. I've never been there but the Hottentots will know of it; go there. Do you understand?'

She nodded miserably.

'Here,' he said, wiping away the tears that were beginning to roll down her cheeks. 'Don't weep for us yet.'

The north bank of the Great River was as tangled as a primeval forest. The growth was prodigious; willows and buffalo-thorn, karree-trees and acacias, and the space between filled with heavy bush most of whose branches wore curved spines. All around was the shrill of birds: the rattle of the wood-cutter banging the bark with his beak for insects, sparrows and thrushes, finches, wood pigeons, Namaqua doves, butcher birds – and deep in the thickets the impatient clanking of guinea fowl.

There was only one way to penetrate it and that was by following the tracks of river horses, as one would the tortuous paths of a maze. This they had done and now James, Fitzhenry, Stone-Axe and Mollende were tucked down behind a shield of bulrushes. Ten picked warriors were hidden in the thickets behind them. James looked across the stretch of foaming yellow water to the Island. What he saw was in no way heartening; it was a natural fortress.

To their left, about a quarter of a mile upstream, was a waterfall about two hundred feet high. At the top of the falls and directly in the middle of the river an outcrop of rock caused the torrent to split. Over the centuries the river had cut its twin paths deeper and deeper so that from the angle they were looking there were in fact two waterfalls divided by massive sandstone cliffs. These, speckled by swallows' nests, dropped down almost sheer to water level but instead of ending abruptly rose again into a hog's back. This was the Island. At its rear it was protected by cliffs, its flanks were secured by the twin streams, compressed after their long drop into narrow channels; in front of the Island was the great spread of the re-united river.

The four men looked at the fortress and its barriers in silence. Each carried a gun except Mollende who had two throwing assegais in his left hand and an iron-shod knobkerrie in his right. Round his neck hung a short-handled knife. They were dusty and unkempt, the result of travelling fast by night and sleeping rough in thickets of grass during the day. James still wore his leather jacket and trousers and, although he was uncomfortably hot, they had protected his body again and again from ripping thorns.

'It's impossible,' Fitzhenry said at last. 'There's been rain in the mountains. The river is much higher than I remember it. There's no way to reach the Island from this side.'

'There has to be,' James said. 'They do it.'

'If you ask me we'd have done better to send Stone-Axe south again.'

'To let the crows have another chance at his eyes?'

'I didn't mean that.'

'No, but it's what would have happened.'

Since they'd left Litakun there had been further friction between them. Several times James had been on the point of turning angrily on the older man but then he had remembered Frances and checked himself. In a way he understood Fitzhenry's dilemma. He felt responsible for Frances and Dr Goodsir. He had done well to get them to the Bachapins in the first place; he was not to be blamed for things going wrong. And yet – James knew that if he had been there from the beginning *something* would have happened by now. He would have *made* it happen.

'Claw!' The Bushman's voice was low and urgent. 'People.'

James focused his eyes on the near side of the Island. He saw something move among the acacia trees.

'How many?'

'T'oa-t'oa-t'oa-t'oa-t'oa.'

'Ten,' James said.

'I can only see two or three,' Fitzhenry said.

'You haven't got Bushman eyes.'

'There!' Fitzhenry said. 'More of them.'

James watched in silence. The Island was heavily bushed on the top of the hog's back but the bush thinned as the ground levelled out at the water's edge. Red and white cattle were grazing everywhere. In among the trees he could see the outlines of grass huts and it was from these that the people had come. In the centre of a small clearing a fire was burning and they squatted down around it.

'They've got women with them,' Fitzhenry said.

'Midday meal,' James said, feeling the need for food himself. He turned to Stone-Axe. 'Hottentots?' The Bushman had turned and was looking into the bush over his left shoulder. Somewhere a bird was crying: 'Cherr – cherr – cherr – cherr.'

James touched him sharply on the shoulder and he turned slowly back. 'Hottentots?'

'Yes, Claw.'

'Cherr – cherr – cherr – cherr.'

'What is it?'

Stone-Axe had risen on one knee and was peering back into the bush of the river bank. And then, from the middle of a buffalo-thorn, hopped a small grey-green bird with a light yellow beak and bright yellow patches on its wings.

It flapped away a few yards, perched again, and made the same calling sound. The Bushman answered the bird with a low whistle.

'Stay where you are,' James said to Stone-Axe, but the Bushman had already slipped from the cover of the bulrushes and was moving towards the bird.

'Stone-Axe!' James hissed angrily. 'Damn you, come here!'

The bird once more flew on a few paces and stopped. 'Cherr – cherr!' it said to Stone-Axe.

224

'Blast you, come back, d'you hear!'

Stone-Axe melted into the thick bush like a ray of yellow sunlight.

'What's wrong?' Fitzhenry whispered. 'What's the matter with him?'

'It's no good,' James said angrily. 'He won't stop now.'

'What's happening?'

'The bird,' James said. 'Honey-guide. It's leading him to wild honey. When he breaks open the hive he'll leave some for the bird.'

'You mean he's gone looking for honey *now*?' Fitzhenry said, unbelieving.

'I've threatened to knock his head off several times but you'll never keep a Bushman from honey no matter what the stakes are. Anyway, there's nothing we can do till dark and he'll be back long before then.'

'But what if he's seen?'

'You can rest assured on that. If he doesn't want to be seen no human eyes will see him.'

James saw Mollende stiffen and follow his glance to the Island. Two others had joined the group. 'White men?' James asked, and Mollende nodded.

The midday sun glared down out of clear skies striking the water at right-angles, producing on it a sheen like polished metal. Every wavelet seemed to give off golden sparks as it moved. James had closed his eyes to slits but even so he had to look away every now and then. The heat in the thick bush became unbearable. He tried to concentrate on what they had come to do.

Ten spears and four guns against twelve guns. They were not the odds he would have chosen. Fitzhenry was right; it was pretty near impossible. But if they were able to cross they'd have surprise on their side and James was a great believer in surprise. The annihilation of the Bushman village had taught him that.

A dozen more spears – half a dozen – and there would have been no doubt about the outcome. But King Mateebe had been withdrawn; almost indifferent about the loss of cattle.

Perhaps it had been Sekootu's influence again. No matter what happened now the Bachapins would get what they wanted in the end.

They scouted the banks, each taking a different area, but when they met again in the cover of the bulrushes none had found a possible crossing place and neither Fitzhenry nor James thought it feasible to try the cliffs at night.

'One of us'll go downstream, the other up and we'll find a fording-place,' James said, 'and then we can have a look at the other side. It might be easier.'

Fitzhenry looked up swiftly at the authority in his voice. 'You've come a long way,' he said. 'It really *is* Lord James Fraser Black now, is it not?'

He was about to reply when there was a sudden rustling in the bush and Stone-Axe appeared. His face and hands were still sticky with honey, his skin was covered in dirt and animal droppings and in the close stillness of the riverbank he stank abominably.

'Where the hell have you been?' James said angrily.

Stone-Axe smiled guiltily and James could see the angry bee-sting bumps on his face and neck. He had followed the honey-guide to a ledge a quarter way down the cliffs and had found not one, but six hives. He had robbed one and then the bees had come after him like enraged hornets and he had been forced to wriggle into the labyrinthine passageway of a rock-rabbit to avoid them. His smell was a ripe mixture of hyrax and urine.

'But Claw,' he continued. 'I have seen a place. Come.'

They followed him through the thick bush, always keeping to the trampled paths of the river horses. Stone-Axe led them along the bank until they came to the foot of the nearest cliffs. He then struck out at right-angles to the river and after about half a mile the bush thinned out and they found they could clamber easily up the slope ahead of them and come out on top of the cliffs.

As soon as they neared the river again Stone-Axe made them crawl through the grass so they would not be outlined against the sky. They found themselves looking at the Island from an entirely different angle. On their immediate left was the first waterfall, then came the buttress of rock that split the river and fell away again into the hog's back and beyond the buttress the second fall. The Island looked just as secure.

'There,' Stone-Axe said, and James followed his pointing finger.

'What?' he said, frowning. 'I don't – wait – wait yes, I see.'

What the Bushman had seen when he was collecting the honey was now apparent. From the height at which they were looking the water was much clearer and in many parts it was possible to see the bottom. Almost exactly opposite the bulrushes where they had hidden James could now make out a sandbank. It ran diagonally downstream from their bank to the tail of the island where the streams joined. No one close by would have been aware of it.

'It's as good as a bridge,' he said and Fitzhenry nodded. 'No wonder they don't bother to set guards.'

'What now?'

'If I'm any judge,' James said, 'they'll be feasting tonight. It must be a long time since they've had that much beef on the Island. We'll cross when they're asleep.'

'And then?'

'Shoot them as they lie. Get close up on our bellies, keep the barrels low and make one ball pay for two. Spearmen will get the rest.'

There was something in the matter-of-fact way he said it that caused Fitzhenry to shiver. 'You've learnt well,' he said.

It was like the Bushman village all over again. They crouched in the thick bush looking across to the leaping fire on the Island. Once or twice they heard a raucous shout and once there was the sound of a shot. The Islanders seemed to be enjoying themselves. James, sweating in his heavy leather clothes stared out through the thick darkness impatient to get started. Occasionally he slapped at his damp skin trying to drive away the clouds of mosquitos that had discovered them.

Towards midnight the fires died down and the silence was only broken by frogs and crickets. He gave his final instructions and they moved down to the river. Even though he had been expecting it the water sent a shock of cold

227

through his body as it closed on his ankles. He went first and the others strung out in a long line behind him. He had tied his powder horn and bandolier round his neck and he held the musket above his head. He moved out into the river, trying to gauge exactly the angle of the sandbank. It crunched under his feet, hard in places and soft in others. At first he was afraid of quicksand but then, when he found that even in the soft parts he did not sink more than a foot, he went on steadily.

Every few yards he stopped to listen and let the others come up with him. They heard nothing but the rush of the water against their legs.

He had begun to shiver slightly. The sweat on his body was drying quickly in the cooler air that hung above the river and the leather clothing felt clammy. Something moved under his foot and he jumped back in horror, almost losing his balance. It was some moments before he was able to continue.

Half-way across he stopped again. They were all tired from the strain of pushing against a swift current. They were now below the area where the fires had been and the Island was in complete darkness, a black hump against the starry sky.

The sandbank had narrowed to a slight ridge and James had difficulty in keeping to the top. Each time he pushed his leg forward the current tried to sweep it into the deeper water at the side; each time he had to force it back. He knew that the bottom of the river would be pitted by huge holes made by river horses; one false step would send him plunging to the bottom weighed down by a full bandolier. Fitzhenry was right, the river must be well above normal.

He heard a sudden noise behind him and he stopped and turned. Fitzhenry was doubled up, coughing into his hands. James swore under his breath. It was the first time he had heard that cough since reaching Litakun. Here in the middle of the river it did not matter so much but once they reached the Island . . .

He waited for the fit to subside and then he pointed to the water. Fitzhenry bent, cupped his hand and drank. After a few seconds he nodded and they moved forward again.

They were now approaching the Island bank and he could

feel through his shoes the change in the river bed. The sand was giving way to rock. He stepped warily, half turning to Fitzhenry and the others and pointing to his feet. He saw Stone-Axe nod and realized he had already felt the change. The rocks were round and smooth and some were covered in slimy weed. James tested each step before he transferred his weight.

There was only a matter of yards to go. Close in by the bank the rocks became slimier and the holes between them dropped away abruptly into deeper holes gouged out by the racing current. Once or twice he stumbled and felt the water surge up to his waist. He held the musket higher.

He felt something brush his face and realized it was an overhanging bough and he was about to reach up to grasp it when his eye caught a faint glint of starlight. He looked more closely. It wasn't starlight, it was metal. And then he saw another glint and another. The tree was festooned with pieces of iron and tin. Anyone grasping the branch which extended so invitingly over the dark water would have set every piece of metal clanking and rattling. He felt his heart thudding under his ribs at the nearness of the trap. No wonder they had not posted guards. He slowly groped his way downstream looking for a landing place.

The bush was thick, black and impenetrable. He went on, avoiding all overhanging limbs. At last, about twenty yards downstream the bank flattened into a thick patch of bulrushes. He examined the area carefully and saw nothing. He stepped ashore. He heard Fitzhenry moving through the bulrushes on his right, the others were still strung out in the water.

Then came disaster.

Their own stealth brought them on top of the water-leguaan before either they, or it, knew it. The reptile had been hidden in the depths of the marshy bulrushes when James almost stepped on it. It was nearly five feet long with a dangerous blade-edged tail and it shot out from beneath his legs with a hiss and a flurry that stopped his heart. Everything would have been all right if Fitzhenry had not been in its path. Before he knew what had happened he had cannoned into the fleeing creature. It stopped and lashed out with its tail, opening up Fitzhenry's trousers and laying the flesh white to the bone. He gave a frightened cry and fell backwards into the fast-flowing current, the trigger guard of his musket catching in the fringing bush. The gun went off with a roar and James felt the wind from the ball as it whistled past his face. Then he heard the splash of Fitzhenry's body.

Without thinking he turned and leapt in after him hearing his own voice shouting to Stone-Axe for help.

Fitzhenry was struggling to remain upright but each time he pulled himself up his feet were swept off the slimy rocks and he went in with a renewed splash. James, holding his own gun in one hand, desperately tried to hook his clothing with the other. The weight of Fitzhenry's body almost tore the claw from his arm.

And then beside him he saw the glistening body of Mollende as the Bachapin gripped Fitzhenry in the foaming water. The huge biceps bulged as he took the strain and gradually Fitzhenry was worked out of the teeth of the current until his feet found the rough texture of a flat-topped rock and he was able to anchor himself. But the noise of the struggle had panicked the Bachapin warriors and as one they turned and splashed back across the river to the safety of the far bank. Even as James became aware of their defection, he heard voices close by. A musket exploded in the bush and he heard the thud of the ball as it struck Mollende, knocking him sideways into the water. Then he had swung his own rifle around in an arc, aimed at a shadowy figure and pulled the trigger, but the wet powder failed to catch and then the figure thrust something forward. He saw the glint of the musket barrel and dived to one side but a great light blossomed in his skull, giving way to utter darkness.

The morning sun burned down fiercely on the two bodies in the clearing. They were lying on their sides facing each other and both were tied by ankle and wrist. They were streaked with dried blood and covered by dark clusters of flies. They lay near the cooking fire in the open space ringed by the Islanders' huts and if it hadn't been for the flies they might have been two dead logs flung down in the dust. Nearby the women prepared the day's food, cutting lumps of beef from a dripping carcass, fetching water from the river, breaking lengths of wood to feed the fire. It seemed, as far as they were concerned, that the bodies did not exist. But this was really only because the bodies had not reacted earlier. The women had tried to humiliate the bodies by poking them with sticks and spitting on them and even throwing dust in their faces, but the bodies had remained unconscious and the fun had quickly palled. Occasionally one of the men would stroll over and stare down at James or Fitzhenry but that was all. No one cared whether they lived or died except that in the long run it would be more amusing if they lived.

Fitzhenry regained consciousness first. He was not aware that someone had spat in his face or flung dust at him, he was only aware of the dreadful throbbing in his leg. He had no idea yet what had caused the gash; he could only remember something rustling in the reeds and then the lashing pain as it struck him.

Some time later, it could have been minutes or hours, James stirred. He bent his head down to his hands and gently touched the furrow caused by the musket ball. He winced with pain. Slowly he opened his eyes. The flies, which had risen at the movement, settled back as a dark smear on his face.

He saw a blurred face in front of him. It seemed to have no outline. He closed his eyes, blinked and tried to focus again. Now there were two outlines that moved apart and then together. After a few moments they fused and he found himself looking at Fitzhenry.

He opened his mouth. His tongue felt as though it were twice its normal size and covered in fur. 'Where are we?' he whispered.

'On the Island.'

A shadow fell across their bodies. He saw two naked feet near his face. Then a voice said in Dutch: 'They're awake.'

'Bring them.'

He felt a knife between his ankles and the leather thongs fell away.

231

'Get up,' the voice said.

He pulled himself up on his knees and suddenly everything started whirling in his brain and he fell forward on his face. He heard a woman shriek with laughter and one of the naked feet kicked him hard over the kidneys. He groaned and pushed himself up. Someone spat and he felt the warm spittle run down his cheek. There was another laugh. This time hands grasped him roughly under the armpits and dragged him to his feet. He realized that the same thing was happening to Fitzhenry.

Up to then he had only seen things in isolation: his hand, Fitzhenry's face, the naked foot. Now he was able to take in his surroundings.

The clearing was encircled by mimosa and buffalo-thorn and between the trees he could see the beehive huts built of grass and reeds. In the centre of the clearing was the communal fire-place and some of the women were standing over the black cooking pots, staring at the two Christians with a curious lack of interest. Others had left the fire and come over to get a closer view. James wasn't sure how many men were around him, perhaps three or four, but he recognized the foot which had kicked him and he looked up into the man's face. He, like the others, was of Hottentot extraction with high cheekbones and a flattened nose but he was almost James's height and strong, and there was the possibility of Christian blood somewhere in his past. He carried a brass-bound musket, which he now dug sharply into James's side. 'Walk,' he said.

James turned, feeling the weakness in his legs, and began to walk slowly to the other end of the clearing. This was the end he had not seen yet and now he noticed that it was closed by an enormous pile of jumbled rocks. They were tall and smooth and the crevices were filled with bushes.

At the base of the outcrop one pillar of rock formed a natural throne with arm rests on either side. A man was seated in it and James was led towards him.

At first he thought the man was also a Hottentot or a Bastaard, his skin was so deeply burnt but then, as he drew closer, he realized that this was one of the figures Mollende had seen from the bank. He was a white man.

He wore a blue kerchief on his head in Hottentot fashion, a leather coat hung open displaying his naked mahogany-brown chest. Leather trousers came down to his knees and were clasped with silver buckles where they joined the tops of ragged white hose. On his feet he wore coarsely-made buckskin shoes. He was a mass of jewellery. On each finger he wore a shiny ring. His ears were pierced and in one he wore a piece of red glass which had been drilled to take a copper thread, in the other a plain gold ring. Around his waist was a black leather belt richly chased with silver and from his neck hung a big sheath knife. His wrists were obscured by bracelets and the lapels of his coat were covered in tarnished brass buttons which made a jingling noise as he moved.

But it was his head that held James's attention. Black hair hung down in long greasy tresses each bound at the end with copper wire. Within this frame was a bony long-jawed face, gaunt and malevolent, from the centre of which stared two burning eyes.

'So,' he said at last in broken Dutch. 'You're alive. More's the pity.' Something about the grating quality of his voice stirred a dim memory but there was no time to allow it to develop. His mind was clearing quickly and, with a whine in his voice, he said: 'We meant no harm, Captain.'

'No harm!' the Chief of the Islanders laughed without mirth. 'I'll give you no harm! Sneaking across like thieves in the night!'

James glanced quickly at Fitzhenry to see how he was reacting but he was standing in the midst of the hostile crowd, almost unconscious on his feet.

'On my honour, Captain,' James went on, 'we had no thought of touching the beef.'

'Cut their throats!' someone shouted.

'Sink them in the river!'

'Leave off!' the Chief of the Islanders said. 'I'll say what's to be done. What d'you want here then if it wasn't thievery? Quick now, or you'll get a bullet like that great heathen friend of yours.'

'We came to join you.'

'You what!'

'We heard of your honour from as far away as the Snowy Mountains. We heard you were working with the Hottentot Africaander and that you remained here when he left. That's why we came.'

The Chief of the Islanders looked puzzled. 'Aye, we came through the Snowy Mountains right enough. But that was more than two years ago. You took a long time in coming, mister.'

'We have been north seeking elephants' teeth. To the land of the Bechuanas and the Bachapins.'

There was a flicker of interest in the crowd.

'So, you've been to Litakun?'

'We passed that way.'

'They know us well in Litakun.'

'They spoke of you, Captain.'

The Chief of the Islanders laughed loudly. 'They spoke of us, did they, mister?'

'They fear you.'

'Do you say so now?'

'They fear for their cattle and they fear for your guns, and above all they fear for their elephants' teeth.'

The Chief ran his tongue over his lips. 'What of the elephants' teeth?'

'There are thousands, Captain. Whole huts have been built to store them against the coming of the Christian traders.'

'Huts full!'

'Three huts full.'

'And yet you come empty-handed.'

'Our trade goods were plundered.'

The interest was beginning to die in the Chief's eyes. 'What's that to me?'

Quickly James said: 'But with help we can get them. We have a plan. There is enough to make all of us rich for life.'

The crowd stirred excitedly. 'Let's hear the plan!' a voice shouted.

'Why not?' cried another.

The Chief of the Islanders was looking hard at James and there was the same puzzlement in his eyes. 'So you have a

234

plan, mister. Well, we'll hear it and if it's a good one we may oblige you by cutting your throat and if it's a bad one we'll think of another way of obliging you. Come, we'll talk.' He rose to his feet.

Then two things happened simultaneously. Fitzhenry, who was being held up by two of the men, suddenly said in clear English: 'You bloody murderer! You gutter scum!' The Chief turned angrily towards him and James saw something hanging from his right wrist which had been obscured by the folds of his coat. It was a small axe with frayed leather binding on the handle. He stared at it for a moment and then his mind went racing back to the heaving deck of the *Babylon* and the murderous look in Rance's eyes.

Royal!

'I know you, mister,' Royal was shouting at Fitzhenry. 'I know you now, and you'll die for that.' He turned to James: 'And as for . . .'

But James, past all caring, had already launched himself at the Island Chief, both hands raised and the curve of the hook glistening in the sunlight.

He had only taken one step when he felt a blow on the back of his neck that brought him to his knees. Rough hands grabbed him and leather thongs bit into his arms and legs.

'Christ!' Royal said. 'It's the boy!' And with a great shout of laughter he turned to one of the huts and called: 'Ogle! Come out, ye lazy devil! We've got visitors! Old shipmates that need entertaining.'

The evening sun slanted across the Great River burnishing the water to copper. A breeze had sprung up and the willows moved gently to and fro caressing the river with long fragile fingers. The high cliffs reverberated to the muffled roar of nesting bush-doves and from a long way away there was the faint clanking of guinea fowl coming down to roost in the trees.

The Islanders had been tapping a barrel of Cape brandy. Some drank it neat from tin mugs, coughing sharply after each mouthful; others cut it with river water. Most were

235

smoking long-stemmed pipes made from bone but there were others who preferred chewing the oily tobacco and the area round the fire was foetid with their spit. Some of the women, now drunk to the point of stupefaction, lay on the ground, their naked limbs sprawling. Earlier in the day, before the ardent spirits had robbed them of all desire, James had seen the Islanders coupling in the dust like frenzied animals.

He and Fitzhenry were tied back to back. Fitzhenry was unconscious and had been for many hours and was therefore lucky. James, although his mind was almost blank with pain and exhaustion, still retained a spark of consciousness and an ability to recall part of what had gone before.

He could remember the blows and buffetings that had become, through repetition, almost casual. What he could not remember was how many times they had sent Fitzhenry and himself, tied together like beasts, sprawling sideways in the dust, nor how many times he had painfully pulled them upright. He could recall being spat upon and urinated upon, he could remember one woman, who seemed almost possessed, forcing a handful of cowdung up his nose. He could remember the hook being torn from his arm and the pink stump held aloft to the amusement of the others. And he could remember the savage delight which Royal and Ogle had taken in his humiliation.

But that was past. Even cruelty becomes boring if continued too long and now they were left alone, almost forgotten on the perimeter of the fire-place. No one bothered to spare them a glance.

Except one. High up on the cliffs, on a ledge no wider than his own body, Stone-Axe lay watching. He had been there all day without food or water. He had not moved a muscle; not even when the rays of the noon sun scorched the sandstone rocks. His eyes had never left James and what he had seen made him feel as though his heart was bleeding.

There was nothing he could do. His gun had been lost in the struggle with the river. He had no bow and no arrows, not even a knife. All he could do was wait. He waited.

'Well,' Royal said, 'it's time we settled you.' He loomed over them, a fantastical figure, clutching a mug of brandy and swaying drunkenly on his feet. Then he shook his head in wry amazement. 'Who would have thought it? Who would ever have thought it? Ogle!' A hulking figure detached itself from the group near the fire and joined him. There was the same look of petty viciousness on his wide face that James remembered so well; now it was permanently etched.

He bent down, grasped James by the front of his leather jacket and jerked him forward. His wrist still bore the scars of the manacle. 'Ye've been following us!' he said fiercely. He had repeated the accusation three or four times that day.

'Following be damned!' Royal said contemptuously. 'They came to thieve the stock. D'you think the likes of them would follow *us*.'

James moistened his lips which were caked with dried blood and dung. He looked at Ogle. 'Aye,' he said hoarsely. 'We've been following you right enough.'

'There!' Ogle said, pushing him backwards and looking at Royal half in anger and half in fear. 'I said so!' All that day he had been eyeing the two of them as though his worst suspicions were being confirmed and James remembered that Ogle had been suspicious of everyone, not the least of Royal.

'I tell you –' Royal began.

But Ogle interrupted him. 'What if there's more? What if there's a whole damned commando out there!'

'You're talking like a maid!' Royal said.

Ogle turned back to James. Drink had made him apprehensive. 'Why did you follow us?' he said. 'For that?' He indicated the stump of the arm.

'Aye,' James replied. 'For that. And forbye there's another reason.'

'And what's that?'

'For the rape and murder of a woman old enough to be your mother.'

'Rape?' Ogle said. 'Murder?'

'In the Snowy Mountains. On a farm called Bitterfountain. Where you left Nollitts to die.'

Ogle's eyes widened. 'You're lying,' he whispered. 'You know nothing of that!'

'I saw the red coat,' James said softly. 'You remember the red coat.'

Ogle stood transfixed for a moment before wheeling on Royal. 'I told you,' he said. 'I told you *then!*'

'*You* told me!' Royal shouted. 'Why you dungheap, what worth has that? Here, drink this,' he shoved the mug under Ogle's face. 'It may put some blood into you.' He turned to James. 'So you know about that, do you, and you'd use it to have us at each other's throats!' He turned to Ogle. 'Can't you see, lad? He'd have us stick each other.'

'I don't like it.'

'There's nothing to like or dislike. Look at them! Have you ever seen a sorrier sight? Don't tell me you're afeared of *them.*'

Ogle stared down at the two figures. The mug of neat brandy had pushed him over the edge of suspicion into indiscriminate bravado.

'I'm afeared of no one on this earth!'

'Amen to that,' Royal said.

Somewhat mollified, Ogle said: 'Well, what's it to be then? Cut their throats and heave them in the water, I say.'

'You see,' Royal said mockingly to James. 'His heart's in the right place after all. But no, I think not. I wouldn't want another crime on his conscience.' He laughed shortly. 'I wouldn't want to burden him with guilt. No, no. I once saw a thing done in Kaffirland that was a perfect answer to any man's conscience. You see, mister, we have a friend on this island. She lives in a cave on the other side and only visits us at night. We've not seen her more than once or twice but we've spied her footprints often enough.'

Ogle said: 'You mean the –'

'It's coming back, is it? Yes, that's what I mean exactly.'

They were alone. Around them was the darkness of the cave thick with the reek of putrefaction. It was a small cave, more of a burrow, and they sat with their backs to the wall near the opening which had now been almost completely blocked by a boulder. For a few moments the Islanders had lingered outside taunting them and then they had left and there was only night.

Slowly James's eyes grew accustomed to the dark. Where the boulder touched the entrance there were gaps wide enough to allow air and beams of starlight. He looked about him. The roof of the cave was about four feet high and it was just wide enough to allow them to sit opposite each other without their feet touching. Their bonds had been cut and he eased himself slowly sideways until his shoulder was touching the boulder. He began to shove. He had little strength left but he used it now until he heard his bones crack with the effort. The boulder did not move a fraction and he guessed it had been wedged in place by a branch or the trunk of a small tree.

He slid back to his original position. He could see Fitzhenry only as a vague figure slumped against the wall. He had never regained consciousness. James let his eyes explore the innermost reaches of the passageway. He could not tell how far back it went but the walls seemed to narrow, making it even smaller. There could be an exit in that direction, he thought. These burrows often wound in and out of the rock like a maze, used by half a dozen different sorts of animal, all with their separate entrances and exits. Once, years ago, he had been hunting rock-rabbits on Bitterfountain with a pack of dogs. They had dashed down a burrow after a coney and then each had emerged at a different point, one nearly a hundred yards away.

He leant back against the rock trying to husband his strength. What were the facts? This was presumably the lair of some animal, a leopard perhaps or a lynx, and since it was obviously not in the cave it must be out hunting. But Royal had blocked the entrance, therefore a second must exist. Royal would know this since he had made sure the animal would be able to enter but the prisoners would be unable to leave. However, James doubted very much whether a lynx or even a leopard would attack them. Once again, what were the facts? Both animals were night hunters. They would kill in the hours of darkness, make their meal, drink at the river and return to the cave to lie up during the day.

So that by the time the animal got back to the cave, it would have a full belly and he knew that at such moments even lions would slink away, taking the line of least resistance. But what if it was a leopard and it hadn't killed? He tried not to think of that.

There was one other fact that he had been clinging to all the long day: Stone-Axe. If he had not drowned in the river – and James thought this unlikely – he would be hidden somewhere close.

It was time to explore the passageway, but first he crawled across to Fitzhenry. The older man was breathing hoarsely through his open mouth. His head was bent forward on his chest. James put a hand on his forehead and it came away damp and hot. Already the wound in his leg was adding its own odour of corruption. James decided not to try and wake him just then. If there was a way through the cave that would be time enough, they would both need all their strength. He turned away and with his one good hand began to feel his way along the walls. The surface was rough and brittle and pieces of it broke off in his fingers. As he moved up the tunnel the smell of stale urine grew stronger. Suddenly from deep inside the cave there was the noise of a small avalanche. Rocks clashed together for a second, then silence. He lay quite still. Had there been another sound as well? A sort of snarling grunt? He held his breath, straining every sense in his body. There! A different sort of noise this time. A rustle? A soft pad-pad? Or was that his heart thumping in his ears? He raised his head slowly and stared into the blackness and saw something that raised gooseflesh all over his body.

The darkness was broken by two pinpoints of light that came slowly nearer. They became eyes. Greenish-reddish eyes; angry eyes. They stopped about twenty feet from him, low down near the floor, too widely spaced for a small animal, too low for a big one. Unless . . . Like a vessel materializing through the fog the body of the animal gradually grew sharper and he felt his breath catch in his throat. It was a hyena. A great spotted hyena, crouching down in terror on the ground.

240

At that moment there was a noise outside. The hyena darted backwards along the tunnel in fright and he could hear her, quite close, scratching and snarling at the second blocked exit. Then Royal's voice called out: 'Now you're all together!' And he laughed. 'She hasn't fed this night.'

His footsteps, slithering on the rocky shale, gradually drew farther and farther away until there was only silence.

In the silence the eyes returned. One second there was complete darkness, the next the eyes flaring in the position James had first seen them, low down near the floor of the cave. He shivered in spite of the warmth. He had not heard her return. But he could smell her now, rank and putrid like the carrion on which she fed.

'Jamie.' The voice boomed mournfully in the confined space as Fitzhenry spoke. The eyes flickered once and then, like a snuffed candle, vanished again. It was uncanny how swiftly and silently the great beast moved.

'Jamie. Are you there, boy?'

'Yes.' He moved over and sat opposite Fitzhenry again. 'Yes, I'm here.'

'Wherever here is.' The voice was weak.

'How're you feeling?'

'My compliments and I'm feeling foul. How does your honour?' There was the familiar slightly exaggerated, slightly patronizing lift to the speech and it took James back across the years to the convict hold of the *Babylon* where he had first heard it. He realized they were occupying, in the cave, almost exactly similar positions.

He felt the slightest movement of air on his left cheek and he swung round. The eyes were back. He grabbed up a handful of gravel and flung it at the hyena. In a flick the eyes were gone but this time they did not take so long to reappear.

'We've got company,' James said, but Fitzhenry did not reply.

He was left alone with the eyes. They stared at each other. His fingers closed round something hard. 'Get out, damn you!' he yelled and flung with all his strength. He heard the object strike with a thump as the hyena fled up the narrow tunnel. He leant back feeling the sweat run damply off his cheeks. 'Cheeky devil,' he muttered, then laughed uncertainly. But within a minute the hyena was back. He was aware of her return by the sound of crunching and he realized that what he had thrown was a bone. He tried to remember what it had felt like in his hand: old, decayed. God, he thought, she's already hungry enough to eat anything. While she chewed, her eyes flicked on and off as she looked away then back. He was never out of her sight for more than a split second.

Time dragged away. Opposite him Fitzhenry breathed lightly in his coma. He had slid farther down the wall and James had shifted his position – nearer the hyena – to give him room. Once or twice he moaned with pain and once his body jerked in a spasm, but that was all.

The hyena had finished grinding up the old bone and now lay on the cave floor, her great squarish head resting on her outstretched paws, her eyes fixed on James.

He had long since stopped throwing handfuls of gravel at her. The last time she hadn't moved, just gone on crouching there, letting the pebbles glance harmlessly off her thick coat and he realized there was a subtle barrier between them which could easily break down. Familiarity would swiftly breed contempt and contempt would breed courage. He stopped throwing the gravel.

With the coming of daylight the cave was suffused with a pearly grey light which made everything seem hazy and unreal. He was stupefied with exhaustion and his powers of constructive thought had vanished. They had been in the cave for nearly eight hours but already it seemed a life-time. There was a dreadful unchanging quality about their situation: the three of them seemed bound together by some macabre umbilical cord of inter-dependence.

With a start he realized that his heavy eyelids had dropped over his eyes. He shook himself awake in a panic. How long had he dozed? It might have been minutes or only seconds. He didn't know.

The hyena was watching him.

He shivered again. He *had* to keep awake. If he didn't . . .

Slowly the hyena's eyes closed. She lay there, alertly sleeping, ready to spring back or forwards depending on the circumstances. He knew how light that sleep could be.

He tucked one leg under him where it would soon become painful. That way he wouldn't be able to sleep.

He jerked awake again. His leg was numb. His heart was racing with fright. He swung round to look at the hyena. The great beast had risen into a crouch, the thick collar hair standing up in bristles along her shoulders and back.

'Get away!' he roared, jerking upright against the rock wall and flinging his right arm in a circle as though to attack her. She whirled in fright and raced back along the tunnel. He heard her scratching frantically at the blocked exit. And then, over the rank death smell, his senses recognized another smell. He turned to the entrance and realized why the hyena had almost been prepared to attack. A plate piled with steaming beef had been pushed through one of the apertures. Alongside it was a big bowl of water. He unknotted the kerchief round his neck, poured some of the water onto it and began bathing Fitzhenry's face. It was a grey face and the cheeks were sunken and James thought again of the convict hold in the *Babylon*, remembering the blue-black patches of scurvy.

When he'd wiped away the dust he dipped one corner of the kerchief in the water and placed it between Fitzhenry's lips, squeezing it like a sponge and letting the droplets trickle down his throat. Fitzhenry moaned slightly and began to suck. Soon he reached the upper layers of consciousness and James held the bowl to his lips, allowing him to drink. After a few moments he turned his head away.

He looked at the bowl and then at James. 'You must be a magician,' he said weakly.

'There's food too,' James said.

He fed him two or three pieces before relieving his own hunger. The hyena was back. She watched every mouthful until the saliva began to drip from the huge jaws.

The sun climbed steadily, sending mote-filled shafts into the cave. The day turned hot. Fitzhenry seemed to have gained strength from the meal.

'Why,' he said at last, 'd'you think Christian charity has finally won?'

James shook his head. 'At first I thought it was Stone-Axe. But it couldn't be. This is some game the Islanders –' He broke off suddenly and banged his hand down on his knee. The sudden gesture caused a nervous tremor in the hyena. 'My God!' he said. 'It's plain enough!'

'What's plain enough?'

'The food. Look, what d'you know of hyenas? You must have come across them before on your travels.'

'Not often, but I've heard the talk, of course. Cowardly things. Biggest cowards in the bush; carrion eaters. Slink about after lions picking up what's left of a kill.'

'Precisely,' James said. 'Cowardly but strong. The most powerful jaws of any animal. I've seen the thigh bone of an eland crushed in one bite. But when they're hungry . . .' His voice trailed off. 'I've always slept between two fires when I've been alone in the veld. Head to one and feet to the other. I've seen too many heathen with only one foot.'

His mind was only beginning to take in the dreadful end which Royal had planned. 'Christ,' he said, 'don't you see? When they're hungry they'll attack anything. Royal gives us food and water. Enough for two men, not enough for one hyena. We give her the food and we die of starvation; if we don't . . .'

Fitzhenry laughed bitterly. 'You're one member less than I, dear boy, and she can have this leg with pleasure.'

'We've got to keep awake,' James said, knowing it would be himself whose eyes would have to remain open. 'That way there's still a chance. Don't forget Stone-Axe is out there somewhere.'

'You have a touching faith in our friend the Bushman. I wish I could share it.'

'We should have given her the beef,' he said, looking at the empty plate. 'At least that would have been something.' But then, he thought, that's what they want us to do. Enough beef for two men; not enough for one hyena. She'd attack them anyway and without food they'd never have the strength to keep awake. There had to be some other way. His mind, revived by the food and drink, went back to the moment he had flung the bone. If she had been ready to eat anything, then how much more so now. *Anything* – his brain began to fret at the edges of a plan.

More food and water was pushed through silently at noon. Both men ate but James only allowed them each a sip of water, keeping the bowl between his knees. While they ate the hyena was unable to keep still. The saliva dripped down in a steady stream. Restlessly she padded backwards and forwards along the far passageway. He knew she would not be able to resist her appetite for too long. They followed the same procedure with the evening meal.

The night closed about them. Grey shadows gradually filled the cave, eventually deepening to black and they were left again with the flaring eyes and their own exhausted bodies. But the daylight hours had not been entirely wasted for James had examined their prison minutely and the most important thing was the discovery that where they sat the ground was littered with bones. He now held what appeared to be the splintered leg bone of an antelope. It was about eighteen inches long and the end was jagged and sharp. He had collected what other bones he could and they lay in a pile next to his right knee. Between his legs were the two full bowls of water, each holding nearly a gallon.

The plan was still only half-formed but he clutched it with the strength of a drowning man. That and Stone-Axe. But where was the Bushman? Was he too sanguine, as Fitzhenry had suggested? Perhaps there came a time when even someone like Stone-Axe shut his mind to consequence and fled into hiding like a frightened animal.

The point was that he was not ready to try anything yet. He needed more time and time meant keeping awake. He pushed the jagged end of the bone into the fleshy part of his leg and winced. He wondered how long it would be before exhaustion dulled all his senses so that he would not even feel the self-inflicted pain and simply drift into sleep, his limbs outstretched, a living offering of flesh. He could not depend on Fitzhenry.

He dug the point into his leg again and shook himself. He began to think of Robbie and then of Lisé, remembering her body slumped across Violin's neck shielding the child from the terrors of the night. Could he let that go for nothing? Just because he couldn't keep his eyes open?

Fitzhenry became worse, mumbling and shouting in delirium and he wet the kerchief in the water once more and shifted across to the other side of the cave so he could rest Fitzhenry's head on his shoulder and bathe his forehead and neck. He welcomed the work. Towards midnight Fitzhenry's breathing became more regular and he opened his eyes. He lay for a long time without talking and then said at last: 'I can smell him, Jamie.'

'Smell what?'

'Death. I can smell him creeping up my body like an old enemy. I cheated him once before – we both did – but I'm not likely to this time.'

'You'll be out of here in another twenty-four hours,' James said. 'I'll promise you that.'

'Perhaps. If anyone can do it you can, you were always a determined lad; a touch humourless but determined all the same. In any case it won't matter much.' His voice had lost its bantering tone and James realized that for the first time he was listening to the real person.

'It's strange,' Fitzhenry went on, 'that it should happen this way. I mean, if you hadn't had to drag me out of the river we might just have got away with it.'

'No blame to you.'

'Luck,' Fitzhenry said. 'A matter of luck. The first time you pulled me out of water we ended up at Paradise. The second – well, perhaps it'll be the other place. I thought I wouldn't care, but the surprising thing is I do.'

'I've always wondered why you took me with you?' James said. 'From the *Babylon*, I mean. You had no reason.'

'You were a surly devil all right.'

'Well then?'

'I suppose because I couldn't swim.'

'That's not so. I couldn't swim either.'

'But it worked, didn't it?'

James nodded in the darkness. 'I've always felt ashamed,' he said, 'for what we did.'

'We?'

'I, then. Leaving you there on the sands.'

'You'd pulled me out, hadn't you?'

'Yes, but . . .'

'No buts. It's all too late for buts. They say "if only" is the saddest phrase in the language.'

They were silent for some time and he wondered if Fitzhenry had drifted off once more, but eventually he began to speak again and his voice was so weak James had to strain for some of the words. 'How old were you when they brought you aboard at the Motherbank?' he asked.

'Sixteen.'

'Yes, that would have been about right.'

'What would've?'

'It's a long story, James, and full of buts and if onlys. I'm not sure myself of the whys and the hows. But did you ever hear of the Irish Rebellion of '78? Of Wolf Tone and the United Irishmen? Of New Ross and Vinegar Hill? No, why should you with your own troubles fresh enough in the Highlands.'

Fitzhenry told him about the unification movement in Ireland that cut across the boundaries of Protestantism and Catholicism. And of the uprising of '78 and the battles of New Ross and Vinegar Hill in which the rebels were crushed by British forces. He told simply of the slaughter of his wife and son in the Ulster purges and of his own capture at Vinegar Hill.

'What they couldn't understand, you see, James, was me, an Englishman, fighting for Irish rebels. And that's where all the ifs come in. If I'd not married Margaret many things would never had happened. I'd never have taken her out of the smoky air of London back to her own countryside. She'd have had another son, perhaps, by someone else and he would be alive and so would she and I'd be adorning a different scene right now. The "if onlys" . . .'

He paused again for a long time. 'She was a determined one that,' he said. 'Part of another age. Earlier, perhaps, or later. She hated Englishmen, yet she married one. I've often wondered what my son Edward would have grown up to be. So you see there was nothing left for me to do, once they'd gone, but to carry on as she would have wished. Can you understand that, boy?'

'Yes, I can understand it. I was thinking something of the same a little while back.' He began to talk about Lisé.

When he'd finished Fitzhenry said: 'We've both been lucky, then. It couldn't really happen again. That would be asking too much.'

'You mean Frances?'

'Yes. You see, I was never able to give Margaret much and I thought I could make it up now, oh, not to her. I don't believe in ghosts to that extent . . .'

'Is that why you helped me?' James interrupted.

'Perhaps. I don't know. Life isn't as clear cut as that.'

'But you love Frances!'

'As much as is left in me. And beyond that there were things I could do. A lot has happened since you left Paradise. There's been an amnesty for people like me. And there's money, not a great deal, but enough, waiting in England. I could have made it up, you know. I could have taken her away from this country and given her comfort for the rest of her life.'

James thought of Frances in the neat society of England and of what she had said to him, but he remained silent.

'Perhaps we can never make it up,' Fitzhenry continued. 'No matter how hard we try. Perhaps there's no need and it's the irony of life that we try and always fail.'

It was almost dawn when the hyena attacked.

In the early hours of the morning Fitzhenry had slipped away into an uneasy sleep and James had moved back to his own position against the wall. The beast, now almost frantic with hunger, was unable to remain still and she padded softly up and down the cave, returning every now and then to the far exit to scratch at the blockage. He wondered how secure the Islanders had left it. It was his one hope and he reasoned that drunk as they had been their energies would probably only have lasted long enough to block the main entrance. He was hoping that the work on the other would have been perfunctory, just enough to keep in the hyena since no one would expect one of the prisoners to tackle it.

His mind, occupied with thoughts like these, must have drifted into a state of waking sleep.

He wasn't certain what had first warned him. The hyena had made one of her restless journeys to the far end of the tunnel and for a few moments he had allowed his senses to relax. She must have come slinking back against one of the walls, her head held half away from the two men, otherwise he would have seen the eyes. He was aware of her first as an alien presence, a strengthening smell, a darker shadow pressed down on the gravelly floor. And even as he realized what had happened she sprang.

He reacted automatically. He shouted at the top of his voice, swung his feet out of the way of her gaping jaws, heard the empty click as the jaws missed his shoe by inches. Then he swung at her with the sharpened bone and she turned in mid-air and there was another snap and her teeth closed on the bone an inch from his fingers. She jerked her great neck, dragging his face up to the foul-smelling fur and then the bone snapped off. She darted back to the rear of the cave and he heard the jaws crunch down twice and then silence. He looked into the angry eyes and felt his whole body trembling. He had nearly lost a foot and a hand. How long, he wondered, before she'd come again?

He had planned to wait until after the noon meal before starting but he doubted now whether either of them would live that long. By then the hyena's hunger would have overcome her fear and she would attack them openly and that would be the end.

He woke Fitzhenry when the beef and water arrived and tried to get him to eat, but his throat was painful and he could not swallow. The smell of the beef caused traceries of saliva to hang from the hyena's jaws. She began to whine.

James ate as much of the beef as he was able and then pushed it through the gap in the rock.

'Why not give it to her?' Fitzhenry said weakly. 'If you've that much faith in the Bushman, what you'll need is time.'

'I've got a different sort of meal for her,' James said.

He now had three bowls of water between his knees. They

had used a little out of one but he estimated that there were probably about three gallons left, more than enough for his purpose. On his right side lay the pile of bones. Now he slowly began to take off his leather coat. It was a heavy coat of buckskin. It had been coarsely tanned in the Frontier manner by placing it in a solution with acacia bark, and in damp weather it still became soft and slimy. In the present dry heat the leather was uncomfortably hard and brittle. Carefully he selected a bone with a sharp cutting edge and sawed at the thin leather thread which held the arm of the coat to the shoulder. He cut a dozen stitches and then, holding the jacket with his feet, ripped the arm out.

The hyena, even more restless than before, watched the movements.

'Here you are, my beauty,' James said. 'Food.' And with that he flung the arm of the coat towards her. She reacted so swiftly that if he had not been expecting it he would have missed it. In one fluid movement she had plucked the flying leather from the air, turned, and fled up the passage. In less than a minute she was back.

He was already at work on the second sleeve. He ripped it out and followed the same procedure. This time the hyena stood her ground. She caught the sleeve in mid-air, gave two incredible swallows, in which the sleeve hung briefly from her jaws, and then her tongue emerged to lick the dripping lips.

Next he threw her half a dozen leg and thigh bones from the pile next to him. She took these in single snaps, the bones disappearing in ragged pieces down her throat.

'I'll give her a few moments to get that down properly,' he said, more to himself than Fitzhenry. He was working on the back seam of the coat. The sharp bone-edge cut through the stitches and again he was able to rip a piece away. This was even bigger than the sleeves and it looked like a great black bat as he flung it through the air.

Snap! The jaws slammed shut, the great muscles in the throat jerked twice, three times, and the piece of leather was gone, swallowed, as the others had been, without chewing. He threw a handful of bones.

'She'll eat anything!' Fitzhenry said softly.

'That gave me the idea.'

The coat had gone and the little pile of bones was diminishing rapidly, yet the hyena showed no sign of having had enough. On the contrary she appeared hungrier than ever, whining and pacing, dropping down on her forepaws, jerking upright, and all the time the juices from her mouth dripped wetly onto the floor and the big red tongue rolled one way, then the next.

He looked down at his shoes. No, not the shoes. If ever they got out of the cave, covering for his feet would be vital. He opened the flap of his leather trousers, pulled them from his legs and went to work on the seams with the sharp bone. The hyena swallowed the separate pieces like a dog plucking biscuits from the air.

He glanced across at Fitzhenry. His clothes were corduroy and therefore useless. 'That should be enough,' he said. 'Now for the other.'

The hyena still stood waiting expectantly but all the leather was finished and so were the bones. Suddenly James shouted as loud as he could and swung his arm through the air. She whirled and was gone. Immediately he picked up the bowls of water and carried them as far up the cave as he dared. When the beast slunk softly back along the tunnel he was sitting in his usual place.

The hyena glanced suspiciously at the bowls, testing the air for treachery, then, her eyes fixed on the two men, she bent her head and began to drink. She had had no water for nearly forty-eight hours and the salty leather had inflamed her thirst. She drank and drank. First one bowl and then the next until finally she had taken almost all the water there was. She lay down next to the empty bowls and licked the droplets of water from the fur round her lips.

'Now,' said James, 'we'll wait and see.'

The beams of sunlight moved across the floor of the cave. The air was drowsy and still. The hyena's head rested on her forepaws and her eyes were closed. Fitzhenry was unconscious. The smell from his leg was now the strongest odour in the cave. Only James was awake. His eyes were fixed on the hyena. Half an hour passed. Then an hour. He waited.

The pain first came to her as a whimper in her sleep. She twitched. Her eyes flicked open. She moved her head restlessly.

'That's only a beginning,' James said softly. 'Only a start.'

Abruptly she gave a slight snarling moan and pushed herself to her feet. Her legs did not appear to be too secure and she swayed slightly. She began to pad up and down. Her head was held low, almost touching the ground. She stopped and tried to pass water, as though it might relieve some of the pressure building up inside her, but nothing came. Fretfully she bent her head and pushed it against the sides of her stomach. He tried to picture the mess of bone, leather and water churning in her stomach. He tried to picture the unchewed leather sucking up the water, swelling and swelling, pressing the jagged edges of bone against the stomach wall.

Suddenly she gave a high-pitched warbling scream that sounded like a madman's laugh and began to whirl round and round in a circle like a puppy chasing its tail. Her lips were drawn back over her teeth in a ghastly smile and the huge jaws snapped together as she tried to bite herself in the belly. Dust rose in the cave until he could barely see her. But the movement must have aggravated her pain; it must have worked up the sharp bone ends more fiercely into her viscera and forced the mucid leather farther up to her windpipe. She stopped and stood with lolling head, fighting to get air into her lungs against the mounting pressure of the hide. Then, her stomach muscles heaved in three great spasms as she tried to retch. A piece of leather protruded from her jaws, its other end still in her stomach. It hung there, covered in blood and foam, while she tried to bring the rest of it up. But the blockage was now too great. She coughed and retched but the leather still hung limply from her jaws.

She came closer to him, as though for help. She was trembling and coughing and each movement must have been like hot knives in her belly. For a second he was struck by the horror of her agony and in spite of himself felt an over-powering urge to take hold of one end of the leather and draw it out of her tortured body. But in the same second his ears picked up a sound from outside the cave. It seemed some distance away and he strained to listen.

It was the sound of people shouting and at first he thought it might be the Islanders enjoying another drunken debauch. But then he was able to differentiate between shouts and screams and the screams were of terror and pain.

Almost simultaneously he heard a scratching at the cave and then Stone-Axe's voice shouting. 'Claw! Claw! It is I.'

'Stone-Axe. Can you hear me?'

'I hear you, O Claw, but speak quickly. The little people are here.'

In the distance the shouts and screams grew louder.

'Can you move the boulder?'

'There is a tree.'

'Pull on it then!'

He heard Stone-Axe take up a new position and then there was a groaning sound as he used the wedge as a lever. The boulder began to shift. James pushed his feet hard against the opposite wall to give him leverage and bent his shoulder to the inside of the rock. It moved a fraction. Then a bit more. Suddenly it rolled out of the entrance, crashing down on the shale and scrub, bounding down the slope. He had a fleeting view of Stone-Axe leaping to one side and then he was knocked flat as the hyena made one last dying run to freedom.

He felt a piercing pain on his cheek, and then another. The hair round his head was humming with angry bees. Stone-Axe was almost unrecognizable. His face was twice its normal size, his lips were swollen and his eyes almost closed.

'Quick, Claw! To the river!'

He whirled his arms about, trying to keep the bees from his face. 'How many hives?' he shouted.

'T'oa-t'oa-t'oa.'

'My God! Six!' He tried to imagine what courage it had needed to break open six hives and then lead the bees down the cliffs of the Island camp – and couldn't. Stone-Axe's arms were still covered with shining, sticky honey; a living target.

James ran three paces towards the river, then turned back to the cave. He had momentarily forgotten Fitzhenry. He picked him up with one arm, slung him over his back and went down the slope towards the river in a stumbling, slithering trot.

Bees were everywhere, in his hair and ears, on his naked back and legs, behind his knees, in his scrotum. Their separate lances became one gigantic, red-hot pain that seemed to sear the skin from his body. The wild black bees of Africa were exacting their vengeance.

As he ran he saw the bodies; first the hyena which must have died within seconds of leaving the cave. Already her eyes and snout were invisible under a layer of bees. Then the naked body of a woman. She must have come out suddenly from one of the huts, seen the air black with bees and tried to run back. She had not got more than a few yards. She lay on her back crusted with bees. Her face bore no resemblance to a human being. The eyes and mouth were lost in the swollen folds of her cheeks which had ballooned out to the same level as the bridge of her nose. Her breasts were like gigantic melons, ripe to the point of bursting.

James ran on. There were other bodies, some wearing beards of bees, some still alive, staggering blindly in circles.

James had pulled Fitzhenry's coat over his own face and raised it fractionally every few moments to see if he was still on the right path. They lumbered past the cooking fires: more bodies, limbs contorted in death spasms, mouths open, swollen tongues, black with crawling bees, protruding from pincushion cheeks. A figure wreathed in smoke erupted from the safety of the fire-place and staggered across the clearing, clothes alight.

And then they came to a sight which made even James falter in his stride. It was Ogle. He was stumbling aimlessly through a grove of mimosa trees, running up against the branches and the thorns, staggering left then right, waving his arms about ineffectually at the cloud of enraged bees that swarmed round his head. It was apparent that he was already blind. Suddenly he collapsed. He jerked once or twice as the acid from countless stings burnt into his system and then he

254

gave one dreadful scream, his body went rigid and slowly his head moved backwards until his shuddering backbone was bent like a bow. Bees were moving in and out of his ears.

James was tempted to stop and put him out of his agony but to stop now would mean his own death. Already he was dazed with shock. The thorn bush gave way to bulrushes, his feet slipped on the surface. The river lay before them.

Without a thought for rocks or rapids they flung themselves through the last few feet and hit the water together. It was no more than a few feet deep. The sudden freshness revived him. He was holding Fitzhenry's head above water and now he raised his own. Immediately the bees descended in a black haze. He ducked, held his breath for as long as he could then broke the surface again. The bees were hanging over the tops of the bulrushes. He waited for them to come zooming down. They seemed to hesitate. Then he saw that Stone-Axe was standing waist deep in the river throwing handfuls of water in the air. The drops glittered in the sunlight and James noticed that the bees kept their distance. He anchored Fitzhenry to him with the stump of his left arm and began to imitate Stone-Axe.

Still buzzing angrily the bees moved farther away, driven upstream by the continued splashing. James used his good hand like a whip, flicking at the surface of the water and sending the drops cascading after them.

The swarm whirled several times like a miniature tornado and then, as though on some command, whisked off the river and were lost in the trees. A strange silence settled on the place.

For the first time he was able to look down on Fitzhenry's swollen face. In parts it had already turned black. It did not need more than a casual glance to tell he was dead.

It was dusk and the bush glowed redly in the last rays of the sun. A slight mist had come up over the river and a breeze moved the strands of willow. The wild bees had long since returned to repair their ravaged nests.

James and Stone-Axe moved round the deserted camp. They had counted a total of eight dead bodies which they had consigned to the river. He guessed that most of the others would have perished in the water. They had found Ogle's body where he had fallen but there was still no sign of Royal.

They had spent nearly an hour extracting stings and now, in spite of the swellings and the soreness of the glands under his arms and in his groin, James was feeling better. His hook was back on his arm, rescued from where it had been casually thrown, and he was wearing trousers and a coat from one of the dead men.

Night was coming quickly and he wanted to be off the island before dark, but first he lit a torch at the still smouldering fire and they went from hut to hut searching for muskets. There were very few and after giving Stone-Axe the best, he threw the others on the fire. Then he set a light to each hut in turn. The dry thatch and reeds burnt fiercely, sending sparks and smoke up into the sky and he knew that if any Islanders were left on the far banks of the river they would know their days of raiding were over, at least in this part of the country: without guns, without shelter and with the secret of the sandbank available to others they would be an easy prey to any wandering Bushman tribe. If there were any survivors James felt sure they would go westward along the river and try to join up with Africaander and the remainder of the Jäger Hottentots. In any case they would cease to exist as a menace to the Bachapins. As for the cattle, they had stampeded all over the island before the rampaging bees and would still be there when King Mateebe sent for them.

There was nothing left to do. He flung his blazing torch on the roof of the last remaining hut and turned to call Stone-Axe. He looked round the clearing but the Bushman was no longer in sight. He stood there uncertainly, feeling the exhaustion sweep over him.

And then he heard the Bushman's shout. It came from somewhere over to his left, behind the pillar of rock which Royal had used as his throne. Clutching a musket in one hand he began to run. His steps were weak and faltering.

'Claw!' the cry came once more.

James pushed his way through the thick bush on the sides

of the stone pillar and saw immediately in front of him and in its own little clearing a hut much larger than the rest.

Stone-Axe was crouching to one side of the hut, the blazing torch still in his hand. He beckoned sharply. 'Claw! A person lives!'

James squatted down next to him and heard faint moans coming from the interior of the hut. He took the torch from the Bushman and together they moved to the entrance. Holding the blazing light ahead of him, he stooped through the doorway. What he saw made him stop dead. It was like entering a treasure cave. The floor was strewn with hand-woven rugs, some of which he had no doubt had come from the belongings of rich farmers. Each rug was covered in a shimmering mass of beads, glass ornaments, semi-precious stones, porphyry, chalcedonies, amygdaloids, greenstones and agates – all winking and shining in the flickering light of the flame. The walls were hung with bolts of cloth swept into drapes and from each bolt hung copper and brass bangles, beadwork, shiny assegais, knives, the teeth of sea horses, snake skins, buffalo horns and ostrich feathers. On the floor round the walls were half a dozen brass-bound wagon chests, their fittings gleaming. And in the centre of the room was what looked at first sight like a four-poster bed. It seemed to be half bed, half couch. It was supported on each side by a magnificent elephant's tooth and covered in a rich profusion of lion and leopard skins. In the centre of the couch was what remained of a man. Slowly James drew nearer. As he did so his nostrils picked up a stronger smell than the rather musty odour of the skins. It was a sweet stench, like that of roasting flesh.

'Kaptein!' Stone-Axe hissed.

James nodded. He had already seen the little axe held in one hand. It was Royal all right but he was now almost totally unrecognizable. He was quite naked and his skin had a brown crisp look about it through which blood was oozing in patches. He sprawled on his back, his head supported by a leopard skin, his blind eyes towards them. There was almost no part of his body that had not been burnt.

'The fire,' Stone-Axe said, and James nodded again. This

had been the smoking figure he had seen. When the bees attacked, Royal must have known he could not reach the river and instead had tried to get as close to the fire as possible knowing the bees would not penetrate the smoke. And then . . . James could imagine the falling log, perhaps displaced by one of Royal's feet, the flames unnoticed licking at his clothes; too late the realization that he was on fire. He could see him beating at the burning garments, running, falling, trying to get up and then, as the flames burnt down, crawling to his palace.

Royal's lips began to move. 'Who's there?' he said and his voice was faint with pain.

'James Fraser Black.'

The lips turned down in a grimace of hatred. 'I should've cut your throat.'

'You'll damage no one ever again.'

'D'you say so?'

'Aye.'

'Well –' he broke off and James watched the twitching body without feeling.

After a few moments he spoke again. 'Am I done for?' The tone was a mixture of fear and hope.

'You're finished.'

'Not even a heathen would let me die like this.'

'What is there to do?'

'Help me . . .' The sentence ended in a scream and James shivered at the agony in it. Royal was silent for some moments and then at last he whispered: 'Help me, boy, for God's own sake.'

In spite of himself James moved forward. Then, too late, he saw the pistol in Royal's left hand. It was pointed at his chest. He watched, unable to move as the index finger crooked on the trigger. The brown crust over the knuckle began to crack, drops of thin greasy blood dripped onto the coverings. The trigger bent backwards. He knew the gun was about to go off and there was nothing he seemed capable of doing to get out of the way. He was fixed, hypnotized by Royal as he had been in the *Babylon*. He waited . . .

The crash of Stone-Axe's gun was like a thunderclap in the

confined space. The ball took Royal squarely in the face, obliterating eyes, nose and mouth, leaving only a gaping red hole. Slowly he collapsed, slithering down the couch until he rested among his pieces of glass at James's feet.

For a few seconds more James was unable to move, then he turned away and beckoned Stone-Axe to follow. He pushed again at the doorway looking back at the rich trappings and the shimmering stones, then he touched the thatch on either side of the door with the torch and finally flung it into the centre of the hut where it lay near Royal's body.

'Come,' he said to Stone-Axe. 'It is time.'

They walked slowly down to the river and it was only when they reached the bank that he realized he had Royal's axe in his hand. He had no idea when he had reached for it; only that it was there. He looked at it for a moment, remembering Rance and Old Lena, the beach below Mouse Mountain, the smell of tar, the towering figure of Vreetman. The past suddenly seemed very close. But for him the past was dead, there was no way back, and with a jerk he sent the axe sailing out over the stream. For a moment its blade caught the final rays of the sun. It seemed to be red with blood. Then it hit the water with a slight splash and was gone.

EPILOGUE

'. . . one may call the interior of South Africa a vast
solitude . . .'

LORD BRYCE: *Impressions of South Africa*

Extract from Narrative of a Journey to the Kaffre Country *by
the Rev. William E. Johnstone (Lyle & Mackenzie, Edinburgh.
1817).*

August 24: A most singular occurrence took place this day.

Yesterday the violence of the wind and inclemency of the
weather, with even some snow, prevented our travelling; and
which, although the sun shone the whole morning, was not
entirely melted by noon. The thermometer was, at that hour,
only 31 degrees and rose no higher during the day than 45
degrees (7.2 C.).

I therefore decided that we should, in order to rest the
beasts (as well as ourselves), stay at our camping place for a
second day. As is my habit when in camp I raised the Union
Jack upon my wagon pole at noon and thereupon conducted a
short service at which, as usual, I was both clergyman and
congregation.

I was about to descend to conduct a second service for the
Hottentot servants (they seem to gain much spiritual strength
from these) when one of them leapt upon his feet and pointed
to a gap in the hills through which, at that moment, I espied
two wagons emerging. We made immediate haste to welcome
these travellers and I found myself stimulated at the thought
of a civilized meeting in so isolated and wild a place.

But my feelings underwent an alteration once they drew up with us; a change as easily apparent among my servants, who withdrew to one side talking among themselves and fingering their muskets. For this was, in truth, a most singular group. It comprised a man, a young woman who, it was obvious to the most circumspect glance, was heavy with child, a small boy of about three or four years of age and a male Bushman badly scarred about the face and arms which imparted to him a most villainous aspect and who seemed, by his relaxed and casual manner, to have adopted airs above his station.

Apart from these there were two or three Hottentot servants upon whom I would have felt little disposed to place my trust.

All appeared travel-stained and weary, though their health seemed in no way impaired judging from the robustness of their appetites. They made a large meal of boiled beef, rice, bread freshly baked from wheaten flour, and between them drank nearly two gallons of new milk which was our total supply but which, of course, I did not grudge them. I did, however, find it strange that the Bushman servant should seat himself with his employers, partaking of the same food and drink, and it was noticeable that his eyes moved from one to another as though fearful that something unusual might happen. This by the fire-side of a man of God!

I thought to make some jocular comment on it but was uncertain of his master's humour and forbore. Indeed, I had been covertly inspecting him since they arrived, for his accent and manner of address bespoke a fellow-countryman.

He was a man of the most fearful mien with lank black hair, a cruel-looking hook which was strapped to the stump of his left arm and eyes as cold as the grey winter sky. And yet in his dealings with his own people, and especially the woman, whom I then thought to be his wife, he appeared to be a person of gentle manners; a feature which both surprised and gratified me.

During our meal he spoke of a journey they were making from the land of the Bachapins which, I understand, is many hundreds of miles to the north-west of here. I am still uncertain for what reason he made so arduous a journey in the first place, since by his very appearance he could not have been carrying with him the Gospel. He spoke briefly of a group of Islanders, a colony of bees and the death of an English doctor in the town of Litakun, the details of which seem to me so utterly incredible and lacking in veracity that I do not propose to set them down here.

After we had finished our meal and given thanks to God we sat by the fire for a time drinking coffee which these people seemed greatly to relish. I had decided to ask no further questions of my countryman – it would be my judgement that he hailed from remote parts even there – fearing I would be the recipient of even more romantic tales, and the conversation languished. Thereupon the young woman, who seemed to be of gentle birth (which made her presence in this wilderness and in this company more difficult to apprehend), began questioning me as to my own journey. I told her truthfully that I was here on the Lord's business. She asked if I was an ordained minister and when I gave out that this was so and that I should be pleased to hold a combined service for the whole party there and then, I perceived a knowing look pass between the two of them.

I heard the man say, 'Well, Fran?' Whereupon she smiled most tenderly and made this reply: 'I think it's about time, Jamie.' I naturally had no means of understanding what this meant at that moment, but was quickly to learn, for the man, whose name became known to me as James Fraser Black, asked if I would perform the ceremony of marriage. To state that I was utterly confounded (taking the woman's condition and the presence of the small boy into account) would be an incomplete summary of my feelings! It seemed to me then, as it does now, that they had falsely taken advantage of my charity. I was about to say something in this fashion when I noticed that Mr Black was smiling at me, if such a freezing configuration of the face could be so described. I decided to remain silent and he thereupon said he would pay me well and spoke of elephants' teeth which were stored in the rear wagon.

Elephants' teeth are extremely valuable at the Cape of Good Hope at the present time and I had been hoping to defray the costs of my evangelical mission by the acquisition of some dozen or twenty tusks. I would not, however, want it to be thought that this in any way influenced my mind for it suddenly came to me that the state of matrimony was equally blessed whether it was completed late or early, before or after.

And so, there in the cold wind, with storm-clouds gathering on the surrounding mountains, I married them.

I wish I could truly state that the sanctity of the service wrought some change in Mr Black but I cannot, for no sooner was it over than he asked me to write out a certificate and caused his Bushman to affix his signature as witness with a cross, under which he wrote the name 'Stone-Axe'. I would have protested at this heathenish blasphemy had my attention not been drawn just then to the unloading of an elephant's tooth and the need to see it safely stored in my own wagon. However, I make my feelings known here.

In the early afternoon they departed and I cannot say that I was sorry, although I had, of course, extended the hospitality of my camp to them for as long as they wished. But Mr Black said they had to get on and when I pointed out to him that his direction was north-east, which was the opposite road for the Colony, he laughed, and said he would not be going back there, 'not yet awhile'. I am uncertain, in fact, whether the words he used were 'would not' or 'could not' but it seems to make no matter. He was, he said, journeying to the land of the Zoolus, a tribe as yet unknown to me and, I would venture, to most other civilized men. When I asked what he hoped to find there he made a curious reply: 'I have found what I searched for,' he said. 'I have found what I need. Forbye the land that flows with milk and honey always lies beyond the far hills.' And with that he spurred his horse.

I stood in the cold afternoon and watched their wagons disappear into the vast solitude that lay ahead of them and then I retired to my own wagon to offer up a prayer for their safety. In the circumstances it seemed the least I could do.

SOME SOURCE BOOKS

Barrow:	*Travel in the Interior of Southern Africa.*
Bateson:	*The Convict Ships (1787–1868).*
Bleek:	*Specimens of Bushman Folklore.*
Burchell:	*Travels in the Interior of Southern Africa.*
Campbell:	*Travels in South Africa.*
Fairbridge:	*Lady Anne Barnard at the Cape of Good Hope.*
Harris:	*The Wild Sports of Southern Africa.*
Holt:	*Memoirs.*
Idenburg:	*The Cape of Good Hope at the turn of the 18th century.*
Lichtenstein:	*Travels in Southern Africa in the years 1803–06.*
Moodie:	*History of the Battles etc. in Southern Africa.*
Sparrman:	*Voyage to the Cape of Good Hope (1772–76).*
Stow:	*The Native Races of South Africa.*
Theal:	*Records of the Cape Colony.*
Thompson:	*Travels and Adventures.*
Thunberg:	*An Account of the Cape of Good Hope.*
Van der Post:	*The Lost World of the Kalahari.*
	The Heart of the Hunter.
Walker:	*A History of South Africa.*
	The Great Trek.

A SELECTION OF BESTSELLERS FROM SPHERE

FICTION

DUNN'S CONUNDRUM	Stan Lee	£2.95 ☐
GOLDEN TALLY	Pamela Oldfield	£·.95 ☐
HUSBANDS AND LOVERS	Ruth Harris	£2.95 ☐
SWITCH	William Bayer	£2.25 ☐

FILM & TV TIE-IN

BOON	Anthony Masters	£2.50 ☐
LADY JANE	Anthony Smith	£1.95 ☐

NON-FICTION

THE FALL OF SAIGON	David Butler	£3.95 ☐
THE AMBRIDGE YEARS	Dan Archer	£2.50 ☐
THE SUNDAY EXPRESS DIET BOOK	Marina Andrews	£2.50 ☐
THE PRICE OF TRUTH	John Lawrenson and Lionel Barber	£3.50 ☐

All Sphere books are available at your local bookshop or newsagent, or can be ordered direct from the publisher. Just tick the titles you want and fill in the form below.

Name _____

Address _____

_____

Write to Sphere Books, Cash Sales Department, P.O. Box 11, Falmouth, Cornwall TR10 9EN

Please enclose a cheque or postal order to the value of the cover price plus:

UK: 45p for the first book, 20p for the second book and 14p for each additional book ordered to a maximum charge of £1.63.

OVERSEAS: 75p for the first book plus 21p per copy for each additional book.

BFPO & EIRE: 45p for the first book, 20p for the second book plus 14p per copy for the next 7 books, thereafter 8p per book.

Sphere Books reserve the right to show new retail prices on covers which may differ from those previously advertised in the text or elsewhere, and to increase postal rates in accordance with the PO.